AT FIRST SMILE

AT FIRST SMILE

MELISSA WHITNEY

ABOUT THE BOOK

Disability advocate Pen Meadows is on a mission; grab a breakfast sandwich, find her gate, and listen to her smutty audiobook. Only, the sexy, tall man in front of her at Tim Hortons may prove a worthwhile distraction. His soft Irish lilt and mix of gruff sweetness make Rowan Iverson unlike any man she's ever met. After a brief meet/cute, and even briefer goodbye, the social media influencer ends up seated beside Rowan on a cross-country flight.

Rowan Iverson desperately wants to get back to Los Angeles without calling further attention to himself. A potentially career-ending incident at hockey's biggest game could transform the NHL's top defenseman into its most hated player. The last thing he wants is for his mess to trip up Pen. A mid-flight detour forces him to realize that his goal to resist her bright smile may be a game he's already lost.

Back in the reality of their jobs and lives in Los Angeles, Pen learns that the man she'd spent one incredible night with isn't who she thought. He's a player and Pen doesn't play games, especially when her heart is at stake. Can Rowan prove to Pen that he is who he wants to be...just hers?

At First Smile
Copyright © 2024 by Melissa Whitney
All rights reserved.

This is a work of fiction. The characters are products of the author's imagination, and any resemblance to actual events or actual persons, living or dead, is entirely coincidental. Although it's fair to say that anyone enjoying a life so full of love is lucky indeed.

Digital eISBN-979-8-9904334-3-4
Print ISBN: 979-8-9904334-2-7

To everyone who's ever been told that they weren't the main character, I see you.

AUTHOR'S NOTE/CONTENT WARNING

My Dear Reader,

In so many ways this is the riskiest book I've ever written. As a legally blind woman that has been losing her sight since the age of six, I have seldom saw myself as the main character (pun intended). There is limited thoughtful/accurate representation of legally blind characters within media, especially characters that are crafted by someone that is legally blind.

As a disabled person, I've always wanted to see myself as the main character. Especially to see myself as the vibrant, feisty, flawed, joyful, and sexy love interest. In so many ways writing Pen's story has been therapeutic and the scariest thing I've ever done. This book is the one that I always wanted to read. One where blindness is part of the story, but not the sum total of Pen's character.

There's both pride and terror in publishing this story. What if I get it wrong? What if readers aren't open to a main character like Pen? What impact will this have on my community? These are the things many authors writing own-voice stories struggle with. Still, here I am. A theme of this book is in community you can do scary things and thanks to the loving support of my husband, friends, family, readers, and fellow writers that believe in me, I'm bringing this story to the world.

While this is a fun, sexy, and swoony hockey romance with a guaranteed happy ending, it does explore some topics/themes that may be difficult for some. This includes depictions of ableism, loss of a parent (not on page, but discussed), a plane emergency (everyone survives and nobody is hurt), open door consensual sex (sorry Uncle Mike), discussion of a disabling injury (brief), a dog attack (the dog is uninjured and the human survives), depiction/discussion of toxic masculinity, loss of a sibling (briefly mentioned and not on page), stalking (not between the main characters), toxic/emotionally abusive relationship (not between the main characters), and cheating (mentioned but does not involve the main characters). As a trained social worker, I have endeavored to explore these topics in a thoughtful/sensitive way; however, I understand that some of these things may be difficult for some readers. Please do what you need to do to take care of yourself, while reading.

I'd also like to apologize in advance to the hockey community for anything I may have got wrong. Trust, my hockey obsessed husband will be the first to point out any penalties. As a proud Buffalo Sabres fan and someone that goes to Anaheim Ducks games regularly with my husband, I did my best to ensure the sport was accurately depicted in the book, but will fully own taking some literary license to make things fit with the story.

While steeped in reality, this book is a world of fiction. Any resemblance to actual people or places is purely coincidental. Any real places mentioned in this story may have a mix of actual and fictionalized details.

I hope that you fall in love with Pen and Rowan as much as I did writing them.

Happy Reading!
Melissa Whitney

CHAPTER ONE

Cane Austen and Me
Pen

"Mommy, what's she doing?" The small chirp of a child's voice draws my attention.

I am not the aforementioned "mommy," but my head tilts toward the tiny human anyway. There's something in the shock and awe in their voice telling me there is a small finger pointing at me.

"It's her stick—"

It's a cane. I don't correct the wrong terminology. Instead, my smile tight and white cane ahead of me, I stroll down the not-yet-fully awake Buffalo-Niagara Airport terminal.

"It helps her see."

Ah, if only it were that magical. It's barely seven a.m. After spending a week with my mother, I lack the temperamental bandwidth to explain to this woman and her child the intricacies of being legally blind. It's a cane. It doesn't help me see, but rather it's a tool to allow me to use nonvisual cues to get from point A to point T. Right now, the point T I'm destined for is the Tim Hortons tucked into the airport's food court.

Aunt Bea always said I was a shining light illuminating the darkness in the world's understanding of what it means to be blind. It's why I've dedicated so much of the last ten years to educate people through my social media page, Cane Austen and Me. To my thirty-thousand followers, I'm the "It" blind girl, documenting my every day and big adventures with Cane Austen, my white cane, helping the non-visually impaired world's knowledge be just a little less obscured about vision loss.

The knowledge that I'm no longer Aunt Bea's little light aches deep in my heart. I can almost feel her soft arms folded around me as she cooed, "Pen, you'll help them understand." No matter how tired I was, she'd have expected me to stop. Explain how the cane works. Tell the child that not all blind people can't see. Set his mommy dearest straight on the blind people facts, helping their little human grow up without misinformation and ensuring that other little humans – ones like me with failing vision – don't repeat the storyline I'd faced as I grew up.

Clear their vision, Aunt Bea's sing-song words dance in my heart.

Sighing, I pivot on my strappy, wedge sandals and head toward the sound of the mother and child. A little boy sits, feet kicking, beside a woman, her long hair gathered into a messy bun, at a half-full gate.

"Hi. I'm Pen." My free hand gathers my long auburn hair, brushing it onto my right shoulder. The action soothes the pulse of anxiety. No matter how many times I do this, it's still awkward as fuck. *Good thing I love you, Aunt Bea.*

The little boy tips his head to his mom, whose forehead puckers in confusion.

Yep, I'm weirding them out. Frankly, I don't blame them.

Most people don't have a lot of interactions with the legally blind. Let alone one who walks up to them and introduces themselves. Thanks to Aunt Bea, that is exactly who I am. Even if there are days – like today – where I wish I wasn't. Where I'd rather fade into the crowd, unseen and forgotten.

"I heard you ask about my cane," I lace just enough sweetness into my words to not send anyone into a sugar-rush. "This is Cane Austen. I'm legally blind, and she helps me stay safe. See how I sweep the cane? It's called constant contact and helps me trail things to guide my path or find things, so I don't trip and fall." With a tight upward curl of my mouth, I demonstrate how I use the cane.

"Are all canes girls?" The little boy's face twists into a pout.

A genuine smile kicks across my face. "Not all, but this one is."

"Why did you name it Cane Austen?" The woman's eyebrows knit.

"So she'll help me find my Mr. Darcy," I quip, making the woman snort with laughter.

It was the same reaction Aunt Bea had. This is my tenth Cane Austen. I've had a new one every year since I was sixteen. While everyone else was getting their first car, I was getting my first cane. The eye condition I have, retinitis pigmentosa, progressed to the point that a cane is necessary to keep me safe. I'd been diagnosed at age six, so I knew my vision was fading to black at a glacial pace…slow but unstoppable. The gradual progression of vision loss didn't lessen the painful realization that, while classmates were getting their licenses and cars, I was facing just another way in which I wasn't like them.

Not allowing me to wallow, Aunt Bea presented me with my first white cane. Blindfolding me – which she found hilarious – she dragged me into the driveway where she gifted me a white cane tied up with a giant red bow. She'd even put a Porsche sticker on it, winking as she affirmed that her niece would travel in style. "You gotta name this bad bitch," she'd crooned, explaining that the cane was my car, and everyone named their vehicles.

The little boy worries his lower lip, as if considering his words. "What does 'legally blind' mean?"

What, indeed? To the world blind means you can't see, but unsuspecting civilians didn't realize that blindness is served on a spectrum. The majority of legally blind people are like me, with some usable vision. There's a whole medical explanation that Trina, my ophthalmologist bestie, would bore people with at parties. I keep it simple, saying I have enough vision to get myself in trouble but not enough to always get myself out of it. Which is why I avoid trouble. As adventurous as Aunt Bea raised me to be, I don't take uncalculated risks.

After finishing my impromptu blindness in-service, I leave the smiling mother/son pair and redirect myself toward Tim Hortons. My flight to LAX doesn't board for another hour, so I have ample time to secure my sought after breakfast sandwich and make it to the gate to lose myself in my steamy romance audiobook. There's something delightful about listening to the swoony and sometimes illicit words of a favorite male narrator, with his hot guy voice, in public places. The idea of exposure makes the risk so much more rewarding. Whoever ends up sitting next to me on my flight home would, no doubt, turn a violent shade of red if they only knew what I was listening to.

Grinning, I stroll toward Tim Hortons. *Bless the airport gods!* I fight the urge to wiggle my hips, spotting only one other person in front of me. The sweet ecstasy of a multi-grain breakfast sandwich and apple cinnamon tea is within my grasp. Besides seeing Trina, Tim Hortons was the only thing bringing me joy on this trip back to Buffalo. After moving to Seal Beach, California with Aunt Bea at seventeen, this Western New York staple was the only thing I missed. That includes my mother, who was already on husband number three at that time, and had *no* problem letting her teenaged daughter move cross country without her.

Whenever Aunt Bea and I went home, the first thing we'd do was hit Tim Hortons. Each Christmas, Mom sent us an assortment of teas, coffee, and hot chocolate from the retailer. Even this last Christmas. Though there's no longer a coffee drinker in the house.

I swallow the growing lump in my throat. Adjusting the large weekender bag on my shoulder, I force my focus to the back of the head in front of me. Only, in order for my gaze to actually land on the back of the man's head requires craning my neck. *How tall is he?* I'm five eight, but he's a giant.

"The card machine isn't working," the peppy cashier says to the tall man.

"Oh." His large hand slips to his pocket.

No doubt the action is to grab the wallet bulging from his back pocket and not to call attention to the way the faded jeans hug his firm backside. One that Trina would joke that she could bounce a quarter off. Although, I could think of far more pleasurable things to do with that ass.

Stop checking out his behind! Pushing my red-frame glasses atop my head, I twist my now extra foggy vision away from the tall man's cute butt. I mean, how would I feel if he was ogling me like I'm the last cupcake?

That might be a nice change. It's been a minute since someone looked at me with the same kind of covetous gaze that I'd used when looking at baked goods after that illbegotten month I tried to give up carbs. Life's too short to not eat a cookie or ten.

"Shit!" he grumbles, closing his wallet. "Is there an ATM around?"

Second-hand embarrassment on his behalf flushes my cheeks. Few people carry cash on them. My always prepared motto means I'm not one of them. No matter what country I'm in, my wallet remains stocked.

The cashier taps the counter. "I think there's one down by gate twelve."

"Thanks. I'll run down and come back," he says, slipping his wallet into his back pocket.

Poor guy. My lips drag into a frown. Traveling is frustrating enough but to toss in an unnecessary trip across the airport terminal is obnoxious.

"No need, I got this," I offer, pulling my glasses back down. "I have cash."

"No, it's—" His words halt as he spins to face me. Beneath the brim of a blue cap, a smile curves at his lips. Its brightness is accentuated by his tidy dark beard.

A sudden swoop seizes my stomach, causing an explosion of butterflies. *That's new. Am I into men with beards?*

A navy Henley molds to his muscular frame. A fresh woodsy scent wafts from him, eliciting scenes of a pre-dawn walk through a dew-kissed forest. His entire aesthetic screams sexy lumberjack. Like someone who would press you against a tree, its rough bark biting into your bare ass, while even rougher hands held you in place.

Good lord, perhaps I need to cut down on my dirty audiobooks.

"That's kind of you, but I have cash. It's just in the bank." A gentle, barely noticeable Irish lilt mingles with his low gruff timbre.

I love the way unique voices tingle along my nerves. Perhaps my dulled vision heightens the way I hear the world, but I revel in the musicality of voices, picking out the unique notes that make each one distinct.

"Those pesky banks holding our cash hostage." My smile lifts, just a little bit more, with his soft chuckle. "It's really no big deal."

"Are you sure?"

"This will give me at least five karma points for the day." Stepping up, I join him at the counter.

"Are you in need of karma points?"

"Well, I did send my mother to voicemail this morning." *Twice.* But he doesn't need to know that.

This trip I lasted three of the five days I'd planned to stay at my mother's house, a new record, before I sought refuge. On day four, I retreated to Trina's, feigning that she had more reliable Wi-Fi for me to work from than the farmhouse my mother lives in with Charlie, her latest husband.

He grins. "I wouldn't want to get in the way of you reaching Nirvana."

"Thanks." I brush my long hair behind my ear, facing the cashier. "Can I get a large apple cinnamon tea and bacon, egg, and cheese breakfast sandwich on a multigrain bagel."

The cashier shakes their head, a big laugh bursting. "That's two apple cinnamon teas and bacon, egg, and cheese breakfast sandwiches on a multigrain bagel."

Twisted toward the man, my eyebrow arches. "Tea?"

He wags a finger. "That judgy eyebrow may cost you some of your karma points."

I gesture at him. "You just don't seem the *tea* type."

"What type do I seem?"

I frown and cock one hip. "Like 'drinks gasoline while eating a burger made out of the grizzly bear he just killed with his bare hands' type."

"That's preposterous," he scoffs. "Everyone knows moose make better burgers."

"I stand corrected." I laugh, pulling out my wallet.

After paying for our food, we slide down the counter.

Drinks in hand, we stand waiting for our breakfast sandwiches. Other customers file up to the counter, while we remain in silence. Not uncomfortable or awkward silence, just companionable. Sipping my sweet, spicy tea, my eyes flick between the staff preparing our food and the sexy lumberjack beside me.

I play the game we all play when meeting someone: using the little external clues to put together a picture of who he is. His clothes are comfortable and well-worn, but clean. One hand grips the to-go cup, while the other brushes the back of his head as if he's nervous.

Do I make him nervous? *No, that can't be.* Men like him make people nervous, not the other way around.

Gnawing on my lower lip, I try to think of the last man I made nervous. Besides Cael, Trina's fiancé who was terrified that her oldest and closest friend wouldn't give him the stamp of approval, the last man with a wisp of nerves around me may have been Alex. *Ugh, Alex.*

"Pen," I blurt.

His head tips to the right. "Pencil?"

Laughter bubbles out of me. "My name is Pen. Well, it's actually Penelope Meadows, but my friends call me Pen."

He grins. "Rowan."

Of course, his name is Rowan. That name radiates big D hot guy energy. Not a Herman or Stanley vibe about him.

"Nice to meet you, Pen." His hand envelops mine, sending a jolt of something zipping along my nerves.

I try not to fixate on that little tingle but have to admit failure. When was the last time my body reacted to someone like this?

"So, are you coming or going?"

Seriously? Coming or going? Who am I? I school my features into a pleasant smile stamping out the blooming wince at my non-stellar verbal skills.

"Excuse me?"

"Are you coming into town or leaving?"

"Both."

"Overachiever," I tease, pivoting towards him, and my arm brushes against his. My senses hum with the quick caress of his muscular body against mine.

He clears his throat. "I drove down from Hamilton, Ontario to catch my flight."

"So, where you heading to?"

"L.A."

"Me too!" I say with far too much pep.

What is wrong with me? I'm like an overexcited puppy. I should be cool and indifferent, not exclaim with the fevered devotion of two ten-year-olds exchanging friendship bracelets on the first day of camp.

"Well, *not* L.A. I live in Seal Beach, but LAX is a direct flight getting me the hell out of here sooner."

Why am I sputtering? *Awkward, party of one.*

"Not a fan of Buffalo?" He shifts, turning to face me.

"I have nothing against Buffalo as a city. People are nice. Love the wings. It's just…"

Stop talking, Pen! Do not emotionally vomit on this poor man. All he wanted was breakfast, not to have you overshare.

"…just prefer being home." I tighten my hold on Cane Austen's handle.

"Buffalo's not home?"

"Not anymore." I shake my head.

Rowan's hat brim shadows the upper half of his face, making it hard to read his expression. Reading facial expressions isn't my forte. Even with the limited vision I do have, it's often difficult to make out the tiny cues that can be found in someone's face. Aunt Bea always talked about the stories in the eyes. Those are stories I'm unable to read. If I'm close enough and the light is just right, I can make out

9

some of the little eyebrow ticks, lip quirks, or forehead wrinkles.

My stories come from the voice and energy. Everyone has a kind of energy they exude. It may make me sound like the lady with a different crystal for each day of the week, but it's something I've learned to trust.

Right now, the energy coming off Rowan telegraphs annoyance, but I don't think it's directed at me. Despite my oversharing, his broad frame remains mere inches away. His obscured gaze fixed on me.

He nods. "I get it. I've only lived in L.A. for three years and it feels more like home than Hamilton where I grew up."

"Canadian boy, eh?"

He snorts at the terrible joke laced in my even worse Canadian accent.

Smirking, I raise my tea to my lips. "So, how did a nice Canadian lad end up in L.A.?"

His hand rubs his neck. "Work."

"What do you do for wo—"

"Christ," he groans, yanking out his cell from his back pocket. "Sorry, this is the fourth call in a row that I've ignored. I need to take this."

"Sure." I smile.

Holding the phone up, he grumbles, "This best be important." Pivoting, he strides away from the counter.

"Ma'am." The cashier holds up two bags with what I suspect are our breakfast sandwiches.

With a nodded "thank you," I take them. In literally five seconds, I've lost Rowan. Scanning the now bustling food court, he's disappeared into the crowd. Do I wait? Do I try to track him down? Do I just take his sandwich in hopes that I run into him again? What if he comes back and thinks I stole his sandwich? Although, I paid for it, so it's not stealing.

"Excuse me, do you see that man I was with?" I ask the cashier.

"He went over there." She points.

"Where? Can you verbally explain?" I hold up Cane Austen in a nonverbal reminder that pointing is not the best way to give direction to the visually impaired.

"Oh, sorry." The blush can be heard in her voice. "Far right corner… My right, not yours."

"Thanks."

Turning, I set off listening for his voice. Moving through the crowd, I make my way toward the far-right corner. Voice recognition is the best way for me to find people in large gatherings. Although, it's not ideal with someone I just met, there's something about Rowan's voice that has imprinted on me, both distinct yet familiar. Like nothing I've heard before but somehow something as well-known to me as my own.

"Damnit, I told you I don't want to do that," Rowan growls.

I halt. Not because I've found him, but due to the frustration underscoring his words. He's pissed.

"This is fucking bullshit."

Really pissed.

With his back to me, he carries on in an annoyed mutter with no idea I'm standing behind him, eavesdropping. It's not intentional, but I'm listening, nonetheless. Granted, my relationship with Rowan is five minutes old, but this anger reads wrong on him. Like an ill-fitting Halloween costume. Also, I'm not going to overthink my use of the word relationship.

Raking my teeth against my lower lip, I clutch the sandwich bag. I should turn, run away, and give the sandwich back to the cashier. Let them give it to the angry man. Not because I'm scared. There's no nip of fear telling me to stay away. Rather, it's more like witnessing someone do something they don't want to do.

"You're being a real motherfucker," he snarls, causing a few onlookers to clear their throats.

Ouch. I don't blame them. His tone is harsh.

Dropping his duffle by his feet, Rowan's rigid stance slumps. His free hand grips the back of his neck. The movement communicates regret.

"I'm sorry. That was uncalled for." Scuffing his sneakers along the floor, he lets out a beleaguered sigh. "I know. You're *my* motherfucker."

Aw. It's almost sweet the way it rolls off his tongue.

"We can discuss this when I get back. My flight gets in…" Pivoting, he comes face-to-face with me, mouth slack. "Pen." It comes out almost pained.

Crap! "I wasn't listening… Well, I was, but not intentionally. I—" I hoist up the Tim Hortons bag. "Breakfast!"

"Thanks," he says, drawing out the word and taking the offered bag.

"Sorry."

The muffled voice of whoever is on the other end of the call crackles between us.

"I should go." Frowning, I turn and hurry away.

So fricking embarrassing. Rowan is clearly having a day and I'm all like "Here I am holding your breakfast sandwich hostage while eavesdropping on your conversation with someone you fondly refer to as motherfucker."

Finding my gate, I fold myself into an uncomfortable plastic chair to devour my breakfast sandwich and fall into my latest audiobook. The sultry timbre of Wesley Williamson – my favorite narrator – helps me escape into the world of thousand-year-old hot vampires with Mr. Darcy vibes. The story being woven in my earbuds helps me leave the last week behind. Leave why I came back to Buffalo, the tension with my mother, and the awkward meet-cute with Rowan.

Rowan. My stomach flip-flops between a sigh and a flutter at the thought of him. I hope everything turns out okay with he and motherfucker. It seemed to have turned the corner before he'd caught me listening in. I scan the boarding area, wondering if he's here. He's not. At least, I don't see him which doesn't mean he's not here. He's bound for L.A. Are we on the same flight? The Buffalo-Niagara Airport is small, but not *that* small. There are several airlines flying direct to Los Angeles in this time window.

"Penelope Meadows, please see the agent at gate eleven's counter." A voice booms over the sound system, interrupting the vampire/awkward girl meet-cute.

Hitting pause, I sling my bag over my shoulder and shuffle with Cane Austen to the counter. "I'm Penelope," I say, reaching the agent.

"Ms. Meadows." The agent beams. "Your seat has been upgraded. I have a new boarding pass for you."

"Upgraded?" I blink.

"You're still in a window seat, but you've been moved to first class. Seat one-A. We'll start pre-boarding in a few minutes for our passengers with disabilities. Would you like assistance going down the jetway?"

First class from Buffalo to Los Angeles? Perhaps I had earned some karma points after all. Thanking the agent and telling them I wouldn't need assistance, I head back to my seat.

Pulling my phone from my pocket, I check my messages. Despite the frown, guilt swirls in my stomach at the four unread messages from my mother. Sighing, I open them and respond.

Me: I'm at my gate.

Mom: Good! Did you click on the links I sent you to those clinical trials?

Eyes closed, I release a hard breath. If it isn't messages about my love life, it's ones about studies to cure my eye condition. *She means well,* Aunt Bea's cautious warning plays on repeat inside me. Opening my eyes, I reply.

Me: I'll look at them when I get home, so I can see them on the larger screen. I'll message when I'm home.

It's a lie, but my energy for this familiar conversation is nonexistent.

I swipe to my message with JoJo, my West Coast bestie. Trina is insistent that I'm allowed two best friends if I designate them by coasts. Trina Lyons, who is two years older than me, was my first bestie due to close proximity. She lived next door until I moved with Aunt Bea to California. I met JoJo Rivers a year later as freshmen in undergrad.

Me: Flight is on time. You still picking me up at the airport?

JoJo: Does a hobby horse have a hickory dick?

Me: A simple yes would do.

JoJo: Then I wouldn't be me. Tongue out emoji.

I snort just a bit. Even with the magnification program on my cell, I have the worst time with GIFs and emojis, so JoJo spells them out for me. It's both sweet and totally self-serving because I'm a hundred percent positive that a majority of the GIFs and emojis that she spells out do not exist.

JoJo: How are you doing, BTW?

God, that's a loaded question. My heart aches just thinking about the many, many responses rattling around in me. How does one respond when their entire world as they know it has been ripped away in a single moment?

Me: Okay.

JoJo: Acceptance smiley face when your friend is pretending they are okay when they're not emoji.

Me: Middle finger emoji.

JoJo: Gasp emoji.

Me: These aren't real emojis emoji.

JoJo: I love you emoji.

Me: I love you too emoji. We'll have all the LAX to Orange County traffic to dig into how I'm doing. I promise.

JoJo: Excited social worker friend emoji.

Hearing them announce pre-boarding, I text goodbye to JoJo and slip my phone into the pocket of my denim jacket. The late June weather is warm, allowing me to sport my favorite pale pink cotton sundress, but the jacket will keep me warm on the plane.

I won't pretend that excitement doesn't crisscross inside me at turning left while boarding the plane. The first-class lifestyle isn't something I've indulged in. Outside of that all-inclusive resort Aunt Bea took me to in celebration of my master's degree. As first-class as I typically get is getting to skip the wait at Bread, my favorite breakfast spot in downtown Seal Beach, because Aunt Bea and I've gone there every Saturday for the last nine years. *Almost every Saturday.*

Ignoring the twinge in my heart, I follow the flight attendant to my seat in the front row, which means more leg room. It also means all my things have to go up top. Pulling out the things I'll want quick access to – bottled water, bag of trail mix, phone, and earbuds – I toss my bag into the overhead bin and plop into my seat.

Head pressed against the window, I lose myself in my audiobook which drowns out the flight's boarding soundtrack – murmured apologies, cleared throats, and muttered, "I think that's my seat," and the repeated chastising of a passenger for blocking the aisle.

Someone takes the seat beside me. The furnace of their body laps against my skin. A fresh woodsy scent makes my eyelids flutter open. Straightening, I turn my face toward my seatmate.

"Pen," Rowan drawls.

CHAPTER TWO

Don't Let this be the End
Rowan

An unbridled grin stretches across my face, taking in the shock illuminating Pen's features. The gold in her brown eyes was bright, mirroring warm honey, like a punctuation mark to her sweetness. Her pink heart-shaped mouth forms an "O" and then lifts into that same big smile that blasted me at Tim Hortons.

"Rowan." She tugs at a piece of glossy hair. A nervous tick that I'd noticed her do a few times in our brief interaction. Each time she did it, I wondered how those dark locks with rich red waves woven through the tresses would feel wrapped around my fingers.

You sound creepy. I clear my throat. "Looks like we're seat-mates," I say, clicking my seatbelt. A decadent, candied aroma wafts between us, cocooning me in her lush scent. *Alright, I am creepy.*

"What are the odds?" She crosses one leg over the other, drawing my attention to toned sun-kissed limbs.

I move my gaze back to her face, trying not to think about those legs wrapped around my waist, her body writhing beneath me. "What are the odds, indeed."

If she only knew. I'd suffered only a moderate amount of shock in finding Pen sitting beside me. It feels stalkerish, but not completely. After she offered to pay for my food, I planned to repay her in some way. My mam may *tsk* "Rowan Michael Iverson, don't insult others by not accepting their kindness," but she also taught me to always take care of a lady. Glimpsing Pen's boarding pass while she dug for her wallet at the counter, I knew that was my opportunity. A way to thank her without seeming like an ungrateful asshole unwilling to accept a stranger paying for their meal. Especially such a pretty one.

No, not pretty – beautiful. A blend of sweetness and strength radiates from Pen. The loveliness of her voice as she'd said, "I've got this," had thrummed in my ears but her incandescent smile gut-punched me. If Greg, my agent, hadn't engaged in his favorite new hobby of blowing up my mobile for the last three days, I could have stayed drinking in her smile for hours.

When Pen scampered away after overhearing my less-than-polite but far too regular conversation with my bulldog agent, he repaid me by having his assistant upgrade her seat to first class. The plan was never to have her seated beside me, but Greg subscribes to his own brand of agenting. Doing what he wants for me rather than what I want for myself. I just want to repay her kindness…and maybe a little part of me doesn't like the idea of Pen crammed into the last row of the plane for the five-and-a-half-hour flight. At this moment, watching her bite her lower lip, the tiniest of pink gracing her cheeks, I may up Greg's percentage, or at the very least send him a gift basket.

"I'm sorry for eavesdropping on your call," she offers, the color deepening on her cheeks.

"Yeah." A slight wince covers my features.

It's not the first time someone has witnessed me lose my temper. Fuck, there's an entire Sportscenter gag reel of my bleeped-out outbursts cut to the beat of Taylor's Swift's "You Need to Calm Down." My dad would joke he went to a boxing match and a hockey game broke out. Somehow in a sport known for its aggression, I get labeled the poster child for anger management.

Still, the thought of Pen witnessing that part of me so soon after meeting churns in my gut. I don't want to hide who I am from her, but the idea of her seeing me as the world sees me...

"I hope things turned out okay with you and motherfuck-er," she says. The sweetest goddamn smile widens on her face.

"Ha!" I bark, unashamed of the booming laugh. "Yeah. He's fine. Greg can be *a lot.*"

"Guess he earned the nickname, then."

"That he did." I smirk, thinking motherfucker may be my nicest term of endearment for my agent of the last ten years. "I'm sorry you overheard that."

"No apology needed. I was the one chasing you down."

"I'm happy you did."

Even if I don't like that she witnessed my mini meltdown, something buzzed in my blood seeing her there. Standing there – bag in hand – her eyes wide with embarrassment, apology, and determination to ensure I got my breakfast sandwich. How many people would offer to pay for a complete stranger's breakfast then chase them down in a busy food court to ensure they got it? Most people wouldn't. Although, I already know Pen isn't like most people.

My brother, Gillian, would warn me that I don't know

her, not really. That I'm blinded by a gorgeous smile and stunning personality. He'd say I'm thinking with my cock. He may be right. He generally is about me. But something tells me in this he's wrong. *Very wrong.*

"Thank you," I offer. She'd run off so quickly after bringing me the sandwich that I hadn't gotten a chance to thank her.

"You're welcome." She just beams.

God, I could drown in that smile. Allowing its warm waves to wash over me cleansing away the last week. The sting of a lost championship, thirsty reporters, disappointed yet not surprised family, and a pissed-off coach dwindle to mere shadows in her presence.

She wraps a tendril of auburn hair around her finger. "I didn't know you were on this flight. I didn't see you in the gate area." Her face scrunches in self-deprecation. "Of course, me not seeing something doesn't mean much."

"I don't know if I should laugh at your blind joke or not." I rub the back of my head.

"You must laugh or *no* karma points for you."

A low chuckle rolls out of me at the serious pout puckering her pretty face.

Her lips tug up into a smirk.

"May I…" I shift in my seat, trying to figure out how to word the question without sounding like a dick.

The first few traits of Pen that I cataloged were that brilliant smile, those honey eyes, shapely figure – I am a man after all – and all that hair. God, my fingers itch to thread into her hair, pulling her close in a deep kiss. The thought ran on repeat while we'd chatted at Tim Hortons. It wasn't until we moved down the counter that I noticed the cane.

"You can ask." She leans back against the plush leather seat.

"I imagine you have people ask you all the time."

"Not really." She shakes her head, a silent laugh sparking in her eyes. "Most people don't ask me directly."

I frown. "What does that mean?"

"They usually talk *at* me, spewing whatever misinformation they have about blindness, gush, 'God bless you' or, most frequently, ignore me completely. Well, they don't *exactly* ignore me completely. I have enough vision to see their stares and pointing fingers."

"Assholes." My jaw clenches.

Her palm rests on my hand, its warmth soothing the angry beast inside me. I fight a strong urge to punch anyone who'd ever looked at this gorgeous creature with pity or indifference. The same angry beast that came out a week ago as I ignored repeated calls from Greg to fix this or else I'll find myself wearing yet another new jersey.

"It's okay, Rowan. My Aunt Bea always said the world is full of assholes, but it's also full of a lot of good people. People who ask questions rather than assume. People who meet my gaze when they talk to me."

Placing my other hand atop hers, sandwiching it between my far larger ones, my gaze meets hers. "How much can you see?"

"May I show you?"

An electric zing pulses across my skin with the sensation of her satin hands wrapped around mine. Folding them into small circles, she brings them to my eyes like makeshift glasses. The TV screen and flap with inflight magazines is eclipsed in the tiny holes I look through.

"Like that, but with a layer of fuzziness. I see things; however, the details can be unclear like looking through a fogged-up telescope. My peripheral vision is pretty much MIA, so I use Cane Austen to get around safely," she explains, releasing her hands from mine.

A shiver slides down my spine at how wrong it feels to

lose the contact. Like somehow my body never felt warm until she touched me.

Ice runs in Iverson's veins. It's the most common descriptor announcers, reporters and, even, some teammates use for me. For ten years, I've been Rowan 'Iceman' Iverson, top defenseman in the National Hockey League. I'd been called a ruthless, unfeeling machine with only one goal: defend.

Pushing those thoughts away, I arch an eyebrow. "Cane Austen?"

"My cane."

"Favorite Austen book?"

"*Mansfield Park.*" Her entire face explodes into a grin. "You?"

"*Emma.*"

"Tea and *Emma.*" Smirking, her body shifts, as if she is giddy.

Can someone be both adorable and fucking sexy as hell all at the same time? I want to pull her into the bathroom, lift her onto the counter, fall to my knees and worship her until she screams my name *and* have her curl up against me watching a sappy movie. The dichotomy of each scenario sighs with a satisfying rightness through me. I want to do depraved things to her, while tucking her close, protecting and cherishing her all at the same time.

"The Colin Firth or Mathew MacFayden version of *Pride and Prejudice?*" I ask.

Gasping, she clutches her hand to her chest. "There's *no* choice. Any real Austen fan knows the Colin Firth version is superior. Sorry, Mathew MacFayden."

I chortle. "My mam would agree with you."

"Your mam?"

"My mother. She's a professor of English specializing in Austen. She got her PhD when I was a teenager, so there was a lot of Austen-related discussion and compulsory reading in my house growing up."

"The vile woman...making you read Austen and starting your proper male education," she teases.

I raise my finger and *tsk*. "Don't mock me. It was a *real* problem. I actually used the word court when dating my first girlfriend in secondary school."

"Secondary school? Mam?" She tilts her head. "I hear a slight Irish lilt, but it only comes in and out."

"I was born in Toronto, but my mam is from Dublin. She came to Canada for university and met my dad. They had a bit of a whirlwind—"

"Courtship," she interjects, with a cheeky grin.

"Yes." I nudge her shoulder with mine. "My brother Gillian was born ten months after they met."

"That is a whirlwind."

"A year later, Finn came along and then me the following year."

Pen motions to me. "There are two more of you? Are they as big as you? Your poor mother's vagina."

I grimace. "Please don't mention my mam's bits."

"Ladies don't have bits," she scoffs. "You gentlemen have that market cornered."

"Noted."

"So, the Irish-ish accent is just something that rubbed off from your mam?" The tiny dimples punctuating her smile pop with the word "mam."

"A bit, but we moved back to Dublin when I was nine and lived there until I was sixteen when mam went back to university in Canada to finish her degree." I hold my breath knowing what the next question will be and deciding if I'll answer. It's not something I talk about with anyone. Even with Finn and Gillian. Outside of Wes, my unwanted and persistent friend, I've barely spoken about it outside the cliff notes version.

"Why'd you move to Ireland?"

Peering into her coaxing eyes, I have no choice. It just comes out. "My dad died, so we moved in with my grandparents."

My eyes close for a moment, drifting back to that flight. Eleven-year-old Gillian sitting beside me, nudging my ribs and hissing, "Shut up." Ten-year-old Finn, the spitting image of our mother with golden hair and blue eyes, presses tight to her side cooing, "It's okay mam." Her tear-logged stare fixes forward while saying, "Rowan, I'm sorry."

"I get it," Pen's delicate fingers thread with mine, pulling my attention to her. A thoughtful expression etched in her lovely features. "We moved in with my Aunt Bea when I was three after my dad died."

I squeeze her hand, allowing the action to bind me to her in this shared understanding of each other's grief. In not just losing someone we loved far too soon – too soon to even really know them beyond the flicker of memories and stories from others – but in the loss of our entire world.

"What's your favorite memory of him?" she asks, her thumb dancing along mine. Each caress is reminiscent of kisses across my skin.

"We had a pond behind our house where we'd swim in the summer and, in the winter when it iced over, we skated. My brothers didn't like skating. Finn preferred being in the house with mam and Gillian...found me annoying." I grin, knowing his feelings hadn't changed over the years.

Though, Gillian wouldn't use the word annoying. He has far more colorful words to describe me now.

"Dad and I would skate for hours. He'd been a hockey player at university until he hurt his knee. He never stopped loving the game. My brothers watched with him but didn't share the same passion as he and I did. On our pond's ice, it was our time just me and him. I wasn't one of his boys but *his* son."

"Are you still into hockey?"

My gaze meets hers. "I am."

"Good." Her smile drips with acceptance.

The open admiration in her eyes unspools the tangled emotions in my chest. That sense of being alone – being unseen – dissolves in the way she looks at me. Like somehow, she sees me. *The real me.* The lonely boy forced to say goodbye to the father he loved and the life he knew. The guarded man that bought his childhood home to sit beside that pond in hopes to hear the whispered voice of the past.

"Just checking in to see if you need anything. Perhaps, a drink? I know you declined during our first pass," The flight attendant asks, pulling my stare away from Pen.

"Ah." I blink, not realizing there was an entire flight outside of the little bubble that Pen and I had fallen into. The rest of the world was drowned out by this woman. I'd not noticed anything. Not the safety announcements. Not the takeoff. Nothing.

Pen's almost conspiratorial glance telegraphs that she'd been very much in that bubble with me.

"Tea, please. English Breakfast if you have it."

The flight attendant nods. "And your wife? What would she like?" He tips his head to Pen.

My wife? The attraction between us is palpable, but we've just met. Even if the initial thought I had when first meeting her was *mine, mine, mine* – as if I'm a fucking caveman – she's not mine.

Though, I don't like the way the flight attendant is looking at her, nor the dismissive way he referred to Pen. Mine or not, I'd expect him – or anyone – to address her directly. To meet her gaze. *No. Fuck that.* He should bow to

24

this goddess beside me because God knows that's all I want to do is prostrate myself at her feet.

I open my mouth....

But Pen steals my words. "His wife"—she clears her throat— "can answer her *own* questions and would also like an English Breakfast tea." Somehow, she's both sweet and fierce in the polite request, making me want her even more.

My gaze flicks from Pen to the flight attendant, flashing him a stern glare. A snarl building in my throat.

"Apologies." He shifts foot-to-foot, the muscles of his throat working.

Her features are soft. "It's totally fine. My hubby gives off *major* alpha vibes, so I get it. Don't let the growly face fool you..." Raising her hands, she pinches my cheeks and coos, "He's a total softy."

I scowl, fighting the grin that curls my lips. Everything about this woman makes me smile. But the scowl is also for her, at the idea that this is not the first time she's dealt with someone not speaking directly to her. That someone only saw her cane, not her.

"He is commanding." The flight attendant blushes. "I'll bring you both some warm chocolate chip cookies with your tea." With a placating expression, he moves to the next row.

"Asshole," I mutter under my breath.

She taps my cheek. "Easy, hubby, or I'll make you give me your cookie."

Fuck, she can have everything if she keeps looking at me that way.

"I guess he's one of those assholes your Aunt Bea talks about."

Wistfulness swims in her expression at the mention of her aunt. "Perhaps. Or he's just a little misguided."

"You have so much grace. I was about to tell him to fuck off."

Shaking her head, she laughs. "I know you were. The anger radiated off you. If I told everyone who got it wrong to fuck off, I'd be all out of fucks to give. Gotta save those fucks for when I truly need them."

I huff an incredulous laugh. "I seem to have an ample supply."

"Perhaps we should get you some herbal tea, then." She pats my knuckles.

Without thinking, I envelop her hand in mine. Her touch is the only calming elixir I need or want.

"You said you're still into hockey...do you still play to stay close to your dad?"

I shift in my seat. "Yes."

"I'm glad." Her fingers tighten around mine. "It's important to hold on to the things that keep us close to the people we love."

I clear my throat. "Do you have something like that with your dad?"

"I was so young when he died. He's just a picture in a frame to me." The corners of her mouth tick down into a small frown.

"I'm sorry."

"It's okay. I never missed him. At least not the way I think you're supposed to. It may be because of my Aunt Bea. She was my dad's twin sister. My grandmother always said they were two peas in a pod, so in a way I had a piece of him through her." Sadness shimmers in her stare.

My thumb strokes along her smooth skin, wanting to ask what darkened her brightness. A wave of selfishness washes through me when I look at Pen. I want to coax free every secret, sad memory, happy thought, and all that lives within her.

"We're like the most depressing seatmates." She chuckles, her face crinkled with what looks like self-reproach. "Maybe we should nix the tea and get mimosas. We need to liven this place up." Her lips pucker, seeming to consider something. "Truth or dare?"

"What?"

She pokes me with her free hand. "You heard me, hubby. Truth or dare?"

"Truth." I grin.

"Tell me a secret." Her forehead wrinkles. "A fun one. I think we've done enough emotional vomiting this morning."

One secret raises its hand, wanting to be told. My eyes fall to her mouth, watching the flash of white teeth bite into that plump lower lip. I want to lean across the armrest and sink into her lips. Make her whimper with a nipping kiss, coaxing her to open for me. To slide my tongue against hers, drinking up what I know – without having ever tasted – would be the most decadent thing I've ever consumed.

"A secret," I murmur, raising my free hand to her face, cradling her cheek. Brushing the rough pads of my fingers against her silken skin, her eyes close like a kitten reveling in the soft strokes of loving hands. On the ice, I play with no regard for anything but what I want. And what I want right now is to claim her pretty mouth for mine.

"Rowan," she says, a tiny hitch in her breath.

"Pen," I whisper, leaning in...

A sudden jerk yanks us apart. My back crashing into the seat.

"Turbulence?" Pen's hand clutches mine.

This feels like more than the standard bumps of air travel. Jolts rattle the cabin, causing passengers to shift violently in their seats. Gasps and screams fill the plane. My arms wrap around Pen, holding her close with the increasingly rough turbulence.

"Folks, this is your captain." The pilot's steady voice

crackles over the intercom. "Please ensure you're seated with your belt buckled. Flight attendants, take your seats."

Two flight attendants grip the seats, trying to make their way down the aisle. A sudden violent shift flings one forward, the other grabs her arm to steady her but misses.

"Please ensure your belts are secure. Put up tray tables." The male flight attendant who took our drink order commands, helping the other one off the ground. Both amble toward their seats.

"What's happening?" Pen's eyes widen, her body burrowing deep into my side.

"I don't know, but I've got you." I run my fingers into her hair, massaging soothing circles on her scalp and praying this isn't the end.

I'd just found her, after all.

CHAPTER THREE

Option B
Pen

We're alive. A little dazed, I take Rowan's hand and follow him off the plane. My weekender bag and his duffle hang over his broad shoulders. I'd not even realized he'd gotten both our bags until we attempted to squeeze into the aisle together. Stepping into the intense midday sunshine, I wince. The stinging rays jolt me into the reality of the last thirty minutes.

The violent turbulence turned into a rapid descent and an emergency landing somewhere in Michigan. I have the vague recollection of the pilot's calm voice explaining that there were mechanical issues necessitating an emergency landing. The entire time, Rowan kept his protective arms wrapped tightly around me.

And he continues to hold on to me, which I don't mind in the least. Descending the narrow ramp to the tarmac our fingers remain linked. It should be weird. We don't really know each other. Still, there's something about my hand in his that seems right.

"Here," Rowan says, plopping his hat onto my head. "It's bright out here."

"What about you?"

"I've got another one in my duffle. I'll grab it when we get inside." His head tilts to the small terminal building at the end of the orange-coned barrier path.

"Thank you." Some rather insistent butterflies make their presence known in my stomach.

Rowan's kind gesture dissolves away the fear still biting my frayed nerves. I don't want to be melodramatic about this, but we could have died. We didn't but.... Instead, I sink into the knowledge that I'm alive, holding Rowan's hand while we zigzag across the tarmac.

Rowan. Was he about to kiss me before the plane did whatever the hell that was? The sensation of his fingers coasting over my cheeks lingers. His fresh woodsy scent enveloping me as he leaned in. It's been a while since I've been kissed, but I could still read the signs.

Entering the building, a frazzled flight attendant instructs passengers to take a seat in the boarding area so they can assist us with getting home. Rowan guides us to a pair of empty plastic chairs and tosses our bags onto them.

Turning, he grips my shoulders. "Are you okay?"

"Yeah. You?" I rasp, blinking.

The surrealness of today is dizzying. Any minute someone's going to pinch me and wake me up from this dream. I'll find myself in my original last row coach seat, having never met Rowan, and my flight safely en route to Los Angeles. The *Sliding Doors* effect with its alternative world in which I almost died in a plane crash but never met this man whose light eyes drink me in is not appealing.

"Are you sure?" His hands cup my face, seeming to search for something.

"Yes." Dropping a folded Cane Austen between us, I mirror his movements, requiring me to rise to my tiptoes. "God, you're tall. Why are you so tall?"

He huffs a quick laugh.

"Are you okay?"

Mouth slanted into a lopsided grin, he tucks me into a tight hug. "I am now."

"It was scary, but we're safe." Eyes closed, I listen to his heart's gentle thud. "Thank you for…"

I'm not sure what to say. *Thank you for holding me, reassuring me, and making me feel safe and even needed.* Somehow, the way Rowan held me on the plane spoke to his need of me. He both comforted and was comforted in one small action. For so much of my life, people want to protect me. They think my disability equates to a belief that I need to be taken care of. There's protectiveness in Rowan's arms but also the plea for me in the thump of his heart. His arms give as much as they take.

"…Just thank you," I murmur.

"Thank you." His chin rests atop my head.

"I think I want to walk home, though."

"Ditto."

No way was I walking home in my strappy wedge sandals. And double that sentiment on hopping on another flight. The only destination available from this airport was Chicago. If I thought one flight was unappealing, taking two was a nonstarter. Some passengers opted to be bused ninety minutes to Detroit to catch flights later tonight. With very little desire to climb into another plane today, Rowan and I take option B. We'll spend today here and rent a car to drive to Detroit tomorrow for a flight home. Option B isn't something the airline offers, but Rowan grunted that he and his "wife" would not be getting on a plane tonight.

The terrified flight attendant practically gulps, "Yes, Mr. Iverson."

Something about the way he says "my wife" causes an unexpected clench in my vagina. I am very much *not* his wife. The only thing I am to him is some random woman who bought his breakfast and sat next to him on a plane. We both know it. The little case of mistaken identity is probably just a ploy Rowan is using to… I don't know but I'm not correcting the little ruse.

I never had a desire to be possessed or claimed by anyone. Lord knows Alex, my ex-boyfriend, had a possessive streak and a desire to know where I was at all times, which led directly to his becoming the ex in his descriptor. Although, the warning bells that had sounded with Alex are dead silent with this man.

Adjusting Rowan's ball cap on my head, I greedily scan his muscular back – visible in his fitted Henley – while he fills out paperwork at the rental car counter. What would it be like to be possessed by this man? To have those strong arms folded around me at night. To allow his hands to trail down my body, heating and claiming every inch. To feel him move inside me, taking and giving all at the same time.

Heat crawls up my neck at the though. Five hours ago, Rowan was just a sexy lumberjack I offered to buy breakfast for. Now, he feels like something more. I'm not sure if it's the shared trauma of our near-death experience or the over-sharing we seem to do so easily with one another, but he feels real. Like a tangible dream I'd not realized I'd dreamt coming to life. And I can't stop wondering… Was he about to kiss me? And if he was, why hasn't he kissed me yet?

My phone buzzes. Slipping it out of my jacket's pocket, JoJo's name flashes on the screen.

"Hey," I answer.

"Are you okay? I've been flight stalking you on the airline app, and it says you had an emergency landing. Where are you? Are you okay?" Panic grips JoJo's tone.

"I'm okay." I force a smile on my face.

Even if someone can't see you, they can hear your smile. Just another Aunt Bea-ism instilled from a very young age. You'd be surprised how often smiling on difficult phone calls calms the other person. I've had a lot of practice with the obligatory weekly chat with my mother. "You're getting married *again*." *Smile.* "It's totally fine you're not flying out for my graduation." *Smile.* "Oh, sorry I'm not coming back for Christmas." *Smile.*

With a real smile – not the one reserved for my mother – I explain to JoJo what happened. Her frequent gasps of "oh my god" validate my "I was almost in a fricking plane crash" bewilderment.

"Thank the sweet baby Jesus you're okay." A relieved sigh rolls out of JoJo. "I don't have the bandwidth to find a new best friend. You were hard enough to train," she teases.

"Love you, too." I snort.

"Will you be on a flight later tonight? I can pick you up. What time will you get in?"

"Tomorrow around eight p.m."

"Tomorrow!" Her shrill response pricks my ears. "They almost kill *my* best friend, and now they can't fly you home to me until tomorrow?"

"Don't go rage posting about the airline," I tut. "They offered a flight, but we decided to take a break from flying after our near-death experience. We're staying here today. I'll explore what Michigan has to offer for my social. You know, blind girl takes on the Midwest. We'll drive to Detroit to catch our flight tomorrow afternoon."

"We? Our? We'll?!" Each word louder.

Shit. I cringe knowing exactly what I've done.

"Last time I checked *you* are not a member of the British Royal Family, so that can't be the use of the Royal We. Penelope Anne Meadows, are you *with* someone?"

"Can we include this in the things we wait to discuss on our drive back from LAX?" I worry my lower lip, watching Rowan accept a key ring from the rental car attendant.

"As if. What's his full name? I need to internet stalk him to ensure he's not a serial killer or a hipster with a man bun."

I resist the urge to cover my face with my hand. My West Coast bestie elevates internet stalking to an art form. With just a grainy cell phone picture taken in a dark club she found the guy she'd made out with one Halloween. In a not-so-happy ending, turned out he was married with three kids. Ending aside, JoJo has skills which she never ceases to use on behalf of her people.

And I'm her people. And she's mine. Since freshman year – thanks to the randomness of the college roommate lottery – she joined Trina in the sisters from other misters bestie brigade.

Snorting, I roll my eyes. "His name is Rowan Iverson."

"Rowan Iverson?" she almost gasps. "That is a *hot* guy name if I ever heard one."

"Yep." I bite back my oversized grin.

"Lady, how good looking are we talking?"

"Devastatingly," I breathe, taking in Rowan's tall figure sauntering my way.

"Well, if you end up at a hotel with only one room and one bed, just remember to use a condom... and tell me *everything.*"

"Life isn't a trope from a romance novel. Also, I'm not having sex with someone I just met."

"Maybe you should. You haven't had sex since Alex—" she

makes a barf noise. "Might be time to get the pipes clean. You know...use it or lose it, sister."

"Goodbye, JoJo."

"Wait! Don't hang up. Can you get a pic of hot guy Rowan? There are like a hundred Rowan Iversons coming up."

"Goodbye, JoJo." Laughing, I hang up.

Reaching me, Rowan dangles the keys. "Ready to head to the hotel?"

"Yes." My belly swoops just a bit, wondering if there's only one room at the inn and secretly hoping my life is like a romance novel.

IT'S NOT A ROMANCE NOVEL. NOT AT ALL.

Discontent sighs through me as Lola, the peppy clerk at Three Dog Night Inn, drawls, "You're just in luck, we had a last-minute cancellation, so we have two rooms available."

"Great," Rowan says, tapping his long fingers on the reception desk's dark wood surface.

Eyebrow arched, my head tilts to him. Was there a faint trace of disappointment in his "great"? *You're hearing things that aren't there, Pen.*

It's been at least two hours since he caressed my cheek and peered into my soul with those eyes that look either gray or green. Since the almost plane crash, he's had ample opportunity to make his move. Rowan doesn't strike me as the type of man to hold back. Like the flight attendant said...he's commanding. Even without the low rumble of his voice and Viking-like physique, a quiet confidence radiates from him. If he wants to kiss, he'll kiss. And I remain very much unkissed.

I need to let this schoolgirl fantasy go. To quote *Sex and the City*, he's just not that into me. This isn't a pity party. I know I'm cute. Like best friend's little sister or the unthreatening gal pal of your boyfriend cute. It's an aesthetic I embrace. There's just *one* thing that sometimes shades that cuteness.

"Will the two of you be checking out the Milford Waterfall while in town?" Lola asks, handing me back my credit card and ID. "It's a big tourist attraction a few miles outside of town. I can give you a map and mark the various trails to get you to the waterfalls."

Lola continues checking us in and going over the inn's features. The small inn, tucked into the brick building-lined downtown street, is a restored colonial-style mansion. Landscape oil paintings in ornate gold frames, a nod to the town's past, decorate the wood panel walls. Antique sofas and chairs with red velvet fabric trimmed in gold fill the cozy lobby. Despite the décor, there's not a stuffy museum vibe. The sweet scent of vanilla wafts in the air, as if someone is baking delicious treats. Alongside the uncomfortable-looking furniture, there are life-size statues of different dog breeds.

"That's adorable." I giggle, elbowing Rowan to check out the pug statue, tongue poked out, flat on their back in front of the lobby's unlit fireplace. "Someone wants belly rubs."

He twists. "What in the hell?"

"They're all over the inn," Lola explains. "The owner's wife makes them. Some are for sale. She donates the proceeds to a local animal rescue."

"Oh my god!" I squeal, shuffling over to a bulldog statue, leg raised, in front of a potted Ficus tree in the corner. "This is amazing!"

"That's Pisser," she calls.

"Of course you are, aren't you." Bending, I coo at the statue. "Is he for sale?"

"You're not buying that." Rowan's laugh-filled words pull my attention.

"Excuse me?" I straighten and offer an indignant of an expression.

Sauntering towards me, he motions to Pisser. "Why on earth would you want a statue of a pissing dog?"

My body hums with the Irish brogue lacing the way he says "pissing." *Mental note: find a way to get him to say pissing a lot.*

"Why on earth *wouldn't* you want one?" I narrow my eyes, fighting a blooming grin.

"Sound argument." He winks, reaching me. Crossing his arms over his chest, his eyes drop to Pisser for a beat and then back to me. "Do you really want it?"

"Sir! Pisser is not an *it*; he's a *he*." Bending, I cover the bulldog's ears.

"Adorable," he rasps.

"What?" I blink.

"That...uh...you think it's...uh...he is adorable." He rubs the back of his neck.

It's an endearing tick. Under his brutishly handsome exterior, he's a little bashful. Without his hat, I get the full effect of his rugged good looks. The combination of his short cropped dark hair and neat beard meld perfectly with the broad shoulders and muscular body. Every inch of him screams man. Rough hands. Sometimes gruff timbre. An energy pulses from him making me think of an Irish bandit who could hoist me over his shoulder and take me to his lair to have his way with me all night long.

And I would revel in every minute of it.

Good god, did I pack my vibrator? Also, what is wrong with me? I'm never like this. *Never.* We're talking about a pissing bulldog statue and heat is crisscrossing my body. It's been a while, but seriously...

"Do you really want him?" he asks, pushing his hands into his pockets.

I straighten. "No. Wouldn't fit in my suitcase or my carry-on bag. But…" I pull out my phone. "Would you mind taking a pic of me with it for my social?"

He nods, reaching for the phone. "Sure."

His hand brushes mine. Goosebumps bloom across my skin with the brief contact. *Can't get the one-bed trope but bring on the accidental brushing hands cliché.*

Cane Austen and I pose with Pisser. Positioning my leg next to Pisser's aiming one, I widened my eyes in faux shock and flash a goofy expression causing Rowan to laugh.

"I took a few," he says, handing back my phone. "Let me know if you want more."

"My followers will love this." I beam, flipping through the photos.

"Followers? Are you an influencer or something?"

"Not like that. My job is in healthcare, but I have a social media page as a disability advocate. I post videos and photos related to blindness and my adventures as a legally blind woman. My handle is Cane Austen and Me." I slip my phone into my pocket. "I started doing it when I was a freshman in college. I guess I just wanted to show the world what it means to be blind through my eyes. For them to see the good, the bad, and in-between."

A warm smile curls his lips. "Cane Austen and Me. I like that name. My mam would too."

"It was my Aunt Bea's idea. She always said that I may lack sight but not vision. So, I'm using my social media to reshape the world's vision about blindness and help visually impaired people see themselves as the amazing humans they are. It was lonely growing up being the only legally blind kid. I'm still often the only one in the room. Part of what I want to do is show other blind people, especially kids, that they aren't alone."

"You're a light in the darkness," he says.

I push back the threatening tears. Aunt Bea's singsong voice saying the same thing echoes inside me. "We should get our keys." I nod, pivoting to walk back to the counter.

"If you two are looking for something fun to do, my nephew Harley will be performing here tonight," Lola offers, handing us our keys.

"That sounds fun." I grin.

"He's really good. Like Ed Sheeran, only sexy. Do you like men who play guitar?"

"Uh…" I try not to visibly grimace at an aunt referring to her nephew as sexy. "I'll get back to you on that."

Rowan grunts something and then grabs my suitcase and his duffle.

We follow the small hallway to an alcove on the first floor with three sets of doors. I'm grateful to not have to lug my suitcase up the spiral stairs to the second and third floor rooms. Though I suspect Rowan would happily lug it for me since he's insisted on pulling my suitcase since the airport.

"This is me." I pull out my key card and swipe. Pushing the door open, I twist and face Rowan. "Oh, your hat."

"Keep it. It looks better on you."

Swoon. "Okay." Reaching out, I take the handle of my suitcase from him. "Thank you."

"You're welcome."

And now it's awkward. We just stare at each other. Neither one of us speaks or moves. We've not made plans beyond checking into the inn. I know I'm going to explore the town a bit. Would he want to join?

"I've got to return a few calls," he starts.

Guess that answers my unasked question.

"Do you have runners in your luggage?"

"Runners?" My forehead scrunches.

"Sneakers."

"Yeah. Why?"

Mischief radiates off him. "I thought we could go on an adventure."

CHAPTER FOUR

Claimed
Rowan

"**G**et your shit together, or you'll no longer wear gold and black," Greg grumbles. His pursed lips and puckered forehead fill the laptop screen.

"What Greg is saying"—a smiling Sasha leans in, her expression soft in contrast to her husband's hard one— "now is the opportunity for us to rebrand you from hockey's bad boy to its nice guy. I'm working with some reporters to capture images of your volunteer work at the shelter and—"

"No." My protest is gruffer than I intend, but the warmth in Sasha's onyx eyes doesn't falter.

In five years, Sasha Ortiz Lawson, Greg's go-to publicist and wife, always meets my borderline curt responses with patience. Despite the sweetness, she might be more formidable than her bulldog husband. With a bat of her long dark lashes and flash of that radiant smile, she disarms anyone's bluster, including her husband.

"Watch the tone with my wife, Iverson. You're not so big that I can't kick your ass," Greg growls.

I wouldn't put it past him to do just that. No doubt I'd get a swift punch to my gut from the former college football player-turned-agent. At twenty-one, NFL scouts salivated at the prospect of All-American Greg Lawson wearing their team's jersey. A bad tackle during a conference title game resulted in a spinal cord injury that stole Greg's prospect to play in the NFL but not his love of the game and sports in general. Instead of the NFL, he went to law school. After graduation, he joined the third best sports management firm in the country as a junior agent.

Despite his reputation as a relentless linebacker, he was an untried agent. Blinded by his wheelchair and tragic story, few athletes signed with Greg. Enter me. At twenty-two, some agents worried I waited too long to go pro, opting to complete my degree at university before entering the NHL draft. I wasn't the sexiest of players. I wasn't drafted until the sixth round. But Greg believes in me, and I believe in him.

There's a strange kinship between us. We started our careers together. Our relationship is reminiscent of team-mates in the locker room – no punches pulled and a lot of colorful language.

"Sorry, Sasha," I offer with an apologetic grin.

Flashing a huge smile, she waves me off. "No apology needed. You have boundaries and I can respect that."

"I know what you want to do, but I don't want my volunteer work exploited. That's separate from hockey Rowan. They've put trust in me and I won't take advantage of that."

Annoyance lines Greg's face. "If the journalists that dubbed you Rowdy Rowan knew you spend your free time working with shelter dogs and kids in foster care, they'd call you 'Really Nice Guy Rowan' or some shit like that."

Sasha places a manicured hand on her husband's bicep.

"Valiant attempt, but let's focus on your strengths, and I'll worry about the branding."

"Doesn't matter if the stubborn ass won't let us use it."

"Remember"—she squeezes his arm— "we promise our players that they give all to the game, but not all of themselves for it."

It's almost the unofficial motto of Greg's agency. It's why I stayed with him when he opened his own shop five years ago. So many players lives are consumed by the factory-like assembly line of the sports world. They become less athlete and more product. Greg expects us to give our all on the field, court, track, or rink that is our stage but never to give ourselves to the game. There's a difference between the sport and sports' industry. One is playing the game and the other simply a game.

The clear line between me on the ice and me in real life has never been an issue. I've always been okay with the reputation I have. I'm aggressive. I'm relentless. I'm focused. But that reputation now chafes against my skin since the disappointed stares from my coach, my brothers, and my mam.

How will Pen see me?

I slump in the chair, snapping my eyes to the clock. I'm meeting Pen in the lobby in ten minutes. I'd promised her an adventure. As soon as the clerk at the check-in counter winked at Pen trying to play matchmaker for her Ed Sheeran-lite nephew, jealousy surged in me. Like a child calling dibs, I wanted to claim Pen for my own. Even though she's not someone to possess. It didn't stop me from asking her out.

God, I'm like Pisser.

Something akin to the nerves I'd had as a sweaty-palmed-teenager going on a first date flips in my stomach. It's not a date. Not technically, but there is an insistent pulse inside me that it could be. That this may be the start of many more adventures.

Women aren't an unknown concept. I've not spent the seventeen years since my first date at fifteen living like a monk. There's been women. A lot of women. Mostly one-night stands, mutual agreements for repeated good times, and that regretful relationship with Emma Sinclaire. I've not been someone pining away for "*the one*."

The one? Those two words twist and flutter inside me. That's more Finn's territory, not mine. I've never been the hopeless romantic like my brother, who falls in-and-out of love with the swift change of the wind. I've never been in love. It's only been seven hours since first meeting Pen. Love at first sight is a myth used by publishers to sell sappy romance novels. It's the Santa Claus of experiences. No matter how much one plays pretend, there's no big-bellied man in a red suit breaking and entering your home to eat your cookies and leave you gifts. Just like there's no love at first sight. No matter how captivating someone's smile is or how much you could drown in their honey gaze.

"What about the girl?" Greg asks, dragging my attention back to him.

I shift in my seat; a furrow notches my brow. Pen being mentioned directly or indirectly in this strategy conversation raises my hackles. We're supposed to focus on rebranding my image to save me from being traded. Why is he mentioning Pen?

"What girl?" Sasha coos.

"Rowdy Rowan met a girl." Mirth drips from Greg's grin.

"It's not like that," I grumble.

"Keep telling yourself that, buddy. You were adamant about having my assistant upgrade her—"

"To first class, not to be seated next to me."

Undeterred, Greg continues, "As well, one would think

avoiding being traded would be incentive enough to get your ass on a plane... but instead you choose to stay with this woman you just met. Never mind the mess we're still cleaning up from you breaking the nose of the NHL's golden boy. What hold does this Penelope Meadows have on you?"

My jaw clenches. "Wow, you've gone a whole five hours without mentioning me punching Landon."

"If you'd share with us why you punched Landon Phillips, I'm sure I could make this go away," Sasha offers.

"He's an asshole." My hand curls tight around the edge of the hotel room's desk.

"That's a given, but I know it was more than that. Like a wolf protecting its pack, you only strike when necessary."

My eyes flick to the door. Sasha has a way of cutting through everything and seeing the truth. It's what makes her one of the best publicists in the business. It's probably how Greg lucked out winning her heart. She may be one of the only people to see through his barbwire exterior to what is, no doubt, a soft gooey inside.

"Fuck his reason," Greg blurts, running his hand over his smooth bald head. "It happened. Let's focus on how to keep Rowan's image in alignment with the family-friendly vibe the new Bobcat's owner has been curating since inheriting the team last year." Greg taps a thick finger against his chin. "Back to this Penelope Meadows."

I stiffen at the mischievous glint in his eyes. "What does Pen have to do with anything?"

"Pen? I see we already have nicknames for each other. Does your Pen call you Row-Row?" He waggles his eyebrows in an exaggerated manner.

I promptly flip him off.

He reciprocates before continuing, "I love my twenty-year-old assistant. Within five minutes, he pulled up her social media. With a name like Penelope Meadows, she wasn't hard to find."

"Wait!" Sasha's eyes widen and she gasps. "Cane Austen and Me? Rowan is dating Cane Austen and Me?"

"I'm not dating Pen," I grunt.

"Not yet." Greg waves a dismissive finger. "Sweetheart, how do you know about Cane Austen and Me?"

"You remember our son?" Sasha quips.

"I'm familiar." Greg flashes a cheeky grin.

"Remember that presentation we sat through at his school two weeks ago that you said you were totally paying attention to and *not* looking at emails on your phone?"

Busted. To anyone else, Greg's stony face might appear unchanged, but the little tick in his cheeks hint at an acknowledgment of guilt.

"His presentation was on positive social media influencers. He did it on her. She's amazing. Such an advocate for the disability community and a role model. Not just for kids with disabilities, but everyone." Sasha takes control of the meeting displaying Pen's social media.

Pen's brilliant smile fills my screen. Images flash of her and Cane Austen on various adventures. Laughing on a tandem bike, a woman with the same brown eyes in the front and Pen in the back. Toasting in a scarlet Regency era dress with a Ryan Gosling look-a-like I immediately want to punch. Beaming in the middle of a group of children all wearing *Camp Abilities* T-shirts. On the top of all the pictures was the one I took just an hour ago with the caption *One lady's Pisser is another lady's new best friend.*

A smile curls my lips. *God, she's beautiful.*

Greg whistles. "You got it bad, Row-Row."

"You know if you take a few photos and tag—"

"Absolutely not." I cut Sasha off.

Greg tosses a warning glare.

"I know." My expression softens. "Sorry, Sasha."

"It's totally fine." She winks at her husband. "He does have it bad."

The muffled click of a door shutting draws my attention. No doubt on the other side is Pen heading down the hall toward the lobby to meet me.

"I've got to go," I announce, turning my gaze back to my agent and publicist's smug grins. "I know you mean well. I know you want to help but leave my volunteer work and Pen out of it. I'll do whatever you think is best—" I point at the screen "—within reason. But I won't exploit what I care about for any rebranding bullshit. Sorry, Sasha."

I may not like playing the publicity game, but I know it's part of hockey. As much as I just want to play the game I love – the one my dad loved – I know I have to participate in this part, especially if I want to stay in L.A.

"*What* you care about? Don't you mean *who* you care about?" she coos.

"I hate you both," I grumble.

"He's a goner. Sweetheart, you may need to draft that wedding announcement," Greg taunts.

Flipping them both off this time, I disconnect. Eyes closed, I run my hands down my face. *Does my son doth protest too much?* My mam's taunting words echo inside me. Releasing a harsh breath, I push away from the desk. After refilling my water bottle, I head down to meet Pen.

Pen stands beside a statue of a Sheltie reading a book with a yellow cover. Her back is to me, and I pause to allow my gaze to sweep down the curves of her body.

Fuck. I may die. Khaki shorts stop mid-thigh, accentuating long, toned legs. Hell, I want to bury myself fully between those legs, finding the Heaven I do not deserve, nor dare to dream about. The fabric stretches around a supple, apple-shaped ass, causing my hands to clench in battle against the urge to curl my fingers around that backside and pull her flush against me.

Greg and Sasha are right. I have it bad.

Pen spins. Her long auburn hair is tied in two long braids beneath my cap. The fitted black tank top, shorts, that hair, and her wearing my goddamn hat is too much. She's the perfect blend of sexy sweetness.

She grins. "Rowan."

"Pen."

My cap. I almost growl the thought. It's like she's a present wrapped up just for me. A possessive voice grunts inside me to scoop her up, to take her back to my room and claim every fucking inch of her. My mouth. My tongue. My hands. My cock. All want to make their mark. To taste, feel, and imprint her on me and me on her.

"Ready?" she asks, biting that plump lower lip.

"Yes." As much as my body pulses to claim her, I know in that instant I'm the one who's been claimed.

CHAPTER FIVE

Falling
Pen

The sun's hot breath kisses along my skin, heating it in the most delicious way as I step out of Rowan's rental car. It only took about five minutes to reach Milford Falls. Two other vehicles are parked in the small gravel lot. An arbor, made with weathered branches, welcomes us to a dirt path. From what Lola explained before we left the inn, the trail twists through a small thicket of trees before it forks into two directions: A gentle hike along the riverbed to the pool at the bottom of the falls or a climb up a steep, rocky hill to its top.

"That's perfect for a pic with Cane Austen and you before we start." Rowan points at a worn wooden sign.

I shuffle closer, squinting to read the words painted in a rich green that mirrors the leafy canopy above us. Running my fingers over the sign's uneven surface, I smile at the message: *Milford Falls, Adventure Awaits.*

"Perfect." My grin can't be contained.

"Absolutely," he rasps, moving behind me.

Twisting my head, my gaze meets his and my breath stutters. Something in the way his affirmation rolls off his tongue makes me think he's not talking about the sign. I'm having trouble reading him. People are like books to me; I generally unlock their secret passages quickly. I've always had the ability to figure them out. Well, minus Alex. Though I wonder how much of that was my deliberate blindness about who he was versus not seeing him from the start.

With Rowan, I don't know. My heart, body, and brain are at odds. My heart flutters in his presence, as if trying to tell me something. My brain cautions I don't know him. Just as the hat he wears obscures his eyes, there's something a little guarded about Rowan.

Then, there's my body, willing to melt into a puddle for this man.

Heat from his proximity licks against my exposed skin. As if the first strike of a match, my nerve endings crackle awake with Rowan's closeness. Gooseflesh blooms. Pulse quickens. Butterflies dance. I'm a living, breathing romance novel cliché.

"I can take it," he offers, stepping back to create unwelcome distance between us.

A slight chill shivers along my spine. "Thanks," I murmur, pulling out my phone.

With my phone in his hand, he takes even more steps back and motions for me to pose.

Cane Austen and I sidle up to the sign. I raise my arms, Cane Austen dangles from my right hand, and scream, "Adventure!"

Laughter rumbles from Rowan as he triggers the shutter. He mutters something under his breath, a grin visible from beneath the brim of his cap.

"What was that?" I blink, taking in the way the navy T-shirt molds over his sculpted torso as he strides towards me.

"Uh…" he pauses, swiping his large hand at his neck's nape. "Who generally takes these photos for you, or do you do the selfie stick thing?"

I take my phone from him. "I'll do selfies from time-to-time, but usually it's a phone-a-friend situation. Aunt Bea used to take a lot, but generally it's my West Coast bestie JoJo or random folks."

"West Coast bestie?"

A soft laugh escapes. "I have two besties. Trina, who lived next door to me 'til I moved to California with Aunt Bea, and then JoJo who I met in college. Both ladies are competitive and a tad possessive of the title 'Best Friend.' Each gets custody of the title based on which half of the country I'm in."

"Who has it now? You're in the Midwest."

"Clearly you." I hip-check him.

He snorts.

"Come on, bestie." I wink, motioning for him to follow Cane Austen and me.

We slip into quiet companionship as we walk. Fat leaves rustle in the gentle breeze, its soft kiss cooling my heated skin as we follow the path. Nature's hum fills my ears. Luscious would be the best way to describe the dirt path, speckled with tiny pebbles, that loops through the clusters of trees, tall grass, and bushes ripe with colorful wildflowers and berries.

"I get why Lola says this place is popular with couples. It would be ideal for a romantic picnic date."

"Yep."

I point to a large tree with leafy branches that offer an awning-like shelter. "That tree is ideal for a private *handsy* make-out session."

He coughs.

You're making this weird, Pen. "Do you have a best friend?" I ask, changing the topic.

"Not willingly," he grumbles.

"What does that mean?"

"Wes." He almost sighs the name. "He's a bartender at the pub I own and rather insistent we be friends."

I fake pout. "How *dreadful,* a man who can make you drinks wants to be friends."

"You haven't met Wes." Playfulness coats his retort. "He's relentless. He makes me process *his* feelings with him, blasts Broadway music at the pub, and makes me watch *The Real Housewives of Potomac.*"

"He sounds like JoJo. Does he have an unhealthy obsession with cats?"

"What constitutes unhealthy?"

"In my opinion, more than one cat. JoJo has three – Mr. Rochester, Jamie Fraser, and Captain Wentworth."

He stops. "She named them after characters from books?"

"After her favorite book boyfriends."

"If she likes men, she may fall in love with him. He's a bartender/actor. He played Mr. Rochester in a Hamilton-inspired musical version of *Jane Eyre* where he rapped a song called 'Bertha's Burning Down the House.' He made me go twice."

"Stop it!" My laugh is almost a cry. "Please tell me there is video of this."

"God, I hope not." Chuckling, he reaches his long arm out and raises up several branches over my head.

Rowan's thoughtful gesture is done with no fanfare. Cane Austen finds ruts, drop offs, rocks, and other obstacles while detecting changes in the terrain, but low branches and things from above that aren't at eye level pose head and face smacking danger. I've been slapped a few times by rogue branches during hikes.

It's nice when someone points it out, but not in a showy way. Alex would have made a big deal. *"If I wasn't here, there'd be a blackeye marring your pretty face,"* he'd drawl. Rowan just does it without making a fuss about it. *Refreshing.*

"Which way?" Hands on hips, his steps cease. "The easier path to the waterfall's bottom or the harder one to its top?"

My gaze flips between each side of the forked path. To the right, the gentle trail leading to the riverbed. To the left lies a rugged path of uneven topography that slopes up a steep climb to the waterfall's top.

I turn, facing Rowan. "Adventure?"

"Adventure." Grin popping, he places his hand on my lower back and guides me to the left.

My nerves sing with the warmth coursing from his palm through the thin fabric of my tank top. There's no question about how my body reacts to Rowan. Desire pools low in my belly, hoping his tender fingers will slip beneath my shirt.

You need to calm yourself! "So, you own a pub?" I blurt, a little breathless. "Is it Irish?" My face scrunches. "Sorry. That might be a stereotype."

"Nah." He chuckles and waves his hand. "It's a little Irish. A little Canadian."

"*Ooh...* Like corned beef poutine and hockey watch parties with pints of Guinness?"

"Something like that." His fingers leave my lower back then wrap about my hand.

The path turns steeper. Clusters of large rocks mar our way. My pace slows as I traverse the rutted and more obstacle-filled trail.

"We could do human guide," I offer, slipping my hand from his.

"What's that?" He stops and faces me.

"Let me show you." I take his bicep and try not to faint on the spot over how big it is.

I know Rowan is fit. My eyesight isn't so bad that I haven't noticed how clothes mold around his chiseled form. He's barely broken a sweat or puffed out a breath during our hike. Whereas sweat forms in unsexy spots along my body and my breath stutters just a bit. I work out, but the hike's increased difficulty and Midwest humidity hit me harder than I expect.

"I take your arm like this." I squeeze his hard bicep.

Did he just groan? *Focus, Pen.*

Biting my lip, I continue, "I'll be half a person and step behind you. You walk like normal and I'll follow. Your body's movement will indicate steps and obstacles. If there's a narrow space, you'll move your arm behind your body and I'll follow. If you're uncomfortable at all with this—"

"I've got us," he jumps in.

It's not just the certainty in his low timbre that eases any doubt in my stomach, but a steady voice inside me. Human guide requires trust. I need to trust my guide will keep me safe, and they have to trust that I'll keep them safe. It's a partnership where either could lead the other astray. It's only been eight hours since I met Rowan. My brain knows this. But my heart...

"I trust you." I smile. "If you're unsure of anything, just use your words. Open and direct communication is key for the human guide and visually impaired person dynamic."

"Funny, Wes would say that's key to any relationship."

"So true. Ready?"

He nods and leads us up the steep climb.

"What's your bar's name?" I ask, stepping onto the rocky plateau.

"Axel's."

"Sounds like a NASCAR bar. My stepdad would love it."

"You have a stepdad?"

"Charlie. He's stepdad number four."

Charlie is a nice guy. Though it's a tad awkward that he rambles on about all things automobile and NASCAR with me. I'm all for treating the visually impaired like everyone else, but read the room. I don't drive and could care less about pistons and horsepower. Still, I'd rather listen to him drone on about that, than be pestered by my mother about my romantic life.

"Your mam has been married five times?"

"Yeah. My mom doesn't like to be alone."

"My mam's the opposite."

"She never remarried?"

My arm raises with the shrug of his shoulders. "Never even dated. We thought she was waiting until we were older. Finn's a hopeless romantic and tried setting our mam up on some blind dates, but she wasn't keen."

"What's not to be keen about blind dates? All mine are blind," I cut in, a wry grin forms on my face.

"Smartass." His throaty laugh twines around us.

"Is she happy?"

"My mam?" He halts, twisting his face to me.

I nod.

"She says she is. Mam has her work. Her students. Her weekly book club meetings. Her friends."

"She also has you boys." I squeeze his arm. "So, Finn is a romantic. What does he do?"

"He got a degree in English like my mam. He's a professor at the same university and writes."

"What about Gillian?"

"He's not a romantic," Rowan deadpans.

I laugh and roll my eyes. "I take it Gillian's not your favorite brother."

"He's the oldest." His face shifts forward and resumes our hike.

Note to self, he did *not* argue my statement.

"Gillian's a chef. He owns a traditional Irish pub in our hometown."

"Wow. A professor and two businessmen. Your mom must be bursting with pride."

He grunts.

"What's Gillian's pub called?" I step over a rock.

"Fiona's. He named it for our mam."

"Shameless man. No doubt naming his place after her secured his favorite son status," I tease.

"My brothers need no tricks to secure that status," he mutters. His statement is almost so quiet that it feels as if he'd not intended to say it aloud.

The questions tap at the back of my closed mouth. *What does that mean? Do you not share status as a favorite son? Why?* I don't know the dynamics of siblings. Despite my four step-dads, I've remained a blissfully solo child for my mother. Trina and JoJo are as close as I have to sisters. But there's a sadness that radiates from Rowan. I just want to smooth it away but fear my questions will only further wrinkle the emotions.

I rake my teeth against my lip. "Why'd you name your pub Axel's?"

"My dad's name was Axel."

My heart squeezes. "You're such a sweet man."

Rowan's muscles stiffen beneath my grip. His body's rigidity seems to protest my soft proclamation.

I squeeze his arm and reiterate, "You're a sweet man."

He stops and pivots to face me. For a moment, our gazes tether. His as equally obscured in his ball cap as mine is beneath his hat on my head.

"Pen." He takes my hand and threads our fingers together.

My pulse riots.

He then guides my hand to a grassy covered outcrop that stops at my chest level. As if waking up, my eyes widen. We're almost at the top. The grassy ledge requires the hiker to use upper body strength to lift themselves to the top, and it stands between us and the riverbed above. The purr of gushing water filters through the trees' canopy.

"I can go first and pull you up or you can go first, and I'll be here in case you"—he swallows thickly— "want me."

My eyes flutter between Rowan and the ledge. It's such a small thing, but it's huge to me. My entire life people have focused on my needs. Not in the traditional sense that we all crave to have our needs met, but in the idea of me needing to be taken care of.

"I'll go first." I fold Cane Austen and pass her to Rowan. "Would you mind?"

"Got her."

Sucking in a deep breath, I place my hands flat on the ledge's silken grassy surface. I squat, then I jump, using the momentum to hoist myself up. *Don't fall. Don't fall.* The internal mantra repeats as I swing my legs up and scramble to the top.

"You got it," Rowan cheers.

Secure on the ledge, I spin to face him, the lush grass rasps against my knees. "Want me to pull you up?" I wink, knowing there's no way I'd be able to pull him up.

"Maybe next time." He hands me Cane Austen and then, like it's nothing, jumps onto the ledge beside me.

"Show off."

With a lopsided grin, he stands and then bends to take my hand and lifts me to my feet beside him. "Just a little further." He squeezes his fingers around mine.

The dirt path along the river is smooth, allowing us to suspend human guide. My arm moves right to left, trailing

Cane Austen against the path's rocky edges, the song of the waterfall hums in my ears. Patches of midafternoon sun break through the thinning grove of pine, birch, and maple trees. After a bend in the path through a small clearing, we come to the river. The once distant babble has become a steady rush. Water ripples toward the cliff's edge. A moss-covered bridge, constructed with misshapen stone and weathered wood, connects the river's two banks.

"This is like something out of a Nicolas Sparks' novel," I quip.

A deep laugh bubbles from Rowan.

"Come on." I take Rowan's hand, tugging him along. His compliance allows a temporary delusion that I have the strength to move him.

The bridge's center features a small observation deck perfect for viewing the falls. A small, dark wooden bench outlines the oval-shaped deck. Walking to the edge, I fold Cane Austen and place her on the bench and then proceed to step on it. The observation deck's stone wall provides enough barrier to keep me safe, but Rowan wraps his large hands around my waist, nonetheless.

My head twists, snapping my gaze to Rowan. Again, he says nothing. No comment about keeping me safe or me needing him. He just tips his head toward the waterfalls.

"Join me." I bite my lip. "The view is better up here."

As if in a silent debate, his head bobs between me, the falls, and back to me again. Finally, he steps onto the bench and moves behind me. His strong hands remain on my middle. Heat from his body licks across my skin. I may combust from the gentle tug of his steady fingers against my shirt. Scant inches separate his front from my back. His large form hovering over me should feel intimidating. The posture is borderline possessive, but not in the way my body craves to be claimed by this man. There's just enough distance between us to make me question any intention outside of protectiveness.

I clear my throat. "My Aunt Bea would have loved this. She'd probably have put it in one of her books."

"She was a writer?"

"She wrote cozy mysteries. You know where the local innkeeper or baker becomes an unlikely detective. All her stories featured people others have underestimated. A lot of them were inspired by people she met or places she went." I press my hand to my chest to quell grief's sharp pang slicing into my heart.

"You think this would have inspired her?"

"Yeah."

"Did you have a favorite of her books?"

I swallow the hard lump in my throat. "It's totally vain, but she wrote a Young Adult series about a blind teenager who solves school-related mysteries. They even made a TV show out of it called– "

"The Unseeing Private Eye," he interrupts.

"You know it?"

"Yeah." His fingers absently trace along the hem of my tank top. "So, Nickel Fields was inspired by Pen Meadows." The chuckle in his tone is distinct and rich.

"She was *always* terrible with character names." I wipe my hand across my face, covering the laughter curving my mouth. "I'm surprised you know the books. You weren't exactly the show's target demographic."

"What's that mean?"

I make a nonsensical gesture with my hands. "I mean, you had to be an adult man when the show first aired. I was eighteen when the first season came out, so you were—"

"How old do you think I am?" he scoffs.

"Seventy-two," I say, fighting back a wry smile.

"Excuse me?"

"Okay, Seventy-nine." I bat my eyes.

"Thirty-two, smartass."

"I'm twenty-six." I adjust the brim of Rowan's hat on my head. "So, guess you're not *that* much older."

"Not that much older," he murmurs.

His hands move from my waist to my arms. My skin sings with the caress of his callused fingers.

"I was living in Calgary. Didn't really have much of a life outside of…work. I'd watched the show but also read the books. With an English professor mam, I'm a read the book first kind of guy. I always liked how brave Nickel was."

I hold my breath for a moment.

"The world saw her one way, but she never allowed their definitions of who they thought she was control her. So many of us aren't that strong."

I let that breath out. "I like that you saw that. Most people just focus on Nickel's blindness."

"It's part of who she was, but not all she was." His fingers tap against my upper arms. "Though, I assume that was the point of your aunt's books and the show. Anyone who only saw that are more blind than Nickel or…" he trails off, a quick intake of breath punctuating the silence between us.

"Me." I lean into him, his muscles contract with my touch. "You're right. It was the point of those books. All of her books, really. Aunt Bea wanted the world to look past what they see on the surface, beyond preconceived notions of what we think people are, to who they really are."

"When did she die?"

Sucking in a deep breath, I close my eyes. "How did you know?"

"You use the past tense when talking about her."

"You *are* the son of an English professor."

He lets out a tiny chuckle.

"She died in November."

"How?"

"Breast cancer." My words wobble just a bit, but I carry on, "She's why I was back in Buffalo. The high school she and my dad attended renamed their library after her and honored her at their graduation ceremony. I was there representing our family. My grandparents retired and moved to Greece ten years ago, so it's a lot for them to travel internationally. I also think it's hard for them to go back to someplace where they once celebrated all the promise of the future for their children, both of whom are now dead."

His arms fold around me, tucking me against his firm chest. "What's your favorite memory of her?"

I settle into his steady embrace, allowing his borrowed question to wash over me. "There are so many."

"Our flight isn't until tomorrow, so we have nothing but time."

Tipping my head back, I take in his coaxing smile. So much about Rowan leaves me topsy-turvy. I just met him, but I trust him. He's guarded, but still looks at me with an openness. My body ignites for him, but my heart settles in his presence. He's strong, but there's a vulnerability in the gruffness of his voice.

I turn my gaze forward. "Saturday mornings. We always went out for breakfast. Even when I was in college and lived at the dorms, she'd come get me to take me to breakfast at Bread, our favorite spot in downtown Seal Beach. We've been going there since we moved to California for her to write for *The Unseeing Private Eye*."

Rowan's chin rests atop my head.

"I still go to Bread every Saturday morning. I sit at our same table tucked in the back corner of the café's small courtyard. I still order the same thing, including the giant baklava croissant we used to share. I can never finish it"—my voice cracks— "but I never take it home."

That cardboard to-go box would only mock the knowledge that she's gone. If she wasn't, it wouldn't sit on the kitchen island like a viper ready to strike, its fangs plunging in and dripping the poisonous truth that she's gone and never coming back.

"Do you feel her... when you're there?"

I swallow thickly. "I don't feel her anywhere. I worry that she's all the way gone. She left her house to me. I live there and still I don't feel her. The memories are there, but she's not."

Tears burn in my eyes. I raise my hand and dash them away, hoping they're not noticeable. Openness isn't a problem for me with most things. Well, with unimportant things as JoJo would point out. I can talk endlessly about my advocacy work, friends, favorite books, and career. Being vulnerable, though, chafes at exposing myself. The moisture coating my fingertips tells me I'm not as strong as I think. That I need. That what...who I need is gone.

His arms fold tight around me, and he whispers, "I bought my childhood house because I thought it would bring my dad back. Like he's somehow still there, but when I go back there's only the memory of him... not him. It took me a while to realize that he's gone, but not all the way gone because I still have those memories." He takes my wrist, raising my hand to my heart. "As long as you keep her here, she's not gone. Even if you don't feel her, those memories keep her alive. It's only when we've forgotten that they're truly gone."

I twist in his arms, facing him. His woodsy scent comforts me. As if just *him* soothes the torrent of sadness inside me.

"Thank you." I place his hand on my heart. "I'll not forget that."

The air between us is charged. My nerves sizzle as if a storm is about to break.

"Pen—"

"You two shouldn't be up there like that! It's not safe. You could fall!" A brusque masculine voice breaks the moment, drawing our attention to a tall older man at the river's edge.

As if to reiterate the meddling man's point, I take a step back. The back of my legs hit the stone wall. Rowan pulls me back to him with such intensity that I slam into his chest. The momentum causes him to pitch backward, taking me with him. His strong arms band around me, holding me tight as we fall to the bridge's wood plank floor.

"Christ!" he grunts, hitting the ground.

My body drapes over him like a rally monkey at a baseball game. Rowan cups the back of my head, while my face burrows into his chest. His other hand rests at the small of my back. The thud of his heart roars in my ears. My legs are splayed on either side of his massive frame.

"So sorry! Are you okay?" I cringe, tipping my face to him.

"Yeah," he groans.

"I'm so sorry. That was stupid of me, I shouldn't have…"

"Pen, none of that… All that matters is that you're okay." Rowan's words are steady with assurance and concern. The hand cupping my head moves to my cheek and brushes away tendrils that had escaped from my long braids. "Are you okay?"

"Yeah. I'm not the one that cushioned *my* fall."

"I'll be your cushion any time. I'm pretty sturdy."

The breath wooshes out of me. My chest heaves against his body, taking in his sweet promise. It both terrifies and allures me at the same time.

"Are you sure you're okay?" His hands skate over my face, down my sides, along my back, at my hips, and graze the swell of my ass. "Shit! Sorry." He throws his hands into the air.

"Rowan, none of that. All that matters is *my* ass is okay." I smile playfully.

A soft laugh relaxes him.

I sit up, peering down at him. "Are you sure you're okay?"

I cradle his cheek and his beard's silken strands tickle my palm. I wonder if the hair on his head is as soft. What would it be like to weave my fingers into his neat tresses and muss them up?

"Strangely I've never been better." His hands rest on my hips.

That static electricity between us crackles, as I realize that not only am I *still* straddling Rowan but my heated core rests against his... And he's hard and large...very large.

I should get up, but I don't move. Neither does he. He doesn't push me off. He doesn't wiggle from beneath me. There's no apologetic or bashful smile. Those strong hands only hold me in place. I can't see his eyes, but I can feel their smoldering stare. It's almost like a dare. The gauntlet has been thrown. Who will make the first move and what move will that be?

Why am I waiting for him to act? Rowan may be a man who commands, but he's also guarded. Why wouldn't he be most guarded about his heart? I know what move I want made and who should do it.

Darting my tongue against my lips, I cradle his face. Both to anchor me to him and to test. Like dipping my toes into the stream to assure the waters will welcome me. He melts into my touch. I bend towards him and...

Stomping feet burst our cocoon. Red faced, hands on hips, the older man appears over our heads. "This is inappropriate. You're in a public place!" the man tuts.

Vagina blocker! I groan and pull away from Rowan.

"We should go," Rowan sighs.

CHAPTER SIX

Fuck Michigan Ed Sheeran
Rowan

The shower's spray beats against my taut muscles. Between the hike and this afternoon's proximity to Pen, I'm on fire. I could fucking combust with need. My body buzzes with the memory of her delicate frame draped over me. The way her ample breasts, hard peaks poking through her shirt's thin fabric, snuggled against my chest. Our hot breath mingled as her honey gaze, with a glint of hunger flashing in the pupils, peered down at me from below my hat's brim. The way that pink tongue darted across her bow-shaped lips. Her candied aroma still lingers in my nostrils.

My hand trails down my stomach towards my cock, still hard despite the frozen temperature of the water. Like a damn teenager again, my dick has been in various stages of erection since meeting Pen. I grip my shaft and close my eyes. My mind drifts to Pen's full lips. Gripping tighter, I let myself fall into the fantasy. Her almond-shaped eyes. Glossy lips wrapped around me, while her dainty hands work my base. Her needy moans and whimpers fill the shower. Jealousy surges at the droplets coasting across her naked body.

I groan, imagining my hands tangling into her wet strands to guide myself deeper. She clenches her thighs together, wanting me as much as I want her. Her arousal mingling with the water swirling down the drain. Like a queen she rules over me.

"My Pen," I moan.

The slickness of my hand is a poor substitute for what I imagine is the ecstasy of her mouth. Pumping faster, pleasure spools tight at the base of my spine.

"Fuck," I rasp as my release claims me.

Hand placed against the slick, tiled wall, I pant and allow my mind to circle back to the reality that it was my hand and not Pen's pretty mouth that I just fucked.

Greg and Sasha teased that I had it bad. This orgasm's intensity warns that they're *not* wrong. I just came harder than I've ever come in my life and all I did was imagine Pen. God, what would sheathing myself entirely in her do to me? Her body writhing beneath me while I take her to the edge again and again prolonging both our pleasure until we each plead for release. Because once I am inside her, I won't want to leave.

This woman has possessed me. Not just with her gorgeous looks, but her entire self. She's brilliant, funny, a little silly, feisty, strong, kind, and sweetly earnest. I've only known her for ten hours, and I barely remember my life before Pen. She's brand new to me, but somehow my heart acts like it's always known her.

There's something dangerous in that. In her. My naturally protective guard is lowering its defenses. I must mentally reinforce my armor around her. Pen's openness has me sharing more than I share with anyone. I've talked more to her about my dad in the past ten hours than I have in the last twenty-three years with my brothers or mam. With Pen, I want to tell her everything. This isn't like me. This is more Finn's territory. My brother falls in love more in a single summer than most people have in a lifetime.

"It's not love. It's just hormones." I shut off the shower and step out.

It's just pent-up sexual energy. In January, as it looked more certain that the L.A. Bobcats were playoff bound, I gave up all extracurricular activities of a carnal nature. No letting off steam with a few of the women I have an understanding with. No taking up Emma Sinclaire's many, many thinly veiled sexual offers. There'd be no repeating *that* mistake.

"Pen wouldn't be a mistake," I argue with myself.

Wrapping the towel around my middle, I swipe my hand over the fogged mirror. My green eyes reflect back to me, the truth written all over my pinched expression. This attraction to Pen isn't just my cock wanting to come out to play after months with only my right hand to keep it company. I like Pen... *a lot*.

I like her so much that after that old man scolded us, as we hiked back down to the pool at the waterfall's bottom, I didn't touch her, didn't pull her back against me. Didn't claim her sweet and sassy mouth. My feelings for Pen keep those instincts at bay.

Those instincts almost vibrate within me. Hold her. Let her unlock me. Wipe away her tears, not pretend I don't see them like I did today as she talked about Aunt Bea. Be the only one taking pictures of her adventures with Cane Austen. Fuck her until the only man's name breaching her lips is mine. I want to ruin her for anyone else but me. But mostly I want to keep her safe, which means not giving into these urges, no matter how hard they thrum inside me.

I'm not the sweet man she says I am. The media circus that is my life right now and my reputation would taint her. She's too perfect to be sullied by me. I know this, yet I am still here thinking about meeting her.

After the hike, we grabbed sandwiches from a deli. I told Pen I needed to work on a few things and would eat in my room.

"I get it." Her small voice almost gutted me. "I should catch up on some work emails too," she'd said, the rustle of the to-go bag in her hand overpowering the car radio's quiet hum.

Hands clenching the steering wheel, I fight the urge to reach over and take her hand. To unwrap her fingers from the bag and bring them to my lips. Even I know I'm throwing her mixed signals, pushing away and pulling her back. I want to assure her how much I want her, although I can't have her. It wouldn't be fair to her.

"Though, all work and no play makes Pen a dull girl." Her lips quirked. "I may take up Lola's offer and have a drink at the inn's bar to listen to her nephew. I'm a little interested in hearing sexy Ed Sheeran. If *you* want to join…" The dismissive shrug of her shoulder counters the breathless challenge in her invitation.

"You mean Michigan Ed Sheeran." The annoyed huff of my response is unmistakable.

Two hours later, here I am staring at myself in the mirror in a losing debate with my reflection. Its counsel is for me to find a movie on the TV or pull out the advance copy of Finn's latest novel, the one that doesn't come out until the fall that I promised him I'd read once the season was over. Instead, I'm thinking about what to wear to listen to a small-town version of a big name musician.

I pick up my mobile from the creamy quartz countertop and text Wes.

Me: Tell me no.

Wes: Why, hello to you bosom buddy. Hand Waving Emoji.

I grunt.

Me: Don't be cute. Just tell me no.

Wes: First, I'm always cute. Have you seen this face?

I groan at the attached selfie of Wes in my tub.

Me: First, don't EVER send me pictures in the bath. Second, are you taking a bath in my bathroom? You were under strict orders to not go into my room while you're watching GB.

Wes: You should know that I never follow orders, which is why I won't be telling you no. Although, guess I'm telling you no to your asking me to tell you no. What am I telling you no about? Is it about Emma? That I'll gladly tell you HELL NO to crawling back into that she-devil's bed.

Me: Not Emma.

Wes: But someone else??

Me: I met someone.

Even as my fingers type those three words, I know I'm fucked.

Wes: Dude, are you actually reaching out to me to process your feelings about a woman? This is facetime worthy. Incoming!

I decline the call.

Me: I'm not facetiming with you while you're in my tub. Boundaries.

He calls again.

Knowing he'll keep doing this until I relent, I answer. "You're the fucking worst."

Wes's dark eyes sparkle with mirth as he fills my mobile's

screen. "You *love* me or else you wouldn't have reached out. Let's dish, boyfriend."

Why the fuck did I text Wes? I should have messaged Gillian. He'd have responded with a *fuck off*. I thought since Wes makes a sport out of telling me no, that he'd give me what I'm so desperate for…. For someone to talk me out of meeting Pen at the bar. Leave it to Wes to tell me no to telling me no.

I let out a beleaguered breath. "Her name is Pen Meadows…"

As the story tumbles out, I know that this is a hundred percent the Pen-effect. Wes calls me the vault. He's made it his mission to pry open my combination lock with little to no success.

"So, what's holding you back? She doesn't sound like a fame fucker like Emma," Wes asks, forehead puckered.

"Pen's not like that," I snap.

"Easy tiger." He whistles. "I say she isn't. I'm looking at her social media, and your girl is like a foxy do-gooder."

"She's too good for me."

"Probably." His dark eyebrows shrug. "Is this because you punched Landon? I know you're taking a lot of heat for that, but what does this have to do with your new lady love?"

"She's not my lady love."

"Maybe not yet, but the growly face you're making at me says she's something." He wags a finger. "Okay, my brother from another mother, let me drop some knowledge on you. You like this woman. Clearly a lot because you're emotionally processing with me, and we know you hate all emotions except for annoyance, aggression, and anger. You want someone to tell you to not do something you want because you're scared."

I open my mouth to protest.

He raises a hand. "Hush, a grown up is speaking."

"I'm five years older than you—"

"Yes, but unlike you, I have the emotional maturity of an eighty-year-old, thanks to my therapist mother. You feel something and that scares you. You're using all the excuses to keep her at a distance. From what you've said, it seems like this woman actually likes you, the *real* Rowan, not the famous hockey player. And the feeling is mutual."

I swallow and take in his words. Since meeting this morning, Pen's only known me. The fame that comes with what I do hasn't clouded her vision about me. She doesn't even know I'm in the NHL. Not yet at least.

"Dude, if you won't give it a shot for yourself, at least do it for her. Give her a chance to decide if she wants to sign up for the Rowan Iverson boyfriend train."

"Boyfriend." The word is a slow pronouncement on my lips as if I'm trying it out like shoes I may buy. That's exactly what I'm considering, because if I let Pen in that's where this is heading. I wouldn't be casual about this... not about her.

"A button-up shirt with jeans. Blue, if you have one – the shirt, not the jeans. Though those can be blue too. Untuck the shirt and roll up the sleeves. Ladies love that look. It's like the male version of cleavage," Wes drawls, pulling my attention back to him.

"Excuse me?"

"It's my suggestion for what to wear when you head down to the lobby to meet Pen. Now, get your ass moving before someone else swoops in and steals your lady."

FIFTEEN MINUTES LATER, I STRIDE DOWN THE HALL TOWARDS the inn's lobby. Clusters of small round tables surround the bar's tiny stage. A half-wall separates it from the small seating area in front of the reception desk. A young woman with short black hair stands behind the dark oak desk, scrolling on her phone.

Scanning the area, I look for Pen. Guests mingle with drinks in hand between the lobby's antique furniture and bar. The quiet hum of instrumental jazz music underscores murmured conversations.

Lola, who's changed from the blazer she wore when we checked in into a canary-yellow dress, bends talking to someone I assume from close-cropped ginger-hair is her nephew, Harley, the *sexy* Ed Sheeran. A large grin stretches over his chiseled features. I guess I can see the appeal, if you're into Greek god-esque good looks. His blue eyes peer past his aunt at someone or something else, obscured by Lola.

Laughing, Lola turns towards the bar and my eyes drop onto what...who...drew Harley's attention. Breath rushes out of me as if I was checked into a rink's boards by a two-hundred-fifty-pound defenseman hurling into me like a bullet train.

Pen sits opposite of Michigan Ed Sheeran. A glossy pink colors her lips, which lift in a sweet smile. A delicate rose glow rouges her cheeks. Her auburn hair is loose, draping around her bare shoulders. The flash of a silver necklace pulls my attention to a hint of cleavage. Her gaze locked with his.

Jealousy explodes inside me. I want to storm over there, take her hand, pull her into my arms, and kiss her. I swipe my hand down my face, knowing that this is partly due to pure envy that her sunshine is directed toward someone else's orbit, but mostly it's simple desire.

To kiss her because she looks so pretty sitting there. The way her skin glows against the Caribbean blue of her dress. How the candlelight from the center of the table dances in the irises of her eyes, making them almost shimmer.

Her hand reaches across the table and touches his arm. An unbridled laugh belts from her.

And I want to fucking die. My jaw clenches and I take a step toward the bar but stop.

You can't do this. I'm ready to walk over there and punch him. He's done nothing wrong. He just sees what I see. How can I expect anyone to be around Pen and not fall into her pull. I've seen it all day. The way her smile disarms and attracts. The cashier at Tim Hortons. The flight attendant. Lola. Hell, even the teenager who made our sandwiches at the deli had a starry-eyed expression as Pen chatted him up about his favorite sandwiches to make.

"Rowan! There you are," Lola shouts across the bar, waving with one hand and carrying a tray of drinks.

Pen breaks eye contact with Harley, scanning the space. A giant grin brightens her features. He doesn't make her smile like that. *I do.*

Buoyed, I straighten my spine and saunter to the table. "Lola." I tip my head to the woman, then turn to Pen. Placing my hand on her shoulder, the caress of her bare skin against my palm shoots warmth up my arm, I bend and whisper, "Pen, you look lovely."

"Thanks." That rose in her cheeks deepens. "You look nice too."

Taking Wes's advice – sort of – I paired a black button-up with blue jeans, the fitted shirt accentuates my muscular physique. My sleeves are rolled to my elbows, just as Wes suggested. I felt foolish talking to him about wardrobe options, but seeing Pen's appreciative gaze sweep over me, I let go of that embarrassment. Thanks to the chandelier above the table, there's enough illumination for her to take me in.

Hand still resting on her bare shoulder, I straighten and

face the knockoff crooner. "You must be Lola's nephew, Marley."

"Harley," he says, right eyebrow arched.

I give him a "like it matters" look. My expression is similar to the face I wear for games. The one that lets competitors know whose house this is. Yep, I'm being a territorial dick. I should be embarrassed. Mam would scowl at my caveman antics.

"There's an empty table beside ours." Harley motions to a table a foot away.

"Thanks." I drag the chair over and place it beside Pen.

Lola's blonde eyebrows lift into her hairline as she looks between me and Harley. No doubt we look like bucks ready to lock antlers over an innocent doe.

"Drinks," Lola clucks, handing a bottle of water to Harley, then a flute to Pen. "Here you go, sweetheart."

"Champagne?" I smirk.

"I like bubbles." She bats her long eyelashes.

"And a Guinness for you," Lola announces, reaching across the table with a frothy pint.

"How?" My head tilts.

"Pen said you'd be joining her and would want a Guinness."

Pen winks. "I knew you'd come."

"Guinness, though?"

"I guess I buy into Irish stereotypes." She sips her drink.

"Perhaps I can assist with your education on Irishman." My low voice rumbles.

"Perhaps." A tiny hitch steals her breath. "Is Guinness okay, though? I can always get you something else."

"It's perfect, luv." I take a swig and let the liquid cool my simmering blood.

Based on Pen's reaction to being called luv, I decide in that moment I'm going to use that endearment as much as possible. Her wide eyes twinkle like starlight. That radiant smile invades every inch of her face, not a single feature untouched by that mixture of delight and bashfulness.

"Pen, what song did you win with?" Harley jumps in.

Oh yeah, this fucking guy. I drag my stare to the douche-canoe with the guitar sitting across from us.

She taps her fingers against the table's smooth surface. "It was a slow acoustic version of Whitney Houston's *I Wanna Dance With Somebody.*"

"I know it. Join me on stage. Make your Michigan debut."

She guffaws, covering her face with her hands. "Nobody needs that."

"You sing?" I ask.

"Pen was a show choir kid like me. We were swapping choir competition battle stories. Turns out our Pen won a New York state solo competition."

Ours? Not yours, buddy. I battle the snarl building in my throat over his presumption.

Pen fiddles with her bracelet, a light pink invades her cheeks. "That was a long time ago."

"She's beautiful and talented." Lola winks, but I'm not entirely sure if it's at her nephew or me.

"It will be fun," Harley pushes.

"She doesn't have to sing if she doesn't want to," I snap, glaring at Harley.

Pen's warm palm rests on mine, but her eyes turn to Harley. "Let me think about it."

"Alright." He stands up, reaches across the table, and lifts Pen's hand to his lips. "I'll hold you to that promise."

My fingers curl tight around the glass.

"I need to set up and I'm suddenly feeling inspired to do a different song for my opening number." Releasing Pen's hand, he winks, and walks away.

Lola leans in, nudging Pen's shoulder. "Oh, I think he's got a crush on you."

"Of course," I grumble under my breath.

Lola's gray eyes drop to me. "Of course, is right. It's a wonder this girl is single. I hadn't even introduced them yet, and Harley was already over here chatting her up. I'm sure she has to use Cane Austen"—she gestures to where Pen's cane sits folded at her feet— "to fight off all the suitors. Imagine being around her and *not* making a move. You'd have to be foolish." She glares at me, steely judgment glints in her stare.

Something swirls in my gut at the dare in her statement. "You're right," I murmur, my stare fixing on Pen.

Pen clears her throat and flutters her hands in the air. "Did you know Rowan owns a pub?"

"Pub owner?" Lola leans back, crossing her arms over her chest. "Is it a *sports* pub?"

The inflection tells me she knows exactly who I am. I shift in my seat.

"It's a little Canadian and Irish. With his love of hockey, I'm sure that dominates the TVs," Pen offers.

"I'm sure it does." Lola's face twists into a knowing expression. "I need to check on Vicki at the front desk, but the next round will be on me. I'll let our bartender know." Lola squeezes Pen's forearm and stands up. "Rowan, you should try the local IPA we serve. It's from Bobcat Brewery. You may enjoy it. It's scrappy." With a wry grin, she walks away.

Bobcat? She knows exactly who I am. I pull the brim of my hat low as if it would somehow erase Lola's knowledge. If she recognizes me, who else does? My eyes flick around the room. Nobody is staring in our direction. The only eyes on us are Harley's, who sets up his equipment on the small stage in the corner of the room, and that stare remains on Pen.

A small palm rests on my knee, dragging my gaze back to Pen's open eyes. "Are you okay?" she asks, her brow wrinkled.

I need to tell her who I am. My hand blankets hers as if I'm hoping to hold her in place. "Pen, I—"

"Oh my gosh!" An excited voice shrills. "Sorry. I know famous people hate when we do this but aren't you—"

Shit.

CHAPTER SEVEN

It's Not For Him
Pen

Rowan's body stiffens beneath my touch, but his hand tightens around mine. Just more of the push and pull that's flown from him most of the day. There's no doubt that he wants me. Finding me with Harley, he'd all but planted a giant flag branded with *Rowan's Girl* in florescent letters. And when he called me "luv" I could have melted. Still, he holds back.

I get it. There're so many reasons to hold back. They stack up inside me. We just met. Despite what my heart protests, we don't really know each other. It's risky, all relationships are. I have these same concerns, but a quiet part of me worries it may be the same reason the boys I liked in high school and college didn't date me. I'm too much trouble. They see past the woman I am, focusing only on my disability and conjure images of needing to take care of me.

"Are you Pen Meadows?" the woman asks, pulling my focus to her.

Rowan's head snaps between the woman and me. His posture relaxes, but he maintains a firm grip on my hand.

"I am." I offer a slight smile.

The woman claps her hands together. "Oh, my word. I still can't believe this. This is amazing. Where are my manners?" A giggle bubbles out. "I'm Stacy Gray. I teach special education at the high school, and my students and I follow you. None of my students are visually impaired, but they relate to you so much. They all have intellectual disabilities and are inspired by the way you embrace your disability as part of your life without letting it define you."

"Thanks," I brush my hair behind my ear with my free hand.

"I almost died when I saw your post from Milford Falls this afternoon. My students have been freaking out on our class's message board that you're in town, but they are going to lose it when I tell them on Monday that I ran into you at the inn. I just came to see Harley play – he's a bit of a rockstar around here."

A low grumble plays in Rowans throat, making me bite back a snort. Clearly, he's not a fan of Michigan Ed Sheeran. I'll admit Harley is attractive. He's all clean-cut boy next door with close-cropped hair and a smooth-shaven face versus Rowan's rugged good looks. The aroma of citrusy soap wafts from Harley, while a haunting woodsy scent clings to Rowan. Harley's timbre is like warmed caramel, while Rowan's gruff, deep voice oozes sex appeal. Even without the snatches of Irish lilt, his voice plays my body like an instrument making me hum with need for more.

God, I wish I had used my vibrator. My body was wound tight after our hike. Between the almost kiss as I straddled him on the bridge and the loss of his physical touch after, every cell blazes. Apparently, even the icy shower I took couldn't quell the fire low in my belly.

"School isn't out yet?" Rowan asks, clearing his throat.

Good gravy, how does that even sound sexy?

"Summer session for special ed students," she says, tipping her head back. "How long are you in town for? I shouldn't ask, but if you're available I'd love to have you come in. The kids would flip. Penelope Meadows," she squeals.

"*We* leave tomorrow," Rowans says, a warm firmness shading his tone.

"Boo."

"But I could record a message for your students. Something you could play for them in class. Or I can post a message to my social media that congratulates them on the end of the school year. We could do it together."

"They'd freak out if you posted it to your social."

"I can take the video," Rowan offers, squeezing my hand.

"Thanks." I slip my phone out and hand it to him. It's almost second nature now. He took several shots of me by the pool at the waterfall's base. He said he'd even captured a short video of me playing with a puppy being walked by an older couple along the riverbed. Its paws, bigger than its little body covered in silken chocolate-colored fur, bounced at my cane's ball tip as if it was a new toy. It was utterly adorable. I didn't look at the pictures or video after. My body was still too keyed up from throwing myself at him, only to be thwarted by that random man who turned out to be a park ranger, to review the pictures and video.

"Would it also be okay to get a selfie with my phone, too?" Stacy asks after we finish recording the short message.

"Of course." My eyes drop to Rowan, who hands me my phone. "Would you mind—"

"I've got you, luv."

Liquid heat surges like wildfire in my veins. The way he says luv and the energy that rushes between us makes me a little tipsy. I've had crushes before, but there's something about the fizziness in my blood that overpowers my good senses around him. Never would I have got in a rental car with a man I do not know to go to a random inn in a town where I know no one and then proceed to go on a hike in the woods with him. That's some textbook *Dateline Special* girl who gets murdered shit. Yet here I am. He could ask me to go for a midnight stroll in the dark woods to an abandoned cabin to see his chainsaw collection, and I'd probably say yes.

This is how you die, Pen...or get your heart broken. Either way I'm going willingly.

"Such a handsome helper. Is he your new boyfriend?"

Rowan's hand brushes at the base of his head. "We just met today."

"New boyfriend?" A furrow notches on my forehead.

"You had a boyfriend on your page, but he's not been photographed in a bit. The one with beautiful blue eyes that looks a little like Ryan Gosling. Dr. Alex something. He's tagged in the pictures with you. Several of the students in my class have major crushes on him. They've been bummed and speculating since there haven't been any photos with him in a while."

Since December thirty-first to be exact. Happy New Year, you're an asshole, now goodbye. My body bristles at the mention of Alex. I'd forgotten about the pictures with Alex that slipped into my social media. There aren't a lot of photos with him. One at a *Bridgerton* themed fundraiser for the hospital I – we work at – and a couple of random shots at some volunteer events. As much as I share my life, there're things I prefer to keep to myself. Cane Austen and Me is about raising awareness and advocating for/about disability, not for sharing the personal things that I like to keep private, including my romantic relationships. Something Alex had no problem sharing all over his social media and tagging himself and me in photos.

"Dr. Alex Walsh. We're just colleagues," I offer the half-truth.

Though colleague adds far more to the current relationship with Alex. He's now the smooth baritone and loud dress shoes who I avoid at the hospital. But she doesn't get to know that. I give a lot to my followers in the name of supporting the way disabled people are seen in this world, but I won't offer my heart nor the massive mistake it almost made.

Snapping the photo, Rowan hands the phone back to Stacy. Large hand on my hip, he tucks me into his side. "While I'm not her boyfriend, we are on a date, so if you don't mind..." he says with firmness in his tone.

It's not a date. He knows that. I know that. Even if I did get myself ready as if it was. He hadn't committed when I invited him to join me, but the jealous way he grumbled about Harley told me he'd be at the bar with me tonight.

The thought had me spending extra time getting ready. I shaved *everywhere*. The strapless tea-length blue dress that I tugged over a matching pair of lacy pink panties and bra hugs my soft curves. I styled my hair to hang straight and loose over my bare shoulders. My body is silky from the brown-sugar scented moisturizer I'd smoothed over every inch.

After Stacy leaves us, we take our seats. The chair across from me that Harley once occupied sits empty, but Rowan retakes the pilfered one he'd tucked beside mine.

"So, this is a date?" My fingers wrap around the glass's stem.

"As far as anyone in this room is concerned," he almost growls.

I snort. "Does that include me? I mean I'd like to know if

I'm on a date or not. You know...open and direct communication."

"If it was a date, could I ask about who Alex is?" He curls his fingers around his pint.

I let out a hard breath. "He was my boyfriend. I broke up with him on New Year's Eve."

"What happened?"

"He was a liar." I fiddle with the blue sapphire pendant on my necklace.

Besides JoJo and Trina, I've not told anyone this story. The only thing my colleagues know is that we're not together anymore. Well and the version of our breakup that Alex – ever the Svengali – has told them.

Rowan's hand rests on my knee. "You don't have to tell me, if you don't want to."

"I want to tell you." I square my shoulders. There's something about Rowan that unspools all my truths.

Despite the topsy-turviness that twists inside me with this man, his energy settles me. I feel safe with him. Safe enough to do things that I don't normally do. Like put on the cutest dress I have, sit in a bar, and order a drink for a man who never promised to meet me, but I knew would be here. To share with him things I've only told my best friends and some things I haven't even shared with them.

"Alex is a pediatric oncologist at the hospital where I work. He's ten years older, good looking, accomplished, and charming. We'd run into each other at the coffee cart and chat. There was some flirting. I work with the Gifts and Volunteer Department. We coordinate fund raising, annual gifts from donors, and the hospital's volunteer program. I'm the volunteer coordinator but dabble in just about everything."

"Of course, you dabble in everything. I'm not surprised. You're utterly impressive with your many talents." His praise is like a breathy kiss from the sun, warming my body.

"Thanks." I continue, ignoring the heat flushing my cheeks. "He approached me during a fundraiser in July and asked me out. It was a bit of a whirlwind. JoJo called it love bombing. He had all these over-the-top romantic gestures. Flowers sent to my office a few times a week. Lavish romantic dates at fancy restaurants. Surprise weekend getaways. Lots of gifts and sweet words."

His head tilts. "Love bombing?"

"It's when someone attempts to influence or manipulate you by showering you with attention."

He leans against the chair's hard back. "And he did that?" It's almost a snarl.

"He tried." I sigh. "I let it blind me. No pun intended. Aunt Bea was getting worse. For so long, she was my entire world. I think the fear of losing her made me cling to the idea of something with Alex, ignoring the red flags."

"What red flags?"

I lean against the chair's hard back, letting it bolster me. "He always seemed to know where I was, showing up and acting like it was a coincidence. He'd chalk it up to this cosmic connection he insisted we had. He constantly texted, wanting to know what I was doing. I always put Cane Austen in the same place, but she'd somehow get moved when we were on trips together or I was at his place, so I'd be forced to do human guide with him until I found her. He'd shrug saying the maid must have moved her or that I must have been so tired from the previous night that I misplaced her."

"Fucking bastard," he hisses.

"That he is." My mouth forms a firm line. "I broke up with him after he proposed to me in front of half the hospital during our annual New Year's Eve gala."

The memory slams into me. Alex's seethed protest,

"You're lucky that someone like me wants you," echoes in my still angry heart. Teeth gritted, the velvet box clutched in his hand, as he snarled insults at me counting all the ways I should be grateful that he wants to take care of me.

"I wasn't ready to get married. As blinded as I was to who Alex was until then, I knew my head wasn't in the right space for marriage. It had barely been a month since Aunt Bea died. In the aftermath, it came out that he was more concerned about his reputation than me. He wanted me for all the wrong reasons. He thought the blind woman with my nice girl reputation and minimal notoriety as a disability advocate would boost his profile. He also thought he could control me...still does."

"Still?" Electricity akin to a raging thunderstorm radiates off Rowan.

"He sent flowers almost daily and magically appeared at places when I was out. I blocked him on all social media and don't post my photos when I'm in SoCal until after I've left that location. He still showed up. JoJo used her sleuthing skills to discover he'd linked my phones to an app that locates friends who've given you permission to track them." I sip my drink, letting the alcohol wet my drying throat. "I never gave him access. He'd found out my passcode, broke into my phone, and linked our phones without me knowing."

"I'll fucking destroy him." Rowan shuffles, like he wants to stand and go after Alex, as if the man was in the room.

I grab his arm to settle him down. "I understand the sentiment, but you'll have to get in line behind JoJo and Trina. They have first dibs and very elaborate plans for his demise."

"I like your bicoastal besties."

"I think they'd like you." I squeeze his corded forearm. "It's all good, though. He's tapered off. Outside the random run-ins at the hospital, I don't see him. I got a new phone and changed my number to be on the safe side. Our department's secretary has designated himself as guard dog to keep him away."

"I know men like Alex, all snake charmers. They flash their golden boy good looks and open smiles and take advantage of the vulnerable."

Vulnerable? I shift in my seat, crossing my legs. I know it's why Alex chose me. The statistics don't lie. Women with disabilities experience physical and emotional abuse in relationships at higher rates than able-bodied women. While he never laid a finger on me, there was manipulation, grooming, and control.

"He saw someone in pain and pounced. You were grieving. Even if your Aunt Bea hadn't died yet, your heart was preparing to lose her." He swipes his hand over his face. "I know JoJo and Trina have first dibs, but I call the scraps."

A grin takes over my face. "I'll let them know." I wince. "God, why do I keep emotionally oversharing with you?"

"Isn't that what you do on dates? I'll admit that it's been a while since I went on a proper date, so I'm out of practice."

"When was your last date?"

"A year ago."

"You haven't been with anyone in a year?" I gape.

"I didn't say that" he scoffs and then let's out an annoyed breath telegraphing that he hadn't planned to share that.

I pick up my glass and feign nonchalance, ignoring the twist in my belly at the idea of Rowan with anyone else. "So, just one-night stands and friends with benefits type of arrangements I take it."

"Something like that." He raps his knuckles against the table. "Nobody since January. I've been focused on work."

"The pub?"

"And–"

"Evening, folks." Harley's velvety baritone steals Rowan's

words. "We have a special treat tonight. There's a celebrity in our mix."

Spine rigid, Rowan's gaze jumps to Harley. His lean frame, washed in the yellow radiance of a single pendant light, leans against a stool atop the small stage in the corner. An acoustic guitar dangles in front of him and his hands wrap around a standing mic.

Rowan grabs my hand, pulling my vision to him. It's dark in here, outside of the soft incandescence of mini chandeliers in random spots throughout the bar area. I purposely picked a table directly under one, knowing the extra light would boost my limited sight.

Rowan's mouth, visible from beneath his hat's brim, forms a firm line. "Pen, I—"

But Harley continues, "For those who don't know tonight we have Ms. Pen Meadows in the audience. Pen is not only a well-known social media influencer—"

My body bristles. I'm *hardly* an influencer. Cane Austen and Me is more advocacy, less influence, at least in the traditional sense.

"—but is also a championship singer. Pen, I know I said I'd let you think about it but in my experience overthinking things leads to regrets. Care to join me for a song?"

My head twists, following the whistles, claps, and cheers that sound around the room.

"Just one song." A self-assured smugness coats his playful crone.

Rowan takes my hand. "You don't have to. I can kill him. We can go."

Chuckling, I shake my head. "No, I'll do it." I stand up.

Rowan's hand remains linked with mine, stopping my steps. "You don't have to do this for him."

My eyes fix on Rowan. "I know."

Harley is an ass. There's no doubt in my mind. I knew it

mere minutes into the conversation with him. The red flags that I ignored with Alex rippled violently in the hot air swooshing out of Harley's mouth. But he's right about one thing.

No regrets. Bending, I press the softest kiss to the corner of Rowan's lips. "This isn't for him," I whisper.

Unfolding Cane Austen, I stride – head high – towards the stage. Harley reaches out his hand and helps me up the small step to the stage.

"You're an asshole," I say through a tight smile.

Hand covering the mic, he murmurs, "I'm very self-aware. Plus, I never had a shot with you anyways, but maybe this will make tall, broody, and handsome over there jealous enough to make his move."

My eyes widen.

"My aunt loves playing matchmaker with the guests, and I help her from time-to-time. Let's make Whitney Houston proud and that man salivate."

"She should call you *sneaky* Ed Sheeran instead of sexy." Laughing, I position myself in front of the mic.

He lets out a hissed groan, "Ugh, she didn't call me that, did she?"

Flashing a sassy smirk, my fingers wrap around the mic's smooth handle. I glance around the bar. Snatches of murmured conversation interrupt the quiet expectation of waiting patrons, their faces blurred in the distance and obscured in the room's dim light.

My gaze drags toward Rowan, his hands flat on the table and eyes on me. I can't see them, but I feel their heat scoring into me. "This is for Rowan," I murmur with Harley's slow strum of the first notes of "I Wanna Dance with Somebody".

My stare remains tethered to Rowan. Fire blazes along my skin with the charged space between us. Each word is sung only for him. In a slow dance, my body moves in cadence with Harley's languid guitar melody.

I yearn for Rowan's rough hands on my hips guiding me in a gentle sway, his front pressed against my back and hot breath promising kisses below the shell of my ear as I sing. Those hands roaming over my dress's soft material and letting the entire room know that while I sing about wanting someone to dance with, *he's* that someone.

With the last note, the room erupts in claps and whistles, piercing the heady sensation that glazed over me as I sang. A small smile, a little bashful, covers my features. Taking a quick bow, I turn and offer Harley a brief hug.

"Magnificent. I think you got him. Bruiser over there looks like he's either going to carry you off to his room or punch me," he whispers in my ear.

"Bruiser?" I guffaw and pull away.

He just laughs like it's the funniest thing I could have said. "If he doesn't make his move tonight, I will," he purrs, helping me off the stage.

"Even if he doesn't, you're not my type. I prefer men who don't play games," I say saucily and stride away with Cane Austen.

"Unless the game is hockey," he drawls and turns to the mic.

I stop and look over my shoulder at him, my face scrunched.

He just smirks. "Pen Meadows, ladies and gentlemen. Give her another round of applause as she walks away having stolen *all* our hearts," he calls out. "Now, grab that someone you want to dance with." Harley strums "Galway Girl" and cements his Michigan Ed Sheeran status.

Asshole. Harley is brash and cocky. While I'd never date a man like him, I find him strangely endearing in the most obnoxious way.

Back at the table, I fold Cane Austen and take my seat. A filled champagne flute greets me. Lola must have dropped off that second round she'd promised, while I was singing.

"You were fucking stunning," Rowan rasps, his Irish lilt rough and heavy.

"Th—th—thank you." I stammer my words.

I lift the champagne flute and take a long drag. The fizzy sweetness steadies me.

"Pen," he starts, but stops.

His head tilts as if considering something. With a quiet mumble of something that I can't make out, Rowan slips his cap off and places it on the table. Those light eyes flash bright in the room's dim glow as if they could illuminate the path forward.

He stands and puts out his hand. "Dance with me... Please."

It's part hopeful question and pleading command.

"Absolutely," I take his hand.

Leaving Cane Austen folded beneath my chair, I allow Rowan to guide me to the center of the small open space in front of the stage. Couples and small groups mingle, twisting and turning to the song's lively rhythm. Harley's voice echoes, but all I can hear is the booming thrum of my pulse. Rowan holds one hand in his and the other firmly on my waist, and then he pulls me in close and then spins me away. My head tips back with unabashed giggles. He's a terrible dancer. His movements stiff and a little off-beat but utterly adorable. Still my heart soars as he twirls me into his arms, out, and back again.

For three more fast paced songs, we weave through the clusters of fellow dancers. In the brief moments he brings me in close, the quiet hum of his voice singing along to the song drifts into my ears. His low off-key melodic timbre has its way with me causing goosebumps to lick down my skin.

Harley's talented fingers seamlessly transition into an acoustic version of Elton John's "Your Song." The almost haunting melody twines around the room, pulling couples together. Big hands clenched at my waist; Rowan brings me close. My arms encircle the nape of his neck. I close my eyes, burrow in just a little more and press my head against his chest. His masculine woodsy scent, body's warmth, and heart's gentle beat cocoon me. One hand still on my waist, while the other slides to my back and presses me tighter. Caged between his firm chest and strong hand, I've never felt so free.

"Being in your arms feels right." My admission is a muffled whisper against his chest.

No sound breaches his lips. The only response is the sensation of a gentle kiss on the crown of my head. It's not patronizing or placating. It's confirmation. His hold's tender firmness punctuates our shared understanding that we're both exactly where we want to be.

A few more slow songs, one laughter-filled clumsy attempt for Rowan to match the fast beat of Harley's rendition of "Uptown Funk," and three more glasses of bubbly we leave the bar. Our chuckles echo against the hallway's hardwood floors and the paneled walls as we head to our rooms. My left hand is in Rowan's, while a folded Cane Austen rests in my right.

"I had fun tonight on our *maybe* date," I tease, a little starry-eyed and tipsy, turning to face Rowan.

My back presses against my room door, it's coolness powerless against the inferno that engulfs my body. Peering up through the fringe of my eyelashes, a coy smile curls my mouth.

His thumb swipes lazy circles across my hand still linked with his. "Me too," he murmurs, his free hand rests on the door jamb above my head. His gaze, on full display with his now backwards cap, mingles with mine.

"What color are your eyes?"

"Green."

"A green-eyed Irishman," I say playfully.

"I'm half Swedish on my dad's side."

"Lutefisk and soda bread." The joke emerges breathy and a little sultry from my lips.

God, I want him. I could just take him, but he needs to kiss me first. As much as I think this attraction isn't one-sided, I need the assurance that I'm not the only one in this. That I'm not the only one willing to risk for this growing connection between us. It's one thing to know someone is attracted to you, but quite another thing for them to want you. To want you so much that they act.

"Something like that." He chuckles.

Kiss me. Kiss me. Kiss me. The plea, no doubt, is visible in my eyes.

Releasing our linked hands, he places his warm palm on my cheek. "Do you have any idea how gorgeous you are, luv?"

My heart roars.

"This silky mane." His fingers twirl a long strand. "Those adorable glasses and big honey brown eyes. These plump lips." His fingertips drag along my lower lip before moving down to my throat. "Such soft skin." He moves lower and traces a heart shape above the swell of my breasts. "And this heart makes me want to fall to my knees and worship you."

Every ounce of breath rushes out of me. My pulse's chee-tah-like cadence is wild and ravenous.

He leans in, his nose nuzzling a sensitive spot below my ear, and inhales deeply. "You have this candied smell like a fucking sweet treat that I know I shouldn't have but am desperate to taste."

"Rowan." Both syllables thrum with a pleading need.

He pulls back. "Pen."

Electricity surges between our locked stares. Desire blooms inside me, slickening my core with arousal. Hard peaks brush against my bra's lacy fabric. My grip on my control and cane loosens. Cane Austen crashes to the hard floor with a loud *clunk*.

"Shit," I gasp.

Rowan blinks. The crashing cane wakes us both from this spell. He bends, picks her up, and hands her to me.

"I'm sorry. I think I've had too much to drink." He rubs his palm over his face. "I should..."

"Should what?"

"Go to bed." He steps back.

My blood turns arctic.

"Goodnight, Pen." He nods his head twice, turns, and then heads to his room across the small alcove. Once there he turns, his gaze meeting mine. A windstorm of confusion radiates off him. "I'll wait until you're in your room, so I know you're safe."

I nod, not knowing what else to say. Unlocking my door, I step in and pivot to face him.

"I'll see you in the morning, luv," he says and then slips into his room.

I could live in the way "luv" falls from his lips. It's warm. It claims me as if I'm still in his arms and not standing alone – utterly confused and pulsing with want – in my room with a hallway and two doors between us.

"Goodnight, Rowan," I whisper and shut my door.

CHAPTER EIGHT

Cold Shower and Regrets
Rowan

"**F**ucking hell," I grumble, closing my eyes.

For the second time in five hours, I seek refuge in the shower. Pen's intoxicating presence crowds every crevice despite her being tucked safely in her room across the hall. The icy spray's sting is powerless to quell the simmering heat in my bloodstream. My heart thrums as I imagine her supple body against me.

"You're daft," I chide myself, running my palm over my face.

I could be with Pen. Our limbs wrapped together while I explore every inch of her. Little whimpers escaping as my hands coast over her body. The rasp of my tongue as I learn that she tastes as sweet as I expect.

The scent of want wafting off her lingers in my nostrils. Like a ravenous wolf that found my meal, I almost salivate with need for her. She's the only thing that will quench the hunger that riots inside me. Just an hour ago, we stood, her back pressed up against her door, her eyes dark with desire. Every sign that my desire for her is reciprocated was there. The hitch of her breath. The staccato rise and fall of her chest. Taut nipples visible through her dress.

Shutting off the water, I get out of the shower and grab a towel. Disappointment flashes in my eyes in my reflection in the mirror.

The almost plane crash. The emotions of the day and shared truths. Too many drinks. It all colluded in a loud voice in my head shouting at me to walk away. To not take advantage. To not be like Alex. *That fucker.* No matter how many pints of Guinness I've had, the only regret that nips at me worse than the idea of waking up without Pen in my arms is the idea of her waking up and regretting being there.

Tugging on shorts and a T-shirt, I pace the length of the room. My body is still keyed up. My phone pings and I lunge for it, thinking...hoping it's Pen until I remember we've not exchanged numbers. It's something I'll need to correct in the morning.

"If she's speaking to me." I let out a hard breath as I'm seized with the realization that I may have left her feeling rejected.

There's no *maybe* about it. I did. The silkiness of her lips pressed against the corner of my mouth is a memory that will linger for a lifetime. The velvety smoothness of her voice singing to me still echoes in my ears. She all but served herself up on a silver platter and I just walked away.

Desperate for a distraction from the churn in my stomach, I look at my phone.

Wes: How'd it go?
Me: Fine.
Wes: Liar.

My forehead creases.

Wes: If it had, you'd be too occupied to answer your phone.

Me: Fuck off.

Wes: Seriously, how'd you fuck it up? I mean after seeing this it's clear she's into you.

I open the attached link, which takes me to a video on someone's social media page. Clicking the video, Pen appears in that sexy good girl dress that drove me wild all night. It appears Stacy took the video and tagged Pen in it. The memory of her almost smokey singing voice crooning the song she dedicated to me dulls in comparison to seeing it live. Sexy. Sophisticated. Sweet. Delectable. Dangerous. They all flash in front of me as I drink her in.

Me: How'd you find this?

Wes: Calm down. I'm not internet stalking your girl-friend. I'm just one of her thousands of followers and set a notification for updates. *Guilty Face Emoji.* Ok, so maybe minor internet stalking.

Me: She's not my girlfriend.

Wes: Yeah, because you fucked it up. She's clearly got it bad for you.

Me: How do you know she's singing to me?

I scan the video to make sure I'm not in it or tagged. I'm not. I flip to my social media to ensure there's no photos or videos of me here or with Pen. Again nothing. The last post on my page is still an apology to my teammates, coach, family, and fans. Not to Landon. I won't fucking apologize for punching him and would gladly do it again.

Wes: Dude, I can tell. Looking at her you can tell she's singing to someone, and it's not the Noah Kahn wannabe playing the guitar. So, why are you texting with me and not with her?

Why indeed? I fling my phone onto the bed beside me and press the heels of my hands against my eyes.

I yank on socks and runners. It's midnight and the inn's small fitness center is closed, but I need to work this off. Regret pulses along my limbs and winds through my muscles. A long run will zap the regret.

Pulling open the door, I stop. Pen stands at her open door and steals my breath. Her long legs on full display in blue sleep shorts dotted with silver stars. The toes of her bare feet painted pink. A camisole, a few shades lighter than the shorts, hugs her full breasts and I try not to fixate on how I can tell she's braless.

Our gazes lock and her heart-shaped mouth forms an O. "Rowan." It's breathless, needy, and fucking unlocks the beast inside me that I've tried to cage all day.

The primal need for her is unleashed. Like a hungry wolf ready to devour Little Red Riding Hood, I prowl towards her.

Eyes wide she swallows. "Please tell me you're going to kiss me."

"Yes." I take her mouth. There's no other way to describe it. Each press and nibble proclaim those plump lips belong to me. I devour her like she's my last meal.

"Rowan," she gasps with the slow lick of my tongue down the column of her throat.

"What, luv?"

"You're really good with your mouth."

"Mmhmm." My mouth trails back up to her lips. "We're just getting started." Coaxing her mouth open, my tongue slides over hers.

Whimpering, her arms circle my neck and I lift her up. Those long legs fold around me. Her pussy scorches through the layers of fabric. Greedy to have her alone, I carry her into the room and kick the door shut behind me. I don't want prying eyes nor anyone who might have recognized me tonight to see us. As drunk as I am about this woman, I have enough clarity to keep her safe. The last thing she needs is a salacious picture of the NHL's currently most hated player defiling her in a sleepy inn's hallway.

With three long strides, I reach the bed. Laying her atop the cream-color duvet, I peer down at her. Her hair a little mussed from my fingers stroking through it while kissing her. Sleep shorts riding up. Her eyes starry. The camisole straps have fallen off her slim shoulders. Her lips are kiss-swollen and her cheeks rosy.

"Shoes by the door," her command is hoarse and a little sultry.

Smiling, I comply.

"I don't want to trip on them in the middle of the night," she says, scooting up and laying her head on the pillow.

"It is the middle of the night, luv."

She waves her hand dismissively.

"Has that happened before?" I crawl onto the bed and settle myself between her legs.

"Do you *really* want me to answer that?" She removes her glasses and places them on the bedstand.

"No." I claim her mouth, hoping to kiss away the memory of anyone else before me. I'm selfish, possessive, and starving for this woman.

She yanks my shirt off and drops it beside us on the bed. "Much better," she purrs. Her hands run along my collarbone, to my pecs, down the ridges of my stomach, and back up. "You are…impressive."

Her legs wrap around my waist. My hand drifts up her bare thigh and plays with the shorts' silky hem. I kiss down her neck and nip at her collarbone. Little mewling noises fall from her lips, spurring me on. My hands curl around her thighs and inch her higher on my torso. My mouth devours hers. Her pelvis moves against my hard cock.

"Fuck," I groan, pressing my arousal harder against her.

"Yes," she moans, her nails dragging down my back. "Right there."

"There?" With increased pressure, I rub myself against that spot again.

"Please…don't stop."

"You don't need to beg, luv." I move against her writhing body.

Thrusting harder, I fuck her through our clothes. Her needy whimpers telegraph that I'm hitting her in just the right spot. Breath stuttering, her nails bite into my shoulders.

"Oh, god," she cries, a gentle shudder ripples through her, halting her movement beneath me.

I comb my fingers into her hair and soak in the sight before me. A sated smile stretches across her face. The pink that rouged her cheeks invade the rest of her sun-kissed skin. A satisfied glossiness glazes her honey eyes. Her legs splay on either side of me, and arms hang loose around my neck.

I roll over and pull her into my chest and she nuzzles limply into me.

"I should have said something earlier, but you in my arms doesn't *feel* right—"

She tips her gaze to me.

"–it *is* fucking right."

She moves her hand to my shorts, the bulge still very visible.

I wrap my fingers around her wrist, gently pulling her away from where she's wandered. "Let me just hold you."

"Are you sure?"

My cock may hate me, but the only thing I want is to hold her. "Very sure."

"Okay." She snuggles in deeper.

"I should have kissed you before."

"After our *maybe* date?"

"Yes." My brow creases. "And at the waterfall. In the lobby

with Pisser. On the plane. At Tim Hortons. Every time I thought of kissing you, I should have done it."

"That's *a lot* of kissing."

My fingers trace her lips. "I plan on doing way more kissing than that."

"I may need to invest in Chapstick stock," she teases, stifling a yawn.

Chuckling, I scoop her up, untuck the duvet and fold it over us. She settles herself into my nook, using my shoulder as her pillow.

"Why didn't you kiss me before?" A sleep-drunk quality coats her question.

I let out a long breath. "I was scared."

"What scared you?"

"Disappointing you."

Her eyes flutter open, and her hand strokes my cheek. "Why?"

My gaze moves from her to the ceiling. The antique-looking fan's blades cut through the dimly lit room sending thin lines of shadows reaching across the ceiling like grasping fingers.

"I've disappointed a lot of people in my life. My mam. Brothers. People I care about. It's funny, though. They have expectations for me but at the same time they're never surprised when I don't meet them. It feels like their disappointment isn't in that I don't live up to their expectations of who I am, but in themselves for believing I am someone I'm not."

"That's not funny ha ha; that's funny sad."

"I know." I brush back her hair, rubbing the silky strands between my fingers.

"They're the disappointment, Rowan."

"What does that mean?"

"They don't see you, the real you. If they really saw you,

then they wouldn't be disappointed by you. They'd know who you are and why you do the things you do. I see you."

I swallow thickly. "We just met."

"That doesn't mean that I don't see you."

"And what do you see?"

"He asks the blind girl." A quiet giggle breaches her lips.

"Smartass."

"Kind. Protective. Guarded. Supportive. Generous. A sweet man." Her eyelids heavy and her hand covers a small yawn. "It's what I see when I look at you."

Fullness surges in my chest.

"Will you stay with me?"

"Yes." My lips press at the crown of her head.

"Yay." She snuggles against me. "See you're not disappointing me."

We lay quiet, her relaxed body curled in my arms. The ceiling fan's gentle hum and the soft melody of her steady breaths silence any doubt that I am where I should be, despite the niggling worry that slithered inside me because of each raised eyebrow, lingering look, or second glance our way.

"I did something recently that upset a lot of people."

"What?" she mumbles.

"I punched someone."

"Why?"

I regret the tension now invading her relaxed body. "He did something to someone I care about."

"Then...you were"—she yawns— "right."

"The thing is, nobody knows what he did and why I punched him. If people knew it would hurt the person I care about more. All anyone knows is that I punched him, and it just reinforces what they think of me."

I close my eyes, pushing away the pinched face of my mother in the stands. My brothers beside her. Finn, eyes blinking and head shaking, while a stone-faced Gillian leans back.

"Protective." A sleepy smile caresses her lips.

"Maybe you do see me," I whisper, praying it's true.

This woman's vision of me is akin to a fresh spring storm, washing away the barren remains of a lonely winter. In her eyes is the promise of rebirth. Am I deserving of that? Of her?

"Pen, when I said I still play hockey..." I look to Pen. Her eyes are shut. Breath steady. Body still. "Goodnight, Pen." I press a kiss to her head. Reaching to the bedstand, I click off the light. Eyes closed, I sink into this moment with this woman, who is utterly undisappointed in me, in my arms and I pray that I won't fail her faith in me.

CHAPTER NINE

Baggage
Pen

My eyes flutter open, taking in the sunshine creeping into the room through the gap between the window's edge and drapes. Rowan's woodsy scent lingers, but the bed is devoid of the muscular frame that held me tight all night. I sit up, the warm duvet falling to my waist, grab my glasses from the bedstand, and scan the room.

"Where is he?"

The question is met only with the ceiling fan's quiet hum and click of the air conditioning turning on.

My body still zings from Rowan's demanding kisses, exploring hands, thrusting hips, and wicked promise. *You don't need to beg with me, luv.*

I kick out of the blankets and scramble off the bed to check the bathroom. I press my ear against the door and hear more silence. Eyes closed, I lean against the wall and relive last night. Before I wade too deep into the waters of doubt, the door's lock disengaging snaps my attention.

"Good morning," Rowan says, stepping into the room, paper bag handles over his right wrist while his hand balances a beverage carrier with two to-go cups.

"You're here." A tiny ache pulses in my throat.

"I woke up about an hour ago. You were sleeping so soundly, so I didn't want to wake you. I grabbed us break-fast." Allowing the door to shut behind him, he crosses to the small table tucked up against the oversized window. "I grabbed us tea, some yogurt parfaits and"—he hoists up a pastry bag— "a croissant. They didn't have a baklava kind, so I got chocolate almond." He turns and halts. "Pen, are you alright?"

Hands wringing, I frown. "I thought you left."

"Just to get breakfast." His green eyes fix on me.

"That was sweet… I'm sorry, I've never done this." I gesture between us.

His head tilts. "Have breakfast?"

My mouth lifts into a small smile. "Have whatever last night was. When I woke up and you were gone… I worried it was a one-night stand kind of thing. Which is silly because we didn't even have sex. Although, you did make me come." I press my right hand against my brow. "*Oh god*, then I fell asleep before returning the favor. That must have been so uncomfortable for you and—"

He closes the distance between us and places his hands on my shoulders. "First, I have no intentions of last night being a one-time anything. Do you?"

"No."

His big grin wakes up the butterflies in my stomach. "Then we're on the same page. Second, return the favor? Making you come wasn't *a* favor that I expect repayment for. Feeling you fall apart beneath me and listening to those little noises you made ensured I went to bed with the biggest shit-eating grin."

"I'm sorry." I let out a stuttered breath. "I'm not usually this insecure. I haven't been with anyone since Alex. He kind of messed me up a bit, and I haven't trusted myself." I bite back the thoughts that churn in my gut. The ones that worry that I made another mistake. "I like you, though," I murmur.

His thumb coasts along my cheek. "I like you, too."

That ache in my throat dissolves.

"I'm sorry I wasn't here when you woke up."

"No, I'm sorry I'm being *needy*." Cringing, I turn my gaze toward the door.

Rowan places his hand on my chin and guides my eyes back to him. "There's nothing wrong with having needs and expressing them. We all deserve to have our desires met. I was a little needy last night and you were there for me, giving me exactly what I wanted."

Like a kitten, I melt into the tender strokes of his fingers along my jawline. "Yeah?"

"Yeah." His hand cups my cheek. "It's understandable you'd be a little gun shy after what Alex did."

I nod.

Tiny embers ignite inside me. Alex taints this moment. Thousands of miles away in this sleepy inn where I stand in front of this sweet man – whose arms cocooned me in a sense of belonging, support, and safety all night – Alex's baritone, smooth but venomous, and clicky dress shoes still stalk me around every corner.

"I can't erase how he hurt you, but I could kill him for making you question anyone wanting you. For him making you believe your only value to him is your social media following or reputation. For making you think someone wouldn't want just you."

"Just Pen."

A smirk twists his features. "Is there such a thing?" His fingers brush into my hair. "Know this: now that I know what it's like to hold you, I don't think I could ever walk away from you."

My teeth clamp down on my lip, fighting the oversize grin trying to bloom. "I like being held by you."

His hands come to my hips, pulling me against him. "God, all I want to do is pull you back into that bed and kiss away any worry you have, but right now I need to feed you. It's almost nine, and we have to check out and be on the road by eleven."

I raise to my tiptoes and press my smile against his. "Did you say you got a croissant?"

"It's Saturday."

My eyebrows kiss. "What?"

"You have a croissant on Saturdays. I assume if we hadn't found ourselves in Michigan for the night, you'd be at Bread." Taking my hand, he guides me to the table and gestures for me to take a seat.

I sit and take in the little breakfast he's put together. Steam billows from the two cups of English Breakfast tea. Layers of yogurt, berries, and granola line the clear plastic cups with our parfaits. A makeshift place setting claims each side of the table with plastic spoons sat atop paper napkins. With Alex, there were decadent room service breakfasts complete with mimosas and a glass vase with long-stemmed red roses adorning the table of the fancy hotel. Rowan's thoughtfulness is like a gentle breeze versus the gale force winds of Alex's love bombing.

Reaching across the table, I thread our fingers. "I like Just Rowan."

And he squeezes back. "I like Just Pen."

FOUR LAUGHTER-FILLED HOURS LATER, WE MAKE OUR WAY through Detroit's Airport. It's been just over twenty-four hours since first meeting and those initial awkward layers that chafe at the start of any new friendship – or whatever this is with Rowan – is nonexistent. Throughout our little breakfast, the ninety-minute drive to the airport, and navigating security, conversation flows easily between us. We talk about growing up. He in Hamilton and then a bustling neighborhood in Dublin and me in a quiet suburb of Buffalo. I make him sing along with my favorite songs on the radio. With each moment between us, I watch his guarded nature fall away. We toss anecdotes along our conversation like breadcrumbs leading us to get to know each other. I talk about boozy brunches on Sunday mornings with an in-person JoJo and a virtual Trina. He laughs about how he and his brother Finn would prank their older brother Gillian as boys.

"You drew a penis on his forehead with a Sharpie?" I guffaw, tossing my bag onto an empty chair at the gate's boarding area.

"He was so blathered, he slept through Finn and I cackling like schoolgirls the entire time."

"Blathered?"

He tosses his duffle beside me. "Drunk."

"Teenaged brothers are ruthless to each other. Trina is as close to a big sister as I had growing up, and the worst thing she did was make me drink decaf tea." I sip the chai latte Rowan bought me at the small coffeeshop at the other end of the terminal.

His hand brushes at the nape of his neck. "Yeah, this was at Christmas three years ago."

I snort. "Why?"

"He's such a prick, so we thought it was fitting. In our defense, there was a lot of whisky involved." He laughs.

"Do you and Finn always gang up on Gillian?"

Our bags take up the chair beside me, so he takes the empty one directly across from me. "Yes and no. Finn's middle ground. He's always game to take the piss out of either of us."

"But Gillian and you never gang up on him?"

His gaze scans the half-filled boarding area. "No."

"You're not close."

It's not a question. Each time he mentions his eldest brother, there's a shift in Rowan's energy. His spine stiffens and jaw tightens. It's the same energy that bristles from me when my mother is brought up.

He leans back, scrubbing his hand over his bearded face. "Gillian's two years older. It's not that big of an age difference but when I was nine and he was eleven it seemed decade sized. When dad died, he became more father and less brother. He's not relinquished that role, even now."

"I used to wish I had a brother." I cross my legs. "You know, someone to beat up the boys who picked on me in school."

"First, may I have the names and addresses of these boys?"

Laughter vibrates in my chest.

His smirk flashes bright from beneath his cap's brim. "Second, used to? Because I have two, I'll gladly share. Finn's easy to like. He's the brother everyone likes best. Gillian is a first-class prick at times, but I think you could handle him."

"If it means a penis on my face, I'll pass." I wince when I hear what I just said. "A drawn-on penis, not an actual—" I draw the outline of an oversized penis in the air with my free hand.

"Christ, Pen." Head tipped back; he shakes with a deep

belly laugh. "Yeah, you can handle Gillian. I just don't know if he'd be able to handle you."

"Am I *that* hard to handle?" I smirk over my cup. "You seemed to have handled me fine enough last night."

"Luv, I've just begun with you."

My skin sears with the blaze of his stare on me. It scorches up my bare legs, over the swell of my breasts, and pauses on my slightly parted lips. I can't see his eyes drag along my body but feel every inch of his perusal as if it brands me in the truth between us. Last night was only the beginning. A tiny fear whispers inside me that I may be love bombing myself, but the roar of my heart in Rowan's presence drowns the protest.

"Now calling our passengers with disabilities requiring additional time to preboard flight sixteen-forty-two to Los Angeles," the gate agent announces.

Rowan stands and slings our bags over his broad shoulders. "Ready?" His hand reaches out for me.

I take it. "Yes."

A slight jitter meanders across my limbs as we settle in the second row of first class. It feels like a lifetime ago since Rowan snarled at the gate agent that he and his wife would be rebooked for today, but it was only yesterday when we adopted that little ruse after the flight attendant mistook us for a married couple.

"You okay?" His callused fingers squeeze mine.

"No. You?"

"Hey, if you can swim with sharks, you can do this." He raises our joint fingers to his lips and kisses.

"I shouldn't have told you that story. You're going to think I'm way braver than I really am. It's all bluster. I'm actually a wimp."

"Care for a drink before takeoff?" the flight attendant asks.

"Yes." I perk up. "My husband and I would like two glasses of champagne."

"Very good," the flight attendant drawls, walking away.

I lean into Rowan, my lips brushing the shell of his ear. "By the way, those are both for me. You know…liquid courage. I just didn't want the flight attendant to get judgy about me double-fisting champagne."

"If you stay that close to me, he may get judgy about me dragging you into the bathroom." Rowan's low timbre ignites my nerves.

"Well, after two glasses of bubbles, I may drag *you* in there and let you bend me over the counter." Sultriness coats my words.

"Christ," he groans, laying his head back against the headrest. "Luv, I think a plane crash is the least of my worries right now." He shifts in his seat, drawing my attention to his lap.

"*Oooh.*" My lips part. "Your mom naked."

His head snaps to me. "What?"

I wave my hand toward his lap. "Think about something unsexy to help, er… deflate that situation. Not that I'm insulting your mom. I'm sure she's a very sexy woman, but I'm assuming that you don't think so." My face pinches. "At least I hope so."

He leans over and plants a laughing kiss. "How are you both adorable and sexy?"

I nuzzle my nose against his. "Ditto."

"JoJo's picking you up at the airport, right?"

"Yeah."

"Do you think"—Rowan twists a tendril of my hair around his finger— "she'd mind if I took you home instead. I realize this is a little greedy of me, but I don't think I'm ready to say goodbye to you at baggage claim."

"First," I say as I stroke my fingers against his beard, "it's not goodbye; it's a see you later. Second, I've promised to process the last week with her. She's a licensed clinical social worker and lives for that shit."

"I get it." A sad smile curls his lips. "How was it being back for your aunt's ceremony?" His fingers skate over the top of my hand.

Threatening tears sting my nose. I turn my head and peer out the window. Below me carts whizz by. Workers in yellow vests scatter across the tarmac.

"If you want to wait to talk about it with JoJo, it's okay. We can talk about anything you want, or we don't talk at all. You mentioned your audiobook on the drive up. We could do that."

Brows knitted, I twist. "*We?*"

"Earbuds come in pairs, one right, one left. We could listen to your audiobook together." Our gazes weave.

"Champagne for the lovely couple." The flight attendant appears with our drinks.

Rowan takes both glasses, and the flight attendant moves away.

"It's not that I don't want to talk to you about this; I just don't want to cry. I know baggage claim isn't goodbye, but we only have a few more hours together. I don't want to spend it on sad things." I take my glass from him.

"Then let's listen to your thousand-year-old vampire fall in love with the gawky librarian." He clinks his glass against mine.

"She's a museum docent." I sip my drink and *tsk* at him. "And don't drink all that. That's my second glass of liquid courage."

He drank it but ordered me a second one after takeoff, so I forgave him quickly.

Heads pressed together and gazes linked, we lose ourselves in my audiobook and in each other. The periodic bumps and jolts of the flight are unnoticeable from the confines of our little bubble. His grin is wide at the cheesy bits. My hands rest on his denim-clad thigh during the tense scenes. His fingers trace my mouth at the parts that make me smile. Our breathing grows ragged at the sexier scenes.

HEADINESS SETS IN AS WE DEPLANE. THE THREE-AND-A-HALF-hour flight reminiscent of a languid game of foreplay. My entire body is humming with need for this man.

Hands clasped, we walk through LAX. If JoJo hadn't already driven from Seal Beach, I'd probably run away with Rowan. A tipsiness washes over me. It's not the two glasses of bubbly; it's him.

We weave through the crush of LAX passengers. No matter the date or time, it's always disordered here, like swimming upstream against an entire school of misdirected salmon. It's six p.m. on a Saturday and the airport buzzes with life.

Rowan pulls me close and tucks me into his side, shielding me from passersby, some who stare while others' focus remains on their phones. I let myself melt into him.

We finally make it to baggage claim. My right eyebrow arches at the increased number of people gawking. I have enough vision to see people pointing and staring, reactions that I often get, but this is unusual. It's brazen. It's rude. Some people even lift their phones and snap pictures.

"What is happening?" My lips purse.

"I'm sorry." Rowan's tone is gruff and a little breathy as if the words sprinted out of him. His hold around me tightens. "Where's JoJo meeting you?"

"At the carousel." I twist and take in the scene.

A barrage of people shout Rowan's name, bright lights flash, and the loud snapping of cameras assaults me.

My eyes squint and I grimace just a bit. "Rowan, what's happening?"

"I'm sorry, Pen... so fucking sorry." He lets out a heavy breath.

"What are you sorry about?" My brow puckers.

"Rowdy Rowan, who's the girl?" someone shouts.

"Iverson, any comment about Landon Phillips being named NHL Man of the Year?" A gravelly masculine voice yells.

"Or the rumors that Landon is pressing charges against you?" Someone else chuckles.

"Fuck." Rowan's muttered word oozes with pain.

"Rowan, what are they talking about?" My gaze bounces around the space.

"Remember I told you about the person I punched—" he starts.

But someone cuts in, "Iverson, any truth to the rumor that Madeline Jacobson wants to trade you?"

"Pen!" JoJo calls, running towards us.

"Is that JoJo?" He squeezes my hand tight.

"Yes." Even over this chaotic cacophony of sounds I recognize my best friend's distinct smoky voice.

"Thank god." He sloshes a breath.

"Rowdy Rowan, is she your *new* girlfriend? Is she part of your plan to clean up your image?" someone mocks.

Image? I bristle.

"Fuck off!" Rowan roars and spins towards the sound.

"Rowan!" I snap, my mouth dropping open.

Reminiscent of a galloping stallion my pulse rages. The crush-drunkenness that fizzed inside me mere moments ago sobers with confusion. My breath shallows at the rampage of shouts and camera flashes.

"What on earth?" JoJo reaches us. Her gaze drops on Rowan. "This is him? This is *your* Rowan," she gapes.

"Iverson! Iverson! Who is she?" The voices grow more demanding.

My eyes widen. "Who are you?"

"Just Rowan." He swallows thickly. "Your Rowan... At least, I hope."

"What about Emma Sinclair, Rowan?" someone laughs.

Who's Emma? Tears brim in my eyes.

"I'm so sorry. I should have never... I'm sorry, Pen." He lets go of my hand and walks away. The further he slips from me, the onslaught of shouts and camera flashes and snaps quiet.

"Pen, did you know who he was?" JoJo asks, looping her arm around my shaking shoulders.

"My Rowan... At least, I thought."

CHAPTER TEN

Suck it Up Buttercup
Rowan

uck! Fuck! Fuck! I grip the steering wheel harder, my knuckles pale, as my Jeep inches along in the snarled L.A. traffic. Teeth clenched, I bristle with the need to get as far away from LAX as possible. I'd let out a hard breath after jumping onto the first shuttle that appeared, but my tense muscles still ache despite leaving the paparazzi curbside. It was a trick Eli Silverberg, team captain, taught me. Unlike Silverberg, with his famous former boyband star husband, I'm not accustomed to this level of attention. Other than the occasional random reporter at events I attend, most of the media around me happens at the rink before and after games or is relegated to the talking heads on sports shows.

Since I'd infamously punched Landon, there's been an uptick in my 'appeal' to the press. Especially since it happened in Toronto, minutes after they'd beat us in game seven of the Stanley Cup Finals. While Toronto is more a hockey town than L.A., it also considers me and Landon hometown boys. I'd gone to university there, while Landon grew up in Bedford Park, a suburb of the city and played at the same university, but at different times. Only unlike me, he'd lasted two years at university before he'd gone pro seven years ago. The media circus after I'd left the arena that night was nothing like I'd ever experienced.

It's why I escaped to my house outside Hamilton. It's why I chose to drive to Buffalo to fly back to L.A. instead of flying out of Pearson Airport. It's been almost two weeks since I punched Landon and the NHL Commissioner announced my five-game suspension to begin at the start of next season. I thought the incident would simmer down, but this...

Pen. The sensation of holding Pen, her muscles coiled tight, still pulses in my arms. Arms that crave to fold around her. To soothe away the gentle quake that rolled along her limbs thanks to the chaos at baggage claim.

"What have you done?" I glare at myself in the rearview mirror.

As traffic finally thins, I ease down the freeway. I could head home to the judgement-free embrace of GB, my two-year-old boxer. His goofy face is always a comfort. But do I deserve to sink into comfort right now?

No.

I could go to Axel's. Wes is, no doubt, perched behind the bar. I can hear his sarcastic, "Are you just going to sit at my bar and brood all night?" On second thought, the popular West Hollywood pub may not be ideal right now.

The unshed tears glistening in Pen's wide eyes as she stared at me haunts my vision. I can't sulk. I can't seek comfort. I need to protect her. From this. From me. Hitting the turn signal, I cross the lanes and head towards the nearest exit.

Forty-five minutes later, I steer the Jeep down a tree-lined street in Sherman Oaks. I brake in front of a one-story house with a charming white picket fence wrapped around the manicured front yard. The house is like something out of a sitcom with its blue shutters, attached double-car garage, and a large bay window that overlooks the front yard. A swing sways from a large maple tree in the front yard.

I hurry up the shrub-lined red brick walkway to the front door. Before I can bring my hand to the turquoise door, it swings open and a tiny body hurls into me.

"Uncle Rowan!"

I scoop up the little human and swing him in a big hug. "Damon."

The seven-year-old is the perfect blend of his parents. His black curls are all his mother but his hazel eyes, with the mischievous glint that's almost always present, are one hundred percent his father.

"He's *not* your uncle," Greg drawls, appearing in the large foyer. "He's my bonehead client."

"Bonehead?" I arch an eyebrow.

He gestures at his son. "Little ears."

"Mom told dad that if he doesn't stop saying bad words, she's going to invite grandma to stay with us for the summer," Damon whispers.

"Which grandma?" I whisper back, enjoying the annoyed expression on Greg's face.

"Grandma Lawson." The kid's huge smile emphasizes his apple cheeks.

Laughter belts out of me at the pained look on Greg's face. My no-nonsense agent cowers only for two people, his mother and wife. Having met Mrs. Lawson at Sasha and Greg's wedding I understand the fear. The barely five-foot tall southern lady ensured I ate all my vegetables that night and some of hers. With Sasha, Greg is more a lovesick man who pretends to be exasperated but is powerless to do anything but make her happy.

A sharp ache pulses in my chest at the memory of Pen's watery eyes at baggage claim. Setting Damon on his feet on the hardwood floor, I scrub a hand down my face. "Can we talk?"

"Let's go to my study." Greg tips his head to his son. "Buddy, let mom know Rowan is here."

His little face turns up to me. "*Oh*, if dad wants me to get mom, then you are in trouble."

"He sure is," Greg snarks, spinning his wheelchair and motioning for me to follow.

Greg leads me down a long hall towards the back of the house. His guidance is unnecessary. I know this path, having walked it many times since he and Sasha bought the house six years ago. Not all of Greg's clients are invited into his inner sanctum. Somehow over the last decade, I've become one of the select few he's invited in. Though that may have been more Sasha's doing. Before being traded to the Bobcats three years ago, Sasha had me over for homecooked meals each time whatever team I was with played in the L.A. area.

Since moving to L.A., I'm here a few times a month. The only other house beside my condo that I have more meals at is Coach Carlson's. He has team members over regularly for BBQs and invites those without families for the holidays. It's the first time in ten years I've had a regular semblance of family and home.

I follow Greg into his study. The pre-sunset light streams into the room from the double patio doors that lead out into the large back garden.

"Grab a seat." He motions to the two rich chocolate-colored wingback leather chairs opposite of his oversized dark oak desk.

I check out the office as he wheels behind the imposing desk. Matching bookshelves filled with leather-bound classics, athletes' memoirs, legal texts, and an entire row stocked with children's books for Damon. While Greg's agency office in downtown L.A. is decorated with framed photos of the sports world's biggest names – team owners, players, and reporters – this space is littered with pictures of Damon and Sasha.

"I figured you'd be coming here. Sasha has been fielding calls from reporters all morning."

"How the fuck did they know I was going to be at LAX?" I growl and plop onto one of the chairs.

"Watch your tone in my house." He wags a thick finger. "Also, what the hell are you talking about? Who was at LAX?"

"Reporters ambushed us at baggage claim. I assumed that's why you thought I was coming." I yank off my hat and rake my fingers into my hair.

"No. I thought you were here because Landon was announced as the NHL Man of the Year this morning."

"Is it true Landon is pressing charges?" I lean over, placing my elbows on my knees.

It's the first time the idea that I might face *real* consequences, beyond a possible trade, my five-game suspension, and impact on my reputation – *what reputation* – for punching Landon. I still don't regret what I did, but just picturing my mother and Finn's expressions and Gillian's "Not surprised, bro" causes a lump to form in my throat.

"Nah." He waves a dismissive hand. "I spoke to Landon's executive team this morning. Also, he gave this whole speech about forgiveness, moving on, and hopes it sets a good example about sportsman-like behavior. The media fucking ate it up."

"Prick," I mutter under my breath.

"Well, that prick's giving you a lifeline."

A furrow notches my forehead.

"When I spoke with his team this morning, they tossed

out the idea of you participating in this charity event he's hosting next month."

"No fucking way."

"That's twice—" he raises two fingers. "One more time and I'll not only kick you out but have *my* mother come stay with *you*. If anyone can teach you some manners, it would be her."

"Sorry."

Greg arches a dark eyebrow. "Seriously, what is it between you and this guy? Did he bang Emma or something? Is that why you broke up with her?"

"No," I mutter.

The breakup with Emma had nothing to do with Landon. It had everything to do with us being two entirely different people with very different wants. I wanted an actual relationship. Like the kind my parents had before Dad died. For the briefest moment, I'd imagined we could have had that, but I was wrong.

"I know you don't like the guy, but suck it up, buttercup. He's the league's darling right now. Lucky for you that golden boy isn't holding you marring his camera-ready face with a blackeye against you...and all he wants in return is for you to participate in the bachelor auction for his foundation."

"Seriously?" I groan.

"It's in Toronto, your home-ish town. This charity provides funds to low-income families to have their kids participate in youth athletics. It's right up your alley."

A snarl builds in my throat. "Is that *all* he wants?"

"And maybe for you to do a PSA with him about violence not being the answer."

"Greg." The way I grumble his name is akin to me saying, "Fuck off."

"Think about it. All it takes is a day shooting a PSA, a night where eligible rich women bid on a chance to take your grumpy ass out, and a few hours taking them out where they soon realize they'd misspent their ex-husband's money on you… And bam"—he claps his hands together— "you're back in Jacobson's good graces, no longer the NHL's most hated player, and the media leaves you alone."

Stunts like this work all the time. Still, the idea of using a charity to make me look good churns in my stomach. I especially don't like doing it with Landon. The idea of appearing on camera with his smug face to spout platitudes about violence not being the answer leaves a vile and sour taste in my throat. It may make me the brute I'm accused of being, but sometimes violence is the answer, and he needed a good punch after what he did.

"Let me think about it." I sigh.

"That's what I thought you'd say." He clicks his tongue. "I told Landon's people we'd reach out next Friday." Greg drums his fingers against his desk. "Who's *us*?"

"What?"

"You said, 'Reporters ambushed *us* at LAX.' Who's us?" His lips curl and that always-present mischief in his eyes almost sparkles.

"And that's what the eight reporters who've blown up my phone the last hour also want to know," Sasha says, striding into the room, her dark curls pulled up into a topknot and her usually sleek business attire has been replaced by leggings and an oversize Dodgers T-shirt.

"Fuck," I mutter, slouching in the chair.

"That's three. I'll let you stay because I want to know the answer, but expect my mother by Wednesday," Greg teases.

"The reporters sent me copies of the photos. You and Pen Meadows make a lovely couple." Sasha leans against Greg's desk and holds up her phone, her onyx eyes dancing playfully.

A picture of Pen, her smaller frame tucked into my side,

appears on the screen. My right hand splays at the small of her back and my other one wraps around her and rests on her hip. A glossiness shines in her honey-colored eyes. My heart pricks with the memory of the tears that brimmed in those beautiful eyes.

"Emma Sinclair who?" Greg whistles. "You look like a wolf ready to rip out anyone's throat that gets close to you two."

"You haven't been photographed with anyone since ending things with Emma, so you can't blame the media for being curious," Sasha explains.

"I don't want Pen involved in this." I try to keep the hard-edge out of my voice. None of this is Sasha's fault and the last thing I want to do is take it out on her. Not to mention Greg's glare warns that he's just as wolf-like about his mate as I am.

Mate? God, I sound like that emo vampire brooding about the quirky museum docent from the audiobook we listened to on the plane. I can already hear my brothers' teasing remarks about how eagerly I land on the idea of Pen being my mate. With his love-logged brain, Finn would spout off on Irish folklore about soul mates. Gillian would slap me upside the head and tell me to stop thinking with my cock.

Maybe I am. How she felt coming apart beneath me as I thrust against her still makes me hard. Even through the barrier of clothes the heat of her pussy scorched with the promise that burying myself to the hilt inside her would be an incomparable experience. My body pulses with more than just the physical desire for Pen. I want to hold her. I want to capture all her smiles with mine. I want to get lost in her stories. I want it all. Her sadness. Her happiness. Her.

You can't have her.

Sasha clears her throat. "If you two are dating then you'll have to contend with the media from time-to-time. I could do media coaching with Pen, but her videos online tell me she may not need it. The media will adore her."

"She has all the grace and charisma you lack. She might even make you seem less of an ornery bastard." Greg chuckles.

Shifting my gaze out the window, I nod.

"What Greg is *trying* to say is that Pen Meadows may soften your image. Make you seem more likeable. If she's open to it, we can issue a statement. Something like this is a new relationship and you'd like the privacy and time to find your way as a couple and…" Sasha's words fumble to a stop.

I shift in my seat but turn my eyes to her assessing gaze.

She points a red-tipped fingernail at me. "What did *you* do?"

"How…" I close my mouth and shake my head.

Of course, Sasha knows. Besides her ability to smooth the edges on the roughest of individuals, she can, with one assessing glance, ferret out your hidden truths. Even if she doesn't know what they are, she always seems to know they exist.

"I left her," I murmur, my stare cast down.

"What?" she almost shrills.

Raising my head, I meet Sasha's glare. "I left her."

"Fucking idiot," Greg mutters, slapping his hand on his forehead.

"Language," Sasha tuts, wagging her finger at her husband before she turns back to me. Lines mar her brow and storm clouds form in her eyes. "You are ambushed by reporters at the airport and proceed to leave Pen, a woman that has – by all my research on her in the last twenty-four hours – never dealt with the press, you left her *alone*?" She draws out the word as if it's a weapon.

Perhaps it is a weapon. The word slices into my gut with the piercing impact of a sharp blade.

"I thought if I left the reporters would follow me and leave her alone." What once seemed like a stellar idea is now acrid in my throat as I say it out loud. My knees bounce furiously, and I grip the chair's armrest. "I need to –" I stand up, but don't move.

What am I going to do? Go back to LAX and look for Pen? No doubt her West Coast bestie JoJo got her out of there immediately. Something I should have done. Instead, I left her to the vultures.

"Call her and explain," Sasha offers. "Although, I'd recommend lots of begging."

"And, perhaps, some jewelry," Greg adds.

"Very expensive jewelry."

"I—"

Her eyes narrow. "You didn't get her number?" She throws her hands in the air. "What the fuck is wrong with you?"

Greg snorts.

"I thought we had more time." I pace the room.

The entire day I'd lost myself in just being with Pen, so much that I'd not done all the things I should have. Get her number. Tell her who I am.

Who are you? Pen's words echo in my heart.

Just your Rowan, whispers back. Am I, though? Rather… Do I deserve to be? Mere hours after telling her that, I don't think I could walk away now that I knew what it felt like to hold her, but I did just that.

"DM her. Explain that you walked away to protect her. I'm sure she'll understand."

Sasha smirks at her husband. "Since when are you the nice one?"

"Balance, my love. If you're going to go Sasha fierce on him, I'll assume your Pollyanna default mode." He smirks back.

I shake my head. "No."

"No?" they say in unison.

Placing my hands on my hips, I suck in a steadying breath. "I won't DM her. It's better this way."

"For who?" Sasha's expression twists into a scowl.

"For Pen." I turn toward the window. "She deserves better than me. You both said it; she'd soften my image. What would I do to hers? How would I impact her life?"

The thirty-five hours I spent with Pen, a respite from my miserable life, is over. I lost the chance for something... I crushed it the moment I walked away from her at baggage claim. Though maybe a bit of the reprieve was lost with each minute that ticked away without being honest with her about who I was. Being a hockey player isn't who I am, it's what I do. A big part. To most people I am Rowan Iverson, NHL defensemen, not Just Rowan.

No matter how much I yearn to go back, I can't. Even if I explain everything and beg for forgiveness, she deserves more. More than a man who hides his reality and then walks away.

"Sasha, please do what you need to do to make this go away. To make"—I swallow the hard lump in my throat—"Pen go away. I don't want reporters bothering her or associating her with me."

"Are you sure?" she says softly.

Her small hand rests on my shoulder, squeezing gently, but I don't turn around. "Yes."

She sighs. "I'll make some calls."

Sasha pads out of the room.

Hands braced on the windowsill, I stare my unfocused gaze on the world outside. The sun hangs low in the sky, readying to say goodbye to the last day with Pen Meadows in my life. I close my eyes and let myself get lost – for just a moment – in the only thing I'll have of her from now on, memories. Her silky lips against my mouth. The melody of her laugh. The sensation of her body curled into mine.

Greg clears his throat, breaking the silence. "In the course of a single play on the field, I lost the future I had mapped out for myself. A career playing in the NFL. The girl I thought I'd marry. My ability to walk. They all were gone in the snap of my lower vertebrae."

I pivot to face Greg.

He seldom talks about his accident, or the life stolen from him by something that happened in the blink of an eye. The well-known story is a cautionary tale for young athletes – the future star cut down too soon. But Greg never let that be his narrative. Looking at his life with his beautiful family and thriving career, I can only imagine that the life he'd wanted at twenty-two pales in comparison with his actual life at forty.

His eyes link with mine. "In the hospital, my mother told me I could wallow in the wreckage of that future or use the broken pieces to rebuild a new one. So, that's what I did. I went to law school. I took a job as an agent, because even if I couldn't play football, at least I could work with football players and occasionally stupid hot-headed hockey players."

My mouth curves into a small smile.

"I built a new future, but I saw it as a consolation prize. I saw myself as one. So, when Sasha waltzed into that board room nine years ago, I told myself that she wasn't for me. Someone like her deserves more than a consolation prize of a man." He gestures to himself. "Hell, most days I think she still does... But she chose me, even when I hadn't chosen myself."

"It's not the same, Greg. I'm no good for Pen. I'm not you. I'm—"

"A man whose vision is clouded with the belief that he'll continually disappoint everyone, a man who doesn't even see himself as a consolation prize, but as a punishment," he cuts in. "Sasha isn't the only perceptive member of the Lawson family. In ten years, I've not seen you develop close friend-ships nor – outside of Emma – have a girlfriend."

"I'm friends with Wes."

"He's your employee and annoyed you into it. Hell, I think he annoyed me into it."

"I'm friends with you."

"We're not friends. I'm your agent."

I huff a dismissive laugh.

"You pay me twelve percent of your earnings, and I tell you the truth. You care so much about people that you hold them at a distance because you tell yourself all you'll ever do is hurt them."

"Are we adding psychologist to your list of agenting skills?" I mumble, crossing my arms over my chest.

"Yeah, and your snarky ass should listen to Dr. Lawson. Date the girl or don't date the girl... but don't lie to yourself that you are doing it to protect her." He rolls from behind the desk and heads towards the door. "We all know who you're really protecting."

CHAPTER ELEVEN

The Cure-All: a Boozy Brunch
Pen

Even heartbreak isn't a good enough reason to cancel boozy brunch with Trina and JoJo. Though, is this heartbreak? As Trina repeated no less than five times, after JoJo called her to debrief on the drive home from LAX last night, I didn't really know Rowan. My heart isn't computing this fact. Last night after JoJo dropped me off, I sank into the oversized clawfoot tub in my en-suite and lost myself in a good long cry with Adele as accompaniment. Add a pint of Ben and Jerry's and I was a crushed-girl cliché.

"No more tears," I command, my eyes fix on my reflection in the bathroom mirror.

I'll pack away all the reasons for each tear. Rowan's deception. My falling for it, for him. The way he left me at baggage claim. Amid all the reasons for my tears, the one that stings the most is that I'll never see him again.

Dashing away one last tear, I grab the hairbrush off the counter and sweep my long hair into a high ponytail.

Perhaps the bouncy hairdo will force a smile on my face, even if it's the one I reserve for my mother.

When the doorbell rings, I pat my hands against my cheeks, hoping they add some color to my pale face. "You know you're sad when *you* can see it on your own face." My mouth forms a small smile at my bad blind joke. "You got this," I assure myself and head downstairs.

Boozy brunch started during my junior year, after I turned twenty-one. Trina flew in to celebrate my birthday. After a night drinking far too many cocktails, me being persuaded to do a blowjob shot on my knees with my hands tied behind my back at a drag show, and flirting with many, many cute boys, we woke up Sunday with the Kilimanjaro of hangovers.

JoJo's answer, "Pastries and bubbles!" She theorized the best way to deal with a hangover is to push it to the next day.

What started as a hangover remedy has become our Sunday tradition. Trina video calls in from Buffalo with donuts from her parent's shop and Bloody Marys. JoJo brings the bubbles and pastries. I host.

I open the door and smile. "Hey."

"Oh babe, you've been crying!" JoJo exclaims, a bottle of champagne in each hand and a bakery bag dangling from her wrist.

"Aargh!" I bury my face into my hands. "I shouldn't be crying this much! Not over a man. I'm a strong ass woman, not a blithering girl-child."

"Oh, Pen." JoJo wraps her arms around me, cold moisture wets my dress from the press of both bottles against me.

"Now my dress is wet," I whine.

"Sorry." Laughing, she pulls back. "It's okay to be emotional after what happened. You haven't been open to dating anyone since Prince Joffrey."

A wet laugh builds in my throat at just one of the plethora of not-so-nice names JoJo and Trina have bestowed on Alex.

"It doesn't take my master's degree to know the tears are a combo of possibly losing someone you really, *really* like and a tiny bit of fear that this is two men in a row who have disappointed you."

"Possibly?"

She shrugs. "I'm an optimist."

"What's there to be optimistic about?" I wave my hands around as if the movement punctuates how very, *very* wrong she is. "He hid who he was and then just disappeared."

"Not to play the sighted ableist card, but you didn't see his face. He was conflicted, pained, terrified, and remorseful. Plus, my spidey-sense and everything you shared last night tells me that he's not Alex. I don't think him withholding who he was had anything to do with manipulation or control. It was about something else."

Fresh tears drip down my cheeks at the echo of the sadness in Rowan's voice as he talked about being a disappointment to the people he loves. I'd reassured him that I saw him. The Rowan I saw wouldn't intentionally hurt me.

Still, he'd said he couldn't walk away from me, but he did.

"He just left me."

"Only after he knew I was there. He made sure you had your people. That you weren't alone." Her tone soft and coaxing.

But I am alone. My best friends are here for me, but the two people who made me pulse with need aren't. One I can never have back. The other I fear I'll never see again and worse, I'm terrified of what will happen if I do.

I swallow thickly. "I don't want boozy brunch to be all about Rowan. I just want to drink, laugh with my friends, and forget about this."

"Denial it is." She sighs. "Go wash your face before Trina

sees you or she'll go all mother of dragons and find out where Rowan lives and burn down his house."

"She wouldn't…" I frown. "I'll go wash my face."

FACE WASHED; I JOIN JOJO ON THE PATIO. BENEATH A GIANT yellow umbrella, we sip mimosas, eat pastries, and grill Trina about her nonexistent wedding plans after getting engaged three months ago. Her scowly, scrunched face, fills the screen from the laptop we've positioned at one of the four place settings atop the circular-shaped glass table.

JoJo *tsks*. "What kind of high performer are you? How do you not have a venue or a date? I already have my venue selected."

"And all you need is the fiancé," Trina deadpans, a smirk replacing the scowl on her lovely face. Like us, she's enjoying the weather by sitting outside on the back porch of the mid-century farmhouse she'd bought last year – pre fiancé.

"Details." JoJo bats the air with her hand.

Adding to the many differences between my besties is their relationship status. JoJo is always single. Despite bad date after worse date, she remains the eternal optimist about all things love. Trina is a skeptic despite always having a boyfriend. Marriage is just something to tick off on her life itinerary.

"Cael and I have a plan. Once he's completed his cardio fellowship next year and I have a year as the attending ophthalmologist at the Retinal Foundation, we'll plan the wedding."

"Wouldn't want something like *love* to get in the way of your career," JoJo quips.

"Exactly." Trina waves a half-eaten donut in the air. "Marriage isn't about the fluffy stuff with Cael and me. It's about partnership. We have very specific career and life goals."

I kick JoJo beneath the table. I don't need to see the details in her expression to know a full-on grimace is etched on her face. She almost vibrates with the need to chide Trina for her romantic blasphemy.

I clear my throat. "Speaking of career stuff. I got an email from my boss this morning. He'd like to meet with me first thing tomorrow."

"Are you fired? Oh god!" JoJo gasps.

"Why do you always think someone is getting fired when their boss asks to see them?" I chuckle.

"An email from your boss to be in their office is the adult equivalent of being called to the principal's office, which is never good."

"I was only ever called to the principal's office for good things. Winning valedictorian when I graduated at sixteen. Being selected for Model United Nations. My almost perfect SAT score. Making it to the final round for a national essay contest." Trina counts off her many teenage accomplishments on each finger.

"Trina, we've discussed being braggy," JoJo tuts.

"Calling women braggy is a tool of the patriarchy to keep us in a social-construct of appearing modest or dumbed-down, so men feel better about their insecure selves."

"You found me out." JoJo raises her hands in surrender. "I'm a patriarchy secret agent."

I kick JoJo again and mouth, *stop*.

She chuckles.

"I was just named employee of the quarter, so I'd imagine they're not firing me."

"See!" Trina points at me through the screen, as if to reiterate her point that sometimes a brag is okay.

I wave her off. "Jamal has been talking about retiring to

spend time with his family. His daughter lives in Chicago and just had a baby. I think he's ready to retire and may be asking me to step up as interim VP of Voluntary Services."

While I'm not as goal focused as Trina about my future, I have a plan. With my master's in health administration, my goal is to ultimately rise to the level of hospital director. During chemo treatments, Aunt Bea would gush to the staff that one day her niece might be their boss. I was both mortified and delighted with her faith in me.

"Pen, this is amazing!" JoJo squeals. "You'd be next in line to be director."

"If I got the job permanently there'd still be like five layers between me and *that* job."

"But if something happened to all five of those people—"

"Don't plan the assassinations yet, lady. It's not the presidential line of succession," Trina guffaws.

"I would never." JoJo clutches at her chest dramatically. "Well, unless…verbal winky-face emoji."

Both Trina and I cackle

Not only does JoJo spell out emojis in texts, she verbalizes them in person to describe some of those little facial tics, like a wink, that I often miss. When someone sits this close to me with good lighting, I can catch some, but still miss a lot. Verbal cues are my primary source of the context and subtext communicated by non-verbal gestures and expressions.

"Well, I'm just happy it's good news. You can't be fired and have your heart broken in the same week. It's just rude!" JoJo bites into a vanilla lavender scone.

"She didn't have her heart broken by the sexy Wayne Gretzky wannabe. It was *only* thirty-five hours. Pen's not that foolish to fall for someone she barely knows." The cringe is apparent in Trina's disdain-filled tone.

"It's not foolish. When the heart knows, it knows," JoJo scoffs.

"Gretzky played center. Rowan is a defenseman," I mutter.

"Looks like *someone* did some googling last night." JoJo leans close and whispers, "Verbal salacious smirk emoji."

I avert my gaze.

"Ugh," Trina groans. "New rule, if I can't achieve-drop, you can't mention men that hurt our friend. Well, unless we're planning their downfall." Her lips purse. "By the way, in your googling did you happen to locate Rowan's address?"

Oh, my besties. I roll my eyes and pour another mimosa.

AFTER ONE TOO MANY MIMOSAS AND ENOUGH CARBS TO START a bakery, I stretch out on the couch. Wind chimes sing in the gentle June breeze. The scent of jasmine floats into the room through the open windows. The sweet scent tickles my nostrils.

It's just me and all my thoughts. JoJo took a rideshare back to her place in hopes of napping off the tipsy aftermath of boozy brunch. Trina, who switched to coffee after her second Bloody Mary, logged off to go plot world domination or whatever she does on a Sunday night.

Possibly. The word hums inside me with a promise I dare not let myself touch. I shouldn't be thinking about Rowan. About seeing him again. I should listen to Trina, forget him, and move on. It's how she's dealt with past breakups. Though, with Trina she's the breaker and not the breakee. Also, this isn't a breakup. We weren't dating. It was just one day.

One amazing day.

Sitting up on the couch, I expel a hard breath. "Ugh!"

Logically I know this is as foolish as Trina cautions. The warning bells that roar with other men have been silent with Rowan. He hid part of himself. He left me. He...

"He's protective," I murmur, bending my legs and wrapping my arms around them to rest my chin on my knees. "There's a reason. There's more to this. I know it."

My eyes flick to my mobile in the glittery pink case on the coffee table. We hadn't exchanged numbers, but he knows my social media handle. I shift to sit on my knees and scoop up the phone. Like a starved woman searching for the tiniest crumb to quell her hunger, I open my phone and pull up Instagram.

Since last night, I've not been online. The last post on Cane Austen and Me is a selfie taken with Harley before he performed and a video where Stacy tagged me as I sang. There are also seventy-five notifications, including an alert that @HarleyGuitarGuy is now following me.

I ignore the notifications and go directly to my inbox where ten new messages wait for me. Scrolling, I see that none are from Rowan Iverson. Unless he's using an alias online.

I open the first message.

Ms. Meadows, my name is Miguel Reyes, I'm a reporter with the LA Press and would like to get a comment on a story I'm writing about the need for universal design in public spaces to support true accessibility. My understanding is Rowan Iverson assisted you during a recent trip due to accessibility challenges as a visually impaired woman. Would you be open to speaking with me?

"What?" My eyes almost bulge out of my sockets.

I open the remaining messages. All are requests from reporters from various media outlets. Each asking about

Rowan helping me navigate airports. Turns out I'm not the new girlfriend. I'm just…

"His charity case." I toss the phone onto the coffee table. "Goodbye Rowan, or whoever you *really* are."

CHAPTER TWELVE

Pen-ance
Rowan

The heavy clatter of weights reverberates around the training room. Daily workouts aren't mandatory during the off-season, but I've not lost the habit. It keeps me at peak physical strength for the upcoming season, even if I'll spend the first five games watching from the stands instead of playing. My suspension means I can't be within fifty feet of the bench, penalty box or dressing room. Completely cut off.

Lifting also offers some momentary mental clarity and respite from all that torments me. With each mile on the treadmill or rep on a weight bench my brain settles into my workout and away from everything else. It's why I drove from my condo to the Bobcat's training center. Every morning, no matter where I am, I wake at six a.m. to workout.

Not every morning. With another triceps kickback, I attempt to push away the sensation of waking up just three days ago with Pen snuggled into me. The melodic hum of her steady breaths. The softness of her body pressed against me. The utter relaxation coursing through my veins at her in my arms and the panic that induced. It's what drove me from her bed.

It's not her you're protecting. Greg's smug face flashes in my eyes.

"Damnit," I growl and drop the weights to the ground with a loud *clunk*.

"Tossing the equipment around won't help you get brownie points that I assume you're trying to get by being here while your teammates are on vacation."

I look up and meet the gray eyes of Madeline Jacobson, the most powerful female team owner in the NHL. In fact, she's the only one. After her father, Cedric, passed suddenly from a heart attack last fall, she inherited the L.A. Bobcats. The thirty-five-year-old is best known for her stint as a Real Housewife and a high-profile divorce from the quarterback for L.A.'s second best football team.

Pulling up the hem of my shirt, I wipe off my face and then stand. "Ms. Jacobson. Sorry. I didn't realize you were here."

She arches a sculpted blonde eyebrow. "I do own the team."

I rub the back of my neck.

"Also, my presence shouldn't matter on you taking your bad mood out on the equipment. Although, I'd prefer you take your anger out on inanimate objects, not the faces of rival hockey players."

Fuck. This is it. A knot pulls tight in my abdomen.

All communication about the trade threat funnels through Greg. He's been the one dealing with management. Besides Coach Carlson's growled, "What the actual fuck were you thinking?" before he turned and grumbled, "Get out of my sight," as he walked out of the locker room, I've had no direct communication with anyone from the Bobcats.

"Why are you here, Iverson," she asks, placing her hands on her hips.

Somehow the woman who's eye level with my chest despite her pink stilettos towers over me. With a flick of her tiny wrist, she can decide my fate like tossing away a nonexistent piece of lint off her tailored white suit.

Forehead creased, I sigh. "I'm working out."

"It's the off-season."

"I like to stay ready."

"Glad you'll be in peak performance to sit out for the first five games." Her tone is curt, but expression placid, the two at odds with each other.

I clear my throat. "I want to be ready for when I'm back on the ice."

"And what's the plan when you can play?"

"Win."

With her mouth in a firm line, she nods. "We have the same plan. I'd prefer we didn't have a repeat of this season."

That knot in my stomach coils tighter as if someone pulls the end of a string. Though isn't that what's happening? My contract isn't up for another season. She's the puppet master who decides if I play and where.

"I—"

She holds up her hand, stopping my words. "I don't want to lose again. Last season was the closest we've come to the Stanley Cup in this team's fifty-year history."

"I'd like to get us that cup." My words are slow and deliberate.

Hoisting the Stanley Cup in the air is every player, coach, and owner's dream. In my decade-long career in the NHL spanning five teams, this season is as close as I'd come.

"What do you regret more...the loss or punching Landon?" Her assessing stare locks with mine.

"Losing." I don't even think. I just speak. The smart answer for a man hoping to keep their seat on this bench is to spout remorse for his actions, but I am not a smart man.

"Do you have any regrets about punching Landon?" She taps the pointy tip of her shoe.

I stand just a little straighter. "I regret letting down my teammates, my coach, and the fans. I regret embarrassing you."

"But you don't regret punching him."

"I don't." I can almost hear Greg's groan to be smart, to lie. I may hold back, but I never lie.

"Did you punch him out of spite for his scoring the winning goal?"

"No." A furrow puckers my brow.

"Why did you punch him?"

"I have my reasons."

"And you won't share those reasons?" Her right brow arches.

I just stare back.

"What if I say it's a condition to not trade you?"

I force myself to remain still. "Then it was an honor playing for the Bobcats."

We face off like dueling gunslingers from an old movie. Expression steely, arms tense. Hands hovering over the trigger, but neither of us shoot.

I love wearing the Bobcat black and gold. Playing in L.A. for the last three years is as close to a home as I've had in years. The stability of being in one place. The security of that leading me to buy a bar and name it for my dad. Working with Stefan Carlson, a man who first coached me at university and brought me to join him when he made the leap to the NHL. Hell, even my Stockholm-syndrome friendship with Wes. I'll not hurt someone I care about to keep that. I've had to rebuild before. Fuck, it's been my life since dad died.

"I can respect that." She sighs, breaking our standoff. "I took over in November. This will be the first full season under my leadership, and I want...I *need* to win. Can you help me win?"

"I'll try."

"I didn't ask you to try." Her brows knit. "Will you play to win?"

"Yes."

"Okay." A grin spreads across her face. Turning on her heels, she saunters toward the door.

I can't help but blink. *What just happened? Am I staying?*

She stops and looks over her shoulder. "Oh, Iverson, tell that new girlfriend of yours I'll be in touch to discuss universal design for the arena."

My nose scrunches. "My girlfriend?"

"Penelope Meadows."

"Pen isn't my—"

Her husky laugh cuts me off. "Oh, Rowdy Rowan you don't think I can spot a planted story from a mile away? I've been on a first name basis with my family's publicist since I was ten."

Universal design? Story? My hands clench and unclench at my sides.

Sasha made calls, but I thought it was to make the pictures go away. There shouldn't be a story.

"You two make a cute couple." She winks then points to my discarded dumbbell. "Try not to break the equipment or I'll take it out of that outrageous salary I pay you," she warns and walks out the door.

As soon as Madeline is gone, I pull my mobile out of my gym bag I'd tossed into the weight room's corner. Plopped back onto the weight bench, I quickly google *universal design*.

It sounds like a term a villain from a dystopian sci-fi film uses to enslave humanity. Rather, it's an architectural term that focuses on the creation of spaces accessible for all. Spaces that don't require accommodations because everyone, no matter their ability, can easily access it.

The article pulls me back to Pen talking about accessible trails as we hiked down to the waterfall's pool. "There's a trail at this state park about an hour away from where I grew up that is wheelchair accessible and has clear borders to trail your cane if you're visually impaired." She'd vibrated with excitement as she described how individuals with physical disabilities could have the same experience as those without while on the walking path.

My mouth curves into a smile. It's not just Pen's passion and advocacy, but the mere thought of her that tugs in my chest. I'd told Sasha to make Pen go away. Sitting here, surrounded by the silence of an empty weight room, I know that's impossible. Since Pen's bright smile blasted me at the Buffalo airport, I've been gone for her. Even if I never see her again, she'll never be gone.

I type *Pen Meadows and Universal Design* into Google. Several links come up. Opening the top result, an article from the *LA Press*, that knot in my gut pulls tighter.

Universal design may be the new goal after a famous hockey player assists a popular social media disability advocate at the airport.

Thanks to Rowan Iverson, L.A. Bobcats star defensemen, Penelope Meadows, a legally blind social media influencer, was able to safely navigate two different airports during her recent trip from Buffalo to Los Angeles.

"This is bullshit." My fingers move before my brain catches up. I dial Sasha and place the call on speaker phone.

"Good morning, Rowan." A smile is evident in Sasha's voice.

"What is this article?"

"Why good morning, Sasha. How are you, Sasha? I hope you slept well, Sasha," she deadpans.

I close my eyes and scrub my hand over my face. *Christ, even her snarks are sweet.* I take a deep breath and soften my tone. "Sorry."

"Good boy," she coos. "So, I take it you just saw the stories. There are three, but a few other outlets picked it up."

"This isn't what I meant." I stand up and pace along the bench. "I thought you'd make a few calls and just make the pictures go away."

"I don't have a magic wand. That's not how this works. If you want one story to go away, you need to feed the press sharks another story. That's what I did."

I rub at my temples. "A story that makes Pen look like a damsel in distress, who needed saving. She didn't need me for a goddamn thing. It also paints me with some knight in armor bullshit. That's not what happened. I don't like using Pen to make me look good."

"That's not—"

"Sasha, you of all people should get this." I kick the bench's leg. The slam of my foot against the metal surface subdues the snarl in my voice.

"Don't you dare try to mansplain loving and advocating alongside my husband who is in a wheelchair," she snaps back.

I slosh a long breath. "I'm an ass."

"You are."

I huff a small laugh.

"But I'm used to overprotective men that get ass-like about their ladies."

"Still, I shouldn't have raised my voice or accused you of not having our best interest at heart."

"Our?"

"Sasha," I groan.

"I thought the *LA Press* piece did a nice job of capturing the experience of people with disabilities while traveling – people like Greg and Pen. As independent as Greg and Pen are, there're still challenges for them in an ableist society. Sometimes those obstacles need to be highlighted to push change. Being in a relationship with someone with a disability means seeing their ability and the ways they are challenged. It's part of who they are. If you don't see both, you're not seeing them."

"We're not in a relationship."

"He doth protest too much," she drawls. "This was the best solution. The headlines are about something that Pen is passionate about. We're using your fame to platform her issue. You may not like how it was done, but it got you what you wanted. To the world, Pen Meadows is just the adorable woman you assisted at an airport, nothing more. Unless…"

Groaning, I pinch the bridge of my nose. "This just feels wrong."

"Of course, it feels wrong because what you asked me to do isn't what you really want. What you really want you won't let yourself have. I'm going to tell you what I told Greg when he'd got all caught up in his head and avoided asking me out for months after we first met… Pull your head out of your ass and do it already. Seriously, Rowan, for a man who spouts about how capable Pen is and how much she doesn't need you, you seem to forget that she's capable of determining what she wants."

I sit back on the bench. "You're right."

"Naturally," she says, cheekily.

"How do we come back from this? How do I make it right?"

Each action stacks like unbalanced blocks in front of me. I did not reveal who I am. I'd left her at the airport, rather than explaining anything. I'd inadvertently used her to make myself look good. Just like her asshole ex, Alex.

"Get out of your head," Sasha chides. "I can hear you hate-spiraling over the phone. Stop telling yourself all the ways you fucked up and focus on how to do something about it."

"How?"

"You need to beg for your Pen-ance."

CHAPTER THIRTEEN

Game of Thorns
Pen

A rainbow of colorful kazoos accompany Lord Bobo McLaughin's boisterous "Happy Birthday" rendition. Staff, volunteers, parents, and pint-size patients crowd into the room for respite with games, toys, and various activities. With Cane Austen – a pink balloon tied to her handle – in one hand and a green kazoo in my other, my smile is large as our hospital CFO, who dresses as a clown for our weekly birthday celebration, gyrates to the buzzing kazoos.

It's one of the best parts about working at Walters Children's Hospital. The not-for-profit hospital offers free medical care for children with chronic conditions, cancer, and other diseases, or who have been in life-altering accidents. Not only does Walters provide world-renowned medical care but also a holistic experience for the kids and their family who spend far too much time stuck in hospitals. As the volunteer coordinator, I spend my days ensuring these families don't have the traditional hospital experience but, as our CEO touts, "The Walters' experience."

"This has to be *my* favorite part of the week," gushes Nelson Lewis, the VP of Major Gifts and Donors and my boss's boss.

"Me too." Grinning, my eyes jump between the clusters of clapping children in paper birthday crowns and Nelson, a smile stretched across his round face.

"This is just one of the many ideas you've implemented in the last three years. The department is lucky to have you. I'm on bated breath to find out what you do as interim director."

I flash him a cheeky "Just you wait" smirk.

It's official. This morning Jamal announced his retirement at the end of the month and that, effective the first of August, I'll be the interim director of voluntary services. He'd told me on Monday, but I was sworn to secrecy until it was announced during today's department head meeting.

"I saw the piece in the *LA Press* on you."

Ugh. I school my features, avoiding the urge to scowl.

Can I go a day without that article being mentioned? It hit Monday night and caused an uptick in my followers, requests from reporters and disability advocacy organizations, and even a few businesses asking for consultation. I shouldn't complain. Cane Austen and Me is all about raising awareness. To make change.

But the gist of the articles churn in my stomach. Some of the reporters leaned into the poor sweet blind girl lost in the airport and the big, strong, and sexy – okay maybe that was my descriptor – hockey player who rescued her angle.

At least, the *LA Press* story had a more thoughtful approach. Miguel Reyes, the reporter who reached out and I contacted Monday morning, did a nice job. His article, with its actual research, focused on universal design versus a blind girl in need of rescue.

Nelson coughs. "I didn't know about your advocacy work. Jamal mentioned you did some social media influencing, but I assumed it was fashion."

"Fashion?" I guffaw.

"The department secretary goes on and on about your outfits." He chuckles. "You're using social media to do good. My teens just use it to complain about doing chores. They have thousands of followers enthralled with their stance on childhood chores being unpaid labor. God, I miss the days before they learned to speak." He rubs his forehead.

I huff out a chuckle.

"Well, it was an excellent piece and reinforces what an asset you are."

"Thank you." I slip the kazoo into my blazer pocket and begin to untie the balloon from my cane. It's a little silly to have such whimsical accessories while talking to my future boss – *hopefully on a more permanent level.*

"Speaking of being an asset—" The tap of his dress shoe pulls my attention back to him. "—we have a new donor, the MVP Foundation. We'll announce our new partnership and large donation at a fundraising event in two weeks."

"That's amazing!" Smiling, I hand the balloon I'd freed to a nearby child and turn back to Nelson, my face twisted in confusion. "What does that have to do with me being an asset, though?"

Searching my memory, I have no recollection of the MVP Foundation. In my role, I've built relationships with many companies and organizations, but this one doesn't ring a bell.

"They specifically asked that you represent Walters at the event."

"Me? Why?"

"The MVP Foundation raises money for adaptive sports programs for children and teens with disabilities," he explains with a dismissive shrug.

"Interesting. I wonder why they asked for me." I nod and my fingers coil around Cane Austen's handle.

It's not the first time – *nor will it be the last* – that I'm specifically tapped for a disability-related thing. In high school, college, grad school, and even here at Walters, I am asked to sit on committees and speak at or attend events that always seem to be associated with disability or blindness. It's a double-edged sword. I don't want to be a token, but at the same time, it's vital to have people see someone with a disability in an important role.

He slips his hands into his trouser pockets and rocks on his feet. "I'd imagine they saw the article, too, and thought this was a good fit. Their donation will allow us to outfit our physical therapy department with some state-of-the-art sports equipment, and the ongoing partnership will establish a scholarship program for Walters' patients to attend the foundation's sports camps. It's a big deal, Pen... Especially for your transition to *interim* director. I hope you're able to attend."

My lips pull up into my "just for mom" smile at the emphasis placed on interim. This is my first test even before starting the new role. We both know it.

"I'll email you the details after I get back to my office." He tips his head and points past me. "Excuse me, I see the chief of staff waving me over."

"Of course."

He walks away.

"I love cake day!" JoJo appears beside me with a half-eaten piece of cake in her hand.

I gape. "How do you already have cake? We haven't served it yet."

"Never underestimate the power of the bat of my brown eyes and flash of my cleavage," she sasses and licks frosting off a plastic fork.

An added benefit of working at Walters is my West Coast bestie also works here. While I'm in hospital management, JoJo serves as a social worker in our outpatient clinic. JoJo jokes that she spends ninety percent of the day helping connect families with resources and the other ten percent pilfering snacks from breakrooms and department birthday celebrations. This is not at all true. She exerts a hundred percent of her energy for patients, which is why I look past her snack thievery.

"Shouldn't you and your questionable workplace cleavage be in our outpatient clinic?" I tease, bumping my hip against hers.

"I'm on lunch break." She bumps me back. "Also, I needed to come officially congratulate you."

A secrecy oath always comes with a bestie clause in my book. While nobody else knew, I immediately told Trina and JoJo after Jamal told me. Our group chat lit up with so many spelled-out excited face emojis from JoJo and links for sales to update my "boss babe" wardrobe from Trina.

"It's still surreal. Like I knew what was about to happen but didn't let myself believe it until I heard the other department heads clapping after the announcement."

She *tsks*. "I could *so* social work you right now for the 'I don't believe good things can happen to me' subtext of that statement, but instead, let me just celebrate you."

I roll my eyes.

"Just four weeks and you'll be the boss," she whisper-squeals.

Heat invades my cheeks.

"You deserve it, lady." She loops her arm around my shoulder. "Especially after the week you've had."

"I'm over it." With a firm smile in place, I join in the claps for Bobo's kazoo version of Pharrell's "Happy".

"Are you?"

I shrug.

It's been my mantra since Saturday. If I repeat it enough, perhaps, it will come true. After consoling myself with half a pan of brownies, I left behind eating my emotions about Rowan and the article. Channeling Aunt Bea, I put on my smile. If I smile hard enough, my heart may believe it.

"You still haven't heard from him?" JoJo murmurs.

"Nope." I plaster a grin on and turn my attention to the children scampering towards the table where volunteers are ready with cake. "Nor do I expect to." I pivot and head out the door.

JoJo shuffles behind me in her pink ballet flats. "What we expect and what we want are two different things."

"What I *want* is to forget Rowan Iverson."

"But you two–"

"Trauma-bonded and got caught up in all the feelings, nothing more." I glance around the empty hall but lower my voice to a hissed whisper. "It's over. Everyone is a winner. I got an orgasm and three major news outlets did stories on universal design, and he gets to play the hero for the helpless blind girl."

JoJo's expression falls. "Oh, Pen."

"It's fine." Spinning on my heels, I move down the hall toward the elevator.

I may have called Miguel and answered his questions, but the story was never for me. It was solely for Rowan. After the internet Rowan Iverson rabbit-hole I fell into Saturday night, I have two theories. One, what happened between us was genuine but induced by the almost-crash. The moment we hit reality, he freaked. Whether it was from his own fears about relationships or Emma Sinclair, the actual Victoria's Secret model who was linked to him until this past January... I have no idea.

What I do know is that he dumped me after landing in

reality, and he's not coming back. No matter what the still crush-sick girl inside me clings to, this isn't one of my romance audiobooks.

Second, is the reputation resurrection theory. Rowan said he punched someone, but failed to share his victim was Landon Phillips, Stanley Cup MVP, NHL Man of the Year, and one of *People*'s sexiest people two years in a row.

"You don't really believe that, do you?" JoJo places a warm palm on my shoulder.

I jab at the elevator's Up button. "I..." Something twists in my belly. "It doesn't matter."

"It *does* matter."

"It was just one night."

"It sounded like so much more than that to me. You opened yourself up to him and even if he didn't tell you everything, it seems like he opened up to you too."

I press my pink-tipped nails into my palms and hope the pain holds the tears at bay. "I wasn't what I thought I was"—I clear my throat— "becoming to him."

"Do you want me to go steal you some cake? We can eat our feelings and online shop in your office?"

Stepping onto the elevator, I shake my head. "I'll pass. I've hit my emotional eating quota for the week." Pushing the button for my floor, I offer a small smile. "It's *really* fine, JoJo. I'm over this."

"Are you?" Her head tilts.

"I will be," I say as the doors shuts.

BACK IN MY OFFICE, I LOSE MYSELF IN WORK. HOURS SPENT drowning in emails and reports is far more constructive than cake. Though my stomach's grumble while I review the MVP

Foundation's event information makes me regret my cake-free office.

"Pen, I need you!" Devon, our department secretary, whines dramatically from the reception area where he sits outside my office.

Grabbing a granola bar from the desk's top drawer, I laugh-shout back. "What?"

Over the last three years I've memorized Devon's various whines. This is his classic "it's not an actual emergency but a tiny blip in the day that annoys me" whine. "I lost the business card for the vendor that came by Thursday. I thought his card was on my desk."

"Which Thursday?"

"Two weeks ago." His tone is sheepish.

"The puppet show or Disney character performer guy?"

There's a long pause before he replies, "Both."

"On it." Taking my phone from my purse, I pull up my camera roll.

It's a force of habit to take a picture of all business cards for easy visual access. Most of these get sent to my work email and stored in a file, but this was taken before I left for New York, so it remains in my personal cell.

As I scroll past my recent photos, my heart aches with the pictures from Michigan. I've not looked at them since Rowan took them. I stop scrolling as a video pops up on the screen. Rowan had taken it at the pool at the waterfall's base.

In it, a tiny puppy jumps and barks at Cane Austen's ball tip. I swipe the cane left and right, allowing the little guy to play. My head is thrown back in laughter as the dog takes the tip into their mouth and tries to pull it away.

"God, she's beautiful." A low timbre, that I know instantly is Rowan, murmurs on the video.

The rumbly Irish lilt wakes up the butterflies in my stomach, the ones that have been asleep or sulking since Saturday.

"That she is." A raspy female voice almost coos on the video. "Is she your girl?"

After a long pause, Rowans says, "No." His tone is sad and full of longing.

"But you want her to be." The woman's tease is reminiscent of a taunting child.

Rowan doesn't say anything. The puppy's bark echoes. In the video, I look up, my gaze dropping to the camera – on Rowan— and a large grin widens on my face.

Watching the video, the memory washes over me. Despite being several feet away, his eyes shaded by the brim of his hat, I could feel his smiling gaze on me.

"Stupid men." The woman chuckles, pulling me back to the video. "If you wait too long to make a move on a woman that makes you look like that at her, you'll lose her."

After a moment of shuffled footsteps, an older woman appears on screen beside the old man with the leashed puppy.

"I don't deserve her…no matter how much I want her," Rowan says before the video ends with the older couple walking away with the puppy and me, wearing his hat, facing him to ask if he's ready to grab food. "Yep," he answers and the video ends.

Staring at my phone, I place my hand on my chest where a sharp fullness pulses.

"Pen? Any luck?" Devon bellows.

"Um"—I swallow thickly and flip to the requested business card pictures— "yep. Sending now."

SEVERAL MORE EMAILS, TWO INITIAL CALLS WITH POTENTIAL volunteers for our crafty kids program, and one annoyed huff from Devon after Nelson asked him to rearrange his meetings for Monday around a dental appointment he forgot about, it's time for me to wrap up. Boarding the bus outside the hospital, I huff out a long breath. In just four stops, I'll be three blocks from my house.

Most Fridays I hit happy hour with JoJo at Harkey's Hideaway, our favorite cocktail bar along Seal Beach's waterfront, but she's on aunty duty. As she's the youngest of three sisters, two of whom are married with kids, JoJo often is the go-to babysitter, a role she adores.

As much as a cocktail or four sounds delightful at this moment, I'm not-so-secretly relieved to have the night alone. The bus's gentle jostle unspools the thoughts I'd tucked back inside after hearing Rowan's unguarded confession.

I don't deserve her. Those words prick in my chest. I close my eyes. The sensation of Rowan's arms folded around me as he confessed his fear of always disappointing the people he cares about washes over me.

"Ugh," I mutter and press my head against the bus's window. The more the thoughts uncoil, the more I am confused. Rowan's words and actions have me upside down and right-side up all at the same time.

Throughout the remainder of the ride and slow walk to my house, my heart and brain wage a war against each other. My brain cautions that I've been fooled by pretty words and promises before. My heart counters that promises never breached Rowan's lips and neither did sugary sweet words.

Reaching my house, I unlatch the front gate. My home is comfortable. A simple, lavender, cottage-style house, one in a row of homes across the street from the beach. A white picket fence encircles the neatly manicured yard with white flowers bursting from bright green bushes. A rocking chair, made from driftwood, where Aunt Bea once sat with her laptop balanced on her lap, sits on the tiny front porch.

It's all she ever wanted, a purple house by the sea. A place where the beach's scent and the mesmerizing melody of ocean waves filter in through open windows. And it's now mine.

Cane Austen and I take the two steps onto the porch. My steps cease and pulse ticks up when I discover a vase filled with long stem red roses sitting on the sandcastle-shaped welcome mat. Lines crease my brow as I bend and pluck up the card propped against the glass vase.

Leaning Cane Austen against the door, I pull up the magnification program on my phone to read the card. "Please, don't be…" I open the card.

Pen,

Congratulations, sweetheart. I hope you'll let me take you out to celebrate.

~Your Alex

I crumple the card. "Aargh!"

It's been at least two months since Alex flowers had appeared on my porch. When JoJo had cut off the heads of the last dozen he'd sent and had her Marine brother-in-law drop it off at his house, it seemed Alex got the message. The flowers. The pop-overs to the house. They all stopped. JoJo even recruited Devon to play guard dog.

Hoisting the flowers into my arms, I take the stairs and stride down the cobblestone walkway that loops around to the back of the house. Midway, I stop, open the trash, and look at the flowers. "I'm sorry. This isn't your fault."

Sighing, I decide not to toss the flowers. They're too lovely. Even if they came from Alex, they are somebody's hard work. Instead, I take them next door and give them to Lenora and Maxine, the retired couple who serve as the street's unofficial neighborhood watch.

BETWEEN THE APPEARANCE OF ALEX'S FLOWERS AND MY knotted emotions about Rowan, sleep eludes me. Pre-dawn light slips into the room through the open window. Cocooned in my sheets, I let the freshness of the cool, ocean breeze dispel the jitteriness that caused me to turn to the door each time I heard a noise last night. I don't fear Alex hurting me, but I dread interactions. For four months after we broke up, he'd be everywhere. There'd be sweeping gestures, gifts, and lots and lots of sweet words.

We're so good together, you know it.

I'm sorry I pushed you too soon, but I just love you so much.

I just want to take care of you. Let me take care of you... Let me love you.

Then there's Rowan. His words don't elicit the same surge of fear inside me. They just confuse me. I know he wants me. No matter how much I offer false comfort that there wasn't something real between us, it's just me lying to myself.

Despite walking away, he wants me. In my heart, I believe the fact of his belief that he doesn't deserve me may be what is keeping him away. This all may be true, but I deserve a man who will push past his fears for me. If Aunt Bea's battle with cancer taught me anything, it's that life's too short. We're not promised tomorrow with the people we care about, and if they aren't willing to fight for that limited time to be with us, then they're not worth exhausting the precious moments on.

Time to move on. I push off the blankets and face the day. Instead of dwelling in the collision of feelings inside me, I do yoga in the backyard, and get ready for breakfast. It's Saturday, so I'll head to Bread for my weekly, albeit now solo, breakfast date. Having flown to Buffalo the Saturday before last, I've missed two weeks in a row of baklava croissants.

Trying not to think about how I'd not missed *all* croissants, I stride down the brick sidewalk along Main Street. Due to the hour, the boutiques and seaside giftshops that line downtown Seal Beach are still closed. A few cafes and coffee shops stir with early morning customers, but it's quiet here.

Bread is tucked between a dog groomer and Chez Jen's, a French clothing boutique. It's a tiny bakery with only three bistro tables in the small dining area. It not only serves the best pastries and lattes in town but offers an array of mouth-watering breakfast dishes. The rows of red umbrella patio tables lining the alleyway that runs between Bread and Chez Jen's gives the popular bakery some much needed additional seating.

Reaching the front of Bread, I smile at the hostess.

"Pen!" She looks up from the tablet on the small podium tucked under an ivy-covered white lattice arbor. "We missed you."

"Hi, Jela." I brush a tendril that escaped from my messy bun behind my ear and look around.

It's devoid of the typical hustle and bustle of a busy bakery's morning. While I came early enough to ensure I wouldn't have a long wait, there're no customers flowing in and out of the bakery's front door. No hiss of the espresso machine from the other side of the counter. No clatter of dishes or hum of patrons talking in the alleyway.

My nose wrinkles. "It's quiet this morning."

"Yeah," she says, her tone a little confused. "Let me take you to your usual table." Lifting the tablet to her chest, she rounds the podium and motions me to follow.

The alleyway is as quiet as the inside confines, the brick buildings on each side and oversize potted palms and Ficus trees create a secret garden aesthetic.

"Your usual table with a little surprise," Jela says, sweeping one hand toward the table nestled between fat leafy palm plants at the back of the alley.

My heart jumps into my throat at the vibrant flower arrangement on the table. Pink, white, and pale purple roses pop against greenery in a clear vase.

"No," I gasp and spin, slamming into a hard chest.

"Pen." Strong hands grip my biceps.

I force my gaze up. "Ro—Ro—Rowan?"

CHAPTER FOURTEEN

Pen's New Boyfriend and My Competition
Rowan

"P en," I murmur, my thumbs skim along her bare arms.

Goosebumps bloom over her soft skin beneath my callused fingers. I drink her in. Those honey, almost doe-like, eyes peer up at me. That glossy pink mouth, which I crave to take with mine, opens with a tiny, hissed moan at my touch. With each gentle caress, her body softens against mine.

"It's you—" Her forehead scrunches. "It's just you."

"Just me." My mouth slants into a small grin. "Just Rowan." I bite back the urge to say, *your* Rowan.

It's too much to dare... but that's why I'm here. Daring, despite the sins of hiding parts of myself and then walking away, that I can earn back her trust and the privilege to be her Rowan.

The breath I'd held the moment she strolled into Bread's outdoor seating area releases with the knowledge that she isn't pulling away. Her smaller frame still nestles against me. The tension that seized her lovely face dissolves with a ghost of her smile. A soft pink caresses her cheeks and makes my hand jealous to follow its path along her now-rouged skin.

"Your beard." She raises her hand and, with tentative touches, skates her fingertips across my clean-shaven face.

Like a petted puppy, my body melts into her touch. "I am surprised you knew it was me without my beard."

After post season was over, I generally just trim my beard. Keep it neat, but shaving it is a symbolic gesture about no longer hiding myself from Pen. At least, that's how Wes puts it. After talking to Sasha on Tuesday morning, I knew I'd been an idiot and would do anything to make things right with Pen. That includes asking Wes for help. The best friend I never wanted is a lady-whisperer, even if he's the only one that calls himself that. With five sisters, two moms, and three ex-girlfriends who are still good friends with him, Wes practically has a PhD in women.

"Lay yourself bare at her altar," he'd advised as he rummaged through my cabinets for snacks. Wes's guidance calls for an unconditional apology. To be unabashed and unafraid. Though fear twists and turns in my veins. Still, I'm here.

"Do you like it?" My brows draw together. "I can grow it back if—"

"No," she says quickly and then bites her plump lower lip. "It's good… All that matters is that *you* like it." She pulls back her hand and brushes a wayward auburn strand behind her ear.

God, I want to do that. I want to curl that silky lock around my finger. I want to run my hands down her body. I want to press my eager smile to her timid one. I want to…

A throat clears. "Pen, are you okay?"

Oh yeah, the hostess. In the flurry of seeing Pen, I'd

forgotten we are in a public place. Despite being the only customers in the bakery's outdoor seating area by design, there's still staff present.

Our gazes remain locked, but Pen nods. "Yeah, Jela. Just surprised."

"I hope a good surprised," I say quietly.

"Jury's out."

"Ok. I'll give you a few minutes for jury deliberation. Take your time, you're our only customers today after all," Jela snarks.

"What? Only customers?" Pen blinks, pivoting towards Jela.

The hostess smirks and motions to me. "Tall and dreamy over there bought out the restaurant for the day." With a wink, she saunters away.

"Rowan..." Pen spins, facing me and gapes. "You didn't... Why?"

I rub the nape of my neck. "To see you."

"How did you know I would be here?" Shoulders stiff, she steps away from me.

"It's Saturday." The hard lump in my throat almost clogs the words from coming out.

Her face scrunches. "Explain."

"I never got your number. Add it to the long list of bone-head decisions I made with you. I am so sorry, Pen." I swallow, forcing the lump down. "I wanted...needed to—" My fingers rake into my hair. "I wanted to tell you everything and I knew I needed to apologize in person. You deserve that."

Her fingers wrap tight around Cane Austen's handle. For strength or to leave, I don't know.

Pen's eyes drag to the flowers on the table. "You're here because I told you about my Saturday ritual." Each word is slow and deliberate.

"Yes." My gaze follows hers and my chest constricts. "I'm a selfish bastard." I reach for her but stop myself.

The last thing she needs right now is me touching her. Even if holding her hand is the only thing that can quell this tornado of emotions storming inside me. For the last year she's dealt with a controlling and manipulative man who stalked her after she broke up with him. A man who would show up wherever she was and make unwelcome grand gestures. A man who sent flowers.

"Alex," I hiss, scrubbing my hand down my face. "Christ, I should have thought. I swear—"

"I know… It's okay."

Is it? My hands clench and unclench at my sides. I want to throttle him. I want to hold her. I want to punch myself.

"Pen—"

The slow shake of her head dismisses my coming words. "What if I hadn't shown up? What would you have done?" Her voice is quiet, but steady.

"I would have just kept coming back week after week." I close my eyes, knowing it was the wrong thing to say. Was there anything more stalkerish? It's the truth, though, and I promised myself I wouldn't hide from Pen ever again.

Facing me, playfulness softens her expression. "That would have gotten costly."

Nodding, my lips rise into a small smile. "Worth it."

"What do you want, Rowan?"

To kiss you. To hold you. To fall to my knees and beg for forgiveness. To spend the rest of my life and even beyond working to be the man who deserves a woman like you. None of that passes my lips.

Instead, I say, "To share a baklava croissant with you."

She arches an eyebrow. Steely resolve hardens her features.

Sweetness may envelop every aspect of Pen Meadows, but

I don't doubt her fierceness. The way she politely checked that flight attendant on the plane taught me that. Unlike me, she's not a growly, rabid mongrel. Still, she's formidable. Perhaps, more. My bite ensures my victim will run away and never come back. With Pen, people simply bow to her demands. And I am ready to fall to my fucking knees for this woman.

"No, not just a croissant. I want to talk."

Mouth drawn into a firm line; she stares at me expectantly.

But the hint of sunshine in her stormy expression emboldens me. "I don't deserve your forgiveness—"

"But you're here anyways," she scoffs.

"Yes." I take a step closer and her candied scent spools around me. "I told you, I'm a selfish bastard. I don't deserve it, but I want it... I want you."

"You left me."

"I know." My eyes cling to hers, despite how much I want to cast down my gaze in shame.

"Why?"

"To protect you." I take another step closer to her.

She remains rooted to her spot.

Our bodies are just an arm's length away. All I need is to reach out and I could pull her into me, pressing her into my chest with the hope that my racing heart conveys all the truths that my clumsy words will never do a sufficient job communicating.

"JoJo was there, so I knew you had your person. I'd thought my leaving would draw the reporters away from you. It's a poor excuse. But, at the time it seemed what was best for you."

She crosses her arms over her chest. "Don't you think *I'm* the best judge of that?"

"Yes... That's why I'm here. I never gave you a chance to

make up your own mind. I was so focused on protecting you that I wasn't completely honest with you."

"Why didn't you tell me what you are?"

"To protect you." My forehead wrinkles. "Wait, *what* I am?"

She rolls her eyes. "Being a hockey player is what you are, it's not *who* you are."

"You may be one of the few who think that."

Face pinched, she lets out a sibilant breath. "Well, most people lack imagination."

My lips drag up at the corners.

She sighs. "What are you protecting me from, Rowan? Yes, you're famous. Yes, your life is messy right now because of punch-gate, but what is it you're really scared of?"

"Me... I'm scared of me." It's almost a croak.

"Oh, Rowan," she whispers, her stiff posture eases and the steely expression melts. "It's not forgiveness you don't think you deserve... It's me."

The words cluster and choke in my throat.

"You didn't leave to protect me, not really. You left to protect yourself. You waited to make your move fearing that you'd somehow disappoint me, but I think you didn't want to let yourself down. That I'd turn out to be just like everyone else and not see you. You didn't give me...*us* a chance." Shaking her head, she starts walking away.

"You're right." Spinning, I follow her. "I'm fucking terrified."

She stops but doesn't pivot to face me.

"I am petrified I'll let you down. I let down everyone who's ever loved or had faith in me. I'm scared I'll break your heart, or you'll break mine." I take a steadying breath. "I've always let that fear control me, keep me away...protect me. I don't want to be safe if it means throwing away a chance to be with you. I am more scared than I've ever been that you'll walk away." I fist my hands at my sides. "But if that's what you want, I understand. I just don't want to hide from you anymore. So, here I am." I swing up both hands. "I'm Rowan Iverson. I play hockey for the L.A. Bobcats. They call me Rowdy Rowan. I've been in every penalty box in the NHL...twice. I punched Landon Phillips and I'm not sorry about it. I've never really been in a real relationship. I tried with Emma Sinclair, but she was more interested in raising her public profile. I wasn't heart-broken about our breakup. That relationship was more about me trying to do what I thought I was supposed to, not about how I felt about her. In the year I dated Emma, I didn't feel an ounce for her of what I felt in just thirty-five hours with you... That I still feel for you. God, I want you so bad and that hasn't dulled in the last week, it's only gotten stronger. I care about you...so, so much and that scares me. And I'm okay with being afraid because you're worth it."

As if in slow motion, Pen turns. Her eyes glossy and lips drawn into the sweetest smile.

My heart soars and I go on, "I'm scared of thunderstorms. I tell people *The Godfather* is my favorite movie, but it's really *Homeward Bound*. I cry like a baby every time Shadow is reunited with Peter."

Her grin widens.

"Finn is my favorite brother, but I'd give my right arm to have Gillian say he's proud of me just once."

"Rowan," she whispers and steps closer.

I meet her steps and take her hand, placing it on my heart. "I want...need to tell you everything."

"Not all at once." A tender laugh coats her words.

"I know." I press her hand tight against my chest. "There'll be times you'll need to pull things out of me, but I'll never lie to you. I'll never intentionally withhold who I am and what's in here again." I lift her hand and splay it over my sternum. "I promise."

Her eyes drop to her hand laid upon my heart.

"I know I hurt you and I don't expect you to forget that. I don't want you to. But if you'd let me, I'd like to earn back your trust."

And hopefully your heart. For the briefest of moments, I'd held her heart. She'd offered it so openly in Michigan and hours later I nearly crushed it. It may take a lifetime to gain it back, but I'm willing to live that life. Because even if her heart slipped from my grasp, I know mine is securely in hers. Love at first sight is a myth used to sell romance novels. I know that. I'm not in love with Pen, but I knew from the first moment she smiled at me I was gone. Call it insta-lust or insta-connection. Whatever it is, there's a charge between us that tethers me to her.

"Let's start with a baklava croissant," she says, her smiling eyes peer up at me.

"Okay." I grin.

Fingers linked, I guide her to the table.

"Look who's channeling their inner Austen-hero energy," she teases, as I pull out her chair.

Smiling, I take the seat across from her. My forehead puckers at the flower arrangement. "Let me—" I scoop up the vase and move it to a table out of Pen's field of vision.

"You didn't need to do that." An adorable pout covers her face. "They were pret—eep!" she squeaks, her eyes grow into giant saucers.

"Pen?"

"Rowan. Something is under the table and licked me." Her whisper is slow and cautious.

"Oh." I scrub my hand down my face, trying to hide my smile. "It's GB."

"What's a GB?"

"My dog."

"You have a dog?"

"He was sleeping under the table."

GB sneaks out from beneath the table and immediately places his head on Pen's lap. His big brown eyes look up at her, imploring for the stroke of her hand.

"Oh my god," she coos, petting him. "He's adorable."

The black and brown boxer wiggles his butt. Contentment sighs across his muscular body with Pen's slow strokes along his neck.

"You should have led with him. I would've said yes a lot sooner."

"Note to self." I chuckle. "GB." I take my seat and whistle for GB to come.

Ignoring me, he nestles against Pen. Her delicate fingers stroke along his smooth fur. Jealousy vibrates in my chest. I can't blame him. I'd be the same way if my head lay on Pen's lap. Though, I can think of less innocent things to do if my head was on her lap.

I'd hike up that mint green sundress, spread her wide, and bury my face between her thighs. Like the starving man I am, I'd devour her until we were both sated. Although, I doubt I could get my fill of the sexy whimpers she makes just before coming.

Focus, Rowan. Fighting my growing erection, I adjust in my seat and cough. "Besides the baklava croissant, what do you recommend?"

She raises her palm. "Wait. One more thing I want to discuss before we do this."

I close the menu.

"The articles."

"I asked Sasha to make the pictures of us go away. She couldn't get them to drop the story, so she pivoted to one about universal design."

"Who's Sasha?"

"My publicist."

Her right brow ticks up.

"I *know*, I have a publicist. She's married to my agent, Greg, so it's more like a package deal." I pinch the bridge of my nose. "God, I sound like a pretentious twat."

"She's married to motherfucker?"

Laughter bubbles out of me. "That she is."

"So, you didn't know?"

"I didn't know until they hit. I would have never let them do a story like that. In fact, I got pretty angry with Sasha."

"Rowan." Her lips purse.

"I apologized. Also, she gave me a tongue lashing."

"I'm sure you deserved it."

"I did." My hand rests on the table, and I let out a long breath. "Please know, that I would never use you for my reputation. I asked for the pictures to be buried to protect you. The last thing I want is to have my messy life tarnish you."

She reaches across the table and places her palm on top of mine. "I know. I just needed to hear you say that. I'm as scared as you are, and part of me doesn't trust myself."

"Because of Alex?"

"Yes. I hate that he still has this hold over me." Her lips drag down. "As upset as I was, I knew deep down that your actions were to protect, not hurt. The portion of me that doesn't trust myself tried to convince me otherwise."

Something tugs in my chest at her confession. "I'm sorry I made you doubt yourself."

"The doubt was there before everything with you. My feelings for you are just making me face them. It was easy to pretend they weren't there, because there hasn't been anyone that made me want to face them…'til you."

I intertwine our fingers. "We can take this slow."

She tilts her head.

"Let me be clear, so there's no doubt, this isn't me holding back. I very much want you. I want to date you. I want a relationship with you. I have zero hesitation about this... But I know Alex put you through a lot and you may need to walk before we run together, so we'll go at your pace."

"You folks ready to order?" Jela reappears, a tablet in her hands.

"Wait. One more thing. At the airport, I saw your ticket and asked Greg to have his assistant upgrade you for buying breakfast. I didn't ask him to have you seated next to me, but I'm not sorry—not in the least—that he did." My green eyes capture her honey-colored ones.

It's not all my truths, but it's a start. As Pen cautions, I don't need to share all of myself at once. Still, this is the last unsaid thing that stands between sharing a baklava croissant with Pen – and, hopefully, more. The others will come. Like a good book, I'll reveal myself one page at a time, but whatever chapter she flips to I'm ready to let her read me, all of me.

"Swoon," Jela drawls. "What will it be, handsome?"

My hand squeezes Pen's. "Whatever she wants."

A beat passes. Our woven gazes engage in a silent conversation. Her eyes seeming to assess and weigh all my truths. While I'm sure mine glint with hope, pleading for the second chance I don't deserve.

"We'll have a baklava croissant," Pen murmurs and clenches my hand.

CHAPTER FIFTEEN

A First Date?
Pen

"Cardigan or—" I pull the thin white sweater off my shoulders and toss it onto the plush, pink-cushioned window bench. "—or no cardigan?" Hands on hips, my gaze bounces between in-person JoJo, and Trina, who's zoomed in virtually for this get together.

JoJo gestures. "Take it in case it gets cooler, but you look scrumptious."

With a laugh playing on my lips, I face the standing full-length mirror tucked into the corner of my bedroom. The teal dress's fit and flare silhouette hugs my curves with just the right amount of sexiness. The twirl-worthy skirt stops at my knees. A tiny, golden teacup pendant dangles below my collarbone, punctuating the hint of cleavage. It's the third outfit change for tonight's date with Rowan and the one that boosts my confidence most.

"I don't know why we activated first-date protocol. Isn't this like date four?" Trina grumbles.

First-date protocol, which started four years ago, isn't something we do for every initial date. It's reserved only for someone we really like, someone ripe with the possibility of a future. Once *P4EVRP* AKA *possible forever person* is sent via our group chat, the troops assemble. Outfits are selected. Hair is styled. Condoms are restocked.

"Technically Pen never formally declared Rowan a P4EVRP. You just brow-beat her into this." Trina's red eyebrows draw together.

"We've gone over this." JoJo's huffed exasperation is still somehow sweet and playful. "I exercised the bestie privilege clause, allowing for intervention."

"You realize you're the only one that ever exercises that clause," I laugh, putting in my gold hoop earrings.

She shrugs. "Hazards of being besties with a social worker."

"Tread softly, Pen, or she'll ask us how we feel about it any minute now," Trina snarks.

JoJo sticks out her tongue and then continues, "Plus, it's their first official date."

"*Whatever.*"

It's taking Trina longer to get on the Rowan second chance train. JoJo's squeal was epic at Sunday brunch. Trina's overprotective nature is akin to a mama lion guarding her cubs. Since age eleven, she's been my big sister from a different mister.

I smooth down my freshly blown-out hair before turning to face the laptop. "Remember, Trina, part of first date protocol includes getting to grill the suitor."

Trina's pout smooths to a wicked grin. "And I'm a grill master."

"That you are." JoJo flops onto the bed and howls with laughter.

I join in, but my laughter soon fades. *Poor Rowan.* "I really like him," I say softly, fiddling with my pendant.

"I know, Pen. That's why I'm worried. The last guy you liked did a number on you," Trina says.

"Rowan isn't Alex."

"I just don't want to see you get hurt." A gentleness replaces Trina's normally steel-edged tone.

"Neither do I, but I may... And I'm okay with that."

It wasn't just Rowan who held himself back out of fear. As much as I went towards him, I still hesitated. I waited for him to make the first move because of the need for reassurance that I wasn't in this alone. The Pen before Alex didn't need that reassurance. The Pen before Alex didn't question her heart. I want to be *that* Pen again, even if it scares me.

"If he hurts you, I'll go scorched earth on his pucking ass," Trina growls before letting out a long breath. "But I trust you... I trust your judgement. Doesn't mean I'm not going to enjoy interrogating him."

The doorbell chimes, and all of our gazes flick to the ajar bedroom door. Even Trina's eyes appear to drop to the door from the strategically placed laptop.

"Showtime." Trina's low tone sounds almost villainous.

Eyes wide, my heart thumps. "Trina, behave. Please."

"Prima-interrogation, remember?" she purrs.

"Come on, Trina, let's go grill this gentlemen caller." JoJo scoops up the laptop and bounds out of the room.

"JoJo, please hit the mute button if she is too Trina-like," I whisper-shout behind them, hoping only JoJo hears me.

"I heard that Penelope Anne Meadows!" Trina tuts.

JoJo just giggles. "Give us ten minutes before you make your grand entrance."

Despite the flutter of confused butterflies in my stomach, I snort. My nerves crackle due to this first date with Rowan.

It's our first *proper* date. At least that's what he'd said after Bread on Saturday.

"May I take you on a first date?" His right hand brushes against mine as we walk towards the pier at Main Street's end.

Despite the insistent pulse to reach out and weave our fingers together, my hand remains at my side. "Didn't we already have a first date?" My lips slant into a teasing grin.

"Not a proper one." His shadowed eyes, hidden beneath the brim of his cap, bore into me.

I can't see them but feel the tender heat of his gaze caress my cheeks. Wildfire sparks across my body.

"First, it's the first time I asked properly. Second, I'm not holding back like before. Third, I'm hopeful it's just the start of many firsts with you."

My lips lift with the memory. Four days later and my hand still pulses to be in his, and my stomach flips with the dizzying effect of his hope for many more firsts with me.

A hope I share.

After he walked me home, I agreed to let him take me out tonight and gave him my number. Sticking to his promise to follow my pace, he's let me initiate most of our text exchanges over the last few days. Most, but not all. The *good morning, how was your day?*, and daily GB update, and photo messages demonstrate his restrained eagerness.

With one last glance in the mirror, I grab the cardigan and head downstairs. Halfway down the stairs, my steps halt and a giant smile blooms on my face at Trina's aghast, "You brought a dog on your date?"

"What's his name?" JoJo asks.

"GB." Rowan's Irish lilt hums in my ears.

"What?" Trina scoffs. "Does it stand for Good Boy? How original."

"Gordon Bombay."

JoJo's high-pitched squeal echoes, "Adorbs!"

"A hockey player with a dog named after a character from *The Mighty Ducks*." The eyeroll in Trina's snark is audible.

"Says the eye doctor with a blind pug named Keller," JoJo snarks.

I cover my snort.

Trina adopted Keller two years ago. Dogs with disabilities struggle finding their forever homes. My sometimes hard-ass East Coast bestie is a gooey mess for the three-year-old black pug. After he came into the shelter where she volunteers twice a week, she knew that she was his person. In true-blue Trina fashion, she bulldozed a speedy adoption, taking Keller home two days after meeting him. It's the only decision she's made that deviates from her thoroughly researched life plan.

"You named your dog after Helen Keller?" Rowan asks, amusement coating his tone.

"Yes."

"Impressive." A big grin is evident in Rowan's rich tenor. "How old is he?"

"He's… Nope!" Trina *tsks*. "You will *not* distract me with my dog Mr. Tall Sexy Hockey Player."

"You are rather good looking. Pen called you devastatingly handsome after she'd first met you—"

My mouth drops open. *I will kill JoJo.*

"—Pen mentioned two older brothers. Do they look like you? Are they single? And into ladies?"

"Uh…" Another short pause. "Finn is. But Gillian…it's complicated."

"Gillian's the chef, right?"

"How much has Pen told you about me?"

Ignoring him, JoJo continues, "I do love the idea of a man who cooks. How complicated are we talking?"

"JoJo, simmer your hormones. We're supposed to be interrogating him about his intentions toward Pen, not about single men in his gene pool," Trina clucks.

This is going sideways. Cringing, I hurry down the remaining stairs.

"What are your intentions with our friend? You already lied to her and hurt her."

I draw to another halt with Trina's question.

"Trina!" JoJo scolds with a loud gasp. "Pen explained what happened."

Forehead puckered, I rush into the small foyer. My mouth opens...

But Rowan speaks, "You have every right to be wary of me. I've not earned your trust. Nor Pen's. Not yet. You love Pen and I hurt her, even if I thought I was protecting her at the time. You ask what my intentions are with Pen... It's to be worthy. I may never reach that goal, but I plan to keep trying."

Sighing, JoJo tips her head to the laptop in her arms. "Well, he has my vote."

"And mine," I say.

Rowan's eyes jump to me, a large grin kicks across his face. "Pen... You're stunning."

Heat tiptoes up my neck and I bite my lower lip. "Thank you."

My gaze drags down Rowan's body. A form-fitting, short-sleeved, collared shirt molds his sculpted chest. Fitted blue jeans hug him in all the right spots making me grateful for the limited vision I have and jealous of the denim's proximity to his body.

"You look handsome." GB scampers from Rowan's side and I bend to lavish him with ear scratches. "And so do you, gorgeous boy." GB's pink tongue slaps me, his sloppy kiss making me giggle.

"GB, kisses come at the end of the date," Rowan teases and tugs gently at the boxer's leash. GB ignores him completely and plants another kiss on my face.

"Jealous?" I peer up at Rowan to see a lopsided grin etched across his chiseled features.

"Nah, he may have won the battle, but I plan to win your heart." The playful comment zings with a promise.

"So sweet!" JoJo squeals.

"Barf," Trina groans.

After saying goodbye to Trina and JoJo, we head out. It's about a twenty-minute drive to Long Beach for a concert in the park.

Originally, he wanted to surprise me, but the control freak in me overruled that. It's not that I must be in control. It just comes with the territory of being legally blind. I need to know where I'm going in order to prepare for how to handle it. I research menus ahead of time, since most places don't have accessible ones. I plan how to get there via public transportation, including when the last bus runs to ensure I can get home. Even with rideshare services, I've gotten stuck for several hours in different locations. Information and planning are my best weapon in navigating a sighted world as a visually impaired person.

I explained this to Rowan on the phone Monday night as we hashed out date details. Unlike Alex, who'd gripe about how my need to know everything killed his ability to be romantic, Rowan simply proceeded to offer all the details, including texting a link to the park's map and event info.

"Ready?" Rowan says, turning off the vehicle and putting on his hat.

My attention moves to the crowds of people streaming into the park and then back to him. "Sure you want to do this? We could go somewhere less public?"

He looks out the window and shrugs. "Yeah, I'm sure."

"I wouldn't want you to be mauled by fans, or uncomfortable."

A deep chuckle rolls through him. "Contrary to what

happened at LAX, I'm not *that* big of a deal. I'm recognized here and there, mostly during the season. With L.A.'s abundance of famous people, I'm pretty small fish. I tend to draw more attention when I'm back in Canada or in smaller cities where hockey is a bigger deal." He frowns. "Of course, I'm more recognizable since punch-gate."

"Has there been a lot of media since LAX?"

He sighs. "Some. Some reporters have shown up at Axel's and a few camped outside my condo, but it seems to have died down. What happened at LAX was a lesser version of what occurred outside the arena after we lost the cup."

"I can't imagine what that was like. LAX was intense enough."

"I'm so sorry I put you through that." He rubs his hands down his face.

"You put me through nothing. Even if you'd told me about being a famous hockey player, you had no idea the press would be there."

He sloshes a breath. "I wish I knew how and why they were there. I'd thought anything newsworthy about me punching Landon would have died down."

"Me too." I nibble on my lower lip.

"Are you worried about going out in public with me? LAX wasn't my norm, but I can't guarantee something like that won't happen again."

Leaning against the plush leather seat, I fiddle with my dress's hem. "I know your famous, but I forget because you're just Rowan to me."

"I *am* just Rowan," he says softly.

"You are, but you're still famous... And sometimes that fame may bring attention. I know this seems odd coming from someone with a social media platform, but I don't really like a lot of attention. At least with my social media, I have the control. I decide what to put out there.

He closes his eyes. "I have no control over that, even with Sasha's skilled assistance."

"I won't pretend it doesn't make me nervous. As a legally blind person I already get a lot of attention when I'm out. Lots of comments, stares, and pointing fingers. There're plenty of people who don't see me as anything but my disability and feel emboldened to share all their thoughts about it with me." I turn my gaze to Rowan. "I'd imagine in many ways what you deal with in the public eye is similar, only with you we can add reporters, podcasters, social media, and fans."

"Yeah." A hint of a laugh coats his response. "To so many people I'm just a hockey player, not a human."

"And they say I'm the visually impaired one." I flash a cheeky grin.

"Stupid bastards." He huffs a quiet chuckle.

"Agreed."

"I don't want to hide our relationship but if you want to keep things lowkey, I'd understand. If we get too much attention tonight and you want to leave...or if you want, we can leave now—"

"I'm not worried." Reaching across the console, I run my fingers over his strong jawline. "After all, your beard went into witness protection." My fingers skim to his lips and dance along their outline. "I think we'll be okay. Nobody's recognized you, yet."

He reaches over and caresses my cheek. "You did." His thumb strokes over my skin.

Like the strike of a match, the air between us ignites. The charged heat engulfs me, raising my body temperature.

"Rowan." His name is a hissed breath.

"Pen."

"I know it's not the end of the date, but..." Channeling my inner-sex kitten I bat my eye lashes.

Rowan makes a delicious growly noise in his throat before he leans in and takes my mouth in a slow kiss. Each press is hungrier than the last. He drinks me up, sip-by-sip, like a thirsty man lost in the desert. My entire body melts into his kisses. His fingers comb through my strands and down to my back, pulling me closer.

"Rowan," I whimper with his gentle bite on my lip, followed by a soothing lick of his tongue.

"So fucking delicious." His mouth drags down my neck, nipping and sucking the sensitive skin.

"More," I moan and lean back giving him greater access.

He pulls away.

"Don't stop," I breathe.

His chuckle is low. "I told you"—he trails his fingers down my neck and traces the outline of my pendant— "you never need to beg with me, luv. I'll give you what you want." He leans in…

But GB jumps up from the backseat and wedges his wiggly body through the front seat gap. His tongue rasps against my cheek with enthusiastic kisses.

"Seriously, dog," Rowan grumbles.

I laugh. "Guess he's not giving up that easy."

Rowan may be certain he'll win the war for my heart, but GB is a fierce competitor. We lounge on the gray blanket dotted with crossed hockey sticks, a gift Rowan tells me he received from Finn after being picked up by his first NHL Team. GB snuggles between us. With his head nestled on my lap, I stroke his smooth coat while he snores gently.

The sun dips low in the sky, firing a burnt orange as it sinks below the horizon. Quiet murmurs from the couples and families settled on blankets and in lawn chairs underscore the melodic voice of a singer who Rowan cheekily calls "Long Beach Ed Sheeran."

"You know Harley is following me on social media." I sip

from a bottle of sparkling water that Rowan included in the small picnic he brought.

"Fucking Michigan Ed Sheeran."

My eyebrow lifts. "Rowan Iverson, are you *jealous?*"

"Of the fuckboy with the guitar?" he scoffs, not answering the question.

With a wry grin in place, I kick his denim clad calf with my bare foot. "You know that fuckboy was on your side the entire time. He was hitting on me to make you jealous, so you'd make your move. Guess his aunt recruited him because she thought you needed some motivation."

"Really?"

"Yeah… In fact"—I tilt my head— "he even knew about your secret hockey identity. When I got off the stage, I told him I don't like men that play games and he said, 'Unless it's hockey.' I thought it was just a stupid joke, but now I realize he knew the entire time."

"I like the way you say my secret hockey identity. It makes me sound like Batman."

"I always found Batman *very* sexy." My mouth curls into a seductive smile.

"Yeah," Rowan purrs and leans towards me. His hot breath ghosts over my lips.

GB lets out a low growl.

Rowan flops back, laughter vibrating in his chest. "Seriously, dog, I'm your human. Aren't you supposed to help me get the girl, not steal her for yourself?"

"You're gonna have to up your game, Iverson." I skate my fingers down GB's neck, who nuzzles in tighter.

"Oh, I have game." He sits up and moves closer, positioning himself behind me. Legs alongside me and GB, he urges my shoulders back until I'm leaning against his chest. Those strong arms of his settle around my middle.

"You're an excellent backrest." Eyes shut, I lean into his embrace.

"It's just one of my many skills."

"Can't wait to experience the others." My voice drips with a breathy huskiness.

"Take that, GB."

A giggle bursts from me.

"Tell me a fun secret." His murmur caresses the spot below my ear.

I grin, thinking of me asking him that very same question on the plane. "I hate carrots but love carrot cake."

"Why do you hate carrots?"

"When I was diagnosed with RP, my mother was convinced carrots were the key to preventing my ultimate blindness, so she made them for every meal. Have you ever had carrot pancakes or an omelet with slivers of carrots in it, because I have." My nose scrunches.

"But you still like carrot cake?"

"It's probably just the cream cheese frosting, but yes."

I feel him swallow. "Does it ever scare you?"

"Losing the rest of my vision?"

His fingers skim over my dress's fabric. "Yes. Full disclosure I did look up RP after you told me about your condition."

His curiosity about my eye disease is to be expected. It's refreshing that he looked it up, so I don't have to explain to him that RP causes permanent blindness. With how upset some people get when I tell them this, you'd think they were the ones losing their sight. From the age of six, the knowledge that one day my entire vision would fade to black has been part of my life.

"Yes and no." I open my eyes and take in the fuzzy world around me. Something about this conversation fills me with the need to soak up all I can, because one day... "When it happens, I know I'll adapt. My entire life has been about adapting. With each degree of vision loss, I figure out a different way to do things, even seeing. Right now, so much of how I see the world already comes via my other senses."

"What does scare you?" His tone is curious and a little somber, but not pitying.

"Losing little things like seeing JoJo's smile or Trina's frown." My lips tug up. "I can feel those things, but it's not the same as seeing them."

"Those aren't little things…those are the big things." He places his chin on my shoulder.

"Yeah." I press a little harder against him -and soak up the sensation of understanding that cocoons me in his arms.

I feel the bob of his throat against my neck. "There's no cure."

"Not yet. There are different trials, but nothing definitive. My mother wants me to try to get into one, but they tend to want to do them with folks whose vision loss is more advanced in case something goes wrong. Doesn't stop her from pestering me about it each time we talk. It's funny, I'm not blind enough for them and too blind for my mother."

"Too blind for your mother? What does that mean?"

I heave a loud sigh. "My entire life, my mother has been obsessed with the idea of curing my vision loss. She's so focused on the things I can't do, that she doesn't see my capability, only my disability. If she's not pushing me to do a medical trial, then she's lecturing me about getting in a committed relationship, so I have someone to take care of me… someone who isn't her."

A familiar ache twinges in my chest at the discussion of my mother. Part of it pulses with guilt about the strained relationship, while the other stings with how my mother leaves me feeling like a problem to be fixed.

"In many ways, she did what she thought was best. She

sought out experts to work with me, like a teacher for the visually impaired, and she let me move to California with Aunt Bea. I was always handed off to someone else like a human hot potato."

"You're nobody's hot potato."

I snort just a little.

"You know what I mean."

"I know." I smile. "Since Aunt Bea died, she's been obsessed with the idea of me getting married. She wasn't happy about me ending things with Alex."

"Does she know what he did?"

"Some. She just focuses on how he'd take care of me or how his gestures were romantic."

"Because stalking and manipulation are the pinnacles of romance." I want to laugh about the low snarl behind his words, but they're just too sweet.

"I think her desire for me to be taken care of blinds—pun intended—her to the truth about Alex..." Sucking in a deep breath, I admit something I've not told anyone, not even my best friends. "No matter how independent I am, she only sees me as a problem to be fixed or handed off to someone else to deal with."

"There's nothing to fix... You're perfect as you are," he whispers, squeezing me tight to him.

"Perfectly imperfect." I inhale deep his woodsy scent.

"The most beautiful people are—" he nuzzles in to my hair "—and you are gorgeous."

The truth of Rowan's words settles inside me. These aren't just sweet words, but a proclamation of acceptance. He embraces me as I am, not as he'd like me to be.

My brow furrows. "Enough mama drama. Your turn. Tell me a fun secret."

"I hate carrot cake, but I love carrots."

My head tips back with a loud laugh. "Look at us. You eat

my carrots and I'll eat your cake. Though, I think I'm getting the better end of this partnership."

He kisses the back of my head. "No, luv, it's definitely me who's coming out the winner."

And cue the butterflies again. "Speaking of winner, what happened with the argument with Greg?"

On Saturday, Rowan shared that he and Greg were going back and forth about Landon Phillips' olive branch in the form of Rowan participating in a charity bachelor auction at the end of July in Toronto and shooting a PSA.

I'm neutral on the PSA but jealousy riots inside me at the idea of Rowan involved in a dating auction. Granted whatever's happening here is early and we're not exclusive but still, I am not a good sharer.

"I need to tell him soon. Landon's people want an answer by Monday."

"His people?" I roll my eyes.

"You forget, I have people too."

"You have an agent and publicist who, based on your description, appear more meddlesome older siblings than your 'people,'" I snark, making air quotes.

"Noted."

"What is the sticking point? The charity auction or the PSA?"

"The PSA. While I'm not a fan of being bid on like a piece of meat, at least that's for charity."

"I'm not a fan of you doing that either." My lips purse.

"Penelope Meadows, are you jealous?" he taunts.

"No. I have GB to comfort me when some rich divorcée buys you like a prize bull at the county fair." I scratch GB's ears.

"I like you jealous." His fingers tap against my bare arms. "You know one way to avoid that from happening is if you come with me and bid on me yourself."

Something flutters in my chest, but I cover it up with a sarcastic, "Ha, ha."

"I'm serious. The event is right before you start your new gig, soon to be your permanent one."

The unabashed faith conveyed in Rowan's words fill me with a kind of giddiness. One that dulls me to the fact that it's our first date and he's suggesting a trip to Canada together.

"It could be a nice way to celebrate. We'd have to attend the event, but we could sneak down to Hamilton, so I could introduce you to my brothers and mam."

"Meet your family?" I sit up, disturbing GB, and turn my gaping face to Rowan.

"Shit." He squeezes the brim of his hat. "Too soon?"

"Ya think?" A nervous laugh falls out of me.

"You're right. I'm sorry. I was thinking out loud." He frowns. "Clearly *not* thinking. I won't bring it up again nor pressure you but let me be clear; I'm hopeful that one day I'm able to introduce you to them...when it's time and you're ready."

My posture softens with the earnest nature of his words. He's not trying to convince or tell me I'm overreacting.

"It's okay."

He nods but remains pensive.

I position myself back against his chest feeling his muscles relax the moment I press into him. "Why does the PSA bug you the most?"

Tentatively his arms loop around my middle. "With the auction, my presence cosigns the charity's work, but with the PSA it feels like I'd be giving Landon a seal of approval. That feels like a betrayal."

"To the person whom Landon hurt?"

"Yes." His chest rises and falls against my back.

"You don't need to..."

I know he wants to tell me what happened. Why he did it. His body telegraphs the start and stop of the words he debates on letting out. "I do."

"No, you don't. You said you didn't want to hide from me, but this isn't hiding from me. You did it to protect someone you care about. I don't need any other details."

"But I want to tell you." His fingers weave between mine. "Stefan Carlson is my coach. He'd been my coach at university. He's always had a lot of faith in me as a player...as a man. When he jumped to the NHL with the Bobcats, he got them to get me traded from Nashville. His daughter, Olivia... Liv, is twenty. I've known her since she was a little girl. After Carlson's wife died five years ago, she's the most important thing to him."

"He didn't," I hiss, suspecting exactly where this story is going.

"I ran into Liv in the hotel lobby the morning before the last game. She goes to university in Toronto and was there to have breakfast with her dad. She was upset and confided in me that she'd been seeing someone, they'd slept together, and then he ghosted her. I didn't know it was Landon 'til minutes after we lost the cup. We were still on the ice, and he'd made a snide comment about taking the cup and Carlson's daughter's virginity all in the same week."

"That fucker... You're not doing the PSA." Face pinched, I sit up. "I take it back; I will be attending this charity event with you just to swat him with Cane Austen."

"Punishing Pen." He grins.

"Rowdy Rowan." I grin back.

"We're quite the pair." He reaches for me and pulls me back into his chest. This time he cradles me, my ear pressed against his heart, listening to its gentle thump. "Doing the PSA with him would help my public image. I know Greg's right about that."

"What's your good name to the world compared to your good opinion of yourself?" I tip my head up to him.

"Indeed." His fingers comb into my hair. "I know it's not the end of our date –"

Grasping his face, I bring his smile inches from mine. "You never have to beg with me."

CHAPTER SIXTEEN

Tell Me to Stop
Rowan

It's been a perfect night. After the concert, I drove us back to Pen's place. The entire drive, my brain came up with scenarios that wouldn't end with me kissing her goodnight at the front door. Ones that would extend tonight just a bit longer. Lucky for me, Pen's as smart as she is beautiful. As we pull onto her street, she bites her plump lower lip and suggests dessert.

"I have ice cream or brownies," Pen says, slipping off her sandals and placing them on the small shoe rack by the door.

I follow her lead and take my runners off. "Why choose?"

She peers over her shoulder at me, mischief twinkling in her eyes. "I like the way your brain works." Pen saunters across the small foyer towards the kitchen.

The two-story cottage-style house oozes charm. White-framed seascape watercolor paintings decorate the robin's egg blue walls and plush inspirational message pillows, the kind my mam loves to buy at open-air markets, adorn the navy couch. Through the open window comes the delicate sound of wind chimes rustling in the gentle breeze. The scent of mint and orange spice drifts across the open-concept kitchen and living room space. If my brother Finn set one of his books in an idyllic oceanside cottage, this would be it.

"Is this Aunt Bea?" Picking up a silver framed picture from the white end table near a plush armchair, my mouth curls into a small smile.

An older woman with auburn hair the same shade as Pen's, only cut short into a sleek bob, stands beside Pen and Cane Austen. In the photo's background the sun sets over Stonehenge. Both women wear bright smiles and T-shirts that read, *But First, Scones.*

"Which photo are you talking about?"

"The one at Stonehenge."

"Yeah. It was my high school graduation gift. Aunt Bea took me to London for two weeks. We'd do a trip every summer to somewhere different... Well, almost every summer."

Setting the picture down, I turn. "How'd you pick what places made the list?"

A sad, wistful expression etches on her face. "Books. We'd read about a place in a novel and add it to the list." She pushes a lock of hair behind her ear. "Did your mom take you on trips as a kid?"

"No. We three boys were a lot." My lips turn down. "Well, mainly me and Gillian. We fought all the time."

"Like bickering or..." She raises her hands into fists and pantomimes punching. Her smile is infectious.

God, she's adorable. "We were known to leave each other with a fat lip or black eye. As much as Finn enjoys helping either of us fuck with the other, he spends more time playing peacemaker or referee."

Her head tilts to the right. "Do you two still beat each other up like that?"

"It's more words or silent indifference these days." Shrugging, I move towards the kitchen island. "I know you lived with JoJo while at university, but did you live with Aunt Bea after?"

It's an abrupt subject change but needed. Talking about Gillian tightens a knot in my stomach. As much as I can talk for hours about Finn, Gillian is a different story. Unlike in Michigan, I'm not hiding this from Pen, but I'm just not ready to unspool that knot, not yet. The guilt and shame that twines the negative emotions surrounding my relationship with Gillian are too much for this moment. Still...

"I'm sorry." I grip the granite countertop's edge. "I'm not trying to be evasive..." My face scrunches. "Or maybe I am. I just don't want to talk about him tonight if that's okay... Unless you want to."

"When you're ready." She reaches across the counter and squeezes my arm.

Placing my other hand atop hers, settled on my arm, I squeeze back.

"JoJo and I discussed getting an apartment together after undergrad, since we'd both be attending grad school at the same place, but Aunt Bea was diagnosed with breast cancer, so I moved back. She hadn't asked but–" With a sad expression, Pen sighs. "It just felt right. She'd always been there for me, and I wanted to do the same."

"She was lucky to have you." My fingers link with hers.

"I was the lucky one." Nodding, she withdraws her hand and turns.

My mouth opens to ask more, but I close it. In the eleven days since Pen had strolled into my life, she's taught me there's a time to push, a time to pull, and a time to just let someone be.

"Individuals or share?" She opens a cabinet beside the oven.

"Share." Leaning forward, I place my elbows on the island countertop. "Want help?"

"I got this." She pulls down a bowl. "Make yourself cozy. Looks like GB is."

Following her mirth-filled gaze, I find the dog sprawled on the couch atop a makeshift bed made from the once neatly organized inspirational pillows. His paws drape off the side of the couch and a quiet snore hums out of him.

"GB," I groan as I straighten. "Down." Snapping my fingers, I motion at the dog, who ignores me completely.

"Leave my boyfriend alone. He's tired after our date."

Rounding the counter, I wrap my arms around her middle and tuck her into my chest. "Am I in a throuple with you and my dog?"

"Absolutely not!" she scoffs. "You're just our chauffeur."

My heart tugs just a little bit more at that. It's not shocking GB fell so quickly for Pen. After all, I have. GB can be a little rough around the edges. He's obstinate and, despite the very expensive dog trainer recommended by Sasha, he's disobedient. Still, nothing but admiration shines in Pen's eyes as she stares at him. Even at the park when he peed on every tree between the parking lot and the grassy amphitheater, she cooed, "Is that your tree too? Classic only child syndrome."

Grinning, I nuzzle into her neck. "In three of my brother's books, the chauffeur gets the girl in the end, so I like my chances."

"Hear that GB? He's trying to steal your girl," she teases, placing a large brownie in the bowl.

You're my girl. Mine. The idea of Pen being anyone's girl but mine fills me with a feral protectiveness I've never experienced with any woman. It's primal. It's possessive. It has me tightening my grip around her waist.

"What does Finn write?"

"Historical romance." I kiss below her ear, enjoying the way she melts into me.

She spins in my arms. "If you're going to distract me, I'll put you to work."

"Gladly." My arms band around her, pressing her soft curves against the hard planes of my body.

Pen's not a small woman compared to others. She's tall with long legs, plump breasts, and a round ass, but in my arms she's delicate. Her frame, which tucks so perfectly into me, appears small against my large muscular one.

Smirking, she hands me the bowl. "Heat this for thirty seconds."

"Yes ma'am." I place a lite kiss on the corner of her mouth and move to the microwave.

"So, Finn writes romance? I don't think I've read many male romance writers. Does he write under Finn Iverson?"

"He publishes under F.M. Iverson." Forehead scrunched, my fingers brush against raised clear bumps atop the microwave buttons. "What are these?" I turn to find a slack-jawed Pen.

"They're bump dots, so I know which buttons are which by touch."

With a nod, I close my eyes and run my fingers over the raised keypad, punching in thirty seconds.

Snapping her fingers, she drags my attention back to her. "Focus, *your* brother is the author of the *American Heiress* series?" She gestures furiously with an ice cream scooper.

"You've read them?"

"*Read them*?! The besties and I are obsessed."

Face bright with excitement, she goes on about her favorite books in my brother's now five – *or is it six?* – part series about early-Twentieth Century socialites and the working-class men who love them. As Pen and I work together to make the brownie sundae, she jumps from book-to-book like a frog leaping between lily pads. Her smile is wide. Her eyes sparkle. Her hands are in constant motion.

"You know I have an advance copy of Finn's latest book." Chuckling, I scoop up a bite of ice cream-smothered brownie from our shared bowl.

Her spoon stops midway to her mouth. "Cassandra and Zachery's story? If you send that to Trina, you may win her over."

The high-back stools that line the front of the kitchen island allow me to sit extra close to Pen, while sharing our dessert. I'm fighting the urge to pull her onto my lap and feed her like the goddamn caveman I am. Though an even more primal part of me wants to shove the bowl between us aside, lay her on the counter, and claim and mark every inch of her. The way she's marked every part of me.

Instead, I nudge her knee with mine. "I'd rather use it to entice you away from GB."

"Never! What GB and I have is epic." She flashes a grin at the sleeping dog before turning back to me. "Seriously, though, that's sweet, but I assume it's not an advance audio-book copy."

I rub the back of my neck. "I should have thought. Sorry."

Her bare foot taps my calf. "It's okay. Most people don't think of it."

"I don't want to be like most people when it comes to you." Cradling her face, I sweep my thumb across her jawline.

Her breath catches. "You're not."

"I can ask Finn for an audiobook copy or, if he doesn't have one, get it from Wes."

"Wes? Your unwanted bestie?"

"He does audiobook narration on top of the acting and bartending. He's done all my brother's books. That's how he ended up working at Axel's. Finn recommended him." My nose wrinkles. "I suspect Finn did it as a prank, knowing how much Wes would drive me—" I stop speaking, taking in Pen's wide eyes.

"Your brother is F.M. Iverson *and* your best friend is Wesley Williamson?"

"Yeah."

"Oh my god!" she squeals. "Trina and JoJo will die. We love his narrations."

I grin. "Well, perhaps you'll let me take you to Axel's Friday night for dinner. I can show you the pub and introduce you to Wes."

"Why, Mr. Iverson are you asking me on another date before we've finished this one?" She picks up her spoon.

"Luv, I'd fill up your calendar if you'd let me." The words sprint from my lips before I can think better of it. This isn't slow. I promised we'd go slow. But when her enticing candied scent envelops me and those honey eyes peer back at me, I lose all notion of proper.

"I'm supposed to do happy hour with JoJo Friday night." She worries her lower lip. "But I could reschedule—"

"Or bring her." My entire body relaxes. "It will give us a chance to get to know each other's friends. Plus, if JoJo is as big a fan of Wes as you say, I could use the brownie points. She may be my ally in the battle to win Trina over and steal you away from GB. Did I mention GB farts in his sleep?"

"How dare you, sir! Not my GB!" She howls with laughter.

His head pops up at Pen's guffaws and I swear he glares at me with a "Pistols at dawn for defaming me in front of my lady" expression.

I offer him an unapologetic grin. *Sorry boy, but she's mine.*

"I'll talk to JoJo tomorrow at work. I'm sure she'd be down to come on our date with us and meet Wes. You know the book we listened to on the plane was narrated by Wes?"

"That explains why I found the whiny emo vampire annoying as fuck."

She spoons up a bite. "Oh hush, you *loved* it. You know you were shipping Lars the Ruthless and Jamie extra hard."

"I am partial to the undeserving brute somehow winning the heart of the good girl." Leaning over, I capture her mouth. The cool sweetness of vanilla bean and chocolate coat our deepening kisses.

"Rowan..." She pulls away and clamps her hands on my face. "...stop saying you're undeserving. Don't put me on a pedestal. It's not fair to me or you. I'm just as flawed. I'm going to say and do the wrong things, too. Let's do each of us a favor and agree that we both deserve to be happy."

I answer her request with another brush of my lips. Threading my fingers into her hair, I take her mouth in a slow, hungry kiss. Her fingers curl into my shirt. My hands roam across her body, and my mouth soon follows. With quick nips and lingering sucks, I trail down her neck, over her collarbone, and to the swell of her breasts.

"Rowan," she rasps, head tossed back to give my mouth greater access for my slow assault back up her throat to her lips.

"We should stop. I promised you slow." My mouth hovers scant inches from hers. "I should probably go. Tell me to stop."

"Do you want to?"

"No."

"Then don't." She slips from her seat and settles on top of my lap. Dress riding up her thighs, she straddles me.

"Fuck," I groan at the sensation of her pussy against my

hardening cock. Even through the layers of denim and her panties, I can feel her damp heat.

"You said for me to set the pace," she murmurs, a huskiness to her voice.

Stare locked with mine, she slides the dress straps off her shoulders and tugs the fabric down to her waist. Taut peaks poke through the sheer lace of her bra. Her ample breasts are pushed up and overflow from the strapless bra's cups. Unclasping the bra, she removes it, placing it on the counter.

Long auburn strands of her hair kiss her bare skin. Her plump breasts rise and fall with shallow breaths.

Placing her hands on mine, she guides them to her. "Touch me, Rowan."

"Pen," I breathe, cupping her. "You're so pretty, luv."

A gentle shiver shudders over her as I lightly tweak her pink nipples. Rolling and pinching one hard bud, I take the other with my mouth, sucking, flicking, and nipping. Her needy whimpers and arching body spur me on. Alternating between both breasts, all my senses feast on her. The taste of her skin. The scent of her arousal. The feel of her heated core rubbing against my erection. The sounds of her breathy moans. The sight of her coming undone.

Her hands slip beneath my shirt, pulling it over my head. Despite the headiness of the moment, she deposits the shirt atop her bra on the counter. "Tripping hazard," she pants between kisses. "My room...is upstairs."

"I can't wait that long." Dragging my mouth up her neck, my hands grip her waist and hoist her onto the counter.

"Aren't we eager?"

"I'm starving for you."

Pushing aside the bowl, clothes, and stools, I stand between her thighs and pull her to the counter's edge. With a wicked grin, I grab the waistband of her panties and ease them down her legs. The lacy underwear is tossed atop the other discarded clothes accumulating on the counter. I open her wide and bunch the skirt at her middle.

"Look at this pretty little pussy." I run a finger down her slick center.

"I have a condom." Panting, she pulls out a foiled packet from her dress's pocket.

Eyebrow arched, I rub slow circles against her clit. "Place it on the counter, luv. I want to take my time with you."

She squirms with the increased pressure against her small nub.

"I don't want to just taste you. I want to devour you." I bend and lick slowly along her wet slit. "Christ, you're so goddamn delicious."

"Rowan." She shakes with a soft cry. "You don't...have to...it's okay."

Forehead scrunched, I look at her. "I have been fantasizing about how you taste since we met." With my thumbs, I brush soothing strokes along her inner thighs. "Do you not like it when someone goes down on you?"

Her gaze shifts away. "I don't know. No one's ever..." Facing me, she sits up. "I'm not a virgin or anything. I've had sex. Lots of sex. Well... not lots. I've just never done *that*"— she gestures to her lap— "sex has always just been...well, just sex."

"Have you not wanted to?"

"No... Well, yes, but I've only been with two men. There was Tim and obviously Alex. Tim was a friend in undergrad who just did me a favor, so I was no longer a virgin. God this is so embarrassing." Wincing, she covers her face with her hands.

My fingers comb into her hair. "Nothing to be embarrassed about."

She swallows thickly. "Easy for you to say. I doubt you were a twenty-year-old virgin. I didn't date in high school and in college... Most of the boys just saw me as the cute friend or the sweet legally blind girl. After college, I was focused on grad school, then Aunt Bea, and now my career. Then there was Alex. He wasn't into oral sex, unless he was receiving it."

Anger burns inside me at the idea of no man ever properly taking care of this woman. Of not worshipping her body the way it should be. Of their selfishness to take without giving. Although, the way I want to consume her, leaving her wrung dry, is utterly selfish. I want nothing more than to leave her in a sated heap, unable to move or remember anyone's touch but mine. To ruin her for any other man.

Hand against her cheek, I capture her stare. "Let me."

"Alright." She nods, trust shimmering in her eyes.

Bending, I plant a trail of kisses from her lips to the column of her throat. "Tell me to stop if I do anything you don't like... Or if I do something you like, tell me and I'll keep doing it."

"Yes," she whimpers at my nipping kisses along her collarbone.

"That's a good girl." Palm pressed against her stomach, I ease her back onto the countertop. "Lay back, luv."

CHAPTER SEVENTEEN

The Proper End to the Proper Date
Pen

The pendant light above my counter showers Rowan's face in a white glow, illuminating his wolfish expression as he hovers above me. Despite the polished granite's coolness against my bare back, wildfire engulfs me. His energy reads predatorial, like a bobcat ready to strike...and I'm his prey, but the gentle, almost reverent, strokes of his fingers along my thighs telegraphs safety.

Pressing kisses down my body, he finally settles at my naked core and hooks my legs over his shoulders. His nose nuzzles along my slick center. "I want to bathe in your scent," he growls, inhaling deeply.

My stomach clenches. "O...kay," I moan with the first flick of his tongue against my clit.

Reminiscent of the first bites of a five-course meal, his mouth starts its focused consumption. Each slow lick, gentle suck, and teasing flick tightens a coil in my core.

"Fuck!" I cry out as his now-aggressive sucks, and the rasp and roll of his tongue on me, cranks that tension tighter.

He looks up. "You like?"

Forehead creased, I whine, "Don't stop!"

His carnal smile is wicked. "Gladly."

"God." Pressure spools tight and my body begs for release as his finger taps at my entrance. "Yes," I whimper, my back arching.

His groans of pleasure as he devours me melds with my needy wines. A breeze drifts into the room, the cool current licking across my heated skin. Somehow, in the sexual haze fogging my brain, I remember the windows are open and I have neighbors.

"Ro—" My hands cover my mouth to stifle my cry with his insertion of a second finger inside me.

Like a feral animal, he growls as he simultaneously fucks me with his mouth and fingers. Legs trembling, the tension builds and builds...

"God!" A quake rolls across my limbs.

"You did so good, luv," he soothes. "Ready for more?" He strokes my sensitive clit.

"More?" Blinking, a breathless laugh falls out of me. "I did good?"

"Luv, you did great. Like a book, your body opened its pages, showing me how to make you come. Your needy moans. Hissed breaths. How you grinded against my face. And how this sweet little pussy squeezes around my fingers." He pushes two fingers back inside me. "Best fucking teacher I've ever had."

Reaching beside me, I grab the condom and hold it up. "Put this on... Now."

"You don't want more of this, first?" He crooks his fingers inside me.

With a gasp, my head falls back against the counter.

Despite the sated sensation that drips through my veins, my body throbs with need for more.

"I told you, luv, you never have to beg with me. If you want me to put on a condom and properly fuck you, I will." His tone is teasingly dark.

"Rowan...fuck me...now."

"Christ, Pen," he groans and takes my mouth in a long kiss, the taste of me on his lips.

Pulling away, he steps back. He unbuttons and unzips his jeans, shoving them down. With a smirk, he folds his jeans and deposits them atop the pile of clothes next to me on the kitchen island.

Those butterflies that I thought were in a sated coma in my belly begin to somersault. It's a small action, but such a thoughtful and sweet thing.

Placing his boxer briefs and socks on the clothes pile, he stands before me completely naked. I reach for him and trace my hands down the cut planes of his body, the muscles twitch beneath my touch. My fingers skim along the soft hair that tumbles down his torso.

"Wow," I almost gasp, running my fingertips along his impressive length.

It's long. It's thick. It's veiny. Beads of precum coat his tip. Wrapping my fingers around him, I pump.

With a groaned "Pen," he presses his forehead against mine.

"Tell me if I do something you don't like, and I'll stop." Repeating his words from earlier, I gently bite his lower lip and then soothe away the sting with a soft lick. "Tell me if you like something I do, and I'll do more of it."

Clasping my face, he consumes me like a ravenous man. His tongue devours and plunders my mouth and I willingly give him everything in return.

"Condom, now," I gasp between kisses.

Breath ragged, he steps back and grabs the foil packet. While he sheaths himself, I push down my dress and toss it beside me.

Positioning himself between my thighs, he taps his tip at my entrance. "Ready?"

"Yes." I grip his shoulders.

Pushing into me, he captures my tiny groans with his soothing kisses. He goes slow, easing into me inch-by-inch, allowing my body to adjust to his size.

"You okay, luv?"

"Yes. You?"

He grins. "So fucking good."

Lifting my legs high on his hips, he moves inside me. He rocks a cadence with slow, rhythmic, and focused thrusts. Gripping my hips, he pulls almost all the way out.

"Wh—"

He slams back into me.

"God!"

"You said you wanted to be properly fucked."

The slow pace is replaced by deep relentless thrusts. In and out. Pressure builds deep in my belly.

He slips his hand between us, stroking me and tipping me over the edge. Clenching around him, I bite back my scream.

"That's two." He presses his lips to my sweat-kissed temple. "Let's go for the hat trick," he says, hoisting me up.

"Three?" I slump against him.

"Someone's googled hockey terms."

"I don't know if I can make it."

"You've got this. And I've got you."

Legs and arms folded around him, he moves us to the oversized armchair, and places me down. Balanced on the chair's edge, my legs draped over the chair's arms, he plunges back into me.

"Oh...god," I whine with the new angle hitting me deeper and in just the right spot.

"That's my girl."

Arms draped around his neck, I cling to him, as he properly and unabashedly fucks me. There's no holding back, no treating me like a porcelain doll on a flimsy pedestal. Somehow, he makes me feel both unbreakable and precious all at once.

Rowan's pumps come harder, deeper, and faster. The grunt and filth-filled praises that spill from his mouth heightens the building ecstasy, ready to burst at any...

"Fuck!" I scream, the orgasm's intensity temporarily causing me to forget the open windows and my neighbors.

After pressing a soft kiss to my temple, Rowan continues his pace. My limp arms just hold on as he chases his own climax.

With a final thrust, he shudders and grunts, "Pen."

Still anchored within me, he hovers above me. My fingers swipe across his sweat damp hairline. Hot puffs of his breath caress my face. His fingertips skim my shaking legs.

After a few moments, he pulls out. Excusing himself to the downstairs bathroom, he gets rid of the condom and returns with a towel to clean me up. Once clean, he scoops me into his arms and cradles me in the chair, the blanket from the couch wrapped around us to create a cocoon. My head rests against his shoulder while he smooths down my sex-mussed strands.

"So, will all proper dates with you end like that?" I snuggle into him, enjoying the way my body seems to mold to his.

"Abso-fucking-lutely." His chuckle is hoarse.

"I could get used to this."

CHAPTER EIGHTEEN

Brunch
Rowan

I t's been four nights since I first found my way into Pen's bed. I haven't spent every night here... Well, almost. Friday after she and JoJo came to Axels, GB and I headed back here. It only made sense as I would be joining her at Bread again for Saturday breakfast. Only this time I didn't need to rent the entire bakery for the day. Breakfast turned into a morning spent with hands clasped, walking along the beach with Pen and GB. Then an afternoon curled up together on the couch listening to an audio-book between kisses, while GB sprawled on the floor chewing the new toy Pen bought him. That soon turned into an evening claiming each other's bodies throughout the house.

Against the wall in the foyer, Pen's legs atop my shoulder, and me worshipping her like the queen she is. My legs splayed as I sit on the couch, gripping her round ass while she rides me, slowly undoing me. Her bent over the kitchen table, flesh slapping with each thrust, and screams muffled against her own hand. Those wild-honey eyes peering up at me while her full lips wrap around my cock, the shower's spray cascading down her naked body, as my hands slip against the slick tile with the way she brings me to my knees.

After, she'd stood at the stove flipping a cheese toasty, "This is JoJo's dream. All she wants is a man that will properly sex her up and make her a grilled cheese after."

Right then, I vowed to work on my cheese toasty game, even contemplated asking Gillian for advice...but think better of it.

Between bites of the single sandwich we'd shared, we lose ourselves in each other, delving more and more into the pages of each other's stories. Not just the important chapters but the small passages that seem so insignificant but make us who we are.

All the little things that make me fall a little deeper for this woman. Like how the simple act of making a cheese toasty pulls out story-after-story, learning to cook with Aunt Bea or the time she and Trina celebrated with hot chocolate and toasted cheese after digging a maze between their houses in the snow drifts from a two-day long blizzard that blanketed Buffalo when they were girls. The little ticks that make up Pen, such as the way she unthinkingly plays with her hair when she's lost in thought or is nervous. How she constantly surprises me with her blend of sweet sassiness.

"Someone's awake," she rasps, brushing her backside against my rigid length.

"Do you blame me?" Nuzzling into the crook of her neck, my hand roams beneath her silky camisole. "Looks like someone else is also awake." I tweak her already taut nipples.

She arches into my touch. "Do you blame me?"

My chuckle is hoarse. "How long do you need to get ready for brunch?" I nip at the shell of her ear.

Taking my hand, she guides it into her sleep shorts. "We can be late."

"And how will that help me win over Trina?" My fingers slide through her slick folds.

"Alexa, what time is it?"

A deep Australian accent comes from the device on the nightstand. "The time is eight-thirty-two a.m."

I lift an eyebrow. "Your Alexa is an Aussie man?"

"It is the *sexiest* of all accents," she teases with a bat of her lashes.

"Are you sure about that, luv?" I murmur into her ear, deepening my Irish lilt as I slip my hand beneath her top. With each whimper she makes as I tweak her taut nipples, my cock gets impossibly harder.

"Alexa, set an alarm for ten a.m." Once Alexa confirms the alarm's been set, Pen flips onto her back and tugs me on top of her. "We have time."

Flipping onto my back, I yank her to sit astride my hard cock. "Good. Now take these off–" I pull at her shorts' lacey hem. "—and sit on my face."

"Yes sir." She flashes a wicked grin. "As long as you take these off. After all it's only fair if you're getting a pre-brunch meal, that I do too."

"Christ." *This woman.*

WE USED EVERY GODDAMN MINUTE THAT ALEXA GAVE US AND stole a few extra before getting ready for brunch. Men aren't generally invited to the ladies' brunch, but I'm the exception, more like Wes and my brother are the exceptions. In my attempt to win over Pen's people, mainly Trina since JoJo is one hundred percent Team Row-Pen, as she dubbed us

Friday night, I've enlisted reinforcements to soften this trio's big sister.

Wes, who hit it off with both Pen and JoJo, will be attending brunch in-person. My brother Finn and Trina are joining remotely. I am not above using Trina's favorite author and audiobook narrator to win her over.

Pen explained that Trina's overprotective nature is a result of losing her younger sister Lauren. Two years before Pen, who is the same age as Trina's sister, moved next door Lauren was hit by a car. She and Trina had been playing in the front yard. In the single instant that Trina bent to tie her shoe, Lauren ran into the street to get the soccer ball she'd kicked.

"It's not that Trina doesn't like you, it's just that she doesn't trust herself to relax," Pen offers, as we stand in the kitchen slicing pineapple and berries for a fruit salad. "She's scared if she looks away something will happen."

I nod, thinking of Gillian. His assessing green eyes, the same as mine, and face always drawn into a stern expression.

"I promise she will warm up."

"Did she with Alex?"

Her lips purse. "I think he's part of her hesitancy. Alex was my first real boyfriend. As I told you, I was a bit of a late bloomer."

I nod. Wednesday night as we sat snuggled together on the chair, she'd opened up more about her dating history. Besides Alex and her friend from undergrad who she'd had sex with a few times, I am only the third man that she's slept with. Of course, I don't care about how many men came before me. My intent is to be the last. Still, I don't like how these men failed to cherish Pen the way she should be. Alex gaslit and emotionally abused her. Her friend from college, while kind to her, didn't take care of her needs sexually, something I intend to ensure never happens again, as long as I'm the current and, hopefully, last man, to be with her.

"Alex had this way of pulling me in. A way of spinning every situation to his advantage. JoJo was the only one whose hackles were up when it came to Alex."

"JoJo?" My right brow lifts.

"As open and friendly as she is, she's able to read people in a single instant. She was a little standoffish with Alex. I liked Alex and so did Trina. I think Trina blames herself for not seeing who he truly was."

Leaning in, I kiss her cheek. "I like that you have protective people in your life. Even if Trina may scare me more than any rival defenseman I've faced on the ice."

She bumps my hip with hers. "It's funny. I should be more nervous. I'm the one who will be meeting your brother in ten minutes."

"He's going to adore you. He already does."

I'd told Finn about Pen earlier this week. One doesn't have a brother who writes romance novels and not tap into his knowledge. Despite his bad luck with finding the right woman for himself, my big-hearted brother is open to all things love. It's why he immediately agreed to join us for brunch. "She must be special if you're calling in the troops," he joked when I spoke to him Saturday morning while Pen showered.

That she is.

As much as Pen protested "too soon" about flying to Toronto with me to attend the fundraiser, the one I'm now officially locked into, and meeting my family, she's comfortable with this. Perhaps Finn being one of her favorite authors makes it less intimidating and more like dipping her toe in the deeper waters of a relationship. I won't push, no matter how much I want her to be mine as much as I'm already hers.

"I'm not just nervous about impressing Trina. You're the first woman, I've introduced to my family."

Her head tilts. "They didn't meet Emma? Didn't you date for like a year?"

"We did...and no, she did not meet my family." Our stares lock.

"But you said he already adores me. Why are you nervous, then?"

"He does." Leaning in, I rub my nose against hers. "Trina isn't the only one a little hesitant about this. I know we both have our fears, and this is a big step for you. Thank you for trusting me...trusting yourself to do this."

"I'm trusting in us," she murmurs, closing the inches between us and pressing a gentle kiss on my mouth. At the chime of the doorbell, she jumps back and squeals, "They're here!"

Game on.

Brunch is less interrogation of me like my first meeting of the bicoastal besties and more fawning over Wes and Finn. Even Trina's stern expression washes away as JoJo joins Wes reading aloud a swoony scene from each woman's favorite one of my brother's novels.

"Go on without me..." Draped over the two stools set in front of the kitchen table as a makeshift stage set, Wes coughs."

"There's no going on without you," JoJo says dramatically, her poor attempt at a posh New England accent makes her sound like a member of the Wahlberg family.

Vibrating with laughter, Pen covers her face and leans against my shoulder. I loop my arm around her, keeping her close and join in the laughter filtering through the room from the in-person and online spectators.

"JoJo, stop!" Trina howls, wiping tears from her eyes.

Undeterred, JoJo continues. Using a wooden spoon she

plucked from the utensil crock, speckled with tiny seashells, she positions herself and points it as if holding a rifle. Her brown eyes narrow and blonde curls tumble over her face. "Let them come. If I faced my disapproving parents, those debutantes, and everyone who's told me I can't my entire life… I can face these wolves."

"Shit—" Finn pinches his nose. "—did I really write that line?"

"Sure did." Trina raises her Bloody Mary on screen. "And it's fucking gold, Boy Brontë."

My brother arches a blond eyebrow. "Boy Brontë?"

"Your nickname."

"Guess it's better than 'Irish Puck Boy.' Finn raises his glass of whiskey and tips his head to the screen. "Thanks, my Buffalo Girl."

Trina blushes, just a bit, before she smooths down her already sleek red bob and shifts in her seat. "They called you Irish Puck Boy?"

"*Not me.*"

Her blue eyes almost twinkle. "Rowan?! I must hear all about this."

"Excuse me—" JoJo claps loudly. "—we are in the middle of a dramatic reading."

Wes sits up. "I normally hate it when the audience interrupts, especially when the actors are in the zone, and JoJo, you're killing it"—she curtsies. He continues, "But I need to know more about Rowan's nickname."

"Me too." Pen nudges me.

"Christ," I groan, scrubbing a hand down my face.

"Sorry, bro." Finn's mouth slants into a lopsided grin.

Hands on her shapely hips, JoJo pouts. "Embarrassing Rowan stories *after*. We agreed."

"I have so many." Finn's blue eyes dance with mirth.

"And I want to hear them all!" Trina rubs her hands together like a villain in a spy thriller.

"Me too." Pen coos, intertwining our fingers. Her sparkling gaze lands on me and her lips tug up into a wide smirk.

Grinning, I lift our joined fingers to my lips. "I'll be the butt of the world's jokes as long as you keep looking at me like that, luv."

Trailing her hand up my arm she cups my cheek and leans in, pressing that heart-stopping smile against mine.

"Fuuuck, I need to write that line down," Finn says, cluing me in that I'd said that loud enough that everyone else heard.

"Clearly, it's a good line. I think Pen's tongue has relocated to Rowan's throat," Trina quips.

"Sorry." Face pink, Pen pulls back.

But I don't let her go too far, tucking her back against me. "Never apologize for that." I trace the outline of her smile with my fingertip. "I told you."

She snuggles into my side.

JoJo places her hands on her heart. "Adorbs!"

"You two are pretty cute, but can we get back to the show?" Wes lays back. "Come on, JoJo, let's channel our inner Onalee and Dylan. Picture a team of wild wolves ready to attack." He whistles. "GB?"

GB looks up from his rawhide bone, tilts his head, and then proceeds to go back to chewing.

"This is why I never work with animals."

Chuckling, Wes and JoJo proceed with their reading.

"This is my favorite part," Pen whispers, as JoJo, AKA Onalee, throws herself atop Wes, AKA Dylan, after running out of bullets.

"Me too," I murmur and kiss her forehead.

The story of the Bostonian heiress that inherits a Montana ranch in 1908 and, despite everyone telling her she can't, runs it and falls for the ranch hand and rodeo cowboy always stuck with me. There's no third act break up in this book. Just a couple who falls in love and meets life's obstacles together, including a pack of wolves that chase them down after Dylan falls from his horse and breaks his leg during a cattle roundup. Onalee is left by herself to fend the wolves off.

"You can't have him," JoJo shouts, the book that she reads from in one hand and the wooden spoon turned empty rifle in the other. She points the wooden spoon at GB, who gnaws on his rawhide, ignoring her entirely. "If you want him, you have to take us both because I won't live without him."

"Did I really write that?" Finn mutters.

"Hush you. It's amazing," Trina laughingly scolds.

"What the hell are you watching?" A gruff voice calls out, causing all of us to turn, even Finn.

My spine stiffens. On screen, Gillian stands behind Finn, his face twisted into a scowl. Despite the neat beard covering my brother's face, we look nearly identical. Unlike Finn with his blond hair, blue eyes, and fair skin, the spitting image of our mam, Gillian and I take after our dad. Our hair is a dark brown, though his is sprinkled with silver at his temples. We both have our dad's green eyes and olive complexion.

"A dramatic reading, which you rudely interrupted," JoJo tuts, wagging the wooden spoon towards the laptop.

Gillian's eyebrows knit together. "Finn, why can't you be normal and just look at porn. Is this one of those Only Fans things?"

"Excuse me, this is completely normal." A furrow mars Trina's forehead. "We're honoring your brother's work."

"Only Fans? Hear that, Wes, we're good enough for people to pay for our dramatic readings?" JoJo's eyebrows waggle.

"Seriously, what is happening?"

"It's brunch with Rowan, his girl, and her friends," Finn offers, gesturing towards the camera.

Rowan's girl. Christ, I like how that sounds. I hold Pen just a little tighter. The way the laptop faces the pretend stage, we're not fully visible. Still my protective nature kicks in, wanting to keep her close.

Gillian's brow creases. "Rowan's girl?"

Smirking Pen leans towards the laptop and waves. "Hi. You must be Gillian. I'm Pen. Rowan's..." Her head tilts. "... Well, we actually haven't discussed labels."

Leaning towards the laptop, I open and then close my mouth. The word "girlfriend" fights to come out. As Pen says we haven't discussed labels. I won't pretend the dip in my stomach at her not saying, "I'm Rowan's girl" doesn't exist.

"She's the woman he's seeing, and you must be the chef brother." JoJo's gaze locks on the screen. "You really *are* attractive. You might be the best looking of the three of you. How are your grilled cheese skills?"

"My what?" Gillian narrows his eyes.

Pen snorts.

"God... JoJo," Trina groans, massaging her temples.

"What?" She gestures towards the laptop and then to me. "Do you blame me? This is one attractive gene pool. Hell, you already dropped three messages into our group thread about—"

"JoJo!" Eyes wide, Trina nearly shrieks.

"I'm intrigued. How do I get in this group thread?" Wes chuckles.

"Ditto." A wry smile covers Finn's face.

"You *should* be intrigued, Boy Brontë." JoJo winks.

"JoJo!" Trina hisses, her face is almost as red as her hair.

"Isn't Trina engaged?" I mumble to Pen, who nods.

"*That* ring on her finger doesn't make her unaware of an attractive man." JoJo winks.

"Which attractive man are we speaking of?" Wes laughs.

"Again, ditto," Finn adds.

"JoJo, why are we friends?" Trina covers her face.

JoJo's face twists into an apologetic expression. "Whoops, sorry, girl."

Shaking with laughter, Pen buries herself into my side. "She has no filter."

"Clearly," Gillian mutters, his features set in a harsh expression.

"It's all part of the JoJo package you have to look forward to, Mr. Sexy Chef Boyardee," JoJo coos, batting her long lashes.

"I'll pass. You're not my type."

"Gillian!" Forehead puckered, Finn spins in his chair to face Gillian.

JoJo's flirty expression falters, her red lips drag down into a frown. It's brief, though. In almost the same moment her lips curl back up. "Your loss." She shrugs. While there's a smile on her face, her eyes don't sparkle with the playfulness she'd had.

"You're a prick," I snipe, my icy stare locked on my oldest brother.

"Agreed." Trina glares.

"I've been told." Averting his gaze, Gillian straightens.

"JoJo, did you want to keep going?" Wes reaches out and squeezes JoJo's arm.

Eyes blinking, she peers around the room and then clears her throat. "Actually, I need to use the bathroom. I'll be back."

"JoJo." Pen stands up.

"Just need to use the ladies." With a tight smile, she places the book and spoon on the table before exiting the room.

Turning back to the screen, I glower at my oldest brother who stands, hands in pockets, staring forward. I open my mouth.

But Finn cuts me off, "You hurt her feelings, Gill. That wasn't kind what you said."

"I—" Tugging at the hem of his T-shirt, his stare shifts around Finn's study.

"You should apologize." Finn's request is firm, but kind.

"No should about it," I jump in with a snarl. "You will fucking apologize to JoJo."

Narrowed gaze locked on the screen, he scoffs, "You're telling me what I will do? The man who never apologizes for his actions."

"Always the asshole."

Pen squeezes my hand, her mouth set in a firm line.

"Enough you two." With a loud exhale, Finn groans, "Did you want something, Gill?"

His stare pulls away from the laptop and to Finn. "Just letting you know I'm back. I didn't realize you were doing a meet and greet with Rowan's *whatever* she is." He waves at the screen.

Pen stiffens beside me.

My jaw clenches. "Pen. Her name is Pen."

Face wrinkled, he shakes his head. "She's the girl from the article, isn't she?"

"What of it?"

"When Mam asked you about her, you said there's nothing going on. You made it sound like she was just some random woman you met while traveling. This looks like more. I get not inviting me to this little party but lying to Mam about seeing someone and then not inviting her... seems cruel even for you. Don't you think you've put our mother through enough?"

An old ache slices into me.

Arms crossed over his broad chest, he quirks an eyebrow. "Unless this is nothing and she really is just another random woman we hear about you being with on social media. For her sake, I hope not. She seems like a nice girl."

"Gill." Finn shakes his head.

"Fuck you!" I growl and go to stand, but Pen's tight grip holds me in place. My stare falls on her.

Her lips wobble. "Rowan, please... Don't." It's barely a whisper.

"Rowan, I got this," Trina seethes. "How dare you! She's not a random anything, you second-rate Bobby Flay wannabe. Despite what JoJo—who's everyone's type and you'd be goddamn lucky if she lowered herself for an amoeba of a man like you—said you are *not* the cutest brother, you are the dickiest one."

"Again, not news," he says, his tone steely.

Finn sloshes a long breath. "Gill, Rowan hasn't told Mam yet because this thing with Pen is still new. I'm sure you of all people understand not telling our mother all aspects of a relationship. Considering she doesn't know you're separated from Layla, yet."

Gillian just grunts.

"Um..." JoJo reappears, her eyes puffy and red. "I'm suddenly not feeling well. Might have overindulged on the pastries. I'm going to head out." She scoops up her purse from the back of a chair.

Wes rises. "I'll drive you."

"Are you sure?"

Nodding, he loops his arm around her shoulder. "Totally. We can discuss our next dramatic reading showcase. I'm thinking next week, we tackle the pond scene from Heather and Jackson's story."

"I think JoJo would be a perfect Heather," Finn says, warmth shimmers in his eyes.

JoJo offers a shaky smile.

"Ladies, give Wes your emails, I'm sending you all an

advance audiobook copy of my newest book. It doesn't come out for another two months, so you'll have to promise to keep it between us."

"Thanks." The three say. Each woman's response is different. JoJo's is quiet. Trina's is thankful, but seemingly not about the free book as much as for the kindness towards her two friends that my brother offers. Pen's is guarded.

"JoJo—" Gillian coughs. "I... I'm sorry if I hurt your feelings."

Her forehead pinches. "That's not an apology. Don't try to be something you're not."

"What's that?"

"Disingenuous."

He blanches.

"You said what you said. Own it." Turning, she and Wes leave.

There are few moments that leave my brother speechless, but JoJo's response seems to have slapped him silent. If my stomach wasn't so knotted up right now, I'd be reveling in the slacked-jawed expression taking over his smug face.

"I'll be in—" Without finishing his own sentence, he walks away.

"Pen, Trina, I'm sorry. He's not"—Finn frowns— "okay, he's mostly like that but he's kind of a pineapple. Deep down there's sweetness."

"Very deep down." My comment is snide and pointed.

Frowning, Finn just shakes his head.

"It's okay." Pen rises, scooping up plates from the table.

"It's not okay." I look from Pen to the screen. "Finn, don't make excuses for him. He's a prick." I stand up to help, but she waves me off.

"I'm the middle brother, it's my job. I do it for him. I do it for you."

"Maybe let your grown ass brothers make their own excuses and apologies," Trina snarks.

"Says the woman that doesn't let her grown ass friends fight their own battles." A warm smile accompanies his chide.

"Noted." She rolls her eyes but returns his smile with an equally warm one.

As Trina and Finn tease each other before saying good-bye, I watch Pen quietly clean up. Her gaze averted and mouth drawn into a tight line. Once I log off the call and shut the laptop, I stride to Pen. Taking the dishes from her hand, I place them on the counter.

"I'm sorry."

Her expression pinches. "For what?"

"For Gillian being...well, Gillian. For telling my mam there's nothing going on with us. She'd seen the article before I surprised you at Bread last week and—" I rub the back of my neck. "I didn't know what to tell her, then."

"I'm not upset by that. Of course, you haven't told your mom about me. We're still new."

"I'm sorry about Gillian." Gripping her biceps, my fingers caress her soft skin.

"It's not your job to apologize for him nor your job to protect us from him."

"I'm not going to let someone speak to you like that." My brows pull together.

"I can defend myself."

"I know that... You're scrappy."

The ghost of a smile softens her features. "So are you. I just wish you'd use some of your scrappiness for yourself."

"What are you talking about?"

"Gillian and you. You're not the man he paints you to be, and it hurts to see you just accept his very wrong words about you."

"I..."

In that moment, every argument with Gillian riots through me. Raised voices. Growled insults. Balled up fists. As angry as I get with Gillian, I've never stood up for myself. Not really. It's just different versions of what took place today. I can demand apologies for others but not for myself.

She steps into my chest, tipping her head up. "You're always ready to protect everyone else, why not yourself? You didn't say anything to him until he hurt JoJo or made a snide comment about me. Why do you allow Gillian to treat you like that?"

I close my eyes. "Because to him, no matter what I say or do, I'll always be the reason our father died."

None of this would be happening, if it wasn't for you. Gillian's words hiss inside me. It's been twenty-three years since he'd uttered those words, his already stern face glaring at me from the top of the stairs.

"He shouldn't have been out there, but he went... For you and now he's gone." He spins and charges into the bedroom we now have to share, slamming the door.

"He didn't mean that," Finn sighs, looking between the now-shut bedroom door and me.

"Yes, he did." I turn and walk away.

"Baby, what does that mean?" Pen's warm palm rests on my cheek, pulling me back to her and away from the past.

My fingers curl around her biceps as if at any moment she'll slip through my fingers. "My dad fell through the ice of the pond in the back of the house we lived in before..."

Before my mam cried for weeks. Before our entire life as we knew it was ripped away. Before everything changed...

Her eyes widen. "The pond where he taught you to play hockey?"

"It was mid-January. The temperature had been below freezing for weeks. We'd not been on the pond yet that season. Dad was testing it to make sure it was safe for us to use. He always said to never go out alone." Tears prick, but I blink to clear them. "We were at the market with mam, when we came home, I saw a new net on the pond but no dad. I didn't think anything of it. It got dark, but he wasn't home. Mam got worried and called my dad's friend, Florence, who was a police officer. It wasn't like dad to just disappear. They found him the next day. He must have fallen through and couldn't get himself out. He was out there getting the pond ready for me."

"Oh, baby I'm so sorry." She folds her arms around me and rests her face on my chest.

The feel of her body against mine is a balm for my stuttering heartbeat.

"I know you say Gillian blames you, but do you blame you?" She tips her head up, her honey eyes are glassy with worry.

I swipe my finger across her jawline. "What happened was an accident. My dad chose to be out there alone, to not heed his own warning, but I still feel guilty that the only reason he was out there was to do something for me... That doing something for me took him away from my mam and brothers."

"And from you."

I nod.

She cups my face. "His choices aren't your responsibility, even if he was doing something for you. He chose to be out there alone. Whether he was out there to set up your hockey net or to catch a fish for the future chef Gillian to cook, he made the decision, not anyone else."

"I know."

"Do you?" She holds tight, not allowing my gaze to turn from her. Her warm eyes glitter with determination. "Because if you did, if you truly understood that, you wouldn't continue to let your brother make you pay for someone else's decision…make you feel like a great disappointment because he doesn't want to deal with who he's really angry with."

If I do anything but nod, the tears and emotions I hold back will flood forward.

"You're both angry with your father and taking it out on each other because he's not here to get loud with… To ask for answers. To push. To curse at. So, instead you take it out on each other and worse, on yourselves."

"I'm not angry with my father." I step back.

"Aren't you?"

"I…" That ever-present knot in my stomach tightens.

"Of course you're angry. Those of us left behind are always a little angry. I'm angry with Aunt Bea." Her admission is quiet.

Stunned, my eyes lock with hers.

"I'm angry that she didn't get her regular mammogram because if she had, we might have caught the breast cancer early, and she'd still be here. I'm fucking furious with her for dying when she probably didn't need to, if she'd have taken better care of herself instead of taking care of me," she croaks.

I reach for her, but she steps away from my grasp, tears welling in her eyes. "Not until you say it. You don't get to hold me, comfort me, for being brave enough to admit something you're not willing to admit yourself."

The words punch into my gut, pulverizing the tangled knot of emotions. "Pen."

She stands firm.

I heave a hard breath. "I'm angry that you're making me do this. I fucking hate that you won't let me hold you right now, especially because I want to hold you to give me strength to be as brave as you and say the things I don't even dare let myself think, let alone speak." My vision blurs and the salty, held-back tears sting.

Pen steps into my chest, her head pressed over my thudding heart, and arms tight around me. Each squeeze of her arms loosens the unspoken truths from inside me.

"I'm furious with Gillian for telling me it's my fault. I hate that Finn only ever said that Gillian didn't mean it but never told me that Dad's death wasn't my fault. I'm upset with Mam for taking us away from our lives just because she didn't know how to live without him. I'm so goddamn angry with him for doing the one thing he told us never to do and leaving us to deal with the consequences. That he died before teaching me to be the man I know he was...the type of man I'm scared I'll never be."

Raising to her tiptoes, she grips my face and captures my watery stare. "I don't know what type of man your dad was, but I know what type of man you are. You're a good man, Rowan Iverson. You're the man I'm falling for. You're my man and I'm"—she offers a sweet smile— "your girl."

"My girl?" The sweet proclamation thrums in my chest.

Wrapping her arms around my neck, she beams. "For the record, I am a strong adult woman who does not enjoy when anyone refers to me as *girl*... But I like the idea of being your girl. Just yours."

"Pen." I capture her lips with mine.

Everything I want to convey is in each kiss, hungrier than the last. *I don't deserve you, but I'll do as you asked and just agree to let myself be happy and you make me so happy.*

I only hope I do the same.

CHAPTER NINETEEN

MVP
Pen

Four weeks ago, Rowan Iverson came into my life. It's hard to imagine a time before then. Since brunch almost two weeks ago, we've nestled into this relationship. Eight of the last eleven nights found me falling asleep curled up with Rowan, GB slumbering at our feet, and waking up in his arms. He and Wes even joined the bicoastal besties for a repeat brunch performance, minus Gillian. Finn took the call behind his locked study door.

As the bus eases down the street, I read the last message from Rowan, my lips tug up into an oversized grin. Even Trina admits that she's never seen me this happy. The one good thing about the interaction with Gillian is that it seemed to have thawed Trina's iciness about Rowan. She won't be rocking the Team Row-Pen T-shirts that JoJo teases she's going to make, but Trina has safely become pro-Rowan.

Rowan: Pick you up at six.

Me: I can take a Lyft. It's such an inconvenience for you to drive all the way out here and then back to L.A.

Rowan: Which means I get MORE time with you and less time waiting for you. Eager face emoji.

A sharp laugh falls out of me causing a nearby passenger to clear their throat. Thanks to JoJo, Rowan has quickly adopted the habit of typing out emojis.

Me: If you insist.

In the almost three weeks since we've started dating, Rowan's primarily come to me in Seal Beach. Except for the first trip to Axel's with JoJo, and then another one last Saturday before the three of us headed to watch Wes in his new show, this is the first trip I'm taking to Rowan's place. Tonight, I'll stay at his condo since we'll be attending the MVP Foundation's event tomorrow.

I'm going as a representative of Walters Children's Hospital, along with the Chief of Staff and my soon-to-be-boss Nelson. As Nelson reminded me as I left the hospital this afternoon, this is my first test in the role I'll soon be officially acting in. Rowan will be there as a celebrity client of one of the foundation's founders.

Me: While highly inappropriate, it was rather ingenious to orchestrate a partnership with the hospital I work at just to try to get us in the same place again.

Rowan: You'd think getting twelve percent of my earnings would be enough for them, but they want to meddle in one hundred percent of my life.

Over tacos at a beachside stand this week while discussing plans for the weekend, we put it together. Greg and Sasha, who founded the MVP Foundation five years ago, were playing matchmaker.

Me: Shall we let Greg and Sasha know their attempt to play cupid was for naught or mess with them? We can

pretend we're not together and see what silly shenanigans they get up to in their attempt to ship us?

Rowan: I'd say mess with them, but there's no way you'll keep your hands off me for that long. Winky face emoji.

Me: Aren't we cocky?

Rowan: Luv, it's your favorite thing about me.

Me: It is a lovely cock.

Biting back my laugh, I can almost hear Rowan's groaned, "Christ!" I do so enjoy shocking him with my sassier comments.

Rowan: So many thoughts about you and my lovely cock. All of which involve that smart mouth of yours.

"Oh dear." Cheeks inflamed, my little gasp pulls the attention of nearby bus passengers.

Rowan: But instead, I need to get into my SUV and head your way. See you soon, luv.

Me: After that comment, not soon enough.

Rowan: You'll need to be patient because I have plans for you that don't involve fucking that smart mouth and tight little pussy. Though I promise those are on the docket for tonight.

I adjust myself in the seat, hoping nobody can read what's on my screen. While I'm not shocked at his casual use of vulgarity, I'm more concerned that the large print that allows me to more easily read my texts, sometimes means a lack of privacy. And I'd prefer the passengers that I ride the bus with daily not be privy to my sexting exchange with Rowan.

Me: As long as eating that sweet little pussy of mine is also on the docket, you can have your way with me, sir.

A thrill tingles along my spine at my saucy comment. It may rile him up, but let's be honest, my sweet little pussy loves the attention.

My smile is wickedly pleased with his *Christ, woman*

response. Leaning against the headrest, a happy sigh fills me. Daydreaming about the many naughty things I'd like Rowan to do to me, I slip my phone into my blazer pocket. Only to pull it out two seconds later as it vibrates awake.

"Baby, if you're hoping I verbalize what I just texted, you should know, there'll be–" I lower my voice to a breathy whisper and cup my hand around the cell. "—no sexy talk while I'm on the bus."

"Well, I certainly hope not."

Jaw slack, I sit up. "Mom."

"I'm surprised you recognize my voice. You haven't called me in almost three weeks," she scolds.

"Sorry." I cringe. "I've been busy."

"Sounds like it."

Rubbing the middle of my forehead, I silently groan. *Why didn't I look at the caller ID before just answering?*

"Who's baby?" Her tone is laced with curiosity and caution.

"Umm…" My eyes dart around the bus, meeting only quiet murmurs and muffled music from earbud-wearing passengers.

Talking with my mother about relationships is akin to a dental cleaning. Somehow, I never floss or brush enough and am guaranteed to walk away with cavities.

"I'd like to hope it's Alex, but he said his two requests to take you to dinner to celebrate your promotion were ignored. Don't get me started on having to hear about your promotion from Alex and not my own daughter, but—"

"It's only an *interim* position, and it hasn't started yet," I interrupt in a miffed tone. "Also, it's so inappropriate for Alex and you to be talking about me. Mother, you have to understand this. We broke up."

"I know that, but he reached out after you hadn't

responded to his messages. He misses you and I'm not going to be rude. What if you two get back together?"

Eyes clamped tight, I hiss, "We are *never* getting back together. You have my express permission to be rude. In fact, it can be my birthday present this year."

"I just don't understand what went wrong with you two. He's handsome, successful, and doted on you. He'd be a good provider... Someone to take care of you."

"I don't need someone to take care of me," I grit out.

The silence on the phone almost paints the image of her pinched features. Each stretched beat replays old retorts from her. *I just worry about what happens after your vision is completely gone. I know life will be easier if you have someone to take care of you.* Each are her worries and wants for me, not mine.

With a hard breath, I school my features into my "just for mom" smile. "Mother, I know you just want what you think is best for me, but please understand that Alex and I are over."

"Well, if you're having phone sex with someone else, I'd imagine they really are."

If only Alex understood that. He hadn't directly approached me since the flowers on my doorstep three weeks ago, but he'd sent another dozen roses last week. I temporarily unblocked him from social media and sent him a message telling him I would not accept any invitations to dinner and asked him to stop with the flowers. He simply replied with *Okay.* My hope is that would be the end of it, but...

"Mom, when did you talk to Alex?"

"Last week." She pauses. "Sweetie, I know you said Alex has been trying to win you back, but you sound a little scared. Is there something I should—"

"Just ignore him if he calls again. Everything's fine." My interruption is both quick and sharp.

"You sound nervous, honey. Maybe I can talk to him—"

"No!" I slosh an annoyed breath. "There's nothing for you to fix. You don't need to worry about me." Absently, I tug at a loose tendril of hair.

"I always worry about you."

I yank tighter on my hair in hopes the twinge of pain will dull my annoyance. "Don't."

Silence stretches between us before she speaks, "So, who's this baby you're sexting with?"

"We're not sexting... Well, not technically."

"Sexting is healthy. Charlie and I—"

"Mother." Groaning, I rub my temples.

"Fine. So, who's this guy?"

"His name is Rowan Iverson."

"The hockey player?!"

Of course my Buffalo Sabres obsessed mother would know who he is. Not to mention it was one of the teams Rowan played with early in his career. A fact he teases this former Buffalo girl about.

"The one that punched Landon Phillips?"

"Landon Phillips isn't what he presents to the world." *Just like Alex.* The bus's automated system calls out my stop and my body relaxes with its promised respite from my mother. "Can we talk about it during our scheduled weekly chat? I'm at my stop."

"You mean the weekly scheduled chats you've skipped three weeks in a row?"

Unfolding Cane Austen, I stand up. "Yep. I promise I'll make the next week."

Hanging up, I exit the bus and head home. Tension coils in my muscles with each step closer to my destination. When I get home and find no flowers on my doorstep, I relax. Maybe Alex got it, finally. JoJo advised going to the police, but there's very little to report. This behavior stopped for months and has just popped up again. He's sent flowers twice. It's not something the police would do something about. I DM'd him and told him to stop. With the flowerless porch, I hope he's done just that.

"HEY GORGEOUS," ROWAN DRAWLS AS I OPEN THE DOOR. HE holds a pair of to-go cups and a pastry bag in his hands. "I grabbed us some tea and a treat for the drive."

"Triple chocolate cookies from Bread?" I bounce on my feet.

Leaning in, he kisses my cheek. "I also grabbed a baklava croissant for tomorrow morning, since we'll be missing our Bread date."

My lips find his.

After a few moments of unapologetic making out at my front door, we head out. An hour later, we park in an empty lot surrounding a large oval shaped building.

"Where are we?" I squint, trying to read the large letters scrawled along the cement structure.

"It's the Bobcats' practice arena."

I take in the snatches of green bushes and trees speckled across the blacktop parking lot. Faded orange letters that I now realize read *LA Bobcats* dominate the building's entrance. Floor to ceiling windows flanked by dark gray pillars make up the arena's front.

"Where you go most mornings." I smile.

Each morning, Rowan heads to the arena to work out. Their training camp doesn't start until mid-August, but he sticks with an almost daily workout regimen, and outside our occasional pastries he adheres to a healthy diet to stay ready for the coming season.

"Are we allowed to be here?" I ask as he opens the passenger's side.

"Scared I'll get you in trouble?"

"I'm more worried I'll get you kicked off the team."

He threads our fingers together. "Worth it."

Hands linked, Rowan escorts me through the building. Games are played at the large arena in downtown L.A., but the players spend most of their time here. This is where their almost daily practices are held. Besides the rink itself, the complex features a large workout room for players, their locker room, and several training rooms for physical therapy.

Posters of current and past players line the hallway leading into the team's locker room. Rowan explains who each player is. I take the opportunity to impress him with my newly-acquired-through-Google hockey knowledge.

Reaching the locker room, I run my fingers across the rows of gold and black lockers. Shiny brown benches line the path through the large room. Rowan leads me to a gold locker.

"This is mine," he says, opening the middle locker.

Affection tugs in my chest at his boyish lilt. "Have you brought anyone else here before?"

"No." He digs for something in his locker.

"Not your mam nor your..." A crease notches my brow. "...Finn."

He shakes his head.

Stepping into him, I press my head to his chest. "Thank you for sharing this with me."

From everything he's told me over the last few weeks, his hockey life is separate from most people in his orbit. His mother and brothers go to the games in Toronto. Finn goes to all of them, but his mom and Gillian only go to the big ones. They've not flown to any of the cities he's lived in over the last ten years.

"I have something for you." He kisses my forehead.

"Is it your cock?" I tease, rocking my hips against his upper thigh.

"Christ!" Head tipped back, laughter rumbles in his chest.

Withdrawing something from his locker, he presents me with a large gift bag. That boyish energy returns to him as I take the heavy bag.

In it, I find a pair of leggings, socks, and ice skates.

With my right eyebrow ticked up, I tilt my head. "What's this?"

"They go with this." He pulls out a hockey jersey and holds it up.

Biting my lower lip, my fingertips trace over the *Iverson* on the jersey's back.

"You'll need to suit up before we hit the ice."

"Wait, we're skating?"

"Of course," he replies and pats my bum lightly in a *get moving* kind of gesture.

Changed, we skate onto the ice. The cool air kisses my cheeks, reminding me of an early winter day in Buffalo. I can almost hear Trina's laugh as we zigzag down the hill behind the house on innertubes.

Looping his muscular arms around my middle, Rowan tucks my head under his chin. "We're at center rink. Besides the nets at north and south ends, both dead center of those ends, there's no obstacles or drop-offs."

"So, basically I have free rein until I hit the boards." I gesture around us.

He kisses the top of my head. "God, I love it when you use hockey terms."

"Icing. Hooking. Penalty kill. Powerplay. Gordie Howe."

Spinning in his arms, I list all the hockey-related terms I can think of.

Chuckling, he clutches my hands, and my knees are a little shaky as we move across the ice. It's not just because this is my first time ice skating, but how adorably sweet this is. Taking his time to orientate me and inviting me into his world.

This is a big part of his life, something he doesn't share with most people. At Axel's, he plays the boss. On the ice, he's the hot-headed defenseman. With Finn, he's both the beleaguered and pestering little brother. I know from overhearing the chats with his mom, that he's the quiet, slightly guarded, but thoughtful son. With Gillian, he's the younger brother desperate for approval from a man whom I believe doesn't deserve that power over him.

Rowan tends to compartmentalize things, but with me, he reveals all his parts. He's simply Rowan and I like every bit of him. The strong. The silly. The sweet. The broken. I like it all.

With slow strides, he guides me across the rink. We circle several times, giving me time to get my bearings.

After twenty minutes, my increasing comfort bolsters my bravery. I don't cling but hold Rowan's hand more for the connection rather than a need for his steadiness as we skate.

Stopping in front of the team bench, he pulls out two hockey sticks and a puck. "Now that you're warmed up, time to train."

Laughing, I take one of the sticks.

Chest pressed against my back, he guides me in the motion of shooting the puck at the goal. After several practice shots, he positions himself in front of the net.

"You're going down, Iverson." I taunt and mock glare at him as I line up my shot.

With a wicked smile, he taps the stick against the ice. "I plan on it."

"Perv," I sass.

He stops shot after shot after shot. Despite the slight annoyance, I'm grateful he's not taking it easy on me.

"Rowan."

"Pen." His voice is low and teasing.

"Are there cameras in the locker room?"

"No."

"Good. I thought you could bend me over the bench and fuck me while I wear your jersey."

"Christ," he groans, standing up.

And I take my shot. The puck whooshes down the ice.

"Did I do it?" I squint.

"Yes."

"Yes!" Stick raised in the air, I jump high and promptly fall, my ass slamming hard against the cold ice. "Oof."

"Pen!" Rowan skates over, leans down, and helps me to my feet. "You okay?" He swipes his warm palm over my butt like he's brushing away ice. He pauses the motion and squeezes my ass cheek.

"I just scored on one of the NHL's top players, I'm winning at life." Winding my arms around his waist, I tip my smile up to him.

"Because you cheated." He hoists me up, my legs dangle in the air.

"There's nothing in the rule book that strictly forbids sexual psychological warfare."

"How much hockey googling are you doing?"

My fingers skim the outline of his lips. "You're just jealous that I'm a brilliant hockey strategist."

"I'll be sure to share with the coach my girlfriend's playbook."

"Girlfriend?" I bite my lower lip.

It's the first time he's called me that. I'd told him that I was his girl, but we hadn't discussed any deeper meaning of the role. Examining our behavior over the last two weeks, it's clear we're in the boyfriend/girlfriend territory. Friends are intermingling. His family knows about me. My mother knows about him, sort of. I'm not seeing anyone else. Neither is he.

"I just assumed." He set me back on my feet, holding on until I'm steady.

"It makes sense that you would. We just haven't discussed it." I brush my hair behind my ears.

"Do you want to be my girlfriend?" He rubs the back of his neck. "God, I sound like I'm sixteen."

I beam. "I want to be your girlfriend."

He takes my hands. "And I want to be your boyfriend. What else is there to discuss?"

"You're a famous hockey player. We've flown under the radar, but I know us being a couple will mean public events. Like tomorrow, for starters. How do we approach it?"

His thumbs soothe against my cold hands. "Tomorrow is a family-friendly event, so the PDA would be minimal, but I'd like to tell people we're together. I don't want to hide us."

"Tomorrow isn't just any event. I won't be there as your girlfriend but as a representative of Walters. With the foundation's connection to you, I'm nervous about how it might make me look."

"I get it." His response is quiet and a little gruff. Letting go of my hand, he turns and scoops up the hockey sticks and puck.

"Rowan, no." I skate after him, slamming into his back when he stops. My arms fold tight around him, and I bury my face between his shoulder blades. "It's not that. I'm not scared to be associated with you. Please know that. I don't want to hide us either, but I'd like to keep this quiet. If anyone asks, we won't deny anything. We won't act like we don't know each other. Nothing like that. But can we just keep this low-key, at least until after tomorrow?"

The muscles in his back stiffen.

"Please understand this is solely about tomorrow's focus being on Walters and MVP, not on us. So often people think I get professional opportunities because of my disability. I'll get comments about how they're ticking a box with me, or I have a special leg up, which is bullshit because I have to work twice as hard."

"And you're scared they'll think you're getting the opportunity because of our relationship and not your hard work?" His voice is quiet.

"Technically, the MVP thing is because of our relationship."

"I'm sorry," he rasps.

"This isn't your fault. You had no idea what Sasha and Greg were doing. I know they meant well. I'm not angry, because at the end of the day the partnership will help a lot of kids." I squeeze tight. "Baby, I will be the first person to shout from the rooftop that you are my man. Just... after tomorrow."

"After tomorrow?"

"Until the thirtieth."

He turns, placing his hands on my hips. "Why that date?"

"That's the date of the charity bachelor auction. I've told you, I'm not a good sharer." My mouth curls into a playful smile.

His hands tighten around me. "Are you saying what I think you're saying?"

"I'd like to go to Toronto with you. Meet your mom and brothers, even Gillian, face-to-face and make sure nobody bids on—"

My words are interrupted by Rowan's mouth crashing against mine. Hands cupping my ass, he pulls me against him. My entire body melts into him. His firm and almost fevered kisses soothe my thudding heart at this brash decision. The disappointment that coiled his body tight has unspooled the desire to want to do this. To give him something he wants but did not push for. He asked. I declined. He let it go. It's still early but each time I pump the breaks, he complies. Even if he wants more, he doesn't push.

However, that's not the only reason I'm doing this. I want to go. I want to hold his hand when he faces Landon. I want to meet his family. I want to be obnoxious about bidding on him, so the entire room knows that he's mine as much as I know I'm his.

"Rowan," I pant, pulling back from our kiss. "I was serious about you taking me in the locker room."

"Pen," he groans, pressing his forehead to mine. "You may be the end of me."

"But what a way to go."

AND IT TRULY WAS. UP AGAINST THE LOCKER. STRADDLING Rowan on the bench. The lick of cool tile along my back as Rowan went down on me in the shower. He'll never look at the locker room in the same way again.

As adult as last night was, today is the complete opposite. The MVP Foundation's event is being held at a sprawling park in Sherman Oaks. To christen the fully accessible playground the foundation built, families of kids who have attended MVP's various adaptive sports camps, wealthy donors, and several famous athlete clients of Greg's agency are participating in a series of sports contests. An official ribbon cutting for the new equipment and the announcement about the partnership with Walters will be held between the contests and a celebratory BBQ.

Rowan drove, but waited in his SUV, to give me a ten-minute head start so I could enter the event solo. Nelson and the hospital chief of staff, who will be in attendance, plan to arrive closer to noon when the official announcement and ribbon cutting occur. I opted to come early with Rowan to watch some of the games, including Rowan participating in a game of goalball, a rugby-esque game where all players are blindfolded.

"Ms. Meadows." A woman with a warm voice strides down the sidewalk that loops through the park. "I'm Sasha Ortiz-Lawson."

"Lovely to meet you, Ms. Ortiz-Lawson. Please, call me Pen." Smiling, I reach out my hand.

"As long as you call me Sasha." She tightens her grip. "I'm so excited to meet you."

I bet you are. My grin gets larger.

"My son Damon is a huge fan. He did a project on your social media for school."

"Really?" My head tilts.

As exciting as the idea is of kids learning more about disability through Cane Austen and Me, it's still a shock to hear things like this. It's why I do it. Still, it's weird.

"Yeah." She waves at someone and then turns her gaze back at me. "I'm glad you came early. I know you're here for Walters, but I'd love to give you a VIP tour of the playground and, if you're okay with it, maybe you could shoot a video or take some photos for our foundation's social media? Of course, you're welcome to use it on Cane Austen and Me. You're a bit of a celebrity to a lot of the kids we work with."

"I'd love a sneak peek." Shifting my feet, I adjust my over-sized sunhat. "But I'm hardly a celebrity. From what I read on the event's info, you have several gold medalists, a Superbowl champion, and some hockey players in attendance today."

"Speaking of *hockey players*." It's almost salacious the way it drips from Sasha's lips "Rowan."

"Sasha," he greets, leaning over and kissing her cheek.

"Rowan, you remember Pen Meadows."

"Yup." His big smile is visible from under the brim of his cap.

"Mr. Iverson," I say, biting my lower lip.

"Ms. Meadows," he murmurs, his fingers briefly brush against the small of my back but quickly return to his side.

"Oh my god! You two are together," Sasha exclaims, motioning between us.

"Can't get anything by you, Sash." He chuckles, but still keeps his hands at his side.

We agreed. No touching. No kissing. No handholding. For the next six hours, we know each other but don't appear to *know* each other in the many, many intimate ways we do.

With Rowan standing inches from me, his heat laps against my body, and I rethink this request. *Stupid, Pen.*

"Sorry to disappoint you. Your romantic subterfuge was for naught," I offer with an apologetic grin.

"I'm not disappointed in the least. Just glad he got out of his own way." She leans over, swatting Rowan's bicep. "Just wish he'd told me, so I could have a statement ready to go in case any reporters—"

"No statements," he jumps in. "We're not hiding this but we're keeping our relationship quiet."

"Just until the thirtieth." My fingers brush against the top of Rowan's hand, drawing his attention to me. *Okay, clearly, he was right. I cannot keep my hands off him.*

"You're debuting as a couple at Landon's fundraiser?" She claps her hands together. "Brilliant! That will officially kill the story about the punch. Your meet-cute and relationship is PR gold. The public would much rather focus on the hockey bad boy redeemed by one of social media's sweetest and, may I add, gorgeous influencers."

Flipping his cap backwards, so I can see his eyes, he locks his gaze on my face. "That's not why I asked Pen to come with me."

Eliminating the space between us, I take and squeeze his hand. "I know." My pull to assure him stamps out any concern about the hospital's chief of staff or my future boss.

"I know, Rowan. You're not that calculating. I've cleaned up enough of your missteps over the years to be very much aware of that." She waves a dismissive hand. "Still, this will cause a bit of a stir. I fielded several 'Are you sure there's nothing going on there?' messages from reporters after the pics at LAX. Photos don't lie and the chemistry between you two is evident. We should discuss a strategy. I know you hate this stuff, but a plan ensures we control the narrative."

"She's right." With one last stroke against his palm, I let go of his hand.

He tips his head back. "I know. Sash, can we discuss this on Monday?"

"Of course. Okay, taking the publicist hat off now." Sasha loops her arm with mine. "How on earth did he manage to win you over? I need to hear everything."

"Uncle Rowan!" A little human screams and barrels into Rowan's arms.

"He's not your uncle," a man in a wheelchair grumbles, following behind.

"Pen, may I introduce you to Damon, Sasha and Greg's son." Rowan hoists the little boy into his arms and my ovaries explode.

At twenty-six, kids are a few years away for me. But seeing Damon in Rowan's arms unleashes a flood of hormones that suddenly make me want to take Rowan into the nearest bathroom for him to put a baby in me immediately.

Good God, Pen.

After officially being introduced to Damon and Greg, Sasha tugs me away for a private tour of the new play equipment. It's amazing. The sprawling playground offers various accessible features. There are ramps allowing for easy access to slides, tunnels, and activity areas. Tactical activities and nonvisual/auditory adaptations allow low-vision folks to easily traverse and engage.

After the sneak peek, I sit in the bleachers with Damon and Sasha cheering on Greg as he coaches his team of famous clients facing the L.A.-based national goalball champions. Despite one Superbowl ring, two gold medals, and a scrappy hockey player who may have sworn one too many times, Greg's team loses to the team of weekend warrior goalball players.

"We should head over to the playground for the ceremony." Sasha stands.

I stand and smooth down my dress's skirt. "Is there time for me to hit the restroom?"

"Yeah. Want an escort?" Sasha asks.

"I got it." Smiling, I take the sidewalk through the park, leading to the brick building on the other side.

It's far enough away to offer a quiet respite in the moments before the ceremony. The hum of activity gentles as I reach the bathroom. A warm breeze rustles the fat leaves of the maple trees encircling the building.

Freshened up, I step back outside. Instead of heading straight back, I take a little break and lean against a tree trunk. I feel its rough bark through my thin cotton sundress. The cacophony of little and big voices crescendo across the park. Moments like this I can't help but think of Aunt Bea. She'd love this. Every single thing about today she'd delight in. Me stepping out of my comfort zone allowing Sasha to take a few photos and videos of me playing with Damon on the playground for both MVP and my social media. Me taking a step professionally for Walters. Me stealing quick touches and brushed fingers with a man that I know she'd adore.

In the distance a voice booms, announcing that the ceremony will begin in ten minutes. Straightening, I step away from the tree and smooth out my dress.

"No need for that. As always you look beautiful, sweetheart."

A shiver rips up my spine. Breath ragged, I lift my gaze toward a very familiar voice. "Alex."

"Pen."

CHAPTER TWENTY

Not a White Knight
Rowan

"I believe this belongs to you." I chuckle as I lower Damon from my shoulders and plop him in front of his mother. We'd been watching his dad playing a pick-up game of wheelchair basketball.

"Hey, kiddo." Sasha bends toward Damon, her dark curls falling over her face, and plants a kiss on his head. "How'd dad do?"

"This many swears," he whispers and holds up four fingers.

"Greg's team took a beating. It's not been a good day for the Lawson Agency." I straighten and scan the park.

Families stream towards the rows of chairs and open spots for wheelchairs surrounding the play structure. Below a balloon arch stands the small stage erected for today. It's almost time for the ceremony. Music underscores the laughter and squeals dancing around the event.

Brow furrowed, I turn to Sasha. "Where's Pen? Aren't you all starting soon?"

"She went to the restroom. Thought she'd be back by now." Sasha's gaze drags to the orange brick building in the distance.

"Let me check on her."

"Can I come?" Damon leans into me.

"Sure, buddy." I scoop his giggling form back onto my shoulders.

"Careful with my child, he's the only one I've got," Sasha calls, her playful tone follows my retreat toward the bathrooms.

"Uncle Rowan, is Pen your girlfriend?" Damon asks, plucking my hat off my head.

I glance up and see him placing it, bill backward, over his own curls.

The oversize cap on his small head reminds me of the first time Pen wore my cap. A hat that she still has, along with a few of my T-shirts, and the jersey I gave her last night.

"Yes, she is."

"Does that mean I can call her Aunt Pen?"

The corners of my lips lift. "Make sure it's okay with her first."

"Okay."

Happiness drips through me at the idea of Damon calling her aunt. It drives Greg nuts that he calls me Uncle Rowan, but I suspect he'll be less critical of Damon calling her Aunt Pen. Over the last four hours, when I wasn't playing goalball or helping kids with some of the mini-sports clinic exhibits, I watched everyone fall for Pen. She and Sasha, thick as thieves already, their laugh-filled cheers drifting from the stands. When I wasn't playing and the blindfold was off, my gaze found its way to her.

So much that Greg slapped me in the head and said in a horrible Irish brogue, "You're well and truly fucked."

Seeing her, head bent in conversation with Damon, I knew I was, indeed, fucked. I couldn't help but imagine Pen in the stands at one of my games, her belly swollen with our baby.

Christ, I am fucked.

"I'm just filling in for VanBuren." A sulky, masculine voice drifts around the corner as we approach the bathrooms.

"Yeah, I'm sure you called in a favor from the chief of staff, who, correct me if I'm wrong, was your former medical school advisor. You shouldn't be here. I was clear in my DM."

My footsteps falter at the hissed venom in Pen's voice. My pulse begins to race, and I try to control my breathing.

"Connections that could help you if you weren't so stubborn. All I want to do is help you. Take care of you, sweetheart. I love you."

Jaw clenched, I place Damon down. "Buddy, go back to your mom."

"Is that Pen?" Damon looks between the building and me, his face twisted with concern.

"It's okay. Just tell your mom we'll be right there."

After a too-mature-for-his-age nod, he runs down the sidewalk. My gaze remains on him until I see him reach Sasha and Greg. The moment he does, I round the corner.

"We were so good together, sweetheart. Why are you being this way?"

"Alex, stop," Pen orders, her back pressed up against the tree, while a tall man with close-cropped blond hair towers over her, his muscular frame caging her in.

"Sweetheart, you used to like when I touched you like this." His fingers twirl a long tendril of her auburn hair.

"Get the fuck away from her, asshole," I growl, grabbing him by the collar and yanking him away.

"Who the—" His words are cut off when I slam him to the ground.

"That woman is not yours to touch. Do you understand me?" Clenching and unclenching my fists, I stalk closer to him.

Blinking, he scrambles up. "I repeat, who the fuck are you?"

"I'm hers," I snarl. "Something you should not soon forget because if you touch her...look at her, I will—"

"Rowan," she gasps.

Her panicked voice halts my threats. As much as I want to grab this man's throat and slowly squeeze the breath out of him like he's tried to do to Pen over the last year, I step back. I don't want to be the monster he is.

Stare still locked on Alex, his breath ragged, Dockers grass-stained, and button-up shirt askew, I move towards Pen. Chest heaving, I pull her to my side. The sensation of her body pressed against mine quells the beast rampaging inside me.

Alex straightens his shirt. "I think this is just a misunder-standing. Pen, I didn't realize you were with someone. You should have said after the two sets of flower deliveries."

"Flowers?" Creases line my forehead.

"You haven't told him about my flowers?" Alex flashes an "Oh gosh, buddy." grin. "Looks like she's been playing both of us."

"You're the one playing games," she croaks.

"I know, luv." I kiss her temple and tuck her closer to my chest.

"Luv?" he scoffs. "Guess she has you under her spell too. She may look sweet but she's a succubus. The moment she has you ensnared, willing to do anything for her, she'll toss you aside."

I take a step forward, but Pen holds me in place.

"I know who you are." His mouth forms a serpentine smile. "Rowan Iverson. Haven't you been in enough trouble lately? Wouldn't want to add assaulting a respected doctor to the list, would you?"

"For her, gladly," I seethe.

"Rowan, no." She clings to my bicep. "He's egging you on. This is what he does...spins things to his advantage. He wants to play the victim, just like he's done with our breakup. Anything to hide what he just did."

"And what did I do?" He huffs a dismissive laugh.

"Ignored my request for you to stay away by asking your former medical school advisor to arrange for you to attend this event, then corner me in a secluded spot. To touch me without my permission."

"Pen, you're being dramatic."

"Perhaps, but we'll let HR figure it out."

He blanches. "Excuse me?"

"See, you've been smart about skirting the line. Keeping things away from the hospital. Doing just enough to keep me knotted up but not enough that the police or HR would do something about it. But you fucked up today. This is a work-related event." She crosses her arms over her chest, a stern expression on her face. "And I have a witness."

"Your boyfriend there." His response is snide.

"And my son." Greg's deep voice pulls our attention.

Greg, eyes narrowed, sits at the edge of the sidewalk, surrounded by three of his biggest clients. Eli Silverberg, my team captain, Carson Ono, quarterback for L.A.'s NFL team, and Kylie Tsan, goalie for the Women's US Olympic Soccer Team, flank him. All three stand, arms crossed, and their glares focused on Alex.

"Damon said there was a man hurting Pen." Greg's stern stare turns warm and drops on Pen. "Are you alright, Pen?"

"I am." With a small smile, she nods. "I'm so sorry for this, Greg."

"Not your apology to make." He gestures a thick finger at Alex. "Pen, would you like the police called?"

My mouth opens but closes with her quick, "No."

"Okay." He nods. "Sasha's waiting to start the ceremony. Do you need a few minutes or—"

"I'm good," she says quickly.

Something tightens in my chest. "Are you sure?" I murmur, caressing her cheek.

"Yeah." She steps back and needlessly runs her hands down her hips to smooth her skirt.

"She's a badass, your lady." Admiration shines in Greg's expression. "Rowan, why don't you escort Pen while we make sure grown-up Zack Morris over there finds his way to his car."

With Pen's hand in mine, we move towards the sidewalk. A glance over my shoulder confirms what I suspected: Alex's blue eyes are fixed on Pen. A snarl builds in my chest.

"I got this." Eli places his hand on my shoulder and steps between Alex and me.

Once we reach the sidewalk, Pen lets out a long exhale and slips her hand from mine. In silence, we stroll toward the stage. Sasha's smile is camera-ready but deep concern shadows her eyes. Like a watchdog ready to rip out the throat of anyone that approaches, I stand at the edge of the stage, my stomach knotted, and every muscle wound tight. Pen – a placid, but pretend, smile anchored on her face – joins her boss, Nelson, and Sasha on stage. Despite everything that just happened she laughs, claps, smiles, and oozes warmth.

Conflicting desires battle within me. To hold her tight, keeping her safe. To ask for answers. Why didn't she tell me about the flowers…about Alex being back.

After the ceremony, I lurk around Pen while she talks with reporters, families, and her boss. Greg appears, letting me know that Stalker Ken Doll is gone. He and Eli waited in the parking lot until they saw his Tesla leave.

"I know that was hard for you." Greg squeezes my forearm.

"I'm not the one he's been stalking," I mutter, my stare following Pen as Damon tugs her towards a buffet table overflowing with desserts.

"True, but I'm pretty sure it took everything in you to not go caveman on him. I wouldn't blame you if you had but thank you. You kept my son safe. You made sure nothing marred this event for the families here. Above all, you kept her safe. What you did today protected her more than if you'd have beat his ass."

"How?"

"She's reporting him. She's taking back her power. If you had hit him, that would have been the *only* story, not what really happened." With a final pat on my arm, Greg rolls towards his son who heaps brownies and cookies onto his plate. "That's enough, Sugar Ray Leonard," he tuts.

"Huh?" Damon's face is quizzical.

"No more sweets," his dad replies as I move away.

"Can we go, please?" I whisper as I come to Pen's side.

"Yes." Her voice is a little unsteady.

Ten minutes later in my SUV, we're parked in the last row of the parking lot. Pen takes off her sunhat and places it on her lap, her fingers fiddle with its smooth edges. Head tipped down, her long auburn tresses fall over her face.

Brushing her hair away, I clasp her chin between gentle fingers and guide her eyes to me. Tears brim in that honeyed stare. "Talk to me, luv."

"I am so sorry." She falls into my arms, sobs wracking her

body. "I should have told you about the flowers. He started back up three weeks ago."

"Three weeks ago? This whole time?" I try to keep my voice calm. "Why didn't you tell me?"

She pulls back and wipes at her face. "I thought I could handle it. He'd sent flowers the day my temporary promotion was announced. I'd hoped that would be it, but he sent another dozen last Friday. I sent him a DM telling him to stop and when no flowers showed up, I thought he got the message." She lets out a beleaguered breath. "Clearly, I was wrong. I feel so stupid."

"Stop." I pull her into my chest. "You're not stupid. You're also not responsible for his actions."

"I'm sorry I didn't tell you," she croaks.

"Why didn't you tell me, luv?"

"I don't want to be rescued… I never meant for you to play white knight, but it happened anyway."

Pressed tight to my chest, I comb my fingers into her silken hair. "I'm no white knight. When I saw him touch you all I thought was ''mine' and no one touches what is mine.' White knights don't think that. White knights don't fantasize about wrapping their hands around someone's throat and…"

Face tilted up, her hand trails up my body and rests on my cheek. "You didn't, though."

I swallow thickly. "I'm no hero, Pen."

"And I'm no damsel."

My thumb swipes along her jaw. "You're certainly not. You're so brave, luv. You faced him today. I was just your backup."

"My teammate." A sweet smile curves her lips. "I promise not to hide things like this from you again."

For what feels like forever and still not enough time, I just hold her. The gentle thud of my heart melds with the cadence of her breath. Muscles relaxed, she slumps against me nearly asleep. At least, I think…

Until she whispers, "Can we get GB and go home?"

"Yes." I kiss her temple and then head to my condo to pick up GB, so we can then drive home.

It's not technically *our* home, at least not mine, but as we get closer to that lavender cottage by the shore, the tension drains from my body.

And the moment she's curled in my arms, naked and sated, the gentle ocean breeze through the open window licking along my bare skin, I know I'm home…as long as this woman is beside me. I may not be a white knight, but I'm hers.

CHAPTER TWENTY-ONE

Just Nice?
Pen

"I brought you this." JoJo appears at my office door, a piece of cake in her hand. "It's Meeka's birthday, so I snagged a corner piece." Meeka is our colleague from PT, and JoJo knows I prefer the corners because there is more icing on them.

With a tentative smile, I nod. "Thanks."

Placing the cake in front of me, she plops onto one of the Windsor-style chairs opposite my desk. "Not to be all social work colleague on you, but how are you doing?"

A hard breath rushes out of me. The emotional popcorn popper of the last two weeks is dizzying.

HR's harassment investigation of Alex ended before it truly started. Five days into the investigation, he resigned from the hospital. The cover story is that he accepted a position at a facility in Texas and would be doing some traveling before starting there in the fall. Despite the spin on Alex's story about his broken heart after I dumped him for a famous hockey player who assaulted him during the MVP event, several staff went to HR with reports about his stalk-erish behavior over the last year. Things he'd done while we were in a relationship and after. Many of which I had no idea about and those still cause a shiver down my spine, including his trying to convince maintenance to let him into my office on three separate occasions.

"Well, at least today's his last day at the hospital," JoJo states, forking a bite of cake.

"Is that why you're here?" My eyebrow ticks up. "Playing guard dog?"

Despite security being made aware of the situation, and HR telling Alex that under no circumstances should he approach me at the hospital, I've been on constant guard. My muscles tighten with each click of dress shoes along the hospital's terrazzo floor, or the scent of that expensive spiced cologne Alex always wears. He's kept his distance, though.

Still, I remain hypervigilant, letting people know where I am, providing regular check-ins via the group thread with the girls or messages with Rowan, and avoiding being alone. After the MVP event, I even contacted the police about a stay-away order. Until he's gone, Rowan or JoJo takes me to and from work most days.

It's all for my safety, but this entire situation strips away my long-cherished independence. I broke up with Alex because he wanted to control me, to keep me in a cage. Right now, it seems as if he's succeeded.

"Is Rowan picking you up today?" JoJo licks frosting off her fingers.

"Yeah." A small, grateful smile remains on my face, despite the sigh.

"Babes…" JoJo reaches across the desk and squeezes my wrist. "I know this is hard for you, but it's only temporary."

Eyes closed, I lean back in my chair. "I know and I'm so

appreciative of everyone's support. You've all been amazing." My eyes open. "I'm not trying to be ungrateful, I just…"

She jumps in when I don't continue my wish. "Want your freedom back, and you *will* get it. You've taken the first steps. You reported him. You're going to therapy."

"I have my first appointment with Dr. Bath this afternoon, before Rowan and I head to the airport."

In the last few weeks, Rowan has been my North Star. He may say he's no white knight, but his actions prove otherwise. Somehow, he navigates the tightrope of being there for me, while letting me do things on my own. As much as this situation with Alex makes me feel powerless at times, Rowan continually offers support without diminishing the control I'm trying to regain.

"I'm so glad you're popping your therapy cherry!" she squeals, clapping her hands together. "I can't wait to process your first session."

"Do social workers just sit around watching therapy scenes from movies on YouTube?"

"It's our porn." Her husky voice drips with sassiness. "Seriously, though. I'm so proud of you. I think talking about everything that happened with Alex will be cathartic for you. Not to mention just having a regular therapist to check in with for a mental tune-up is just smart. You know how much I adore Dr. Senesac."

Brushing my hair behind my ears, I nod. I hadn't been to a therapist since I was a kid.

With my RP diagnosis, my mom had me meet with the school psychologist weekly with a focus on vision-loss adjustment. Although, the school's psychologist had little experience with disability, so they had me go through the five stages of grief and talk about my dead dad.

"Moving on… Have you decided how you'll wear your

hair for the fundraiser?" JoJo almost vibrates with excitement.

"I'm thinking up, but I'll decide that day. Trina has scheduled appointments at the hotel's spa for makeovers."

"Jealous! I can't believe Trina and you are going to a fancy-pants, celebrity-filled fundraiser without me." An audible pout punctuates her words.

Neither can I, especially that Trina's going. She'll be driving up to attend as Finn's plus one. To support his brother, he bought two tickets. By support, he plans to heckle while Rowan is auctioned off and Trina plans, with champagne flute in hand, to join right along. Rowan's growing on her like a fungus she enjoys mocking.

"I know Trina is engaged and they're just friends—" she makes air quotes. "—but have you noticed she giggles with Finn? Like full-on teeny-bopper giggles."

With a smirk, I shake my head. "Leave it alone, JoJo. You always think there's something where there's not."

"But I'm seldom wrong... Also, if she drops her dud fiancé for sexy Boy Brontë, it would make my life much easier."

My nose scrunches. "How?"

"Double wedding. Row-Pen and Fit." She waves her hands like a *Price is Right* showcase model.

I snort. More about the idea of Trina abandoning her life plan to run off with Finn, rather than the idea of a future with Rowan.

Since the MVP event, he and GB have pretty much moved in. On the days when JoJo has chauffeur duty, it's nice coming home to GB, tongue lagging, at the front door and Rowan in the kitchen preparing dinner. It's even nicer to snuggle in his arms, an audiobook playing, as we drift asleep, only to wake up still curled into him in the morning.

"Will Trina be at the meet the mom brunch?"

"Nope." I take a bite of cake.

"How about grump brother?" The eye-roll is evident in JoJo's dismissive tone.

"Yeah. Rowan's mom wanted it to be a family thing."

"I'd say good luck, but I'm pretty sure Rowan will destroy Oscar the Sexy Grouch if he looks at you wrong."

I bristle. "I have the ability to speak for myself."

Reaching across my desk, JoJo squeezes my forearm. "That you do, but it's also okay to let people who care about you speak up on your behalf. As long as they don't speak *for* you."

"What's the difference?" Face scrunched, I tilt my head.

"On behalf of isn't doing it instead of you. It's just cosigning or supporting you. *For* is not letting you speak. Alex spoke for you. Rowan speaks on your behalf. Big difference—" Arms wide, she says loudly, "Huge!"

JoJo's words echo through my brain as Rowan and I stand in front of the reception desk of the downtown Toronto hotel. For the next seventy-two hours, the fancy hotel with its marble floors, trickling fountains, and jasmine-scented lobby, is our base camp.

The receptionist, their head tipped my way, asks, "Will she want a key too or just one for you?"

Rowan says nothing. His hand rests on my lower back, fingers stroking gentle circles. The action reinforces that he's got my back but is waiting for me to speak. Just as he's done all day. Between the TSA agents, airline staff, customs officials, servers at the LAX restaurant we'd had an early dinner at, and taxi driver from the airport it's been a night full of asking about *she* without speaking to the *she* in question.

Forehead pinched, I grumble, "She'll have *her* own key" My tolerance to play the nice blind girl is nonexistent.

The receptionist clears their throat. "Very good."

Rowan's warm breath caresses the shell of my ear. "I'm sorry it's been a parade of assholes today. When we get upstairs, you can take all your frustration out on me. My body is yours to do with what you want."

My mouth slants into a wicked smile. "Can I tie you up?"

"Christ, woman." His low rumble pulses through me.

We barely get through the hotel room door before Rowan's mouth crashes to mine. Our hands roam and our lips devour. Lifting me, my legs wrap around him, as he places me atop the small breakfast nook table near the room's entrance. He pushes up my dress and glides his hands up my thighs.

"Rowan…wait," I pant. "I need to freshen up first."

He slips his fingers beneath my already damp underwear, runs them along my seam, and then pulls them away. "Mmmhmmm," he groans with pleasure as he licks my essence off his fingers. "I think you're perfect as is."

"Christ," I gasp, my body hums with desire.

"You're not the only one who can be sassy." He nips at my lips.

"You like my sassy mouth," I purr, running my finger languidly down his torso, along the bulge in his jeans, and back up. "Especially wrapped around your lovely cock."

"Is that an invitation?" He sucks on my neck, making my head fall back. "If so, I'm RSVPing 'Yes'… Right after I properly worship you."

Hands placed at the center of his chest, I push him back. "Give me ten minutes." I jump down, grab my roller bag, and head to the bathroom.

Ten minutes, give or take a few minutes, later I emerge from the bathroom. The quick shower washes away the emotional and physical grime left over after a day of traveling. It also gave me a chance to put on a special gift for Rowan.

Rowan sits on the king-size bed, his bare back towards the bathroom, hunched over his phone. My stomach swoops at the sight of his clothes in a neat pile atop the cushioned bench at the end of the bed.

"Baby," I say in a sultry voice.

He turns, stands, and drops his phone. The heat of his gaze licks like fire along my skin.

Hands on my hips, I stand – almost like an offering – in front of the desk. Rowan's oversize cap sits on my head, my long hair loose, a form-fitting black tank top with *LA Bobcats* *#5* in gold lettering stops above my belly button, and a pair of black booty shorts trimmed in gold, hug my round ass.

"*Nice.*"

"Just nice?" I pout. "Perhaps, if you get the full effect—" I turn and jut my ass out. "—is this just nice?"

"Pen," he almost moans.

Looking over my shoulder, I bat my long lashes. "You like?" My hands caress over the raised letters across my backside that I know, thanks to JoJo and her Cricut, read *Rowan's Girl.*

A low growl builds in his throat before he crosses the room in what feels like half a second. His arms wrap around me from behind, tucking me into his chest, his erection pushing against me. His hands wander up my body, cupping my breasts as his mouth drags down my neck. I arch into his touch as he tweaks my nipples through the tank top's thin fabric.

"Do you have any idea how fucking sexy you are?" he rasps in my ear. "What you do to me?"

Rubbing my ass against his hard shaft, I let out a breathless laugh. "I have some idea."

"I don't think you do, but I'm going to show you," he murmurs.

His tongue strokes down my neck as he eases the tank top from my shoulders, freeing my aching breasts. Leaned against his firm chest, need pools low in my belly with his massaging fingers' work of my taut peaks. His hands glide over my exposed breasts to my stomach, along my hips, and cup my backside.

"Bend over." His firm, but gentle order slickens the arousal between my legs.

Pulse thudding, I bend and brace my torso atop the desk. Its smooth surface cool against my heated skin. My head twists to the side.

"You're so pretty, luv," he whispers, his hands skim my spine to my ass where he strokes reverently. His fingers trace the words scrawled across my underwear as if committing them to memory.

"Rowan," I whine as his fingers slide beneath my panties, finding my throbbing clit.

"This sweet little pussy is weeping for me, isn't it?"

"Yes," I moan, as he taps another finger at my entrance while he continues to stroke me. My backside moves chasing his thrusting fingers.

"Does my needy girl want more?"

"Yes."

He slides another finger inside me, my body clenching around him. "Do you know what a beautiful sight this is? You coming all over my fingers wearing those." His right hand squeezes my ass, while he fucks me with his left hand.

"Oh…god," I whimper, the orgasm rolling through me.

"That's *my* good girl." He bends and whispers in my ear, his low timbre drips with possessive admiration.

"I am yours." It's almost a croak. I've never wanted to belong to anyone. To have anyone possess me, but with

Rowan, I am utterly his and somehow it both frees and terrifies me like the moments between jumping from the plane before the parachute launches while skydiving. I don't know if I'll crash or glide to safety but somehow the free-fall is worth it.

"I know, luv." He kisses between my shoulder blades before he raises me up.

Turning me in his arms, he slips his hat off my head, tosses it onto the desk, and brushes wayward strands from my face. In the room's dim glow, I can't see his light eyes, but I can feel how they burn for me, how *he* burns for me.

"And I'm yours. From the moment you smiled at me at Tim Hortons, I was yours. I was always meant to be. My entire life has been unsettled. Like I was a broken compass not sure where I was supposed to go." He traces the outline of my mouth. "Then, this smile came into my life like the north star guiding me home. Pen, with you I'm home."

Breath ragged, I place my hand over his heart. It pulses against my palm. The unspoken "I love you" whispers in each gentle thump.

"Make love to me," I breathe.

His mouth is on mine in seconds. We're a tangle of limbs, tearing off the remainder of my clothes as we move to the bed. Pushing Rowan onto his back, I climb onto the bed and straddle him. My hair tumbles over us like a curtain shielding the darkened room from our deepening kisses. Somehow, our kisses are both sweet and a little desperate. Like we're trying to both savor and devour this moment.

Easing onto him, that decadent stretch teases as my body accommodates his size.

"You feel so good, luv," he hisses with pleasure.

"So do you...so good." Biting my lower lip, I rock in a gentle rhythm.

"Pen." He grips my hips tight, ceasing my movement. "Condom."

Sucking in a breath my gaze drops to where we're joined. For the first time he's unsheathed inside me. I've never had sex without a condom but...

"I'm on birth control. I was tested after Alex." My hand rests on his. "I trust you."

In the darkness, I can feel his stare locked on my face. The silence between us is punctuated with assessment. There are risks, even with birth control.

Tightening his hold on me, he moves me against him. Our hips come together in a slow dance. As the pressure builds deep in my core, I rock faster. Hands splayed on his chest, my head tips back, and a pleasurable tension winds tight within me.

"Pen," he grunts, thrusting up.

"Rowan!"

Slipping his fingers between us, he tips me over the edge. As my climax riots through me, he flips me onto my back. Resting my legs high on his hips, he moves inside me.

My unseeing gaze weaves with his. "I love you."

Halting his movement, he cups my face between his hands. "I love you, Pen. I love you. I love you." He emphasizes each sentence with long, languishing kisses.

I tip my hips up encouraging him. He pushes in and then withdraws in focused deep thrusts. That same coil tightens deep in my belly and my fingernails bite into his back.

"God!" I cry.

With a violent quake, Rowan shudders and spills himself into me.

For several moments, our panting breaths are the only sound in the room. In the darkness, I see so much but feel even more.

CHAPTER TWENTY-TWO

Face-Off
Rowan

Midday sunshine halos Pen's hair as it streams in through CN Tower's panoramic windows. Rich strands of bronzy-red and warm brown spark in the waves on her head. She squints from behind her red-framed glasses against the glare. I fight the urge to just stand here and drink in the sight of her or slip my cap atop her head, shielding her from the brightness.

She really is the most beautiful woman I've ever seen. And she loves me. It still feels unreal. Even this morning, buried to the hilt inside her, our gazes tethered, and her murmured, "Rowan, I love you," as she slumped against me sated and spent, I clung to her as if she was a dream that I'd wake from at any moment.

It's like the moment the fog dissipates and reveals a velvet sky full of stars. I always knew stars existed, but the moment the gray disappears, and they twinkle above, you look up and realize how breathtaking they truly are. Loving Pen is like that.

"Here—" I take my hat off and place it atop her head. "—it's extra bright up here."

She bites her lower lip. "What about you?"

Looping my arms around her middle, I nestle her into me. "I got everything I need right here."

"Smooth, Iverson," she teases with a breathy laugh. "But aren't you nervous someone will recognize you without it?"

In L.A. I mostly fly under the radar during the off-season. This summer I haven't been as incognito, but the media fascination with punch-gate has waned over the last few weeks, especially with the world's biggest popstar now dating a pitcher for one of L.A.'s Major League baseball teams. Landon and I are old news.

Toronto is different. Hockey is a big deal year-round. It's also where I'm originally from, so I get recognized way more. Three people stopped me for selfies and a few Toronto fans shouted, "You suck, Iverson!" as we walked to Tim Hortons this morning.

"I've had the hat on all morning, and it's proven a terrible disguise." I chuckle, resting my chin at the crook of her neck.

She spins in my arms and presses her big smile against mine. "You're kind of a big deal here. Do you ever think about moving here?"

"Like playing for Toronto?"

"Yeah. Your contract is up at the end of the season. Punch-gate aside, you have some of the best stats when it comes to avoiding chances allowed, shot attempts, and goal generation in the league."

"Luv, how much research are you doing on hockey?" Smiling, I swipe my fingers along her chin and take in her pleased grin.

"So much that after the CN Tower, I want you to take me

to the Hockey Hall of Fame, so I can see where my boyfriend will be inducted one day."

Pleasure and pride surge in my chest.

"Seriously though, do you think about playing for Toronto? It's a hockey city. Your family is here. It's home," she says, her gaze dropping.

"You're my home." I cup her cheek. "I'm planning on staying in Los Angeles... Staying with you."

"What if..." She swallows thickly. "What if the team doesn't offer you a new contract?"

It's the risk I took when I signed my contract three years ago with the Bobcats. Most players with my stats and age wouldn't have signed a short-term contract, especially one that didn't include a no-trade clause. I did it to play under Stefan Carlson again, and it was the stipulation of the organization which was weary of my reputation as a little too aggressive while they were rebranding as a family-friendly NHL team. Thankfully, Madeline Jacobson, the new owner, seems to only care about me helping her win.

I band my arms around her, holding her tight. "If the Bobcats let me go at the end of the season, I'm staying in L.A. I have plenty of money to retire early. Axel's is just one of the many businesses I've invested in over the years."

She tips her head up. "I'm not worried about your earning potential. I can always be your sugar mama."

Laughter barks out of me.

"But I know how much you love hockey. I wouldn't want you to give that up to stay in the L.A. area for me."

"For us," I murmur, pressing a slow kiss on her lips. "I don't have to play in the NHL to have hockey in my life. There are local leagues. Hell, I've got a girlfriend with a brilliant hockey strategy brain; perhaps she and I will start a team for Axel's."

"You love me that much?" she whispers, her voice tentative.

"Yes." Certainty punctuates my words.

Part of me may be waiting to wake up from this dream. To discover that none of this is real. That she doesn't love me. That she's not mine. That I never met her. Even if this is only a sweet dream, I am rock-solid in how I feel about Pen and how hard I will hold on to this and make it my reality.

A flash of white teeth scrape across her bottom lip as she nods. "Can we take a picture for Cane Austen and Me?"

I skim my hands along her spine. "Sure. Where do you want to pose? By the window, so I can get the city backdrop?"

"No… Not a posed picture of me, but a selfie of us."

A furrow creases my forehead. "Are you sure?"

"Yes… Are you?"

"Luv, I've never been more sure of anything in my life as I am about us."

Rising to her tiptoes, she presses her lips against mine. For a few moments, we just lose ourselves in each other until someone clears their throat. With a sheepish grin, she pulls back.

Not sorry at all. My grin is more wolfish than sheepish.

"Is this something you'll post now or wait until after tonight?"

We met with Sasha a few weeks back. There'd been a lot of back and forth about when to have our first public photo. With everything going on with that douche canoe Alex, I didn't want to add any extra pressure on Pen, so we opted to just debut at the fundraiser and if folks spin this as a stunt, which Sasha warned some people may, we'd weather that storm. I don't care what people write about me, but I do care about what they say about Pen.

"Tonight, they'll take photos of us. Sasha has the press release ready. I know it's not what we're doing, but it feels so formal…it feels… not us. You say I'm home for you, but with you it's like I'm soaring. It seems right to have our first public photo be something *we* take together high above the city that you hail from, where I'm quite literally on top of the world with the man I love."

Like a team. My pulse thuds. "On our terms." I smile.

"Our terms." She pulls her mobile from her back pocket and hands it to me.

MY THUMB CARESSES OVER MY MOBILE'S SCREEN. TUCKED below my chin, Pen beams. My arms wrap around her and my hat, now backward, rests back on my head. A glow from the streaming rays of sun outlines us. Thousands of likes and comments flood the picture linked to both our social media sites.

"Bro, you're trending," Finn says, slapping my back.

Slipping my phone into my suit pocket, I pick up my pint. "It's hardly trending.

At least, I don't think it is. Sasha's texts, with several angry face emojis that we'd not given her a heads up before posting, mentions inquiries from several media outlets. The *LA Press* and other media outlets have reached out. Even with Emma, who was famous in her own right, reporters didn't approach us to do stories, but thanks to the previous stories about our meeting in the airport, they are fascinated by me and Pen's relationship.

Finn nudges my ribs and leans against the mahogany bar. "The world loves romance. My books wouldn't be so popular if they didn't, and Pen and you are a swoon fest."

"Speaking of romance what's going on with Trina and you?"

"She's engaged."

"My question stands." I sip my Guinness.

"I repeat my response." He looks towards the hotel bar's entrance, no doubt looking for our dates.

After the Hockey Hall of Fame, I brought Pen back to the hotel. Trina then promptly stole her, calling out, "Don't worry Irish Puck Boy, I'll bring her back to you," as they ran off to the hotel's spa.

"We're just friends. Plus, I'd never interfere in someone's relationship. Not my style," he says, ice clinking against the glass as he finishes his Old Fashion.

I place my hand on my older brother's shoulders and squeeze. "I know. You're the honorable brother."

"Good God," Finn groans and stands straight.

My gaze follows his and my breath stutters. At the entrance stand Pen and Trina. The light from the chandeliers seems dark compared to their radiance. Trina's red bob, normally smooth, is styled in fat beach waves. A satin emerald-green dress molds her statuesque figure, the slit that runs to mid-thigh reveals a flash of leg. Beside her stands Pen, her long hair is pulled into a loose chignon, bunched in curls on her right side, a silver pearl encrusted comb holding it all together. A sleeveless silver dress hugs her breasts and flares below her knees.

"They're gorgeous," Finn murmurs.

"And both are taken." I slap my brother's back.

"I'm aware. We're just friends."

"I think I'd be uncomfortable if my friends looked at me the way you're looking at Trina."

"Shut up," he grumbles and smooths down his black tie as the ladies approach us.

"Gentlemen," Trina croons, reaching the bar. Pen comes to my side.

If Trina knew my thoughts as I looked at Pen, she'd reconsider calling me a gentleman. All I want to do is whisk Pen away for a night where only I get to experience her beauty. Where I can hold her close as we dance beneath the stars. Then, I'll spend the night consuming every inch of her until the only sound that passes her lips is my name as she cries it out over and over again before she collapses in a heap in my arms.

I'm greedy for this woman in ways that make me more Neanderthal than Mr. Darcy.

"You're stunning." I capture her mouth in a languid kiss.

"Come on, Boy Brontë, buy me a shot. If they're going to be like that all night, I'll need to get liquored up." Trina's quip is playful.

After a round of Patron shots, we catch our rideshare to Casa Loma. The Gothic Revival mansion resembles a medieval castle but is a private residence turned museum. A maze of gardens surrounds the stone structure with two massive towers. Events like weddings and Landon's fundraiser are held here.

"It's like Downton Abbey," Pen says as we enter the castle.

The fundraiser sprawls out from the first-floor restaurant into the atrium and outdoor gardens. After grabbing drinks, we mosey around the event. I spy a few familiar faces. Eli Silverberg and his husband, Malik, are there. My heart swells as he embraces Pen like they're old friends despite only first meeting at the MVP Event.

"Did you see Coach is here?" Eli tips his head to where Stefan Carlson stands, his daughter, Liv is next to him, a tight smile that is more of a grimace on her face.

My eyes narrow as Landon crosses the room, an unabashed expression on his face, and seems to head right toward Carlson and his daughter. Stomach knotted, I fix my stare on Landon.

"Looks like Landon is making a beeline to him." Eli chuckles. "Probably going to try to sweet talk him into the bachelor auction."

"Well, he is a silver fox," Malik deadpans, making the small group, except me, laugh.

"Carlson? Is his daughter with him?" Pen asks, her hand tightens in mine.

Brows knitted, Eli tilts his gaze around me. "Yep."

"Rowan, want to introduce me?" she asks, her thumb strokes across my skin, easing the bristly effect that seized me knowing Landon is approaching Liv.

I lift our joined hands and press an appreciative kiss. "Of course."

It doesn't take psychic abilities to know what's in Pen's head at this moment. She's able to read me like nobody else.

"It's going to be okay, baby," she whispers, leaning into me as we move across the room.

"Rowan!" Liv's mouth blooms into a bright grin, her slender arms fling around me like a vise grip.

"Liv!" I laugh, squeezing her back.

She pulls back. "Oh, my word, I cannot believe it. Is this your girlfriend? She's even prettier in person. I nearly died when I saw the social media posts earlier today. I have to hear all about how you met." She turns to Pen.

Pen reaches her hand out. "Hi Liv, I'm Pen—"

"We do not shake hands, we hug." Liv envelops Pen.

The tension unspools from every inch of me. Seeing that Landon has paused several feet away relaxes me.

"Iverson." Carlson nods at me.

"Coach."

"I see you've been *busy* on your break." His gray eyes bounce between Pen and me.

"Daddy, don't be crass. This isn't a locker room," Liv teases, poking her dad.

Affection glints in his eyes. "My apologies." He extends a hand to Pen. "Stefan Carlson, nice to meet you, Pen."

She grins. "It's lovely to meet you. Rowan has said so many wonderful things about you."

He huffs a laugh. "I'm sure that will change when training camp starts in a few weeks."

The knot in my stomach seems to untie with each smile and joke as Stefan continues to speak with Pen. Almost two months ago I sat in the visiting team's locker room in Toronto, a dull ache in my chest, as Stefan walked away after saying, "Get out of my sight."

"Coach Carlson. Iverson. Glad that you both could make it." Landon steps into the group, his predatory gaze dropping on Carlson's daughter. "Liv."

My jaw clenches.

"*Liv?* I didn't realize you knew my daughter." Carlson's eyebrow raises.

"We met in March at an event at the university. I always enjoy giving back to my old collegiate stomping ground."

Liv's eyes drop to her feet.

"Liv, can I steal you for a minute to help me find the restroom," Pen almost blurts.

"I'm sorry." Landon chuckles. "How rude of me. I'm Landon Andrews." He extends a hand toward Pen.

"Penelope Meadows." She takes his hand but releases it as soon as it is socially acceptable to do so.

"My girlfriend," I add quickly, pulling Pen closer.

"Girlfriend? Really? Giving up that monk lifestyle since losing?"

"Well, Friar Tuck here forced you to a game seven." Pen bristles beside me, a quiet growl builds in her throat.

"That he did." Chuckling, Landon's stare drags down Pen

and lands on Cane Austen, who rests in her right hand. "Iverson, are you using this lovely lady to get out of the bachelor auction?"

On the surface, the joke appears lighthearted, but I bristle with the thinly-veiled judgment that underscores Landon's words. Storm clouds form within me and I open my mouth.

But Pen is quicker. "Nope. I'm using him for his body."

Liv snorts. Carlson chortles. Landon gapes.

Laughing, I press my head against hers murmuring, "Christ, woman."

"What? It's quite lovely."

"On that note—" Liv steps forward. "Pen and I are off to do girl talk in the bathroom."

With a quick kiss, Pen saunters away, arm-and-arm with Liv.

"How on earth did you meet her?" Landon's forehead scrunches.

"Tim Hortons."

"I may need to frequent Tim Hortons," Carlson says, awe in his tone.

"I take it this means I'll need to find a new bachelor to replace you. Coach, ready to get back out there?" Landon says, pushing his hands into his pockets.

"No," Carlson says gruffly.

"Come on, it wouldn't be the most embarrassing thing to happen to you in the city of Toronto." A snake-like smile slithers across Landon's face.

Balling my fists, I mentally count to ten.

"Relax, Iverson, it's just a joke." He waves to someone.

Carlson's palm lands on my shoulder. "Let's go get a drink."

Grabbing a drink at the bar, Carlson and I soon find ourselves in the garden. Fairy lights drape along every surface. A fresh, floral scent melds with the hint of the rainstorm forecast to roll in overnight. Music floats through the gardens from the string quartet playing in the atrium inside.

It is utterly romantic and instead of taking this in with Pen in my arms, I'm standing at one of the many high-tops positioned around the gardens with my coach. A man whom I admire and would do anything for. A man that I'd disappointed, even if I did it for him.

"I hear you've been at the training center almost daily during the off-season," Carlson says, his fingers tap against his glass of Scotch.

"Yes."

"Good." He raises his glass to his mouth and sips.

"I'm..." The thump of my heart drowns out the quiet, murmured conversations around us. "I'm focused on the game. I'm ready for this season."

"Once your five-game suspension is over, you mean."

"Yes." My eyes remain on his, and I swallow thickly. "I know if I hadn't got a penalty in the last two minutes, Toronto may not have scored, and I'd have been playing, rather than in the box. I'm sorry I let the team down... let you down."

His steely stare assesses. "I could give two fucks about that. We were at game seven because of you and Silverberg. You two carried the team all season. What I do care about is what happened after the game. Are you sorry about that?"

I'm two months north of what happened. The smart answer is "yes." It's what Sasha and Greg advise. It's what any smart man would do, lie.

"No."

"Disappointing." It's almost a snarled breath.

"I know." My gaze falls to my pint glass.

"I've known you since you were eighteen. You're scrappy, but you're an honorable man, a good man. Not the beast that

I saw seething with anger, a man whose teammates had to pull off Landon."

Eyes closed, the images of that moment flood back. Blood trickling from Landon's nose as he lay sprawled on the ice, his face twisted in angry shock. My teammates holding me back as I growl, "If you dare, I'll end you," while Toronto players jump into the fray.

"You worry about disappointing me, what about disappointing yourself? That's why I'm angry. These aren't the actions of the man I know."

Pain radiates in my chest, and I rub against its tightness, hoping to quell it. I know why I did what I did and why I can never tell him.

"Guess you're lucky that despite your zero remorse for your actions, Landon has chosen the high road. He may be a smug bastard at times, but you could learn a thing or two from him about being a good man."

"You have that the wrong way around, Daddy. Landon can learn how to be a good man from Rowan." Liv's shaky voice yanks our focus. She stands, wringing her hands, beside Pen, who squeezes her bare shoulder.

His head tilts. "What does that mean?"

With an encouraging smile, Pen nods at Liv, who looks between her and her father.

"Daddy, remember how I told you about the guy I was seeing at the end of the semester."

"The halfwit you said ghosted you and you didn't want to talk about him?" His eyes darken like a stormy sky.

"Liv, you don't—"

"But I do, Rowan" she cuts me off. "I don't know how you knew it was him, but I knew the moment you punched him that you'd figured it out. That you'd done it because of me."

"Who? What is she..." Carlson's face twists with fury. "Landon? It was Landon Phillips?"

"Yes," she whispers. "I'm so stupid. I thought he really liked me but—"

"You're not stupid. Assholes like Landon know exactly what they are doing," Pen soothes, her arm coming around Liv.

"Sweetheart." Carlson strides to Liv, pulling her close. "If I had known, I wouldn't have brought you. I'm so sorry."

Swiping at her eyes, she steps back. "I wanted to come. To face him and show him he'd not hurt me, even though he did. I also wanted to thank Rowan." She turns to me. "You could have told everyone why you did it, but you didn't. You kept my secret. How did you figure out that it was Landon?"

I look to Pen, whose soft expression encourages me to speak. "Landon said something crude after the game and..." I swallow thickly not wanting to finish the sentence.

"Say it," Liv orders, her face stone.

"He said he wondered if it was worse for Carlson to have lost the cup to him or to know that his daughter lost her virginity to him."

"That fucker!" Carlson's rage-filled gaze jumps to the stairs leading into the gardens from the porch, where Landon descends along with Eli, Malik, and a photographer.

In a swift movement, I reach for Coach and halt his steps. "Don't. You're better than this. Better than me."

The hard edges of his expression melt as his stare locks with mine. "I was wrong. You are exactly who I thought you were: a good man. You defended her honor. You protected her despite the exorbitant cost to yourself. Now, let me do the same." He yanks out of my grasp.

"I was wrong. I didn't protect her, and neither will this," I hiss.

He stops and turns his face back to me.

"If I'm sorry for anything, it's for not letting Liv fight her own battles. Not allowing her to face him and just stand as her backup."

Carlson looks between Landon who strides towards us, a laughing expression on his face, and then back to Liv, her fierce glare locked on the man who'd hurt her. Somehow, the little girl that she appeared while tucked under her father's protective arms mere moments ago dissolves. Spine straight and hands clenched at her side she's the image of a warrior ready for battle.

"There you all are. I thought we could get a picture. You know, show there's no hard feelings. Good sportsmanship and all that." A smug expression etches across Landon's features.

"You don't know the definition of good sportsmanship." Liv glowers.

"Excuse me?" Landon cocks a dismissive eyebrow.

"Were you being a good sportsman when you dated me, got me to fall for you, slept with me, and then ghosted me?"

"You what?" Eli growls and steps towards Landon, only to be held back by Malik. "What the fuck, man?"

"He sure did. Mr. Man of the Year is a manipulative bastard who used a twenty-year-old girl to get one over on her father. Were you still upset that he benched you when you played for him at university until you got your grades up, or that out of all the free agent players who played for him, he didn't ask you to join him at the Bobcats?" Eyes narrowed, Liv steps up to Landon. "You're a pathetic little man."

"Who you still slept with," he hissed.

"Watch it, fucker," Carlson snarls, coming beside his daughter.

"Or what?"

Placing a hand on her father's chest, Liv's mouth curves.

"Oh, don't worry we'll give you exactly what you gave me in bed…nothing."

"Coach, we got you and Liv's back. Whatever you want," Eli says, he and Malik move to Liv's other side.

Intertwining our fingers, Pen guides us to stand on Carlson's side. "Us too," we say in unison.

Carlson looks at his daughter. "Your call, Liv."

She looks at Landon like he is gum on her shoe. "Not worth the effort. Let's go."

Fifty minutes later, our little ragtag team, now including Finn and Trina, sit in the hotel lobby. Two dozen Timbits surrounded by coffees, ice caps, and two apple cinnamon teas from Tim Hortons cover the surface of the table we've claimed. We're seated on the cluster of plush sofas surrounding the round table.

Pen is nestled on my lap, my arms looping around her middle, as she munches on our shared cheese toasty.

"Thank you," I whisper against her cheek.

Twisting to face me, she bends close. "For what?"

I trace my fingers along her jaw. "For helping Liv."

"All I did was listen."

"It was so much more than that. You supported her to own her story, to speak up. You helped her regain her power."

"I'm just following my teammate's lead. Thank you." With the sweetest goddamn smile, she offers me the sandwich.

"I love you." Bypassing the sandwich, I slant my mouth over hers. The salty taste from the cheese toasty blends with her natural sweetness in the most decadent flavor.

"Are they always like this?" Eli chuckles.

"Yes!" Both Finn and Trina guffaw.

Mouth still locked with mine, Pen flips off Trina and Finn, making me fall just a little bit more in love with her.

CHAPTER TWENTY-THREE

Brothers
Pen

"You about ready?" Bemusement coats Rowan's question.

"Almost." Teeth scraping against my bottom lip, I take in my reflection in the bathroom mirror. My hair, pulled half back, is styled in loose waves. The sapphire-blue sheath dress that JoJo helped me select, drapes my curves in a flattering, but not too sexy way.

It's just enough to give me the confidence I need to meet Rowan's family, mainly his mom. She's only been a muffled voice from Rowan's phone, when I eavesdrop, just a little, on his weekly calls with her. Rowan assures me that she'll love me, but still a jitteriness ignites my nerves.

"You're perfect." Rowan comes behind me and winds his arms around my waist.

"You're biased."

He nuzzles into my hair. "A hundred percent... Doesn't mean I'm not right, though."

The presence of his arms calms the anxious swirl inside me. Nobody has ever had this power, not even Aunt Bea. The last few weeks dealing with the situation with Alex has frayed my nerves. But each night coming home to Rowan awakens those same nerves in the best way. I don't have to pretend with him that everything is okay, like I do at the hospital. Nor do I have to be on constant guard. With him, I get to just be me... Just Pen.

"You make me feel perfect," I murmur.

"You make me feel so much."

A quiet throb almost whispers in my chest with how full it is. Sometimes I fear I may burst with how much I love this man.

"I have something for you." He squeezes my middle.

"Is it your cock?" I sass, rubbing my backside against him.

"Christ, woman," he laughingly groans.

"You *love* it."

"I love you."

"And I love you."

He slips a small rectangular box out of his back pocket and places it in my hand.

Eyes wide, the breath swooshes out of me. "Rowan...is this..."

He squeezes my middle. "It's not a ring. We're not there yet."

Yet? The word both taunts and comforts. I'm not sure what scares me more, that it may happen or the idea of it not.

With Alex, even after six months of dating, I couldn't envision a future with him. Beyond the excuses that it was too soon when he proposed, and I wasn't ready, I knew Alex wasn't my tomorrow. With Rowan, he's my today and I can almost feel the warm kiss of a breaking dawn in the way he holds me.

With a click, I open the box revealing a pair of earrings.

Squinting, I trace each earring's shape. Forehead wrinkled, I gasp, "Are these…"

"I had them made. It's a hockey stick and a white cane twisted to form a heart."

Every bit of the emotion in my chest rushes to my throat, making it nearly impossible to speak. Tears prick, but I blink them away. Taking out my gold hoops, I put on the silver dangly earrings.

Spinning to face him, I offer a big grin. "How do I look?"

His thumb glides along my jawline. "Perfect."

"I love you." I place his hand on my heart, its beat reminiscent of a horse's gallop. "So much."

"You say that now, just wait until my mam pulls out the photo albums."

"Please tell me there was an awkward phase and you weren't always a sexy god?"

ALAS, ROWAN'S ALWAYS BEEN A SEXY GOD. MY EXPRESSION bounces between annoyance and gaping as I sit beside his mom on the couch in the family room. Using the magnification feature on my phone, I flip through page after page of adorable boys who became cute teenagers and then turned into gorgeous men.

"Fiona, where are the embarrassing pictures? The ones with bad haircuts and acne?" I guffaw and turn to a picture of all three brothers in suits for a family wedding. "Don't moms live for embarrassing their children? I know my mom loves to pull out the pictures from when I cut my own bangs when I was twelve."

"Oh, but my boys do a fine enough job taking a piss out of

each other. They don't need me to do that," she says, her warm Irish lilt hums in my ears.

The anxiety that swirled in my belly throughout our ninety-minute drive to Hamilton is now a calm ocean. Warmth radiates from Fiona. The moment we entered the house, she folded her arms around me and then bestowed on to me a *Society of Headstrong Obstinate Girls* sticker, an outline of Elizabeth Bennet below the script letters, for Cane Austen, which I promptly put on.

It's clear her boys' height comes from both she and her late husband, but her fair complexion and blonde mane seem to have only been gifted to Finn. Rowan and Gillian's darker features are almost carbon copies of the pictures of Axel in the photo album.

"Don't worry, Pen." Finn places the tea service on the coffee table. "I have all the best Rowan stories. Did I tell you about the time Gillian convinced him that mayonnaise would stop the itching from the poison ivy he'd gotten?"

"He didn't?" I cover my mouth to stifle my loud snicker.

Fiona pours two cups of tea. "I found him stark naked smothered in mayo in the kitchen." Handing me a cup of tea, she tips her head towards her other two sons. "These two hooligans were laughing like hyenas."

Finn now sits in the chair to the right of the couch. Gillian, who's said only two to three words all afternoon, broods in the corner. His head tilts between us and the bay window that overlooks the front yard.

"I was seven! Of course, I believed my big brother." Rowan groans beside me, his arm looped around my waist.

"For a time, whatever Gillian said, you believed." Finn chuckles, reaching across the table for a scone.

"A power he took advantage of," Rowan snipes quietly.

"Perhaps." Fiona clears her throat. "But what I also remember is a big brother that used my cookie cutters to make reindeer tracks in the snow on Christmas morning before you woke, so that you thought Santa had come."

Rowan shifts beside me and coughs. "I didn't know that."

"I told you he's got a soft nougaty inside." Finn's tone is playful but shaded with a twinge of smugness.

"Sure." Rowan's mutter elicits a quiet but annoyed breath from Fiona.

I squeeze Rowan's forearm. "It really is sweet," I say, offering Gillian a soft smile. I can't help but wonder what happened to the boy who got up early to extend his younger brother's belief in Santa just a little bit longer.

Rowan reaches for the plate of pastries. "Do you want a scone, luv?"

"Yes please, baby."

"Luv? Baby?" Fiona almost squeals as she slaps her hands together. "Terms of endearment and family introductions, this is serious."

"Easy, Mrs. Bennet," Rowan tuts, playfully.

Fiona's entire being lights up at the Austen reference. It's easy to see the fondness she has for her sons and they for her. Even if Rowan worries that he disappoints her, there's a closeness. The length of their hug. The inside jokes. The playful banter. It all paints the image of a mother-son bond.

"What kind are they?"

"There's cream, and this one here...Mam?" Rowan asks.

Gillian clears his throat. "Carrot cake scone with a white chocolate glaze."

"You made carrot cake scones?" My head tilts to the right.

"Rowan said you liked carrot cake."

"You make Pen and Rowan's favorites, but where's mine?" Finn taunts, his mouth full.

"Cream scones are your favorite?" I look at Rowan.

"Yep." He spreads lemon curd onto his scone.

"Thank you, Gillian." I blink. *Nougat much?*

"You're welcome," he mutters, almost as if it pains him to receive a compliment.

Breaking off a piece of still-warm scone, I pop it into my mouth. "Mmm... So good."

"Luv, please don't make that noise in my mam's living room," Rowan whispers, his smirk pressed against the shell of my ear.

"Jealous?" I coo, batting my lashes at him.

"You and that smart mouth." He presses a chaste kiss, but his possessive grip at my waist teases me with the promise of all the ways he plans to make me scream his name.

"Get a room," Finn quips.

"Hush, Finn, they're sweet," Fiona defends.

"Diabetic," Gillian mumbles.

"Since last night, I've watched them do nothing but kiss or eye-fuck each other," Finn groans.

"Watch it!" Rowan chucks a piece of scone at him.

"Boys," Fiona scolds with a soft laugh.

Finn catches the tossed piece of scone and pops it into his mouth. "Seriously you're going to have to double up the birth control or you'll make Mam a grandma before the year's out."

"I do like the sound of that. Pen's lovely hair and Rowan's green eyes," she gushes.

"Mam, it's too soon for that talk," Rowan protests, but his palm rests against my lower abdomen making the butterflies somersault.

"Sorry."

"It's okay. I agree that any future children should have Rowan's eyes. They'll work better," I deadpan.

There's a beat of silence until Gillian snorts a laugh. "Your girl is funny, Rowan." His gruff timbre softens with warmth.

"She's many things." Rowan presses his lips against my cheek.

"I can see that."

Today is a far different interaction than the first time I'd met Gillian. The scornful dismissal is replaced by approval and wistful longing, not for me but for someone else.

He stands. "I should go prepare dinner."

"Can I help?" I ask.

"No," he says quickly, but not harshly.

Rowan bristles beside me and I press into him, feeling his muscles relax.

Gillian sloshes a long breath. "I mean, no thank you. You're the guest. You should…"

"Do what she wants and if she wants to help you in the kitchen, so I don't have to deal with your homespun version of *Hell's Kitchen*, then I, for one, am appreciative," Finn fills in the blank.

Another round of silence stretches as Gillian seems to consider my offer or Finn's reasoning. I'm not entirely sure why I offer to help. He's hurt two people I love. Still, the breadcrumbs he's offered this afternoon hint that he may not be as gruff as he appears.

"Okay," he says in defeat.

I follow Gillian to the kitchen towards the back of the house. It's not the red brick farmhouse that they'd lived in before their dad died, which Rowan drove me past before we came here. Fiona moved into the two-bedroom townhouse after Finn bought his house five years ago. By that time, Rowan was on his fourth or fifth new city and Gillian lived with his wife.

"Is this a dish you make at Fiona's?" I mention his restaurant as I chop a stalk of celery.

Gillian stands at the stove, poking at the pans of ground lamb and beef. The sizzle hisses in my ears and the flavorful scent fills my nostrils.

"It's an Irish pub, so shepherd's pie is standard," he mutters.

"Is it Irish only? I know Axel's has some Swedish dishes in honor of your dad."

"Just Irish." His reply is curt.

Interesting. My stare jumps to him, but his back is toward me.

Focused back on the cutting board, I lift it and use the knife to slide the celery pieces into the bowl. "It's not open today? Is that why you're here cooking?"

"It's open."

"Finn says you're a bit of a tyrant in the kitchen."

"That he does."

"I think he's over-exaggerated your tyranny. I've been your sous chef for the last twenty minutes and I find you're less tiger and more pussycat."

He huffs a laugh.

"Who's running Fiona's while you're here?"

"Layla."

Oh. I wince.

Rowan may not be as close to Gillian as he is with Finn, but he is aware of Gillian's complicated marital status. He's shared that Gillian is staying with Finn because he's separated from his wife Layla, his partner at the pub.

"I'm sorry," I say softly.

"So am I." He sighs. "I see Finn told Rowan."

"Yep."

"Figures," he mumbles.

"Rowan says your mom doesn't know. Finn is keeping your secret from her."

He lets out a hard breath. "It doesn't matter. It will all come out soon enough."

"Oh," I say.

He grunts.

I grab an onion and start to chop. "My mom's on her fifth husband. She's been divorced three times." *Really, Pen?*

"Five husbands? Three divorces? How does that math work?"

"My dad died. He was her first husband." The pungent onion aroma awakens my tear ducts. The gathering tears are not about my dad.

"I didn't know."

"How would you?" I shrug. "Rowan and you aren't really the chatty brothers."

Again, he grunts.

"Case in point."

"And you say your friend JoJo has no filter," he scoffs with a teasing lilt.

Eyebrows lifted, my head tips his way. "Funny how somebody who isn't your type left such an impression."

"I didn't…That's not what I meant…." He lets out a long breath. "I'm not good with words." He pivots and faces me. "Did I really hurt JoJo?"

"You did."

"I am an asshole," he murmurs, remorse radiating from his tone.

"I won't disagree." I offer a cheeky grin. "But I think your impact was only temporary. JoJo wears her feelings on her sleeve and by the next day she was back to her charmingly unfiltered self."

"Good." He nods. "Just another reason that I'm not her type." It comes out as if it was only meant to be a thought and not something he'd meant to say out loud.

Her type? My brows shoot up.

He pulls something out from his back pocket and places it on the kitchen island beside the cutting board. "Would you mind giving her this?"

"What is it?"

"A letter."

"You wrote her a letter?" I gape.

He raises his hand and coughs. "Yes."

"Why?"

"I don't know... I just did." He turns back to the stove.

Chopping the onion, my eyes drift to the envelope on the counter. "Is it an apology? Because I won't take it to her if it's just excuses—"

"It's an apology. I truly didn't mean...what I said wasn't what I meant. I'm just... I'm just sorry." he says, softly.

"You should be." I blink back the brimming tears from the onion's sting. "I'll give her the letter, though."

"Thank you." He puffs out a soft chuckle. "You're feisty. Rowan needs a partner like you. Someone to keep him on his toes."

"That's funny." It slips out without humor or thought.

"That Rowan needs someone to challenge him?"

"No, that you've written an apology letter to someone you met for sixty seconds but make no amends to your brother." *No, Pen! What are you doing?*

"You don't know me."

Eyes closed, I decide that I've already stepped in it, so I may as well wade all the way into the murky waters. "You're right, I don't know you, but I know your brother. Do you?"

His back remains rigid and turned toward me. He says nothing.

Swiping the chopped onions into the bowl, I continue my work as I speak, "Don't feel so bad, he doesn't know you either." I discard the onion peel and wash my hands. "Do you want to know him?"

"Yes," he croaks.

"Good, because he wants that too, even if he doesn't act like it." Tears drip down my cheek.

"It's too—"

"Don't do that. You know better than anyone that we're

not promised tomorrow with the people we love. Do you love your brother?"

"Of course." He spins to face me.

"Then it's not too late. He's in the other room. There's time. I think you already live with regrets after losing one important man in your life."

"You're a tenacious little bit of a pain in the ass, aren't you?"

I swipe at my eyes and give him a watery smile. "Some say determined."

"Shit! Did I make you cry?"

"No. Onions," I sniffle-laugh as I grab a clean paper towel, lift up my glasses, and dab at my eyes.

"Pen? What's wrong?" Rowan rushes into the room, his voice drips with concern as he pulls me into his arms. "What the fuck did you say to her, you bastard?"

"Rowan, no." I yank myself from his hold. "It's the onions."

"He's a bit overprotective, isn't he?"

"Like an adorable pit bull." I smile and place my hand on Rowan's cheek.

"I think I adore you, Pen Meadows."

"You're growing on me, Gillian Iverson."

"I'm sorry I overreacted." Rowan takes my hand, raises it to his mouth, and presses a tender kiss to my palm.

"I know, baby. It's been a rough few weeks, and we've both been on high alert, but I'm not the one you should apologize to."

"Sorry, Gillian," he mumbles.

"It's alright."

"It's more than alright, it's a start." With a pat on Rowan's cheek, I offer a hopeful smile. "I'm going to grab your mom and Finn to go for a walk while you help your brother in the kitchen."

"*Excuse me?*" they say in unison.

I twist my gaze to Gillian. "It's still today... Not yet tomorrow." Turning back to Rowan, I press a gentle kiss against his lips. "I love you. You can be mad at me later for this." Grabbing the letter from the counter, I leave the room.

"For what?" Rowan's question drifts down the hall, but I don't look back. It's not my past that needs to be dealt with, it's theirs. And I may be risking our future for it.

CHAPTER TWENTY-FOUR

Shepherd's Pie
Rowan

Blinking, I watch Pen disappear down the hall. Her melodic voice drifts back as she asks Finn and Mam to go for a walk. I want to follow, but my feet are rooted to the red and black checkered tiled floor. Something in the way she said "you can be mad at me for this later" commands me to stay. For what? *I don't know.*

"Why has it been rough for you two?"

At my brother's raspy question, I spin. "What?"

"Pen said it's been a rough few weeks for you two." He gestures to the empty entryway as if she still stood there. "Was it because of you punching Landon?"

"No," I snap and turn toward the glass patio door, fixing on the gentle sway of the maple trees in the backyard.

Of course, his first thought would be that it had something to do with me, that I was the cause. *Aren't I, usually?*

Don't do that, baby. Pen's sweetly firm voice whispers inside me.

With a long heavy sigh, I brace my hands on the kitchen island. "Sorry to disappoint you *again*, but I'm not the reason."

"What does that mean?"

I cross my arms over my chest. "You've been pretty clear what an utter disappointment I am to you."

"You're not—"

"But I am," I cut in, struggling to contain the anger that rages in my veins. "You were the only one not surprised after I lost the cup and then punched Landon. Like you were just waiting for me to fuck it up."

"That's not true."

"It is. It's how you've looked at me every day since...." I close my eyes.

"Since when?"

"Forget it," I mutter and turn to walk away.

He reaches out and grabs my bicep, halting my steps. "No. Fucking talk to me."

I could easily break free of my brother's grip. He's strong, but I'm stronger. However, the desperation shading his eyes immobilizes me.

"Since Dad." The knot in my stomach tightens, painfully gnarling my emotions.

His face pinches. "That's not true."

"Bullshit."

"I may have been tough on you, but I was doing my best. For God's sake, I was a little boy too, trying to help you become a man. Nobody showed me how because the person that was supposed to was gone," he shouts.

"Because of me, right?" I hiss, my words slam like a punch.

Blanching, he takes a step back, but his hand remains tight on my bicep. His mouth opens and closes a few times with no words breaching.

With a deep inhale, I let it out. "You told me it was my fault. You said if it wasn't for me, he'd be alive."

His grip clings. "I was an angry little boy who'd lost his dad."

"So was I." I jerk my arm from his grip. "You're my big brother. I looked to you for comfort and instead found blame."

"I was angry—"

"Fuck you," I snarl, bile stinging in my throat, and turn.

"Rowan, wait."

"I'm not listening to your excuses."

"Fucking stop." His arms come around me and yank me back into him.

"Let go." I pull, but he tightens his bear-like hold.

"No."

"I don't want to hurt you," I grit.

"Go ahead, drop me. I'll just get back up. I'm not letting go until you listen…. Please." His voice trembles.

"Speak."

Without loosening his hold, he speaks, "I was angry at him. It took me a long time to realize that, to admit that. I'm still furious with him for going out there by himself."

"Me too," I croak.

"It was easier to take it out on you. You've always been more his son than me or Finn. Mam always says we both got our looks from Dad, but he gave you his heart."

I swallow thickly.

"You're just like him. All heart. Once you commit to something, you're all the way in. You love deeply… Just like him. Never has that been clearer than today seeing you with Pen. The same unabashed smile that Dad always wore rested on your face. It's the same smile he had with Mam—" His voice cracks "—and with you."

"You're his son, too."

His arms relax but remain folded around me. "Not like you. Finn and Mam have always been close. Dad and you were close. I… I was jealous. That day… He'd ask me to help him get the pond ready, but I said no. Ever the prick, I didn't realize it was his attempt to include me. Instead, I went to the store with you all. If I had—"

"It's not either of our faults," I say quickly, raising my hands to his forearms and squeezing.

"His death isn't, but what happened afterward is on me. If anyone is a disappointment, it's me. I failed you. I failed him in the one thing he expected me to do: be your big brother."

Regret overflows within me. Its sting chokes away my ability to speak.

"I can't fix the wrong that I've done, but I want to try to do better… To be the brother you deserve. I don't deserve your forgiveness, but I'm asking anyway."

Those words are almost verbatim of my plea to Pen a month ago. That sweet honey gaze peering up at me as she mulled over my apology in the middle of Bread. Two very different situations, but somehow the same. It's forgiveness. It's love.

"Why now?" My voice is hoarse.

"Because it's still today and I don't want another tomorrow to come not knowing that we're okay. I know I don't show it in the right way or say it, but I love you. What you saw in my eyes after you punched Landon wasn't about you…it was about my failure."

My face wrinkles. "Your failure?"

"If Finn hauled off and smacked someone, I'd know why. With you, I didn't know, and that's on me. Fans in the stands that day thought it was in response to losing. Even if I knew deep down that wasn't the reason, I didn't know why, and I didn't know how to ask because I let our relationship deteriorate to this point."

"How did you know it wasn't because we'd lost?"

"Because you're like dad, you only attack to protect."

We only use our fists to stop, not to start. Dad's deep bass voice whispers in my heart. How often had he said that? The memory of him kneeling in front of Gillian, a trickle of blood dripping from his nose after getting in a fight on the playground, and me wiping away my tears after being knocked down, flashes in my vision. Gillian had darted from the basketball court towards the bottom of the slide where I lay sprawled after Tommy O'Hare pushed me from the ladder, so he could go.

"You're like him too," I whisper.

I hear him swallow, but he doesn't acknowledge my words and continues, "Your protectiveness comes out when you play. Every game you play, it's the same."

"Every game?"

"I have never missed a single one of your games." He murmurs as if it's a secret.

"Why didn't you say?"

"I don't know." He shrugs. "But I'm not going to say anymore. I want to know you and I want you to know me."

"Okay," I rasp, raising my hand and taking his.

He squeezes our intertwined palms. "Okay."

We stand there for what feels like minutes. Each thump of his heartbeat against my back ticks away the time.

"You said you wouldn't let go until I listened… I listened."

"And they say that I'm the prick," he grumbles, humor colors his tone.

"Well, I'm just trying to be like my big brother," I say, stepping away from him. I don't make it too far.

He spins me and pulls me into a tight hug. "I love you, even if you are a smug prick sometimes."

"Again, just following your lead." I squeeze him back. "I love you too, Gillian."

"Ok, now that *that* is over—"

A raucous laugh falls out of me.

"—why have the last few weeks been rough?" He lets me go.

God, I'd almost forgotten about his original question. I rub the back of my head. "Pen's ex stalked her."

"Bastard!" he mutters.

"Agreed."

"Since you're not in jail, I take it he's still alive."

Clenching my teeth, I dig my fingernails into the laminate surface.

"Unless you've fled here to escape the authorities. I hate to break it to you, bro, but Canada will extradite." Somehow my brother's tone teeters between his normal gruffness and a teasing lightness.

"I didn't touch him."

He places a palm on my shoulder. "You're stronger than me."

"I wanted to. It took everything in me to not end him. He stalked her like she was a trophy to possess rather than a queen to earn the privilege to be in the presence of."

"A queen you'll charge into battle for." He smirks.

"Absolutely." I lean against the counter. "She's so fucking brave. Everything he put her through, and she faced him… And she still opens her heart to me. Christ, even before they broke up, he…" A snarl roars in my chest. "…He tried to snuff out her light."

"He failed miserably."

"That he did." I scrub my hands down my face.

"We could—" He motions to the cutting board. "I'm a chef, nobody has to know what happens to the body."

An unexpected snort belts out of me.

His wry grin is almost disturbing.

But my mouth still lifts. "He's gone, now. She reported him. She took her power back."

"Your girl is like hard candy, strong but sweet." He squeezes my shoulder. "I'm sorry for how I acted when I first met her. I was—"

"Being your typical prickish self." My scoff is firm but not unkind.

He blows out a long breath. "I've made an art form of it. Just ask my soon-to-be ex-wife."

"I'm sorry about Layla and you."

He'd been so happy with Layla. They'd met in culinary school and seemed perfect for each other.

"I really am sorry," I repeat.

"Me too." He steps away and motions to the counter. "You chop the carrots and I'll finish browning the meat."

"Pen doesn't like carrots."

"First, you're pussy-whipped."

Not arguing.

"Second, I'm making two shepherd's pies. A large one for us and a mini one for Pen."

Warmth surges inside me, melting the last drop of tension away. No doubt after I gave Mam the list of Pen's food preferences, he'd decided to do this. Even before whatever conversation they'd had or the brokering of our fresh start, he made special scones for her and planned to make her an individual shepherd's pie. It's not for Pen, even if it's clear he likes her. He's done this for me.

"Dad used to do that, too. He knew Finn didn't like sausage patties, so he always made him links when he made us breakfast." My gaze flicks to my brother, who stands with his back to me at the stove, his head bobs as if taking in the thinly veiled truth that we're both like our father in more ways than how we look.

At the sink, I wash my hands. Patting them dry, I move to

the cutting board on the kitchen counter and begin to chop the carrots.

"Medallions, right?" I ask.

"Yep."

"Just like Gran's." A wistful smile tips up the corners of my mouth.

All three of us boys learned to cook in my Gran's kitchen. She'd make us help her with Sunday roast after church. As we got older, Finn and I found more and more excuses, but Gillian remained by her side, learning her recipes and proclivities for vegetable shapes based on what dish she'd make.

"Gran's bread pudding." I groan, the decadent taste of Irish-whiskey-drenched sultanas floods my memories. "Do you still offer Gran's Sunday roast at Fiona's?" I swipe the chopped carrots into a bowl.

Every Sunday Gran made roasted beef drizzled in flavorful gravy, potatoes, Yorkshire pudding, vegetables, and bread pudding. In honor of Gran, Gillian serves it each week at his restaurant.

"Yes."

The burner clicks off.

"But not for long."

"Why?" A furrow settles on my forehead.

"I'm giving up my share of the restaurant to Layla in the divorce."

My eyebrows nearly shoot into my hairline. "What? Fiona's has been your dream. Can't you two share or—"

"Layla's pregnant."

"You two have to work this out if she's going to have your baby."

"It's not mine."

The breath wooshes out of me. "Fuck."

"My sentiments exactly." He grabs a bowl of potatoes, an eerie calm masking his features.

My face twists with disbelief. "How? Who?"

"Our silent partner, Becket. Turns out his silence is all about keeping secrets. Like the fact he's fucking my wife."

It all clicks together. Becket, a childhood friend of Layla's, partnered with them when they opened Fiona's. With his MBA and their culinary experience, it appeared the perfect partnership. Still, Finn always raised an eyebrow at Layla's closeness to Becket. The inside jokes. The lingering hugs. The way he insisted that Becket looked at her. We'd tease that his romance author brain simply saw love stories everywhere.

"God, that's rough. I'm really sorry."

Wordlessly he starts to whip the potatoes for the topping.

"What will you do?"

"I don't know. Part of me just wants to pick up and leave. To start over somewhere, but…"

"But what?"

"Mam."

I wave a dismissive hand. "Mam is fine. She doesn't need anyone to take care of her. Not to mention, Finn is here. Christ, he's a professor at the same university with her."

"Same department," he adds with a chuckle.

"He really is a mama's boy."

"Does our fresh start mean we can finally team up against Finn?"

"Fuck yes. I have years of pranks to get retribution for."

Finn may have played referee and failed peacemaker, but he also took advantage. For years he enlisted one of us to mess with the other.

"The tables have turned." Mischief glints in Gillian's green eyes.

Happiness about a partnership with Gillian, even just for

pranks, thrums through me. It means to truly be brothers in all the ways that matter. The ways that we'd not let ourselves be for far too long. We have so much time to make up for.

"Axel's needs a new head chef," I say, standing up straight. It's a bit of a lie. We don't have a head chef, per se, just a series of cooks that funnel in and out. Still…

"Do you want me to help you find one?"

"No. I want you to be it."

His gaze jumps to mine. "Are you serious?"

"Like a heart attack."

"We just—" he motions between us.

"I know… Even more reason. It's a fresh start. For you. For us."

He gapes.

I continue, "You can stay at my place. I'm at Pen's all the time. Plus, training camp will start soon, so I'll barely be there. You'd run the kitchen. I have a manager who handles all the rest."

"There are so many reasons to say no."

"You only need one reason to say yes."

He tips his head. "The kitchen will be my domain to run as I see fit?"

"Yes." My mouth slants into a smirk.

"And you're really at Pen's all the time, because the idea of moving from one little brother's home to anoth er's is humiliating."

"Yes." Laughing, I shake my head.

"Okay." He puts his hand out.

And I take it. "Okay."

As the comforting scent of the baking shepherd's pie wafts around the room, the murmured voices of the rest of our party returning from their walk fill the house. Gillian sits outside on the back deck. I've come back in to grab each of us another Guinness. I place the bottles of stout on the kitchen island to open, and to wait for who I know will appear in *3...2...1*

Pen enters the kitchen, hope and concern etched on her face. "Hey."

Crossing the room, I pull her into my arms and kiss her senseless. Her pliant lips meet each press before she opens for me. Fingers woven into her hair, I pull her deeper into my thankful kiss. I know what she did and the worry that twisted itself inside her over the last hour. I feel it in the way her body slumps against me in relief.

"I take it that your conversation went well," she says, breath ragged.

I glide my thumb across her jaw. "It did. Thank you for pushing me."

"I'm sorry if I... Well, let's face it... I overstepped. I'm sorry for that. I saw an opportunity and took it."

"Are you sorry?" Playfulness coats my accusation.

"Yes and no." Her fingers dance along my forearm. "I'm sorry that I didn't pull you aside and suggest you talk to Gillian. That I didn't tell you that he was more open to fixing things than you thought. For that, I'm sorry. But I'm not sorry I seized the opportunity... at least not now that I can see the heaviness that you carried is gone. Sometimes love is about making someone eat their carrots."

"What? You hate carrots," I guffaw.

"It's something Aunt Bea would tell me about my mom. That, sometimes, people do things that are good for us that we, for whatever reason, don't want to or can't do. Carrots."

"Well, I ate my carrots, and so did Gillian."

"Good." Her eyes sparkle with smug satisfaction.

"You said I could be mad at you later." My low voice almost rumbles.

Her mouth forms an O. "And what does *being mad* at me look like?"

Skating my hands down her lush curves, I grip her ass. "Is tying someone up still on the table?"

"I believe that was for me to tie *you* up, but..." She bats her eyes.

"Seriously? You best really spend all your time at Pen's because I'm not going to last long if each time I walk into the condo you two are like this," Gillian grumbles as he enters the kitchen and saunters to the island to grab one of the bottles of Guinness.

Pen's eyebrows draw into a line. "Condo?"

"Yeah. About that..." I grin.

CHAPTER TWENTY-FIVE

Bite
Pen

The decadent scent of cinnamon, vanilla, and turkey bacon waltzes up the stairs and fills my nostrils. Smile stretched across my face, I wrap a towel around my head and slip on my terrycloth robe. Slippers on my feet, I pad downstairs to find one of my favorite scenes.

"Am I still dreaming or is there a shirtless man cooking breakfast in my kitchen?" I coo, stepping behind Rowan and wrapping my arms around him.

"I'm not shirtless." He laughs.

My hands coast beneath his T-shirt. "Not yet," I purr.

"I can fuck you or feed you. Sadly, we don't have time for both."

The way "fuck" rolls off his tongue makes my vagina clench. The physical connection between us sizzles as much as the bacon frying in the pan.

No man has ever read my body like Rowan, knowing exactly what I need and how to give it to me. Whether it's hard demanding thrusts or languidly diving deep within my body, he always wrings every last drop of pleasure out of me. He can fill my ears with dirty words as he fucks me or lather me with sweet kisses as he makes love to me. It doesn't matter because once sated and spent, he tucks me into his chest and whispers, "I love you, luv."

"So, fucking or food." I grin. "Are you making French toast?"

"Yep."

"Feed me, please." I nuzzle the space between his shoulder blades.

"I don't know if I should be complimented that my French toast is better than sex or severely disappointed in my sexing you up game."

A wet nose brushes against my leg and I let go of Rowan to greet GB. "Good morning, handsome."

"She chooses French toast over sex with me and now leaves me for the dog," he jokes.

It's amazing how quickly we fell into this little routine. It's been a month since we first exchanged I love yous in Toronto. It's been two months since we started dating. Rowan and GB spend most nights here, except last week. With training camp starting, we thought it would be best for him to stay at his place. I didn't want to be a distraction. Of course, I insisted GB stay with me.

We made it four nights before Rowan came back. It does involve an hour drive for him to get to the Bobcats' training center each day, but he doesn't mind. He uses it to listen to our current audiobook buddy read.

"Mmm," I moan, the swirl of sweetness from the agave drizzled French toast floods my tastebuds. "Yeah, I was so right to choose this over sex with you."

"Keep this up and there'll be no more sex for you, period," he teases, his light eyes meeting mine over his coffee cup.

"Really?" Freeing my foot from my slipper, I run it up his calf.

"*Pen.*"

"What?" I bat my eyes.

"Do you want to make us late?"

"Who, me?" I place my hands on my heart.

"We don't have time for this," he says, bemused.

With a cheeky expression, I slide my finger across my plate, the pools of syrup coating the tip. "You're probably right." I lift my finger to my mouth and slowly lick before slipping it past my lips, sucking as I make tiny mewling noises, "So, good."

"Christ, woman," he groans.

"Aunt Bea used to say good men will fuck or feed you, but great men will do both."

"*She* said that?"

"Something like that." I lean in and slip my hands beneath his shorts, caressing his thigh.

"Pen." He pulls me into his lap.

"Eep!" I giggle. "Sir, we don't have time for this." My tease is half-hearted.

"Exactly." He takes his fork and spears a bite. "Which is why I'm putting a stop to it. Now, eat."

"So bossy this morning." I take the offered food.

"Says my very sassy girl." He grabs a piece of bacon from his plate.

Like it's nothing, we proceed to eat from his plate, me on his lap at the kitchen table.

"You *love* my sass." I lick syrup from my lips.

"Pen, I love everything about you."

A fizziness bubbles through my veins.

"Well, except for this new-found obsession you have for buying GB clothes."

"But he *loves* it!" My gaze drops to GB in the green shirt

with tiny pineapples dotting it that I'd put on him while Rowan finished cooking breakfast.

"Does he?" Rowan's head tilts and eyes look past me. "That dog will do anything to make you happy."

"Like someone else I know." I fork a bite and offer it to him.

"Guilty as charged." He takes the bite.

"Well, I'll be in jail beside you." My heart swells.

Each day I fall just a little more for this man. It's like I dove into the ocean and just as I think I've reached the bottom, there's more to go.

"Also, I think it's the relief that's making me extra sassy."

The interviews for the director of voluntary services position wrapped up yesterday. No matter what decision is made, I can breathe. I know I did the best I could in the interview, and I'd knocked it out of the park the last month as interim director. Outside the MVP Foundation's partnership, which came in pre-me, and Sasha later revealed was more coincidence as they'd been working with Jamal for several weeks prior, I've established a volunteer program with a local high school and secured donations from several businesses.

"They'd be idiots not to select you." Rowan's palm squeezes at my waist.

"True," I say saucily. "If they don't, they don't."

"*Still?*"

"Still." I sigh. "I really hope they choose me."

My false bravado fools nobody at this table, especially Rowan. He's so in tune with me. Even if he doesn't know exactly what goes on in my head, he's able to discover my emotions, the hidden and not-so-hidden ones.

"When do you think you'll hear?"

"Nelson wants to decide by Friday."

"Then Friday I'm taking you out somewhere special."

"What if I don't get it?"

"I'll still take you out somewhere special." He folds me into his chest. "Only we'll have dessert for dinner, all the dessert."

Shifting in his lap, my hands slide up and cup his face. "Now, I kind of hope I don't get it." My fingers trace his smirk.

"Luv, you can always have dessert with me."

"You are my dessert." I press a soft kiss to the center of his chest. "My healthy breakfast." I kiss the column of his throat. "My afternoon cup of tea." His chin. "My vegetables." The corners of his mouth. "All the things." The center of his forehead.

"Fuck it." With swift movement, he drives to his feet and carries me out of the kitchen. "We can be late."

I WAS ONLY TWENTY MINUTES LATE FOR WORK, WHICH ISN'T A big deal since I've never been late. However, Rowan hit the tail-end of L.A. rush-hour traffic, making him forty minutes late for practice, which means he could be fined. Something he insisted was worth it as he bent me over the side of the couch and drove into me.

Me: How much is that second round in the shower going to cost you?

Rowan: No fine.

Me: No punishment? Relieved emoji.

Rowan: I didn't say that. Carlson is old school, so I have to stay late to run drills and clean the locker room.

Me: Still worth it?

Rowan: Fuck yes emoji.

A loud giggle rolls out of me with his totally made-up

written-out emoji. I wrap up my text exchange with Rowan whose break is ending.

His penance will have a ripple effect, meaning he won't be home for dinner tonight since he'll need to stay later than planned for a meeting with Gillian and Yasmine, Axel's manager. Gillian arrived two nights ago and starts as Axel's chef next week.

"Can I get this signed?" Devon plops something beneath the closed circuit TV on the small table next to my desk.

"Sure." I swivel in my chair towards the screen and roll my eyes. "Seriously?"

A print copy of the *LA Press* sits on the tray and is magnified in high contrast white on black. A headline reading *Love at First Sight?* runs above a picture of me and Rowan.

There's been moderate interest in our relationship. After the initial social media post, a few outlets requested interviews. It's still strange to us that anyone would be interested, but Sasha says we have all the makings of a romance that the public loves to root for. He's famous. I'm not. I'm a disability advocate. He's famous for being an able-bodied athlete.

Most of the attention was supportive. There'd been a few stories speculating that the relationship was a ploy to revamp Rowan's reputation until pictures from the MVP Foundation event of Rowan, his arms around me, as we walked to his car and some of us kissing outside the Lawson Agency taken before our appearance in Toronto surfaced. A pissed-off Sasha found out that the pictures were taken and leaked by Greg's assistant, who'd also been the person to tip off reporters that Rowan Iverson and his new social media influencer girlfriend would be arriving at LAX. They'd thought they were helping protect one of Greg's clients.

It solved the mystery and Greg's assistant was fired. Despite me and Rowan protesting, Greg explained that he needs to have complete trust in his staff. Even if the leaks helped, it violated our privacy, which the Lawson Agency has zero tolerance for.

Continuing with our "on our terms" stance about our relationship, we declined all the interviews. We're not hiding or pretending, but just living our lives. We post things to social media. Not a lot, but some things. We go out in public. I plan to be at all Rowan's home games and a select few away games. We get some attention, but nothing too destructive to our daily life together.

Despite our declining interviews, several outlets ran stories about us, but that's died down after the Dodger's star pitcher proposed to his famous popstar girlfriend last week after she'd sang the national anthem at his game.

"Aren't we old news, now?" I groan. "Also, this article is like two weeks old."

"True, but one of our older volunteers had it and asked me if you'd sign it," Devon says sweetly, handing me a twenty/twenty pen from my desk organizer. "Make it out to Hazel."

"Isn't Hazel your grandma's name?"

"She volunteers to make me dinner twice a week and I work here, so she's a volunteer," he deadpans.

Laughing, I sign the newspaper before I head to my next meeting. The day drags just a bit as I go from meeting to meeting. Besides a quick drive-by chat with JoJo as I grab a tea at the coffee cart, the other bright spot is texted photos of GB from the dogwalker that Rowan hired for while we're at work. As I slip my phone back into my blazer pocket, it buzzes with an incoming message. I take it out.

Devon: Where are you?

Me: Leaving the social work office. What's up?

Devon: Nelson's looking for you. Cortes is in his office.

With that my pulse quickens. Nelson reports to Mark Cortes, associate director. Before any directors are selected, the VP will always run it by their senior leader. If they're looking for me, it's either to tell me I got the job or, which is customary for inside candidates, to inform me in person that I wasn't selected. It's not required but it's the polite thing to do and part of the culture here.

Me: On my way.

Reaching the suite that houses the department of major gifts and donors, I suck in a steadying breath before pushing through the glass doors. I find the reception area empty. Devon must have stepped out. Heading past Devon's desk, I move down the narrow hall towards the voices drifting from Nelson's office in the back of the suite.

"I still can't believe everything that happened between her and Dr. Walsh." A raspy male voice says.

At the mention of Alex, I stop in my tracks, about ten steps away from Nelson's door.

Someone coughs. "It's terrible to lose such a good doctor, but I'm glad he left on his own accord. It could have been *very* ugly."

"I'm glad he's gone," Nelson says. "He may be a good doctor as you say, but stalking a woman like that, especially a blind woman…disgusting."

Especially? What the actual fuck?

"Agreed." The other male pauses. "I always forget Pen's blind, because she's so capable."

The words sting and bite into me, reopening never-healed wounds. This is just a version of something I've heard many, many times before. *You're so capable. I forget that you have a disability.* On the surface, the words read like compliments, but what they're really saying is that they don't expect me to be successful, let alone meet the basic standards.

Nelson chuckles. "She's so impressive."

"There you are!" Devon calls, causing me to jump and spin.

"Yeah," I say, letting out a long breath. "I was just heading to Nelson's office. You said he was looking for me." I make a verbal show of it, speaking extra loud, as if I just arrived and hadn't been listening outside the door.

"Pen, is that you?" Nelson shouts, his tone is warm and friendly.

"Yep." With a firm smile in place, I enter his office.

"You know Mr. Cortes." He motions to the other man, who sits in one of the leather chairs across from Nelson's desk.

"Yes. Mr. Cortes." I reach out my hand.

His grip is firm and warm. "Call me Mark."

"Please, take a seat." Nelson gestures and I take the seat beside Mark. "We were just talking about what an amazing job you've been doing as interim director of voluntary services."

Spine straight, I cross my legs at my ankles and smile. "Thank you." A polite expression hides the churn in my belly.

"We'd like to make it permanent. Pen, we're selecting you as director of voluntary services. The official announcement will be made Friday morning," Nelson says, clapping his hands together.

I nod. "Thank you."

A deep belly laugh falls out of Mark. "You've stunned the poor woman."

Sure, we'll go with that. "Yeah. I wasn't expecting that," I offer, keeping my tone light and airy.

"Since we're not announcing the promotion until Friday, we'd like you to keep this quiet until then." Nelson clears his throat. "That includes *you*, Devon. I'm sure you're out there eavesdropping."

"Roger that," Devon shouts.

It's not hard to keep the promise to not tell anyone. The norm is for me to run to my group thread and tell the girls or, my new go-to over the last two months, call Rowan. I should be jumping for joy, but right now I don't know how I feel about this.

LATER, AS I SIT ON THE BUS ON MY WAY HOME THE MOMENT replays on a loop. It should have been an exciting moment, a triumph. I want this job. This is something I've worked hard for. To be impressive because someone doesn't believe you can do the basic functions of a job isn't what I've strived for. High-five me for my achievements, not that I did them despite your lack of belief in my ability.

Deboarding the bus, Cane Austen and I move down the sidewalk and into the neighborhoods that lead to my street. The chaotic sounds of an early evening swirl around me. Cars whizz by. People say hello as they shuffle by. A dog barks in the distance. I ignore it all, losing myself in my thoughts.

"It's just par for the course," I mumble to myself and turn down the residential street.

There are rows of fenced yards to my right and the street, filled with parked cars, to my left. With every step, I allow the tension to ease out of me. Soon I'll be home with my guys, where I can just be Pen. Not the surprisingly capable disabled woman.

Loud barks break into my thoughts. My head tilts towards the sound to try to place it.

I screech as a sudden sharp pain bites into my right hand. "Fuck!"

Eyes wide, my gaze drops to my hand. A white dog, its snarling mouth engulfing my hand, growls back at me. Biting down harder, pain sears as it shakes and tugs at me. Cane Austen slips from my grip and tumbles to the ground.

"Let go!" I howl, swinging my bag at the dog.

With a whine it releases me. Holding up my oversized tote bag as a shield, I crouch down and feel for my cane with my right hand, which radiates with pain.

"Get away from her!" A deep voice shouts, echoed by the slap of shoes against the cement sidewalk.

"Oh my god, are you okay?" A woman yells.

"I'm o—" I locate the cane, but I can't grasp it with my hand, which pulses in pain. Blood, warm and thick, drips down my arm. Sucking in a sharp breath, I croak, "I'm not okay."

CHAPTER TWENTY-SIX

Powerless

Rowan

"**A** vegan version?" asks Yasmine Nor, Axel's manager. Leaned back against the booth's plush leather, a smile kicks across my face, as she flips through Gillian's proposed menu changes. I'd told my brother Axel's kitchen is his. As we sit in a corner booth in the dining room, it's clear he's taken me at my word. After years of free-ish reign at Fiona's, it's not surprising that he'd have ideas. Lots and lots of ideas.

"Yes. As well as a gluten-free option." Reaching across the table, Gillian points to the proposed fixed menu for a Sunday roast. "In fact, I think we need to revamp the entire menu to provide more vegan and gluten-free options. It will mean some changes to the kitchen to ensure no cross-contamination."

"I thought this was supposed to be just a friendly meet and greet?" Yasmine snorts, one sculpted eyebrow arching.

"We met. We greeted. Let's work." Gillian taps his fingers on the table's smooth oak surface.

Leave it to my brother to not mince words or waste time.

After a long pause, Yasmine grins. "I like your style. Let's get to it."

Of course, my no-nonsense manager and Gillian would hit it off. Yasmine runs the front end of Axel's with the precision of a stunt driver. She's not scared to make changes or take risks, but they're always calculated to ensure the best outcome.

Laughing, I flip through Gillian's other requests. Turns out my brother, who's supposed to be getting settled in his first week in L.A., has come by Axel's every day since he's arrived. He's inspected the kitchen, reviewed the menu, and met with staff.

"Axel's should be a place for everyone, no matter their dietary restrictions." Gillian clicks his pen before scribbling notes on the paper menu.

"A place for all." Yasmine's face lights up. "I like that! We could use that for a marketing plan to promo some of these changes. I know some local food influencers that could highlight us." A wry expression covers her face. "Perhaps, someone's popular social media girlfriend can—"

"Pen's not that type of influencer," I interrupt with a chuckle.

"Actually," Gillian clicks his tongue. "There are many individuals with disabilities or chronic conditions that require specialized diets. It's totally up her page's alley."

Face scrunched, I lean in. "Are you following my girlfriend on social media?"

"Yep."

"You don't even follow *me*," I tut playfully.

"Well, *she's* interesting." Despite the insult, warmth shines in his eyes.

Amusement slants my mouth into a lopsided smile. The trepidation of this fresh start still lingers between us. I won't pretend it doesn't, but moments like this I relax into, not just a future, but a here and now with my big brother.

"Speaking of Pen, looks like she's calling." He points to my buzzing mobile atop the table, a picture of Pen and GB flashes on the screen.

"Be right back." I grab the phone, stand up, and start to walk away. "Hey, luv."

"Hi…um… I'm sorry to call during your meeting," she says, a gentle quiver skitters in her voice.

Concern hits me like a slapshot, and I halt abruptly. "Are you okay?"

"Yeah…uh…I'm okay."

She's lying.

"I got bit by a dog and—"

"What?" I spin.

Gillian and Yasmine stare at me with lifted brows.

"Where?"

"My hand," she says.

"I mean—" I exhale a breath and rub my temples. "Where did this happen? How?"

She swallows hard. "On my way from the bus stop."

Fuck. If I'd not been late this morning, I'd be home. I'd be with her. This may not have happened.

"I'm so sorry—"

"Hold on," she cuts me off, muffled voices drifting over the line.

"Pen, who's that?"

"The paramedics."

"Paramedics?" My heart thunders in my chest.

A pen clatters to the table as Gillian shoots to his feet. Within a breath he's beside me, face drawn with worry.

"Baby, it's okay. They're going to take me to the hospital.

It's just a precaution. I swear. I just wanted to make sure you knew. I'm okay, I promise."

Only she doesn't sound okay. Each measured word quakes with the truth underneath her verbal brave face. She's scared, and so am I.

"Which hospital? I'm on my way."

"No, it's ok. I'll—"

"Which hospital?" I repeat. The fear coursing inside me overpowers my ability to just listen. I'll apologize later, after I have her in my arms.

"Sacred Heart," she pauses, a slight catch in her breath. "I love you."

The hidden almost whimper as she says that guts me. My strong girl is working so hard to not break, but I hear pieces of her brave front crumble in every hissed breath and trembling word.

"I love you, too." I swallow thickly. "I'm leaving now."

"Okay," she whispers.

"I'll call JoJo, so she can be with you 'til I get there."

"Okay." A small sniffle breaks through. "Rowan, I'm going to get in the ambulance now."

"Let me know when you get there."

"Okay... I promise I'm ok."

"I know...but *I* won't be 'til I see you. You know how it is; you're the strong one, and I'm the needy fuck." I force a smile into my words, hoping it eases the worry that underscores her tone.

"Rowan?" Gillian's hand lands on my shoulder as I end the call. "What's wrong?"

I rake my fingers into my hair. "Pen was attacked by a dog. They're taking her to the hospital... I need to go." Slipping my mobile into my back pocket, I turn.

"Hold on." Gillian tugs me to a stop. "You're in no state to drive."

"I'm fine." I pull away and stride towards the door.

He jumps in front of me. "Give me your keys."

"What?"

"I'm driving." He extends his palm. "You'll be no good to Pen if you get in an accident or pulled over because you're driving like a man desperate to get to the woman he loves."

"He's right, Rowan," Yasmine cautions.

"Fine." I hand over my keys.

/

GODDAMN L.A. TRAFFIC.

Ninety minutes later, Gillian pulls up in front of the ER. "You go in. I'll park and meet you inside."

"Thanks." I unbuckle and open the door.

"Game face," he says, repeating what he'd told me on our way here.

For the entire drive, I funneled through all the emotions. Guilt about not being there. Worry she is hurt worse than she says. Anger that this happened.

Gillian lays a hand on my forearm. "Get those emotions out here. Because once you walk into that room you'll need to be there for *her* feelings, not your own."

I inhale sharply, then let the breath snake back out. I repeat the cycle and then step out of the car.

Each thump of my heartbeat as I enter the ER drowns out the murmured conversations of the half-filled waiting room and overhead announcements. Scanning the room, I don't see Pen or JoJo, so I hurry to the reception desk.

"Pen Meadows," I rasp, reaching the clerk.

The clerk blinks and grabs a clipboard from behind the counter. "Are you checking in? You'll need to fill this out."

"No, my girlfriend is here. Pen Meadows."

"Oh, okay," Chuckling, the clerk pulls up something on the computer.

"Can I go back and see her?"

"Patients are only allowed one loved one back there at a time."

JoJo must be back there with her; she'd messaged when she arrived an hour ago. If I can't be with Pen, at least one of her other people is there. Still, worry spools tight in my stomach. That knot won't be undone until I see her, until I touch her.

"Can you tell me how she's doing?" I scrub my hand down my face.

"Sorry, I can only release info to immediate family."

"She is my family, and I'm hers," I snarl, my fists balling at my side.

"Sir, if you'll take a seat in the waiting room, I can check with the nurse assigned to her case who can speak directly with the patient."

"I'll wait here."

"Sir, I have other people behind you. Please take a seat or—"

"Or what?" I hiss.

"Or nothing." A strong hand curls around my shoulder. "Because you're going to take a seat, and we're going to wait while this nice clerk does their job," Gillian commands firmly.

My brother tugs me away. As if I'm a toddler in the midst of a tantrum, I stomp along. Flinging myself into an orange plastic chair, I slump against the seat, crossing my arms over my chest.

"Text JoJo and tell her you're here." He plops beside me.

Within a few minutes of my text, JoJo enters the waiting room. A calm expression covers her face. She looks as if she'd come straight from the gym in pink yoga pants and a black tank top with white letters that read: *I like Big Squats and I Cannot Lie*. Loose blonde curls escape from her messy bun.

"Yoga pants." Gillian's awed murmur draws my attention.

"Hey," JoJo says, a soft smile on her face.

I stand up.

And so does Gillian. "JoJo."

Her brown eyes bounce to him, annoyance glinting in them, and then back to me. "She's alright. The dog did a number on her right hand. Her hand is sprained. Additionally, her ring finger and the back of her hand are damaged. They've flushed the wounds but won't be doing stitches to close them. They're splinting the finger and bandaging the wounds in hopes it will close in a few days. It will take a week or so to heal. She'll also be on some strong antibiotics to combat potential infection. They gave her a tetanus shot, and after they go over the release paperwork, she'll be free to go."

"She's okay?" I ask, my chest rises and falls with ragged breath.

"Yes."

"Can I see her?"

"Here she comes now." Gillian squeezes my shoulder.

I dart my gaze to the ER doors, where a frowning Pen, with Cane Austen folded on her lap, is wheeled out by a laughing nurse.

"Luv—" I break away and go straight to her. "You're okay." I cup her face, my thumbs skating along her smooth skin.

Bright blue gauze is wrapped around her splinted right ring finger. Red scratches crisscross the top of her hand where it's not covered by the bandage. A plastic bag, with the blazer I know she'd been wearing today, specks of blood on it, sits underneath her cane. Another bandage covers where they'd given her the shot on her upper left arm.

"I'm fine, baby." She offers a sweet smile. "Which is why I don't need a wheelchair."

"Hospital policy." The nurse chuckles.

At this point, I've had enough of hospital policy. "Let's go home."

After we get Pen's antibiotics at the pharmacy, we head home. Gillian pulls into the drive and JoJo parks behind him. Opening the door, I fight the urge to just scoop Pen into my arms and carry her inside. When we'd gone to the pharmacy she croaked, "I can't use my cane." As we got out of the vehicle, the quiver of her lips forces the air from my lungs with a whoosh. Those honeyed eyes are glossy with unshed tears.

"We'll do human guide." I press a tender kiss to her temple.

I help her navigate her way to the front door. GB trots up to us. His butt shakes wildly, and his tongue lolls out of his mouth.

"Down, boy," I say firmly, snapping twice for him to sit.

He lowers to his haunches. GB's not known for his obedience, but his head tilt towards Pen telegraphs his concern.

Letting go of my bicep, Pen shuffles to the couch and sits. Within seconds, GB runs to her.

"GB! No!" I snap my fingers.

He lays his head in her lap, and she folds over him for a cuddle. "Hi, handsome. I missed you."

He licks her face, and a sweet laugh falls out of her.

"If GB was with you, he'd have given that random stray dog the business," JoJo teases, entering the house. Gillian follows her through the door.

"I'm glad he wasn't. I wouldn't want him hurt." Pen scratches his brow with her uninjured hand.

Every time I think there's no more room inside me for how much I love this woman, she does something like this

319

and greater love seeps into lesser-known, unfilled crevices. She worries about everyone else.

"You look exhausted." JoJo sighs. "Why don't I help you change into something comfy while Rowan makes some food? Don't want to take your antibiotics on an empty stomach," JoJo says.

With a kiss on GB's head, Pen stands. "Thanks, but I don't need help." Her tone is firm, but not unkind.

"Alright."

A few minutes after Pen goes upstairs, JoJo heads out saying she'll check in tomorrow. Gillian helps me in the kitchen – and by *helps* me, I mean he takes over.

"She's taking a while up there." He places a toasted cheese sandwich on a plate.

My thoughts exactly. "Let me check on her."

Muffled sniffles drift through the closed bedroom door as I approach. I stop and close my eyes. *God, I hate that sound.* All I want is to pull her into my arms and hold her tight.

I step inside the room. "Hey, luv." Her head snaps up as I announce my presence.

Pen sits in her bra and panties on the edge of the king-size bed.

"I can't get my bra off," she says, her voice cracking.

Coming up behind her, I unclasp the bra. As it slides off her, I press a tender kiss between her shoulder blades. "I got you."

"You're good at that."

"Unclasping your bra?"

A soft laugh whooshes from her. "Getting me."

Sitting beside her, I fold her into my arms and let myself do what I've wanted to do since she'd called, just hold her. She slumps against me, and our tension seems to melt away.

"I promise I'm ok. This is only temporary." She holds up her hand.

I brush wayward tendrils of hair away from her face. "I know it's temporary, but I'm not."

Our gazes lock and my hands coast along her silky skin. All I want to do is pull her into my arms and never let go. To protect her from anything that dares to hurt her. But I can't. No matter how much the caveman inside me wants to, I can't protect her.

It's a truth I've ignored since the moment the plane nose-dived. Despite her being secure in my arms, I couldn't protect her if the plane crashed. I couldn't protect her from Alex. I couldn't protect her from this dog or the next one, the literal or metaphorical. All I can do is hold her and take care of her in the aftermath. For the first time in my life, I know I am powerless.

"I should probably put some clothes on," she says.

Running my fingers along her spine, I smirk. "I'm not complaining."

"Perv." A smile brightens her face and further unwinds the tension inside me.

Kissing the center of her forehead, I rise and walk to the dresser. I pull out a pair of sleep shorts and one of my T-shirts, which is her current loungewear go-to.

"Thanks," she says, taking the shorts and pulling them on with her uninjured hand. With a bit of a wiggle, she tugs the T-shirt over her head. A hiss falls out of her as she pushes her injured hand through the sleeve.

"Gillian made a toasted cheese." The sweet aroma of chocolate chip cookies wafts into the room. "He also put in some break and bake cookies. We both thought you deserved a special treat."

"It's been a day." Grabbing a hair tie from the dresser she attempts to brush her hair, the injured hand not allowing her to gather it up. "Seriously!" she winces and tosses the hair tie onto the bed.

I scoop it up. "May I?"

Eyes closed, she nods.

Coming behind her, I comb up the long strands with my fingers. "Ponytail or messy bun?"

"Either." She shrugs. "I can't take off my bra. I can't do my hair. I can't even use my cane."

"Baby, it's only temporary."

"How am I going to go to work tomorrow if I can't use my cane?"

Enveloping her in my arms, I tuck her against my chest. "Maybe take the rest of the week off. You have plenty of leave and—"

"Great," she scoffs. "Just as I get offered the promotion, I'm out because—"

"They offered you the job today?" I try to keep my tone curious and not accusatory, but the question still whispers inside me. *Why didn't she tell me?*

Yes, she was attacked by a dog. A lot has occurred between her being offered the job and now, but Pen has texted me throughout the day. Practice was over at four, an hour before she'd left the hospital, and she'd not called.

"Yeah… I didn't call you right after they offered me the job because I needed time to process. I don't know how I feel about it," she says with a hard breath.

"We could have processed it together."

"Sorry," she croaks. "You're right."

"It's not about right or wrong, it's about being a team." I brush soothing strokes down her back.

She nods.

"What happened?"

"It's not anything I haven't dealt with before, but I overheard Nelson and the associate director talking about how impressive I am and that they forget that I'm blind because I'm so capable."

My hold around her tightens. "I'm so sorry."

"It just hurts to know what they really think…what their *real* expectations of me are." A tremor shakes her words.

You cannot protect her from this. The thought is on repeat inside me. Still, I want to storm down to that hospital and… But I won't. Instead, I press my lips to the top of her head and then rest my chin there, keeping her cocooned as she speaks.

"And now I have to take the rest of the week off because I can't use my cane, knowing that this isn't something they'd have to deal with from a"—she releases a sharp breath— "non-visually impaired person."

"You were attacked by a dog, that's all they need to know."

Sniffling, she raises her bandaged hand. "It almost stings worse than this… to know how they really see me. It's taken all the joy out of what should have been a big moment for me."

"They're the blind ones."

"Yeah, but they have the *right* kind of blindness…the kind the world's okay with."

An ache reverberates through my chest. There's no time machine that will let me go back to prevent this pain from finding her, but is there something I can do in the aftermath to take care of her in the way I want to, the way that ensures this hurt doesn't find her again?

"I just want to forget it, forget today," she croaks.

"Pen—"

"No, it's fine. I'm fine. I'm just emotional. I'll be okay after I eat and rest." She turns to face me, her red-rimmed eyes peer up and a small smile tugs her lips. "Today has sucked, but I'm so grateful for you. All I want to do is go eat cookies, cuddle on the couch with you and GB, and forget about this," she murmurs, snuggling into me.

"Of course." This is within my power. I'll take it, even if it guts me that the only thing I can do about her tears is wipe them away.

CHAPTER TWENTY-SEVEN

Just Desserts
Pen

Stretching out on the couch, I run my bare feet along GB's velvety fur. His happy moan hums in my ears. The entire afternoon, since the dog walker brought him back, has been just us two in a semi-vegetative state.

Not since I had the flu my freshman year of college, have I spent two straight days doing nothing. It's only temporary is the new mantra on an endless loop in my head. I'll see my primary care physician Saturday morning, and if it appears my knuckle is healing, they'll remove the splint giving me back more use of my right hand. I still can't really grip my cane, so I've been homebound since the attack.

Homebound but not alone. Rowan hurries back here as soon as practice is over. JoJo came by last night with sushi from our favorite spot for a bicoastal bestie virtual dinner date. An evening preempted by Wes and Gillian showing up with homemade bread pudding, a recipe from Rowan's grandma.

Between eye rolls and muttered comments, JoJo *begrudgingly* ate two helpings. The letter from Gillian is in her possession, but she tells me she hasn't read it yet. I won't push the issue, but Gillian is growing on me. Rowan has a big goofy grin on his face whenever they're together.

As lovely as the little impromptu virtual dinner party was, I can't wait until my hand is back to normal. It's amazing how many things require the use of my right hand. Using a spoon. Washing my hair, which I'm not complaining too much about since Rowan washed it for me last night. The magnification program on my cell is impossible without a fully functioning hand, impacting my ability to stay up with Cane Austen and Me. JoJo helped me post an update to explain my mini-hiatus, which will be at least until next week.

I'm startled by the ringing of my cell phone. "Mom calling," my phone announces.

"Ignore," I say out loud, pretending my phone can fulfill that request.

Last night was supposed to be my scheduled weekly telephone date, which I'd missed due to dinner. Of course, it's always easy to find excuses to cancel a call with Mom. A yoga class with JoJo. Dinner date with Rowan. Taking a shower. So many excuses.

"Mom calling," my phone announces again.

Again? Brow furrowed, I sit up. As much as I don't want to, I reach for the phone. Mom never calls twice in a row unless it's something really important. "Hey," I say, pushing the speaker option and placing the phone on the coffee table.

"Are you alright?" she asks, her tone is rushed and worried.

"Yeah." I contemplate my bandaged hand. "Are you?"

"No, because my daughter gets attacked by a dog and I

have to hear about it from Trina's mom at the post office rather than from my own daughter," she snipes.

Cringing, I pinch the bridge of my nose. "Sorry, Mom… I'm fine, though."

"Are you?"

"Yes." An eye roll accompanies the "Just for Mom" smile etched across my face.

"Is Rowan there? Has he been taking care of you?"

The question swirls inside me like a gust of wind sucking up all the emotional debris. Gratitude for my supportive and loving boyfriend. Shame at how much he's had to do to help me over the last two days. Impatience for this temporary situation to be my history and not my present.

Everything else pales in the burgeoning anger that my mother's first thought is about someone else taking care of me.

"He's at practice." I dig my fingernails into the palm of my uninjured hand in hopes it keeps the brewing storm at bay.

"But he's been there taking care of you?"

Eyes closed, I sigh. "Yes."

"Good. It makes me feel better to know you have him. It's just scary to know that you're out there alone," she says, her worry-filled tone is soft.

Rubbing my temples, I count to three before replying, "I can take care of myself."

"Everyone needs someone to take care of them. With Aunt Bea gone, I just worry about you."

"You don't need to worry."

"I know, honey. You've got Rowan."

"I have *me* to take care of me," I hiss.

"Honey—"

"Stop! Just …stop," I snap.

A sharp intake of breath is her only response.

"I wish you saw me as something more than just a

problem to be solved." Standing up, I begin to pace. The cool hardwood under my bare feet does nothing to extinguish the fire raging inside me.

"Honey, that's not how I see you."

"Eat your carrots, Pen, they'll help your eyes. You should get this experimental procedure that has a point five percent chance of working. Pen, you should marry Alex; he'll take care of you." I wave my arms and I mimic my mother's midwestern accent. "If you can't cure my blindness, you want someone else to take care of me."

"I just want to help you," she sniffles.

Part of me wants to say anything to stop her tears. To put on my usual smile and say, "I know, it's okay." It's what I did on Wednesday as I sat with a pretend happy expression on my face while Nelson and Cortes talked to me about the promotion. It's what I do so often with others.

They're the blind ones. Rowan's words almost wrap around me as if they are his strong arms.

"Maybe you should have focused more on *your* visual impairment, than mine. Focus on seeing your daughter as capable."

"Honey, I'm... I don't know," she stammers.

"I've only ever been a problem for you to solve or ship off to someone else to deal with."

"What does that mean?"

"School therapists. Vision specialists. Summer camps. Aunt Bea. If you couldn't have my eye disease cured, you'd stick me with anyone else just so you didn't end up with your helpless blind daughter. Well, I'm blind, but I'm not helpless. No matter what you or anyone else thinks."

The words sprint out of me as if soldiers, swords ready, charging into battle. It's not just the resentment that's quietly brewed inside me over the years with my mother, but a lifetime of others' perceptions that fuels my fury. My new therapist will have a field day at our session next week.

"I will not apologize for wanting what's best for you... For getting experts to help you. That's my job as a mother." Her water-logged tone is fierce.

"What about just loving me as I am, rather than for what I'm not?"

"I know how fucking amazing you are."

My frustrated pacing ceases with her forceful protest. Mom isn't a demure "get my smelling salts" kind of woman, but she's not prone to cursing. They only get pulled out when the Buffalo Sabres lose or if she's angry, *really angry*.

"If I'm so amazing, then why ship me off to California?" I hiss.

"That's not what I—"

"It fucking is. You let your teenage daughter move across the country without you and never came to see her!"

"You wanted to go!" she shouts back.

"And you made no protest."

"You're right." A quiet quake ripples along her words. "Aunt Bea and you were so close. She was so much like your dad, and you bloomed with her. I thought it was best for you."

Forehead puckered, I glare at the phone as if it's her. "It was also good for you. It fixed the problem. I was someone else's burden."

"That's not true."

"Then why are you obsessed with me finding someone to take care of me?"

"Because I want you to have what I had with your father...and what I have with Charlie. It took me a few frogs to find my second chance for a happy ending after your dad died." There's no mistaking the sad wistfulness in her words.

I lean against the wall. "A relationship isn't a happy ending."

"True, but it makes *that* happy ending so much sweeter." She releases a contented sigh. "My desire for you to have someone has nothing to do with your disability, and I'm sorry I've made you feel like it does."

"It isn't just your insistence on me finding someone, but how you always focus on my eyesight."

"I won't apologize for wanting you to have everything, including your vision." She sniffles.

"I have my vision, it's just different than yours." Eyes closed, I slosh out a breath.

"And it works a lot better than mine, as you said mine is the impaired one."

"We just see things differently."

"When you were first diagnosed and the doctor said you'd lose your eyesight, all I could think is that you were so little and already lost so much. Your dad. Now, your eyesight. Perhaps, I was a little zealous in compensating that loss."

I scoff.

"Ok...*a lot* zealous." She sighs. "I don't want this to be our relationship. For you to resent me for making you feel like a burden because of my actions."

"Neither do I." I swallow down that thick lump clustered in my throat.

"That's a start."

"Where do we go from here?" Opening my eyes, I push up my glasses and dash away a few escaped tears.

"With a trip. How about Charlie and I come see you." She clears her throat. "It's long overdue. We can talk more... Figure it out, together."

"Alright," I say, the word slow and hesitant.

It's not that I don't want to move forward with my

mother, but I know a lifetime of emotions knotted up in a strained relationship won't be resolved in one call. I want the type of relationship with my mother where anxiety doesn't gnarl inside me each time she calls. The type where I am her daughter to just be with, rather than a problem to solve.

"I'm glad you're open to this," she murmurs.

GB jumps up with a bark at the doorbell.

"Someone's here. Let's chat this weekend. Figure things out.

"I'd like that."

Saying goodbye, I hang up. With a quick wipe of my face, I stride to the door. GB trots beside me, his nails clicking against the floor.

"Door manners," I coo, scratching at his head as he sits beside me. GB may not always listen to Rowan, but he's a perfect little gentleman for me, unless food is involved and then he's an adorable monster.

"Hey, Pen, it's Wes."

I open the door to find him on the porch, a pink pastry box in his hand. The emotions from the call with my mother are replaced by a giant grin. Wes's velvety baritone is utterly distinct, allowing me to recognize his voice, but I adore how every time he greets me, he identifies who he is, so there's no mistake.

"This is for you." He opens the box.

"Is that…"

"A baklava croissant from Bread."

Bouncing on my feet, I take the box and gesture for him to come in. "So sweet… but you're going to have to help me eat this. Did you come all the way out here just to bring me this?"

"Nope." His tone is teasingly playful, like a child who knows a secret.

My eyebrow arches. "What shenanigans are you up to?"

"Being the *best* damn best friend ever." He pulls out his phone. "I have a message for you."

"Hey, luv." Rowan's low timbre drifts from the phone's speaker. "I promised my girl I'd take her out tonight, and I always keep my promises. Wes is here to take you for some pampering before he brings you back for our date tonight. I know you hate not having all the details and you can be mad at me later for that, after I spoil you, of course."

The promise in the almost rumbly way he says "spoil you" zings right to my core.

"But I will let you know that everywhere you'll be going is someplace you know very well. See you soon, luv." There's an unmistakable grin in his voice.

"Alright, gorgeous. Let's go." Wes offers his arm and I take it.

While surprises aren't my fave, a girl could get used to this. Wes first delivers me to Amarpreet's, my favorite day spa in town, for a pedicure and a blowout. Just as the stylist is putting the finishing touches on the loose waves she's styled my auburn hair in, JoJo appears.

"What are you doing here?" I blink.

She holds up a large shopping bag and points to my body. "You don't think you're going to wear *that* on your date, do you?"

True. Yoga pants and a tank top aren't my standard date night outfit. Though I'm pretty sure I could show up in one of the flannel *Little House on the Prairie* style nightgowns Aunt Bea used to wear and Rowan would still find me attractive.

In the changing room at Amarpreet's, JoJo helps me with the sexy red lace strapless bra that matches the barely-there panties. Rowan may have paid for this, but this selection is pure JoJo.

Dolled up, I stand in front of the mirror. A red satin dress hugs my breasts and hips and the sweetheart neckline accentuates my ample cleavage, thanks to the bra's gravity-defying push-up power.

"I would bang you so hard," JoJo purrs, patting my behind.

"I can't believe Rowan roped you all into whatever he's planning." I bend and slip on the red kitten-heeled shoes JoJo brought with the outfit.

"Of course. You deserve all the sweet stuff. Not just after the dog bite but after everything with Alex. I know this summer has been a mix of the amazing and not-so-amazing." JoJo takes my folded, discarded clothes and slides them into the shopping bag atop the bench in front of the lockers for patrons.

"Rowan's plan… This is just all so much."

"Sweets, it's never too much when you love someone. Rowan loves you. We love you."

A satisfying sensation cocoons me. This amount of love is like a decadent dessert. It's sweet and delicious, but I'm scared too much will churn in my belly. So much of the foundation for my understanding of love was built by my mother. Even with our strained relationship, I know she loves me. We're going to forge a new path, but for so long her love had been focused on fixing and taking care of me.

My friends and Rowan's love envelops me in the knowledge that, though they may take care of me, they love me as I am. Still that foundation is strong. An uneasiness creeps up my spine, but I smooth it away with each caress of my palm over the dress's smooth fabric.

"Hey." JoJo moves up beside me, placing her palm on my shoulder. "What's going on there?"

"Just trying to figure out where the date is. You know me, I like all the details," I say, hoping the lie isn't evident.

"So, we're just going to pretend you're not freaking out about something?"

Groaning, I toss my head back. "Why am I friends with a filter-less social worker?"

"Because I'm fabulous." She shimmies her hips. "But since you were attacked by a dog, I'll give you a get out of being social worked free card. Though, I will remind you it's far healthier to process things. Your choice; emotional health" … she lifts her right hand… "or denial." She lifts her left hand.

"Denial, please. This dress is far too pretty to be upset in."

"Fine." She sighs. "Can we at least talk about what sexy business you have in store for your man tonight?"

"If we can talk about *why* you haven't read Gillian's letter?" I challenge, waggling my eyebrows.

She points her pink-tipped finger. "If we're not processing your stuff, we're certainly not processing mine."

"Why, Ms. JoJo… are you now swimming in denial river?"

"I'm a social worker, we're in everyone else's shit so we don't have time to deal with our own." She laughs. "Now, let's get you to your man."

Entering the house, my heels click against the hardwood floor. JoJo and Wes dropped me off saying my date would meet me inside to escort me to the final location for the night. A blended aroma of vanilla, cinnamon, and chocolate fills the room. The quiet hum of an acoustic guitar drifts in through the open windows.

"Rowan?" I call, stepping further into the living room from the foyer.

"Hey, luv," he greets me.

The breath wooshes out of me. At the edge of the kitchen island, Rowan leans in a dark suit. GB, in a silver bow tie, sits beside him, his head tilting between us.

"You look... Wow. Just, wow."

"Not nearly as gorgeous as you," he murmurs, closing the distance between us. His big hands come to my hips and pull me against him.

"What *you* do to suits," I purr, running my uninjured hand along his muscular arm, taking in how the fabric hugs his defined physique. "You have to wear a suit before and after all your games, right?"

His hands trail up my body and swipe across my wicked grin. "Something tells me, you're going to enjoy the hockey season."

"*So much.*" I bat my lashes. "Where are we going for our date?"

"Follow me." Threading his fingers between mine, he guides me towards the patio door.

Stepping out, I gape. Strings of lights zigzag above us and wrap around almost every surface. The back garden radiates in white light, allowing me to take in everything.

"What is this?" My cheeks almost hurt from the intensity of my smile.

"I wanted to take you somewhere that you'd feel comfortable to get around without Cane Austen. I got Gillian to make all your favorites." He motions to the food-laden patio table. "It's not the taking you out that I planned, but technically we're outside, so I figured this counts. I hope this is ok."

"It's *so* ok." My mouth meets his.

The first few chords of a slow version of "I Wanna Dance with Somebody Who Loves Me" begin to play, pulling my attention away from Rowan. My gaze falls onto a man, an acoustic guitar in his hand, tucked into the backyard's corner.

"Hey, Pen," the man says as he continues to strum his guitar, his familiar voice tickles my memory.

"Harley?" Blinking, my eyes jump between Harley and Rowan.

"I called in a favor." His voice is filled with amusement.

"You flew Harley in to play a private concert for us?"

"Michigan Ed Sheeran has grown on me." A smirk punctuates his tone. "Dance with me, please?"

"Yes."

Rowan leads us down the two steps from the patio to the little brick walk that cuts across the center of the small yard. In the middle, beneath the twinkling lights, he holds me close. His fresh scent melds with jasmine from the garden and the cool ocean breeze. Looping my arms around his neck, I nuzzle into his collarbone. His palms rest at the small of my back. There's something perfect about the way we fit together.

"I remember the first time we danced." His fingers rub lazy circles against my back. "From that moment, it was clear I was always meant to dance with you," he says softly.

"I love you so much," I whisper.

"As big as the moon."

My head tips up, a chuckle escaping. "What does that mean?"

"Dad would say to Mam that his love for her was as big as the moon. It always seemed a little cheesy, but I don't mind being cheesy with, or for, you."

"As big as the moon." Rising to my tiptoes, I press my smile to his.

After our dessert-only dinner and more dancing, Harley leaves. Rowan scoops up the platters of treats and returns them to the kitchen. GB snores on the couch. Plates clank as Rowan puts the leftover brownies, cookies, and cheesecake away. Leaning against the counter, I soak into the domesticity of this.

In such a short period, this has become my life. Not the

surprise romantic evening with an impromptu concert and decadent sweet-filled dinner, but one with this man. Going to bed together. Waking up together. Just doing life together.

"Rowan—" The stampede of my heart almost drowns out his name. "Do you want to move in with me?"

He turns and stares at me, a Tupperware container half-filled with cookies in his hand.

"You're here all the time and…" Raking my teeth against my bottom lip, I huff a breath. "What am I doing? It's too soon. I'm sor—"

"Not too soon," he cuts in, his words rushed and breathless. "Yes."

"*Yes?*"

"Yes!" He places the container down and rushes to me, arms wrapping around my body.

"You don't think it's too soon?" The question is partly to make sure he's sure and also to reassure myself. Despite the anxiety pulsing along my nerve endings, a calmness settles over me.

"Luv, I've been ready to move in since our first date, so as far as I'm concerned this isn't soon enough."

A loud giggle escapes. "You're ridiculous."

"Only for you."

I grin. "Ditto."

"Now if you don't mind, I need to properly celebrate this occasion." He spins me, pressing me against the wall. With a nip to my lips, he slides up the dress's skirt.

"Rowan," I moan as his mouth drags down my neck. "I like your way of celebrating."

He traces kisses down my body. Kneeling before me, he looks up, the light catching his eyes. His stare almost caresses me like worshipping hands. With a slow teasing movement, he drags down my barely-there underwear.

"Tripping hazard," he says, shoving them into his pocket.

My laugh is stolen by a breathy moan as he nips and soothes with kisses along my inner thighs. Gripping me, he hooks both my legs over his shoulders and inhales deep at my core.

"So goddamn sweet." His pleased groan rumbles against my bare center before he takes his first lick.

Despite having had me many times, somehow each time he devours me as if he's never tasted nor will ever consume anything so good again. His tongue laps against me like a thirsty man, drinking up every last bit of my pleasure.

"Oh god!" I cry, my fingers yanking at his thick dark hair.

Body still trembling, he lowers my shaky legs to the ground. But they're not there long. Within seconds, he unzips and pushes down his pants and boxers. He hoists me up, my legs wrapping around him. Pressed against the wall, he drives into me.

"Christ," he groans, moving inside me. "It's like this sweet little pussy was made just for me."

"It is... I am."

"And I'm made for you... Only you." His fingers bite into my hips and he raises me higher on him, thrusting up hard and deep.

Body taut, I cling to Rowan as he fucks me with almost relentless but somehow indulgent drives. He rasps sweet praises in his sexy Irish lilt about how good I feel and what a good girl I am. The tension builds at my center.

"Ohhh," I whine.

"I got you, luv." His fingers move between us and stroke my clit.

"Yes!" Shuddering, I slump against him.

His movements turn fast and uncoordinated as he chases his release. "Fuck!" he cries, spilling into me.

For a moment we remain there. Me tight against the wall. Him holding me. Our ragged breaths are the only sound.

"Oh my god, do you think GB saw that?" I say breathlessly.

His head twists. "Yep."

"We're terrible dog parents."

Laughing, he cups my cheek. "I love you, so much."

"As big as the moon."

CHAPTER TWENTY-EIGHT

An I in Team?
Rowan

"Rowan," Pen whimpers, her head falling back against my shoulder.

The way she says my name as she falls apart is the most addictive sound in the world. Reminiscent of a favorite song, her lyrical mules and whines sing to me.

With lazy circles, I stroke between her legs, pink shading her white skin, and a gentle shake rolling over her. Tucked against my chest, my other hand cups one plump breast, tweaking the hard peak.

"God, I love Saturdays," I murmur and bite gently on her earlobe. "I get to take my time with you—" I pinch her nipple and apply just a little more pressure to her clit. "—to enjoy every inch of you."

"God!" she cries, her body seizes with relief.

There's never a moment when Pen isn't beautiful to me. After she first wakes, her long hair tumbling from her pony-tail. After yoga class with JoJo, sweat glistening on every inch of her. Lounging with GB, a pair of old leggings and one of my too-big-for-her T-shirts. A new red dress like she wore last night when she asked me to move in. Right now, a sated smile and blush painted across her cheeks, as she lays against me.

While moving in together doesn't seem to change anything, as I've practically moved in over the last two months, it somehow changes everything. Now, this is our home, not Pen's place.

This may seem crazy to anyone on the outside looking in. Technically we've only been together for two months. Still, this is right. The calm that settles over me with her in my arms solidifies that I am exactly where I'm supposed to be.

"What are you thinking?" she whispers, caressing along my forearm.

"About us living together."

"Are you having second thoughts?"

I kiss below her ear. "No."

"It would make sense. It's a huge commitment."

"Luv, I've pretty much moved in already."

"But this makes it official." She shifts, rolling over to face me, and winces after bumping her still-injured hand. "Like what does you moving in look like?"

"I'd imagine it looks like what it currently does, but with more of my stuff here."

"We should probably talk about household management stuff."

"Like finances?"

"No...well, yes—" her head tilts. "I don't know. The house is paid for, thanks to Aunt Bea, so it's just utilities and taxes to worry about. I wouldn't expect you to pay anything. Guess I'm thinking more about chores and how the house is set up. Things like that. I want you to feel like this is *our* home."

"First, I will contribute to the household finances."

Her body goes rigid, tension coiling her muscles. "I don't need you to pay for me."

"I know that." I kiss her temple. "But we're a team, so fifty/fifty?"

She nods, seeming to mull that over before she agrees. "Fifty/fifty."

"The rest we can figure out over the week. We can discuss chores and what I should bring from my condo."

Her face scrunches. "Are you going to want to decorate with neon light beer signs?"

A laugh belts out of me. "Pen, you've been to my condo, have you noticed lit beer signs?"

"Maybe you hid them as a ploy to lure me into the delusion that you don't have terrible taste."

"I have great taste," I protest, tickling her.

Giggling, she wiggles against me. "Truce!"

I kiss her.

"You do have excellent taste, you chose me." That big smile beams up at me.

"Luv, I had no choice when it came to you." It's not a line, it's the goddamn truth. From the moment that smile slammed into me at the airport, I was done... I was hers.

"That line just earned you a treat." Her uninjured hand skates down my stomach.

"We need to shower and head out for your doctor's appointment."

Today, Pen's provider will examine her hand to make sure it's healing. If it appears that her wounds are closing, they'll remove the splint. She'll still have a week or so for her hand to properly heal, but the splint removal will give her more dexterity with her hand, regaining the ability to type, use her cane, and do other things.

"Not even one day living together and the magic is already gone," she quips and sits up.

"Tell my fingers that," I say wryly, slipping the fingers, still coated in her, into my mouth.

"Who needs a right hand?" she pants, crawling atop me.

WE WERE ONLY FIVE MINUTES LATE FOR PEN'S APPOINTMENT. Not that it matters since we're still waiting. Though I'm not complaining. Pen's head rests on my shoulder, my arm looped around her, as one end of our earbuds is in her ear and the other in mine. We're listening to the climactic end of our latest buddy read, a hockey romance. She finds it endlessly entertaining to listen to me grumble about all the things the writer gets wrong. Still, a smile stretches across my face at the cliched grand gesture.

"Aw, she told him they're pregnant with a baby-sized jersey," Pen gushes at the book's epilogue.

My stare skips around the room. A toddler, tiny hands clutching a stuffed llama, bounces on what I assume is his dad's knee. Their brown eyes and broad smiles are nearly identical.

The vision of a little boy with Pen's auburn hair, my green eyes, and chipmunk cheeks, sitting on my lap pluses joy inside me. After my mother's comments about one day being a Gran during our Toronto trip, Pen and I have discussed children. We both want a family, but not for a few years. Pen wants to be more secure in her career before we add the title of mom to the many roles she already plays.

"Penelope Meadows," the nurse calls.

Slipping the earbud from her ear and handing it to me, Pen rises. "Ready?" She reaches out her uninjured hand to me.

Nodding, my palm envelops hers. "Yep."

A contented sensation twines around me with each step we take, our hands clasped. In Pen's books, there have been romantic gestures similar to what I did last night. This is the simple, the everyday things that aren't written about by authors. It's just a doctor's appointment. Still, the moment she reached out her hand, inviting me to come into the room with her, almost knocked the air out of me. I'm her teammate, and she's mine.

"This is closing up nicely." Dr. Alvarez grins, warmth glinting in her hazel eyes.

"Really?" Pen winces as Dr. Alvarez prods at her injured hand, clear fluid oozing from the wounds.

I've seen worse in my years of playing hockey. Broken bones. Bloodied noses. Knocked out teeth. Cut calves after a skate blade slices into a player's leg. Still seeing the woman I love, her hand raw, red, and oozing…

"You going to be okay there, tall and dreamy?" Dr. Alvarez quips, a dark eyebrow quirking.

"Yup." I cough, shifting in the plastic chair.

"We're going to remove the splint. I'll have the nurse clean you up and re-bandage. He'll go over instructions about keeping it clean and letting it breathe when you're not out and about. It should take about a week or so before you regain full function of the hand."

"No more splint?" Pen vibrates with excitement.

"No more splint." Dr. Alvarez rises and pulls off her gloves.

"Freedom!" Pen cheers in a terrible *Braveheart* impression, making me and the doctor laugh.

As we leave the clinic, Pen's grin can't be contained. She unfolds Cane Austen and almost coos to it. "I've missed you! Have you missed me?"

To celebrate we head to Bread. Saturday wouldn't be Saturday without a visit to Bread. It will still be a few days before Pen is back to full use of her hand, but to see her big smile, even with the little winces as she uses her cane, my chest fills with happiness.

"Pen! Rowan!" Jela chirps, greeting us at the hostess stand in front of Bread.

Several waiting customers tip their heads toward us. A few whisper and nudge each other. We're mostly ignored by the regulars who see us each week, but every now and then someone recognizes us. For the most part, people leave us alone, but sometimes they approach, gawk, or take a sneaky photo.

"Oh my gosh, Pen! What happened here?" Jela points to Pen's bandaged hand.

"Bar brawl. You should see the other guy," Pen deadpans.

"I bet you swatted them with Cane Austen," Jela teases, a crooked smile covering her face. "Seriously, what happened?" She motions to our usual table.

I pull out Pen's chair and she sits. "I was attacked by a dog."

Eyes the size of saucers, Jela gasps. "What?!"

Jela's shocked breaths and startled *oh no's* grow louder with each detail of Pen's story, one branded into me. That night with her cocooned in my arms, she re-lived it. Somehow Jela's horrified expression to Pen's retelling punctuates how scary it was. There's no embellishment like one of Finn's stories. But the gentle shake in her hand as she speaks illustrates her fear. That fear gnarls itself inside me.

This whole situation is an unfortunate happenstance, as Finn put it. Just the wrong place at the wrong time. All of it made worse by Pen overhearing her bosses discuss her capability. The idea of her going back to work on Monday churns in my stomach.

Pen assures me that this isn't everyone at the hospital, but she's also shared that this is par for the course, just something she deals with. It pisses me off, despite my understanding. God, I want to storm in there, but as Sasha has warned me, "You can't fight her battles for her."

The whole thing slipped out Friday morning when Sasha appeared at the rink with a reporter doing a spotlight on Eli. I told her about what happened to Pen, the dog bite and the asshole comments. Greg faces similar things and Sasha remains supportive of what he wants to do, no matter how much she wants to go scorched earth on anyone who hurts the people she loves. As sweet as Sasha is, she and I have that in common.

"Good thing you've got handsome here to take care of you," Jela says, placing a hand on my shoulder and offering a gentle squeeze.

"Yup." A tight smile anchors Pen's expression.

"The usual?"

"Yup."

As Jela saunters away to put in our order, I reach across the table and take Pen's hand. "You think you'll feel up to a walk on the pier after lunch?"

It's only been two days, and I know she craves a return to normalcy. I want to give that to her. These battles are Pen's to fight, I know that. It doesn't mean I won't help where I can. This temporary injury chafes against her independent nature. It's a struggle to find balance with my desire to protect her without clipping her wings. Though, she'd never let anyone clip them. Everyone who tries fails. This woman is a spitfire and I fucking love that about her.

"Uncle Rowan!" Damon hoots, his tiny body running towards our table.

My eyebrows shoot up.

Sasha and Greg follow, big smiles on their faces.

"What are you doing here?" I stand up. "Sasha, Greg, and—"

Before I can say Damon's name, he's bypassed me and jumped into Pen's arms squealing, "Aunt Pen!"

Guess I'm no longer the favorite. I chuckle.

"Damon. Pen's hand, remember," Sasha tuts, tenderness shimmers in her eyes.

"Oops. Sorry, Aunt Pen."

She kisses the top of his head. "It's all good. You didn't hurt me."

"How are you?" Sasha bends, kissing Pen's cheek.

Pen raises her hand. "Good. It will be all healed up in a week or so. I'm already back to using my cane."

"What are you guys doing here?" I rub at my nape.

"You two talk about this place all the time, so we thought we'd check it out," Greg says.

"You drove all the way from Sherman Oaks for a croissant?" My eyebrow quirks.

"It is a *really* good croissant," Pen quips.

"We also wanted to see Pen and bring her this." Sasha holds out a glittery giftbag.

"How'd you know we'd be here?" A crease lines my forehead.

"I have tracking devices on all my clients." Greg's hazel eyes lock on mine, a steely expression on his face.

"Daddy saw you two walking to the restaurant as we were driving towards Aunt Pen's place." Damon giggles.

"Kid, I was trying to be intimidating." Greg sighs.

The staff pushes the table next to us over allowing the five of us to sit together. We share two croissants before eating our meals. Pen and Greg chatter on about the World War Two podcast they're both obsessed with. Damon drinks milk out of a coffee cup to mimic the adults with our coffees and teas. Since the MVP event, Pen's been volunteering at several Foundation events with Sasha. We've also spent more social time with Sasha, Greg, and Damon.

"I have to admit something… We didn't just come to bring you a gift," Sasha says, a sheepish expression in place.

Pen's head tilts, a furrow forming on her forehead.

"Greg and I want to offer you a job with the MVP Foundation. As Assistant Foundation Director. Your professional experience and passion for this work make you the ideal candidate."

It makes sense. The MVP Foundation aligns with Pen's platform. Besides volunteering with them, she and Sasha are even meeting with the Bobcats about an adaptive sports night at a game this season. Turns out, Madeline Jacobson, the team's owner, isn't all talk. She's personally met with Pen and Sasha to discuss the event, and what changes would be needed to make the arena more accessible.

"Pen would be a great fit," I say tentatively, my gaze moving to her.

Greg taps his thick fingers against the table's wrought iron surface. "Not to mention your public persona. We won't pretend that isn't appealing."

Sasha shoots Greg a glare.

"What?" He shrugs. "I don't blow smoke up anyone's ass."

"Daddy swore," Damon whispers, his hands covering his big smile.

Pen blinks. "I'm honored, but I have a job."

"Hear us out. We can offer you twenty percent more in annual salary compared to what you're paid at the hospital." Greg leans in like a cat ready to pounce on a helpless mouse.

It's his typical position in negotiations. He's assessing when to strike to get just what he wants. Only Pen is *no* mouse. Even if a big part of me roots for him to win this battle, I know my girl.

"How do you know how much I make?"

Greg smirks. "It's my job to know everything."

"Ego much?" Sasha rolls her eyes before continuing,

"There are other perks. A flexible schedule. Also, most of the work you'll do can be done remotely, so you can work from home or even from hotel rooms when someone is traveling for away games." She winks.

"I won't be traveling with Rowan. He needs to focus on the game. Also, the players are required to stay with each other. Plus—"

"Plus, no more random dogs to contend with walking from the bus," Greg interjects, a wry grin etched across his face.

Pen nods.

Greg goes on, "And you'd work for an organization that truly understands what you bring to the table... Everything you're capable of doing."

Pen's lips purse.

Sasha tosses Greg another death glare.

He flashes a crooked *oops* smile back at her.

Uneasiness braids in my stomach. I shift in my seat, my gaze dropping to Pen.

Her mouth is a firm line as she nods. Pen's left hand slides from the table's surface to her lap and grips the fabric of her skirt. Her eyes are intense as they remain fixed on Sasha as she goes on.

"Don't answer right now." Sasha reaches out and squeezes Pen's forearm. "Think about it this week. Talk to Rowan." She tips her head towards me as if we're conspirators in this, in whatever plan she and Greg have hatched.

"You've given me a lot to think about." Pen picks up her mug and takes a long sip of tea.

Pen is the picture of politeness. All smiles and warm conversation throughout the remainder of breakfast. But I notice the way her hands curl around the mug's handle. The shallowness in her laughter. How her eyes don't meet mine.

Later as we say goodbye and walk away from Bread, I

clear my throat. "Did you still want to go to the pier?" I already know the answer.

"I'd like to go home, please."

"Okay."

The walk back is quiet, though the thick tension between us roars.

"I swear I didn't know they were going to do that," I say as we reach the front door.

"You didn't seem that shocked when you said I'd be perfect for the job," Pen grumbles, unlocking the door, she pushes it open. GB runs up to greet us.

"I *was* surprised, but that doesn't change the fact that you'd be a good fit." I follow her in.

"Good fit for whom?" She spins, lightning flashing in her eyes.

"What does that mean?"

"Not three days after this—" she raises her bandaged hand. "—and I tell you about what Nelson and Cortes say, Greg and Sasha just happen to show up at Bread to offer me a job." She slams Cane Austen into the corner by the front door and storms towards the living room.

A furrow notches my forehead. "I had no idea they were going to do that."

Whirling, she faces me. "But you did talk?"

"I..." Sighing, I slump against the entryway between the foyer and living room. "...I did. It all came out Friday when Sasha was at the arena. I was just sharing with a friend my concern over what happened to you, nothing more."

"I'm sorry." Her expression softens. "I just don't like to feel ambushed."

I cross the small distance between us and place my hands on her bare arms. "I know and I'd never do that. It hurts that you'd even think that."

"I'm so sorry... I don't think that... I was just caught off guard and..."

"It's okay." I lean in to kiss her, but she places her hand on my chest and stops me.

Her gaze locks on my face. "But you'd like me to take the job?"

The question climbs down my throat and sloshes in my stomach. It's a test that I know I'm going to fail. "I won't lie to you... Yes."

With a bob of her throat, she nods.

My fingers skim her silken skin. "It is a good offer. You'd be doing the work you love with people who respect you."

"With *your* agent and publicist's foundation." She glares.

"It's not like that. They are doing this because of you, not—"

"They're doing it for you." She lets out a humorless laugh and pulls away from me.

I blow out a breath, releasing a little of my frustration about the situation. "Sasha and Greg aren't going to hand over a position in the foundation they love just because you're my girlfriend. Knowing them, they'd had the idea prior to this and seized this opportunity. As good-natured as Sasha is, she's as strategic as her husband. They are doing this to get you to work with them, not for my benefit."

"But it does benefit you. You get to know that I'm taken care of." She tosses up her arms and stomps towards the kitchen, GB trotting behind her.

"What's wrong with that? Of course, I want you taken care of." I rake my hands into my hair.

"I can take care of myself," she snaps back.

"That's not in question."

"You just said you wanted to take care of me," she shouts.

"Yes! We're a team. Though sometimes I think that only

351

applies when *you* want to take care of me. Like you did with Landon and Gillian."

"Landon?"

"I know you spoke to Liv. That you convinced her to say something to her father."

"It's not the same," she scoffs.

"Why?"

"You know why," she hisses.

"That's bullshit and you know it." My heart thuds loudly in my chest. "I love you. It has nothing to do with me thinking you can't take care of yourself. I'm not Alex. I'm not your mom," I shout back.

"I know you're not them." She grips the counter's edge.

"Do you?" My voice is hoarse.

"Yes!"

"Maybe it's easier to assign that role to me than yourself."

"Excuse me?" She freezes, hurt swimming in her eyes.

God, I want to fold her into my arms and assure her that all will be okay, that I'd not meant what I said, but it's the truth. There's a tightrope that I walk between supporting Pen's independence and my desire to take care of the woman I love. Only, there's no net below to catch me if I stumble.

"You've made me eat my carrots a few times, even though it's the same behavior you hate about your mother... And I love that about you. That you push me, but it can't be one-sided. We're either a team or we're not."

"I'm not like my mother," she hisses.

"I think you're more like her than you think."

"With my mother it's always been about fixing me, about what she feels is best for me. It's not about what I want. She doesn't work with me. Not like us. We're a team!" She gestures between us.

"We weren't at that table. The moment Sasha and Greg

offered you the job, you pulled away from me. You assumed I'd orchestrated this."

"I know you didn't do that. I'm sorry I went there. It's something I'm working on with my therapist." She lets out a hard breath.

"I know you are, luv," I rasp, my stare locks with hers. "I know it's hard for you to trust that someone's love and care for you isn't about fixing you. You lost your dad—"

"My dad's death has nothing to do with this."

"But it does—" I step forward and place my hands on her shoulders "—You lost him and you were left with a mom that made you feel like something to fix, rather than someone to love. Then Aunt Bea died.".

"What does Aunt Bea have to do with any of this?"

"With her, for the first time, you were secure to be needed and to need. She loved you just as you are, as do I. You're not scared that I'll take care of you, you're terrified you'll get used to it, and I'll leave you like Aunt Bea did."

She flinches.

"That's why you really push against me." I cup her cheek.

"She has nothing to do with this."

"But she does. It's not just the people who clip our wings that keep us in cages. For so long, she was the most important person in your world. As independent as you are, you depended on her for so much. All the things I depend on you for. Love. Support. Team. Then she left you, and you didn't have those things anymore. Trina and JoJo may be your sisters in all the ways that matter, but I don't think you have the relationship with them that you had with your Aunt Bea, or with me, despite you sometimes pulling away."

"I don't pull away. I asked you to move in."

"Yeah, and it's a huge step for you but your fear is still fighting your heart. You bristled at the idea of me paying for anything. You're scared. It's why you don't always tell me things, like Alex and the flowers or the job offer. I know that fear makes you think you have to handle these things on your own, we can deal with things together. Just let us really be the team you say we are. For real, not just when you want to take care of me."

She yanks away from me. "I think you should go home."

"This is my home, *our* home."

She says nothing, just stares.

"Let's talk about this." I step towards her.

She holds up her palm. "Let me be alone with this."

"But you don't have to be. Please, let us be a team. I know it's scary, but together we can do scary things. We already have."

"I want to be alone."

"We—"

"You said you'd never make me beg." Iciness coats her voice.

Pain radiates in my chest as if she'd slammed her fist into it. "Do you really want me to go?"

"Yes." Her lips quiver, but fierce eyes lock with mine.

"Fine. Come on GB."

CHAPTER TWENTY-NINE

Gone
Pen

The clack of GB's nails against the hardwood as he follows Rowan out echoes as the front door snicks shut. Now, the house is quiet, other than the thump of my heart.

Rowan's words and his fresh scent lingers in the air. A plush dog bed, tucked in the living room's corner, lies empty except for a discarded chew toy. Just a few steps from the bed is a bookshelf filled with Aunt Bea's books and framed pictures from our many adventures. They're all gone, but still here.

Is he right? The same emptiness that had engulfed me after Aunt Bea died swirls around me. She wasn't my world, but the person that navigated it with me. Since her death, the thought of traversing it with anyone else wasn't a reality, until Rowan.

This isn't goodbye with Rowan. A breakup over a single fight is silly. If that happens, we have no business being in a relationship with anyone, let alone with each other. Still, I know this is more than just a single fight. It isn't a lone squall in an otherwise calm sea.

Pressed against the wall, I slide down to the floor. Its coolness caresses the backs of my bare legs. I bend my knees and bury my face on them.

A loud knock halts the storm of tears. Dashing them away, I rise. My pulse thuds as I run to the door.

"Ro—"

"Hi, honey."

"Mom?" My brow wrinkles. "What are you doing here?"

"We said we'd talk this weekend."

I gape. "On the phone."

She makes a dismissive gesture. "Plus, we said the next step was a trip. Charlie's with me, but I sent him to explore the neighborhood, so we could chat."

In nine years, she's never been here. Not for any of my graduations. Not for Aunt Bea's funeral. Not even for a random vacation.

"May I come in?" Her tone is tentative but hopeful.

Without fully processing that she's at my door, I step aside and motion her in. "I assumed when you said a trip, it would be something we'd plan, together."

She stands in the foyer and shifts from foot to foot. "I didn't want to wait to rebuild with you. It's already been too long. Also, there was a tiny bit of me worried that chat this weekend wouldn't happen, so I—"

"Decided you knew what was best for me again." My mouth purses.

"This is the behavior that you've been talking about." She rubs at her temples.

"It is... I know you mean well, but you can't just decide what's best for me, for us. This isn't the relationship I want with you."

The irony of my words isn't lost on me. In this argument, I am Rowan, which means in the other I was my mother.

She steps closer. "But you do want a relationship with me?"

"That's all I've ever wanted… But not one like this."

"What kind do you want?"

"One where we're a team. Like what I had with Aunt Bea and what I want with Rowan." My voice cracks with the ache that twinges in my chest.

"I want that too." She wrings her hands.

"We can't just want that kind of relationship. We have to make it, together."

"Alright. How do we start?" Hope fills her question.

"We talk. We ask each other what we want, and we actually listen… Me included." Hot tears roll down my cheeks, knowing this is what Rowan wants. For us to be a team, but instead I pushed him away.

"Honey, I'm so sorry, please don't cry…" She places her hands on my shoulders.

"It's not you." I swipe at my face.

"Is it this?" She reaches and grasps my right arm. "Are you in a lot of pain? This looks bad."

"It's fine." I pull my arm away.

She raises her hands. "I know… I know, you don't need anyone's help." Her words push into me like a dagger.

"I do need people," I croak.

"We all need people, the *right* people," Mom says, a shake in her voice.

My gaze meets hers.

"I know I haven't been the right people for…well most of your life."

"Mom."

"It's true. I push what I think is best for you without considering your wants. I am sorry for that, but I'm a parent.

357

I'll always want the best. Please know that my desire for your eyesight to be fixed doesn't mean I think *you* need to be fixed."

"What if I'm fine with my vision as it is?"

"That's what you want? What you need?"

"Yes."

She heaves a long sigh. "Then I'll stop."

"Thank you."

Her arms wrap around me, pulling me into a tight hug. A sweet lavender scent from her perfume and the soothing strokes of her palms against my back eased the tension spooled tight in my muscles. Today is the first step of many. I don't doubt a future of missteps and wrong turns, but for the first time ever I'm hopeful that we're in this together.

After a few moments, I pull away. Both of us are swiping at our faces.

"Knock, knock," Charlie greets us, slipping through the still open front door.

"I thought you were going to grab a coffee in town?" Mom twists to face him.

Charlie pats his back pocket. "Hard to do when my wallet is still in your purse."

"If you'd use that fanny pack I bought you, this wouldn't keep happening," she tuts with a cheeky lilt as she digs into her bag.

He tips his head to me. "Hey, Pen."

"Hey, Charlie." I wave.

"Whose black BMW X5 M is parked in your driveway?" He lets out an impressed whistle. "It's a beauty."

"Rowan's." My eyes drag to the ajar front door. "Wait, his car is still here?"

Grabbing my cane, I slip past Charlie, my pulse roaring, and run down the two short steps. Rowan's SUV remains parked in the driveway.

"He's not gone," I murmur to myself.

"Is everything okay?" Mom calls from where she stands by the front door.

"Yes and no," I breathe.

"What happened?" Her sandals slap against the brick steps as she descends.

That familiar impulse to deal with this on my own ignites, but I snuff it out. The path I'll traverse with my mother and the one I want with Rowan means pushing past the fear that told me to do it on my own.

"We may be more alike than I thought." I blow out a hard breath. "Like you I did what I thought was best for him."

She nods.

"All he wants is for us to be a team, but I pushed him away because I'm scared to need him, to depend on him." My admission is quiet and shaky.

Her arms envelop my shoulders. "I was the same way after your dad died. It took three more husbands until I figured it out. When you truly love someone it's the most vulnerable you'll ever be and it's scary as hell."

"That it is."

"Also, vulnerability isn't your comfort zone." She leans her head against mine.

"It sure isn't." I close my eyes.

"Does the fear ever go away?"

A sharp laugh huffs out of her. "No. You just learn how to embrace it and how to share it. The right partner doesn't make it easier, but holds your hand when you do hard things."

A loud bark draws our attention. Lifting my head from my mother's shoulder, I pivot. GB scampers down the sidewalk with Rowan behind, his steps are slow and hesitant. Then he stops. At this distance, the sun's glare and his cap hide his expression.

"What do you want, honey?"

My pulse roars. "For Rowan to hold my hand."

Mom pats my bicep. "I'll be inside."

"Rowan!" I call, running towards the gate between my walkway and the sidewalk.

Before I'm able to open the gate, he's there.

Tongue lagging, GB jumps up, his front legs resting on the gate's top.

"Down, GB," Rowan commands, gently tugging him down before he swings open the gate.

"I'm so sorry." Leaning my cane against the gate, I fling myself into his arms, encircling his nape. "You were right. I was scared. I'm still scared. But I'd rather be scared with you than without you. To face these things together. I want to be a team with you, a *real* one. You take care of me, and I take care of you." I almost pant it all out as if I'm running a sprint. In so many ways, I am. I'm sprinting towards what I want, *who* I want.

"I'm scared too, but I can face anything as long as I have you at my side."

"I love you." My fingers trail up and skim across his smile.

"I love you too. For the record, I don't like arguing with you."

"Ditto." I laugh.

"Whatever you want to do about the job is your decision."

"But you want me to take it."

He sloshes a breath. "Yes. Does that make me an asshole?"

"No. It makes you honest."

"Even if I have a different opinion, I'll always support you. Please know that."

"I know." I take his cap and place it on my head. "And even if I don't always act it, I am on your team and you're on mine."

"Always."

The brightness of his expression melts away the remaining lingering tension and fear. There's much to discuss and figure out, but I know we'll do it together.

"I'm so glad you didn't go home."

His hand strokes my cheek. "Luv, I did go home."

"But you're here."

"Exactly." He nuzzles my nose with his.

I close the scant inches between us, taking his full lips into a slow embrace.

EPILOGUE

Audiobooks
Rowan
Nine Months Later

"That will be fifteen-seventy-five," the Tim Hortons clerk says, looking up from the cash register.

I reach for my wallet in my back pocket, only to have Cane Austen slam into my calf. "Ouch. Careful or you'll have to explain to Carlson why I can't play next season."

"I can take him." Pen flashes a daring smile and adjusts the brim of my Bobcats hat on her head.

Pen wearing my hat will never stop bringing me to my knees. It's almost as sexy on her as the oversize LA Bobcats Stanley Cup Championship T-shirt she wears. Another article of my clothing she's stolen from me. Though, I'd give this woman anything she asks for.

"Plus, I believe the deal was that I would be paying for everything on our celebratory trip." She hip-checks me.

For the last two weeks, we've celebrated the Bobcats'

Stanley Cup win in every room of my Hamilton house. The old tradition of escaping there by myself after the season is now replaced with my new favorite thing; escaping anywhere with Pen. Between the intense hockey season and the silver medal win in the Olympics midseason, we've only snuck in a few mini trips. Mostly a day or two at a bed and breakfast somewhere.

With Pen's role at the MVP Foundation, her flexible remote work schedule allows us to do a few more trips together this summer. Minus the week we'll be together working at MVP's summer camp. Since starting with the foundation in October, Pen's not only increased donations but expanded its programming to fund an adaptive sports league for kids in the L.A. and Orange County areas.

"GB has more likes than you." Pen snorts, enlarging a post on social media of GB, wearing a *My Daddy is a Stanley Cup Champion and All I Got Was This Shirt* T-shirt.

It's not just Pen who's the social media darling in our house. She and Wes started an account for GB to raise awareness about shelter dogs and the importance of rescuing them. He's become a bit of a local celebrity, attending events to raise money for animal causes.

"I might ask JoJo to make me one of those shirts too."

"I did enjoy the special Property of Rowan panties she made for you," I murmur in her ear and nip at the lobe.

She giggles. "Behave, we're in public."

"That didn't stop you outside the arena after we beat Toronto."

Eyes wide, she nudges my ribs. "That was a singular event due to you winning Lord Stanley's Cup."

Laughing, I pull my phone and earbuds out of my duffle. "We've got time before our flight and Finn sent me an advance audiobook copy of his upcoming release."

"Yes!" She wiggles in her seat. "God, I don't know which

brother I like more, the one who feeds my historical romance addiction or the one who just feeds me."

Warmth fills me at that. Not just seeing Pen's closeness with my brothers, but my own with Gillian. We're not as close as Finn and me, but we've formed a nice friendship. On Sundays, after boozy brunch with the bicoastal besties, Pen and I join Gillian for Sunday roast at Axel's.

"Mom will be totally jealous. She's finally caught up with the series and is dying to know about Alicia and Tom's story." Pen takes one of the earbuds and pops it in her ear.

"Did I tell you my mam and your mom are going wine tasting next week?" I put the other earbud in my ear.

"Who'd have thought our moms would hit it off."

The way our families have come together is just another way in which we fit. Even with the rightness of this relationship, we put in the work. There are difficult conversations. We argue. We get annoyed. But at the end of the day, we're a team. We tackle everything together.

"Ready?" I ask.

"Yep."

I hit play and Wes's smooth baritone filters into my ears.

A giant grin blooms on Pen's face.

"The thoughts swirl around me as the Tim Hortons cashier's disappointed gaze takes me in. Great just another person I've disappointed, I think."

"Tim Hortons?" Brow wrinkled, Pen raises her head at Wes's words.

"Then the sweetest voice breaks into my thoughts, offering to rescue me. Just as I turn to decline, her smile slams into me, stuttering my breath. The most beautiful honey eyes peer up at me through red-framed glasses..."

"Rowan, what is this?" Pen blinks rapidly.

"Our story." I grin, running my fingers along her lips.

Wes goes on to describe our first meeting. *"Love at first sight is a myth to sell romance novels, but your smile made me rethink everything. In that instance, I wasn't yet in love with you, but I was well on my way. This is just the start of our story, but now I'll turn it over to the actual Rowan and not just his handsome, amazing best friend."*

"That's my cue." I pluck the earbuds from us and turn off the audiobook.

"What?" Eyes blinking, her breath stutters.

Dropping to one knee in front of Pen, I pull out the ring I've had burning a hole in my pocket. "I realize the Buffalo Airport isn't the most romantic place to propose, but it's where our story started and it's where I want it to continue. Penelope Meadows, I want to write a very long story with you."

"Oh my god." Her hand goes to her trembling lips.

"Will you marry me?"

"Yes!" She cries, flinging herself into my arms.

We tumble backward onto the carpet in the gate's waiting area. I nearly drop the ring but hold onto it between tearful kisses. Tears that aren't just hers.

"Sorry." Her grin isn't at all apologetic.

I sit us up. Pen straddles my lap in the middle of the airport to the cheers and applause of other travelers.

Smirking, I open the ring box. "It's a Celtic knot-shaped white gold band with a blue sapphire center."

Her fingers glide along the ring. "Lovely."

I slip it on her finger.

She holds her hand up. "A perfect fit."

"Yes, we are." I lean in and capture that smile in a slow kiss, that smile that has stolen my heart every day since the first day and will continue to steal it every day more.

Thank you for reading *At First Smile.* If you'd like to explore more of my books, turn the page for a sneak peek at the first chapter of *Finding Home*, Book 1 in the Home Series

SNEAK PEEK - FINDING HOME

CHAPTER ONE

"Ah! There is nothing like staying at home,
for real comfort."
~Jane Austen, Emma

"Explain this to me like I'm four," Viet said, one dark brow arched. "You'll go to your hometown for a week for your cousin's wedding, fly back here, and then fly back again for another week for your uncle's fiftieth? All within the same month? Do I have that right?"

Willa ran a manicured finger around the rim of her glass. "Why don't you just stay in New York the entire time?"

"I can't take a month off!" Elle scoffed.

Eleanor "Elle" Davidson regretted her rare decision to leave her downtown L.A. office before seven to make happy hour with her friends, Viet Vo and Willa Andrews. Their badgering was akin to the Spanish Inquisition. Only with more rosé and less physical torture.

"Aren't you the boss?" Willa signaled the server to bring another round.

"Yes." Elle looked around as if Sloan-Whitney, the healthcare system she worked at, had secret HR spies at the bar. She bent closer and whispered, "I'm the boss bitch." And there it was… She was officially tipsy.

"Yes, queen!" Willa snapped her fingers.

"I may lose my feminist card for that one."

"More importantly, aren't you the National Director of *Virtual* Medicine? If anyone should be able to work remotely, it should be you." Viet tipped his glass toward Elle.

Willa shimmied and raised her hands in the air. "Brilliant! Would you Airbnb your place? My cousin is a visiting nurse and needs a short-term rental in August. I can guarantee he's very clean."

"What?" Elle tried to blink away the rosé fuzziness.

"Your cousin Ned? Yes, please! He's hot, despite his old man name." A pale blush swept across Viet's face.

"You're a married man." She *tsked* and then turned to Elle with a wink. "But Ned is single and hetero-leaning."

Like a modern-day version of Jane Austen's Emma Woodhouse, Willa was ever the matchmaker. Just like Emma, she was bad at it. *Really Bad.* Over the years, Elle had been subjected to a string of Willa curated meet-cutes. None of which were cute.

"I do love that Ned is a boy nurse." Elle batted her hazel eyes, the rosé warmth spreading across her limbs.

"He prefers man nurse."

"And what a man!" Viet raised his Old Fashion.

"Thank goodness he's my cousin by marriage or this would feel a little Lannister Family Rules to me," Willa joked.

"Back to my opening thesis. Elle, it makes sense. You've been trying to get your headquarters to be more open to remote work. You could pilot it." Like the highly paid corporate lawyer that he was, Viet laid out his argument.

"You just want to use your spare key to catch Ned in his underpants." Elle aimed her now empty glass at Viet.

"I think Willa may be more apt to do that as she mentions how they aren't related by blood each time his name comes up." Viet waggled his finger at Willa, who flipped him off in response.

"Besides, you *hate* flying. When we went to London last summer, you needed three glasses of wine to get on the plane. You especially hate non-direct flights. Don't you have to take two flights and a wagon train to get to Perry, New York?" Willa mocked.

It was unoriginal, but Elle gave her the finger.

"Also, Uncle Pete," Viet murmured, playing his trump card.

Damn it. Elle closed her eyes. Guilt churned in her belly.

Her best friend of eighteen years knew Elle better than anyone. Even if he didn't know all of her. Who did, after all?

He knew how important her surrogate family of Uncle Pete, his wife Janet, and their son Tobey were to Elle. A simple silver framed photo of Elle in a cap and gown beside a grinning Pete and Janet, while a smirking Tobey gave her bunny ears, was the lone family picture displayed in her condo.

Pete, Janet, and Tobey were far too important to Elle to be dealt the last fourteen years of bad excuses that she used to not visit. They deserved better.

"Ok," she whispered her defeat.

"Hand me your phone." Viet held his hand out, palm up.

"*Why?*"

Viet's forehead puckered. "Eleanor Marie Davidson."

"Oh, you got full-named." Willa laughed, sipping the fresh cocktail that had poofed into existence without Elle noticing.

Perhaps, the wine fairy would bring Elle a fresh glass to numb the dread of being forty minutes from the nearest cocktail bar for a month. More importantly, to dull the anxiety about being in a town where painful phantoms haunted each corner. How much rosé could she pack in her luggage?

"Fine," she muttered and dropped her phone into Viet's hand.

"I'm texting Uncle Pete to tell him the news."

"Wait, I need to get my boss to sign off." Elle reached for the phone.

But Viet was faster. "You're a boss bitch. You'll make it happen."

"Fine." She puffed out a breath. "Willa, let Ned know he can stay at my place."

"Oh, I texted him five minutes ago. He's pumped."

"What if Viet's emotional terrorism hadn't worked?"

"Plan B was for you to fall in love with Ned via close proximity."

"You read too many romance novels." Elle took Willa's drink from her and sipped.

Stupid alcohol. She narrowed her eyes at the cocktail, scrunched her nose, and handed it back. It was the three glasses of rosé's fault that she was doing this. At least, that's what she'd tell herself.

"No such thing! I've had some of my best orgasms thanks to Denise Williams." She fanned herself with the card-stock menu. "Anyways, I'll find you a *dream* Airbnb to live in while you're in Perry-dise. I wonder if I can find one with a hot farmer waiting for a city girl to melt his pants off with her steamy sass!"

"Check the filter options," Viet deadpanned.

"This will be more like a Stephen King novel, only Carrie returns to get doused with even more buckets of blood." Elle rested her head on the table, its cool smooth surface sobered her to what a terrible idea this was.

"Except in this version Carrie returns as a badass healthcare executive with killer fashion sense and a hot bod." Viet placed Elle's phone beside her head.

"Totes! Also, you style your hair *way* better than in high school."

Face pinched, Elle raised her head. "Why did I show you my senior yearbook?"

"It will be fine." Viet covered Elle's hand with his, warmth seeping through her. "You're going home."

Only she wasn't going home. She was going back to where she'd grown up.

Want to read more of Elle's adventures in Perry? You can buy the book here

ALSO BY MELISSA WHITNEY

In the Hello and in the Goodbye

(Available wherever you get e-book, paperback, and audiobook)

The Home Series

Finding Home - Book One

(Available wherever you get e-book, paperback, and audiobook)

Coming Home - Book Two– January 2025

Making Home - Book Three –October 2025

The At First Series

At First Smile

(Available wherever you get e-book, paperback, and audiobook)

Stand Alone Titles

Happy Ever Afterlife, – April 2025

ACKNOWLEDGMENTS

There are so many people to thank for the role they played in making this book happen, but first I must thank, Cane Austen. Yes! Cane Austen is one hundred percent real and my white cane. With my cane I'm assured to never truly do anything alone. It's my ride or die (because if I get hit by a Tesla she's going down with me). For so many disabled people mobility devices support our independence. So, naturally when I wrote a white cane I needed to bestow it with her name.

Not all blind people name their canes, but it's something I started in my early-twenties to help endear a tool, that I once thrashed against, to me. Growing up disabled, the last thing I wanted to be was different and the cane advertised that difference. Naming my cane worked and you'd be hard pressed to find me out and about in most places without her.

A theme in this book is the sense of not going at things alone, a team. Boy, I hope I did my job as an author to communicate that. Team is so very important for all of us and I have an amazing one. So, here are some of my heavy hitters...

Liam, my love for you is truly as big as the moon. Thank you for your continued support on this journey.

Meghan, "I will always find you!"

Gemma Brocato, my editor and author mama bear, where would I be without you? Thank you for not just editing my words, but guiding me both in craft, business, and the ups and downs of the author world.

The ladies of Happily Booked PR, thank you for your amazing support in helping my stories find their readers.

Autumn, you are the kindest of souls and I am truly grateful for your support and guidance.

My RomCom Divas (Irene, Andrea, Layla, Ivy, Stella, Alicia, Reina, Britney, and JL) thank you for your support, guidance, and laughter.

The pugs, thank you for your many snuggles and inspiration for all the furry babies I put in my books!

Earthly Charms (Su), as always your covers are amazing!!

To my amazing narrators Harlow Wilde and Benjamin Sands, who brought the audiobook to life! As an audiobook reader, I am in awe of their talent and thankful they've shared it with me to ensure this story is accessible for all readers.

And to the MVP of my team, my readers. My stories would only be paper without you. Thank you for your belief in me and embrace of the worlds I create through words.

ABOUT THE AUTHOR

Melissa Whitney hails from Western, New York, but lives in Southern California with her husband and three rescue pugs. When not brewing the perfect cup of tea, hunting for a pastry, or listening to her latest audiobook, she writes swoony and steamy romances. Melissa's work explores themes of trauma, disability, grief/loss, and the complexities of human emotions and experience told through a romantic, sometimes comedic, swoony, and steamy lens.

To learn more about Melissa visit www.melissawhitney writes.com to sign up for her newsletter. As well, you can follow her on social media @melissa_whitneyauthor (Instagram), @melissasuewhitney (Tik Tok), or Melissa Whitney Author (Facebook Page).

Printed in the USA
CPSIA information can be obtained
at www.ICGtesting.com
LVHW020005081024
793227LV00036B/1175

9 798990 433427